FARWORLD

AIR KEEP

BOOK THREE

J. SCOTT SAVAGE

SHADOW
MOUNTAIN

To Vicki Martin Savage (1938–2012),
the happiest person I know.
I love you forever, Mom.

Text © 2013 J. Scott Savage

Illustrations © 2013 Brandon Dorman

Visit us at ShadowMountain.com

Library of Congress Cataloging-in-Publication Data

Savage, J. Scott, 1963- author.
  Air keep / J. Scott Savage.
    pages cm—(Farworld, book three)
  Summary: Marcus and Kyja continue to search for the Elementals they need to unite to open a drift between Earth and Farworld, but the Air Elementals have a strange sense of humor and with Farworld in the grip of a terrible drought and daily earthquakes, the two friends face untold challenges.
  ISBN 978-1-60907-325-1 (hardbound : alk. paper) 1. Fantasy fiction.
[1. Foundlings—Fiction. 2. People with disabilities—Fiction. 3. Magic—Fiction.]
I. Title. II. Series: Savage, J. Scott (Jeffrey Scott), 1963- Farworld ; bk. 3.
  PZ7.S25897Air 2013
  [Fic]—dc23   2012043373

Printed in the United States of America
Worzalla Publishing Co., Stevens Point, WI

10   9   8   7   6   5   4   3   2   1

See the Lords of Water—
Beyond the waves they leap

∞

See the Lords of Land—
Beneath the ground they sleep

♌

See the Lords of Air—
Above the clouds they creep

♌

See the Lords of Fire—
Around the flames they reap

∞

Water. Land. Air. Fire.
Together, the balance of Farworld they keep.

CONTENTS

PART 3: AERISIANS

PART 4: BATTLE AT TERRA NE STARIC

WHAT CAME BEFORE

WATER KEEP

Marcus Kanenas is a nobody from nowhere. He is found abandoned near a Greek Orthodox monastery in the Sonoran Desert as a baby. His body has been so badly broken that he is nearly given up for dead. Even after he recovers, the police are unable to discover the identity of the tiny infant. The only clue is a mysterious symbol branded on his shoulder.

Badly crippled and confined to a wheelchair, Marcus is often the butt of cruel pranks by the other boys in the various schools he attends. The only things that save him from being picked on even more than he is are his willingness to stand up to any odds and some unusual talents that seem almost magical.

Kyja lives in a world called Farworld where everyone from babies to farm animals has magic—except her. Not only is she incapable of performing any magic whatsoever, but she is immune to its effects as well. Her only friends are Riph Raph, a small dragon-like creature, and Master Therapass, the wizard who helped raise her.

While trying to find some sliver of magic inside herself, Kyja learns she is in terrible danger and is forced to flee the city of Terra ne Staric. She sees Marcus in a vision and realizes he is about to be killed by a dark wizard named Bonesplinter.

Desperate to save the boy, Kyja clutches the amulet she has worn since she was a baby—an amulet engraved with the same symbol as the one on Marcus's shoulder—and sees a golden rope in her mind. She pulls on the rope and brings Marcus to Farworld.

After narrowly escaping an encounter with a large scorpion-like creature called a mimicker, Kyja and Marcus meet up again with Master Therapass. The wizard reveals a secret he has been hiding for the last thirteen years.

Marcus was born in Farworld, fulfilling a prophecy. Legend holds that a boy with the brand Marcus wears will save his world from destruction. Aware of his birth, a group of evil wizards known as the Dark Circle conspired to have him killed. Master Therapass and a warrior named Tankum managed to save Marcus from certain death by opening a portal and sending him to Earth.

But in order to keep the scales balanced, Master Therpass had to bring a person of equal importance from Earth to Farworld—Kyja. Just as Marcus may hold the future of Farworld in his hands, Kyja may hold the future of Earth in hers. What Master Therapass did not foresee was that once Kyja was in Farworld, she could not be sent back because she is immune to magic.

In order to restore the balance, Marcus and Kyja must return to their own worlds. They soon realize that Marcus isn't completely *in* Farworld at all. Kyja's accidental summoning left part of him trapped in a gray area between the two worlds, where he will be unable to survive for more than a few days without returning to Earth.

The only way for Marcus and Kyja to save their worlds is for them to open a passageway between both worlds called a *drift*. This requires the help of four elementals, beings which control water, land, air, and fire magic. But the elementals won't even talk to humans, much less one another.

Marcus and Kyja travel toward Water Keep—home of the water elementals—pursued by the Dark Circle. When Master Therapass is attacked by a Summoner, Marcus and Kyja escape by jumping to Earth. It appears the geography of Earth and Farworld are somewhat similar, so Marcus and Kyja can move in one world by traveling to the other world and jumping back. But, like Marcus, Kyja can't stay away from her world for more than a few days without getting sick so they have to jump between worlds often.

The Dark Circle—which has already created a passageway usable only by evil wizards—chases them in both worlds. After being captured by a cave trulloch named Screech and nearly dying in the cavern of the Unmakers, Marcus and Kyja ride a frost pinnois named Zhethar to Water Keep.

Once they arrive at Water Keep, Kyja and Marcus learn the elementals, who call themselves Fontasians, have no interest in helping the cause. In fact, they condemn the children to death for entering the city without permission.

Marcus and Kyja risk their lives to save a trapped Fontasian named Morning Dew. Intrigued by the children's actions, several of the water elementals leave Water Keep and save Marcus and Kyja from the Dark Circle army waiting outside the city walls.

Cascade, the water elemental who controls all moving water, agrees to join Marcus and Kyja on their quest. Marcus hears Master Therapass's voice in the music of flowers and thinks the wizard might still be alive.

LAND KEEP

Marcus and Kyja, together with Cascade and Riph Raph, leave Water Keep in search of Land Keep. Marcus is getting better at using magic, but he is haunted by a recurring dream in which he destroys Farworld. During their search, they come across the Keepers of the Balance. The Keepers use creatures called snifflers from the realm of shadows (the gray place between Earth and Farworld) to take magic from those who are weak and give it to those who are powerful.

Kyja accidentally touches a sniffler, and, without realizing it, begins to draw away Marcus's magic. After they flee into a swamp, Marcus is captured by a harbinger. The harbinger takes Marcus into a huge underground cavern where he meets a boy named Jaklah, who tells him the people in the cavern are either criminals or those who ran from the Keepers.

As Kyja, Riph Raph, and Cascade search for Marcus, they are joined by an unexpected visitor. Screech has been following them since the cavern of the Unmakers. He offers to help find Marcus. Kyja leaves Cascade and Screech in the swamp and descends to the underground cavern where Marcus is trapped.

They discover the door to Land Keep and manage to open it. Once inside, they learn that Land Keep has been abandoned for thousands of years. Because they are deep underground, Marcus can't jump back to Earth, and he is getting sicker and sicker. They can't return to the swamp without being attacked by the harbingers. Their only choice is to enter a doorway that leads to a kind of oracle called the Augur Well.

Inside the door, they meet an odd little man named Mr. Z, who explains that they can't get to the Augur Well without passing the land elementals' quests. As they attempt to pass the tests, Marcus grows weaker while Kyja's magic gets stronger. In the last test, Kyja is forced to give up the thing she values most—her newfound magic—to save Marcus's life.

When they finally reach the Augur Well, the oracle tells them they will never find a single land elemental. At first, they are crushed, but eventually they discover the well's true meaning. There is no such thing as a *single* land elemental because each is a combination of two creatures.

Marcus and Kyja become honorary land elementals, free all the captured people, and return the harbingers to their original forms. After learning that Master Therapass has been imprisoned by the leader of the Keepers, Zentan Dolan, Marcus and Kyja realize they must return to Terra ne Staric.

Kyja takes Marcus to Earth, where he heals; the two drive a motorcycle and sidecar across the country. Jumping back to Terra ne Staric, Marcus and Kyja are betrayed by Rhaidnan, a close friend of Kyja's, and turned over to the Keepers who now control the city.

At first the Keepers—who have been absorbing the magic of other people for years—are too strong to defeat, but when Cascade and a pair of land elementals named Lanctrus-Darnoc arrive, the battle turns. Lanctrus-Darnoc brings the stone statues of all of Terra ne Staric's most powerful wizards and warriors back to life, including Tankum—the warrior who died saving Marcus. Marcus and Kyja use the confusion of the battle to enter the tower in search of Master Therapass.

As Kyja hurries to the dungeon to rescue the wizard, Marcus is drawn to the top of the tower. There he finds the Innoris a'Gentoran, a gauntlet only he can use. Mesmerized by the gauntlet's power, Marcus realizes he can destroy the Dark Circle and heal himself at the same time.

It is only when Kyja reminds him that the wizard told them their weaknesses are also their strengths that Marcus realizes the gauntlet is powered by stolen magic. Marcus manages to destroy the gauntlet, returning the magic to those it was stolen from, and the zentan attacks him.

Rhaidnan steps in front of the zentan's blade, sacrificing his life to save Marcus. Master Therapass and Tankum arrive in time to fight Zentan Dolan.

After the battle, Marcus and Kyja meet a tall man named Graehl. It turns out that Screech was once a man, but had been turned into a cave trulloch by the Keepers as a punishment. Now that he is human again, he vows to help Marcus and Kyja on their quest. Master Therapass sends Cascade and Lanctrus-Darnoc on an unknown journey.

The wizard tells Marcus and Kyja that the gray place between their worlds is called the realm of shadows. It is extremely dangerous for Marcus to pass through the realm of shadows because one of his parents was from there. Marcus must return to the monastery on Earth until Master Therapass can find a way to bring him through the realm of shadows safely.

At the end of book two, the master of the Dark Circle changes Bonesplinter into a Summoner and contacts a pair of land elementals and a water elemental who are apparently working with him.

DROUGHT

JAKLAH WAS THINKING ABOUT WATER. Filling his mouth. Running down his parched throat. Splashing over his sun-burned face and dripping from his hair. Unlike the small supply of warm, dusty liquid sloshing in his waterskin, the water in his imagination was fresh and so cold the very thought of it brought goose bumps to the backs of his arms and cramped his stomach.

Not yet seventeen, Jaklah was one of the youngest soldiers in the army, but the drought that had dried up entire rivers and had shrunken lakes to little more than ponds affected him as much as the older men. His eyes, gritty with dust, hurt every time he blinked. His parched skin itched constantly, and his lips cracked until they bled.

Marching across clumps of dead grass and weeds so dry they exploded into tiny brown clouds with every step, he let his mind summon up a crystal lake—icy, blue, and endless. He'd stop on the shore, inhaling the deep, wet aroma. Then he'd stick in just one toe, shivering at how good the water felt on skin that hadn't experienced

I

more moisture than could be wrung out of a damp rag in what seemed like forever.

He'd wade in far enough to cover the tops of his feet. Then out to his shins. Waves would slosh against his knees. Finally, when he couldn't stand it any longer, he'd throw his hat, tear off his shirt and breeches, and—

Caught up in the wonderful vision playing out in his head, he didn't notice the rest of the army coming to a halt around him until he ran face-first into the broad back of a stone statue.

Tankum, a curved blade sheathed behind each of his shoulders, didn't so much as turn around as Jaklah collided with him. The stone warrior stood with both feet planted in the baked ground, arms folded across his chest like a boulder that just happened to be in the shape of a man. "Brace yourself."

At the warrior's words, Jaklah's heart began to race. Was this it? After weeks of searching, had they finally come across a band of Keepers and their pet snifflers? Or even better, an unmaker—one of the creatures said to have come from the mysterious world of shadows? His hand went to the nicked iron sword at his waist as he scanned the terrain.

Nothing. Not even the blurring of air and light that was said to signal the presence of the shadow creatures. Why had the army stopped? The stone wizards and warriors stood in rows and columns safely apart from one another, the horses were hobbled to keep from running, and the men and boys who had joined the army knelt or lay flat on the ground. Only then did Jaklah remember what time it was. His eyes went to the sky.

The sun was almost directly overhead.

With a panicked yelp, he dropped to the ground. He found no

bushes or rocks to clutch onto, so he dug his fingers into the cracked and broken dirt, hoping that would be enough.

For a moment everything was perfectly still, as though Farworld itself waited. Then it came, starting as a low rumble in the distance, growing in sound as the stalks of dead grass shook and crumbled to dust and pebbles rattled and bounced. Jaklah pressed to the dirt and closed his eyes.

Beneath him, the ground rolled and bucked like a wild stallion determined to throw its rider and trample him underfoot. Dust filled his nostrils and caked his throat as the world around him shook and roared. Horses whinnied in terror; wagons groaned.

He'd experienced these quakes every day for the past six months—as long as it had been since the last rain—but he was still terrified of each one, sure *this* would be the time the world opened up and swallowed him.

As though hearing his thoughts, the ground gave a final heave, and a sound like rocks being torn apart roared in his ears.

"Look out!" a soldier screamed. Jaklah's eyes flew open.

Not a dozen steps away, a split nearly the length of a man across and ten men long had divided the ground. Jaklah's friend Theyin stood at its edge, straining to catch his balance. Wheeling his arms, he tried to keep from falling into the great black mouth stretching open before him. He wasn't going to make it. Face white with panic, he slowly tilted toward the crevice.

"Hold on!" Jaklah shouted. "I'm coming."

Before he could get to his feet, a flash of stone and steel blurred past. Jaklah had never seen Tankum run, and it came as a shock to watch the living statue move so quickly his feet barely touched the ground. But even so, he would be too late.

Theyin's last shred of balance gave out, and he tumbled into the opening. The warrior was only a few steps away, but he'd never be able to reach Theyin without falling into the chasm himself.

"Help!" Theyin cried, spreading his arms as though he might somehow be able to sprout wings and fly to safety.

Without slowing at all, Tankum raced to the edge of the crevice, grabbed Theyin's belt in his great stone hand, and launched himself into the air.

"Not possible," Jaklah whispered, his hand going to his mouth. He had no idea how much the stone warrior weighed, but he'd seen the man's footprints leaving indentations in the dirt, each as deep as his little finger was long. Yet, somehow, even with Theyin's full weight in one hand, Tankum had bent his stone legs and launched himself over the crevice.

One foot crashed onto the far edge of the opening, and Jaklah gasped as dirt and rocks crumbled away beneath it; he was sure soldier and boy would plummet into the darkness together. But Tankum's momentum carried them forward, and a few seconds later, he sat Theyin gently on the grass as though they'd done nothing more eventful than go for a brisk walk.

Jaklah crawled to the opening and looked down. The crevice was so deep he couldn't see the bottom. Keeping safely away from the edge, he circled the hole and hurried to his friend on the other side. "You all right?"

Theyin sat on the ground, trying to catch his breath. "I'm . . . not sure."

Around them, men were getting to their feet, untying horses, climbing into wagons, and checking their gear. Several of them eyed the break in the ground warily and muttered under their breath.

Jaklah reached out and pulled his friend up. "When I saw that crack open, I thought you—"

Theyin held out a hand, cutting off his words. "Don't say it. Don't even think it. I haven't been that scared since . . ." He ran a hand across his brow. "To tell the truth, I don't think I've ever been that scared."

Jaklah pointed to the front of Theyin's rough-woven breeches. "At least you didn't wet yourself. The other soldiers would never have let you live that down."

"Slim chance." Theyin pulled the cork from his waterskin and took a measured sip. "With as little as they give us to drink, my body wouldn't dare spill a drop. There's not enough moisture in me to break a sweat."

"Forward, march!" Tankum shouted. The statue's feet shook the ground like an aftershock of the quake as he strode forward. Theyin and Jaklah walked a few paces behind him.

"You think it's true what some of the men are saying?" Theyin asked. "That the land elementals are behind the quakes?"

"Nah." Jaklah had seen Lanctrus-Darnoc, the half boar, half fox creature that had come out of Land Keep with Marcus and Kyja. According to Tankum, they'd helped save Terra ne Staric from the Keepers. "They're on our side."

Theyin tried to spit the dust from his tongue, but his mouth was too dry to create enough saliva. "They say the water elementals are on our side too. But they don't seem to care about the fact that folks are dying of thirst."

Jaklah didn't know what to say to that. The weather had gone crazy everywhere. Half the reason he'd joined the army was to escape the floods at home. But now here he was, dreaming of getting more than a mouthful of water at a time. Could the water elementals have something to do with the bizarre weather?

"My heart's still pounding," Theyin said.

"At least you had something happen," Jaklah muttered, his voice thick with bitterness. He knew he wasn't being fair. His friend had nearly died. But the other reason Jaklah had joined up was to get revenge on the Keepers who had stolen magic from his friends and family for so many years. So far, army life had been nothing but day after day of boredom. He kicked a rock. "Guess we'll never see any action."

He'd forgotten Tankum was still there until the warrior turned to look back at him. "That eager to wet your blade in another man's blood, are you?"

Jaklah flushed. "It's not that. It's just . . . well, what's the point of us being here if we aren't going to fight anyone?"

Tankum pulled out one of his long, curved steel blades and ran its keen edge across the tip of his stone thumb. "An army's job is to obey orders. Sometimes obeying orders means fighting—to the death, if necessary. Other times it means keeping violence away by our very presence."

Jaklah had never looked at it that way. Tankum had fought in many battles. Maybe it was time to do less talking and more listening.

The sun was still several hours from the edge of the horizon when Tankum abruptly called the march to a halt. Jaklah looked around. Why were they stopping? Except for the quakes, they never quit walking before dusk. The other men seemed confused as well.

A stone wizard with big ears and an even bigger nose took out his wand. "What is it?"

Tankum shook his head. He sniffed the air and put a palm to the ground. "Something's wrong."

For the second time that day, Jaklah's hand reached for the hilt of his sword. Following the warrior's example, he smelled the air. He detected the faintest scent of something familiar. Despite the hot, dry air, the smell made him think of the swamp near his home—now turned into a lake.

"Look!" One of the men pointed toward a dark spot in the dirt. Jaklah stepped through the crowd to get a closer look.

"Is that what I think it is?" Theyin asked. The dark stain on the ground was round and less than a stone's throw across, but it appeared to be growing.

Several of the men dropped to their knees and touched it with their fingertips. "It is," one of them said, his eyes wide with surprise. "It's water!"

Jaklah rushed forward and flattened the brittle grass, ignoring the way it jabbed his fingers. He touched the dark soil with his palm. It was definitely wet.

Two men began digging into the ground, trying to get enough of the brown water to cup in their hands. Even as they did, it became clear that it wasn't necessary to dig. Like a spring, the water bubbled up through the ground, first soaking the dirt, then puddling around the base of the grass.

Theyin scooped a handful and held it to his mouth. "It's cold." He hooted. "And delicious."

Soldiers shoved each other to reach the water—cupping it in their hands, soaking pieces of cloth and squeezing the water into their mouths or lapping it straight from the ground. Theyin was right; it was ice cold, and despite the grit and dirt, the best thing Jaklah had tasted in weeks.

The men started shouting and splashing, wetting their faces and dousing each other. One man dropped his pack and sword, tore off his shirt, and rolled across the ground, giggling like a child.

Only the statues seemed impervious to the water's allure. Unlike the humans, they could neither drink nor eat. Tankum, who continued to sniff the air, stepped away from the growing pond. "Get back," he growled.

When the men failed to respond, he shouted, "On your feet!"

A few men stood, but most of them ignored the warning. "What is it?" Jaklah asked, getting up.

The warrior suddenly drew his second blade. "Away from the water. Now!" The army of living statues pulled out their wands and weapons.

Jaklah's throat ached for more to drink, but he took the warrior's advice, grabbing Theyin's arm and pulling his friend backward. About half of the men did so as well. The other half continued to drink despite their commander's orders.

"Is it the water?" Jaklah asked Tankum. "Is something wrong with it?"

Tankum's brow lowered, the muscles in his stone arms bulging as he gripped his swords. "Something's . . . coming."

Jaklah looked around. There was nothing as far as he could see. But he did feel something—a tingling in his limbs. The hairs on his arms and legs were standing straight up.

Some of the men who had continued drinking must have felt it too. A few stood, looking around with confused expressions, before hurrying to join their companions.

The ground shuddered under Jaklah's feet. Another quake? Usually they happened only at morning, mid-day, and evening. But once or twice the ground had trembled at other times. If that was all, why was Tankum holding his swords out before him, a low rumble growing in his throat?

The water gushed faster from the ground, washing up chunks of grass and clods of dirt. Now all of the men who'd continued to drink began getting up. They stumbled through the thick, silty water that had risen to their knees. Only the man who'd pulled off his shirt took no notice—he continued to splash and frolic.

"Look there." Theyin pointed toward the middle of the pond. Bubbles boiled in the mud.

"Get out of the water!" Jaklah screamed. Several soldiers started forward, but then froze as something thick and brown rose from the murky liquid. It took Jaklah a moment to realize that he was seeing an arm. Could there be a man down there? But the arm was too big. A man with arms that size would need to be . . .

A second arm emerged, dark as mud and lumpy, not like a real man's at all, but like some kind of monster's. Out of the murk rose a head as big as a boulder. Its face was blank—no sign of eyes, nose, or mouth. Yet Jaklah felt hatred radiating from it so strongly, it might as well have been glaring straight at him. The creature climbed from the water, growing as tall as a man, then two men, then the size of a small tree.

Soldiers yelled out warnings, and for the first time, the swimming man seemed to understand that something was wrong. He turned, saw the creature towering above him, and stumbled backward—straight into another pair of lumpy arms. The shirtless soldier reached for his sword. Before he could remember he'd dropped his weapon, the second pair of arms yanked him under the water.

Bodies emerged from all over the muddy lake now. Clay giants pulled themselves out of the ground. Ten, a dozen, thirty—Jaklah lost count as he drew his sword with a trembling hand. The clay golems turned and started toward their army.

Just before Tankum raised his pair of swords and moved forward to meet the charge, he glanced at Jaklah. "Looks like you'll get your action after all."

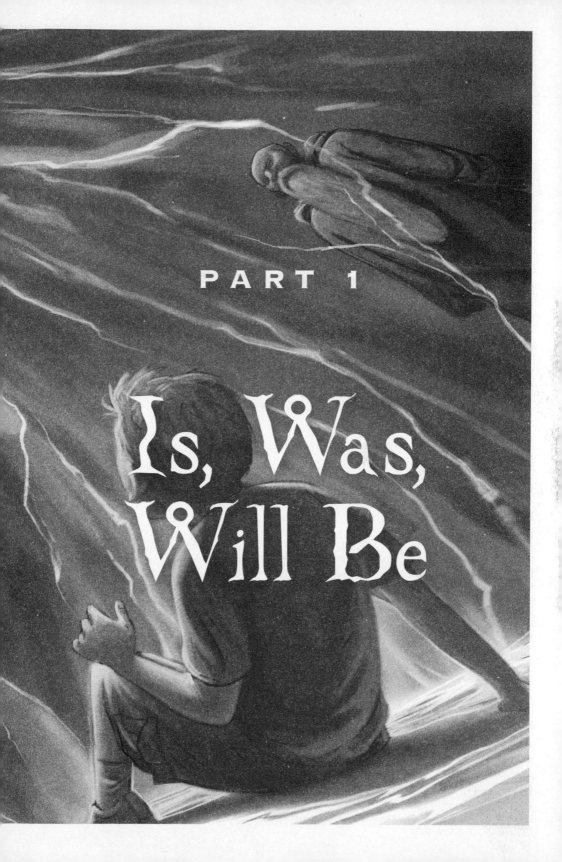

PART 1

Is, Was,
Will Be

CHAPTER 1

BOOKS AND BEETLES

*F*LICK. SNAP. CRUNCH.
FLICK. SNAP. CRUNCH.

"Would you *stop* that?" Kyja swept away the pile of maps in front of her and scowled into the dark corner of the underground room.

Riph Raph spotted another of the eight-legged water beetles that had come here to avoid the blistering heat outside. His tongue flicked, and he snapped the red-shelled insect into his mouth, then crunched it with his beak. "Did you say something?"

"Ohhh!" Kyja slammed a fist on the big wooden table. "You are *so* annoying."

The skyte flapped his stubby, teal-blue wings and hopped up to where Kyja had been studying stacks of maps and books for hours on end. "Pardon *me*," he said in a tone that was anything but apologetic. He looked around, found a beetle hiding in the shadow of a thick book, and speared it with one talon. "Here," he said, the creature wriggling. "I wouldn't have hogged them all if I'd known you wanted one."

"I don't," Kyja said, tired of his jokes. "I want you to let me think."

Riph Raph ate the beetle, then licked his beak with a long tongue stained the same bright red as the insects he'd been catching. "I didn't realize my trying to eat enough to stay alive while you keep us locked in this *dungeon* was bothering you."

Kyja wiped a dusty hand across her face. Riph Raph was right. She'd been at this so long she'd lost track of time as she tried to locate any mention of air elementals and where they might be found. Plenty of people had searched for them, each with a different theory of where Air Keep was located. But as far as she could tell, none of them had discovered so much as a single clue to the elusive creatures' whereabouts.

She'd worked straight through dinner, and if the candle, burned down nearly to its holder, was any clue, she'd probably missed breakfast as well. Keeping track of time was impossible in these rooms deep beneath the tower. This area, used for storing documents too old or unreliable to be worth keeping upstairs in the library, wasn't actually *in* the dungeon, but it wasn't far from it.

"I'm sorry," she said. "I'm just frustrated. Water Keep wasn't that hard to find, and we at least had rumors of where Land Keep was located. But I can't find a single theory on Air Keep that isn't based on a dream or a story someone made up. Then there's that stupid poem. *See the Lords of Air—Above the clouds they creep.* How am I supposed to get above the clouds? I can't fly!" She pounded her fist on the table, causing Riph Raph to jump.

"What's making you angry is the turnip head," Riph Raph said.

"What?" Kyja looked up sharply from the table.

The skyte shook his floppy ears. "You're blaming maps and books, but what's really frustrating you is that the wizard won't let you bring your boyfriend with the turnip-shaped head back to Farworld. He's all you think about."

Kyja felt her face redden. "Marcus is *not* my boyfriend. And he *isn't* all I think about. I've been practicing fencing and archery. I've been searching for Air Keep. I've been helping the wizards try to discover what's causing the ground to shake and what's causing the drought. Until you brought him up, I hadn't thought about Marcus in . . . *weeks!*"

Riph Raph nodded as though considering her argument. "Then I guess you won't want to check on how the wizard's doing with his search for a way to protect Turnip Head from the realm of shadows."

Kyja clenched her fists. What she wanted to do was give Riph Raph a hard whack on the head with one of these big dusty books. But that would just convince him all the more that he was right. In a tight voice she said, "Marcus does not have a turnip-shaped head. And I am not going to check on how Master Therapass is coming with his research on the shadow realm."

The skyte crunched on a bit of beetle.

At last Kyja licked her fingers and pinched out the candle. Except for the flickering light of a torch in the hallway, the room went completely dark. "As it turns out, I *do* need to speak with the wizard. But only to update him on my search for Air Keep. It has nothing to do with Turni—I mean, Marcus."

Riph Raph made a sound that might have been caused by a piece of insect shell caught in his throat. Or it might have been a laugh.

———◆———

Five minutes later, Kyja raced through the kitchen, where Bella, the tower cook, was blustering up a storm at a red-faced guard.

"How am I supposed to bake anything when there's no milk because the cows have dried up and you give me only a half barrel of water to last an entire week?" the stout woman shouted, waving her large wooden spoon. "You do realize I'm trying to feed an entire tower, don't you?"

"Don't blame me. I'm not the one who stopped the rain and dried up the river. The high lord says that's all there is," the guard said with a grunt. "Another week, and there won't even be that if we don't get some rain." He eyed the barrel, licking his parched lips. "You think maybe I could get a tiny . . ." He mimed drinking from a ladle and Bella hit him on the top of his head with her spoon.

"Get out!" she hollered. "And tell the high lord he can expect stringy beef with hard carrots and no biscuits for dinner."

As Kyja started toward the spiral staircase leading to the tower, Bella noticed her. "Come here child," the cook whispered.

"No time," Kyja said. "I have to talk to—"

Bella cut her off, taking her arm with fingers strengthened from hours of cutting vegetables and rolling dough, and led her to a corner cupboard. After checking to make sure no one was watching, she pulled out a small clay jug.

"There's no more than a swallow or two," Bella said. "But it's the last there is." She pulled the cork from the jug, and the heavenly smell of apple cider wafted through the air.

"No, I couldn't," Kyja said, although her stomach gurgled with desire at the smell. "Drink it yourself. Or give it to one of the children. I'm fine."

"You're not fine." Bella pulled down one of Kyja's lower eyelids. "When did you last have anything to drink?"

Kyja couldn't remember. Ten or twelve hours? A day, maybe? She'd meant to drink her ration yesterday morning—a half cup of warm, brackish liquid. But then she'd seen a boy crying in the street, so thirsty his eyes couldn't even form tears, and she'd given the cup to him instead.

"That's what I thought," Bella said. The cook put the jug to Kyja's lips. "Go on. Another day, and it will turn sour anyway." Kyja gulped down the few swallows gratefully. She hadn't realized how dry her mouth was until her tongue tasted the sweet liquid. She poured the last trickle into her hand and fed it to Riph Raph.

As the skyte lapped the final drops from her palm, the tower floor began to shake. Bella reached for a counter, and the jug slipped from her hand, crashing to the floor with a jangle of broken pottery. That wasn't the only crash. From around the kitchen, anything not firmly held down or locked away rattled and shook. Although all breakable items had been placed at the backs of the shelves, two dishes and a bowl still managed to rattle off and crash to the floor.

Kyja clung to Bella, waiting out the quake.

"If this keeps up, there won't be a single cup or bowl left in the whole town," Bella said when the shaking finally stopped. "Of course, that won't matter if there's nothing left to eat or drink." She looked down at Kyja as though realizing the girl was still there. "Didn't you say you had somewhere to go?"

"Yes!" Kyja ran to the doorway, and Riph Raph flew out the window. At the base of the staircase, she stopped and turned to Bella. "The water will come back. Cascade won't let us starve."

Bella nodded, her double chins wobbling. "I hope so, child. I hope so."

As Kyja hurried up to the tower, she remembered climbing this same staircase on her way to magic lessons. It had been only a little more than a year ago, but it seemed much longer. Back then she'd been convinced that with enough practice, she could learn to cast spells and use potions like every other kid her age. She hadn't known she was really from a place called *Earth,* where no one cast spells. She hadn't known she was destined to save that world—and Farworld—by creating a doorway called a *drift* between the two. Elementals had been something from a children's poem.

And she hadn't known about . . . *Marcus.*

Kyja swallowed and increased her pace, the steps blurring as she leaped up them. For the last six months, she'd concentrated on her studies and weapons practice, trying not to think about Marcus. But how could she, when, for all she knew, he was in the hands of the Thrathkin S'Bae—the Dark Circle's evil wizards—or worse? Master Therapass wouldn't even let her check on Marcus with his aptura discerna, saying that using it would only make it that much harder for her to resist pulling Marcus back to Farworld.

But what could possibly be taking the old wizard so long? He'd said it would be a few weeks at most before he found a way to bring Marcus safely through the gray place between their worlds, the shadow realm. He'd said Marcus was fine. But what if he wasn't? What if Master Therapass was lying to keep her from using her one power? Once, Bonesplinter had nearly gotten Marcus by turning into a huge, black snake. If Kyja hadn't discovered her ability to pull Marcus to Farworld at just that moment—

Riph Raph waited on the windowsill as Kyja reached the level near Master Therapass's study. Bits of brown mud clumped on the skyte's beak. He must have stopped by the Two Prongs River before flying up to meet her.

Kyja skidded to a stop, panting. "Is there any water at all?"

"Nothing. What I wouldn't give for a long drink and a succulent fish." The skyte flapped his ears. "You're in an awfully big hurry to tell the wizard that you haven't learned anything."

"I was . . ." She couldn't think of any reason to explain her running and had to satisfy herself with waving a hand at him. "Just be quiet."

Ignoring the skyte, she waited long enough to catch her breath before entering the wizard's study. As she did, she was struck again by the clutter. Powders and potions were spread across the room—on tables and shelves, in boxes and bottles. Scrolls, some open, some rolled tight, covered every surface. Trinkets, charms, skulls, wings, talons, cloaks, crystals, and cabinets were scattered like a child's toys.

The room had been cluttered enough when she first started coming to practice magic. But when the Master had been thrown in prison by the zentan, leader of the Keepers, many of the other wizards had decided that his belongings were theirs to take. Now, bit by bit, he was gathering his things back—and putting them any old place. Surprisingly, nothing appeared to have been broken by the quakes. She guessed it was because of some sort of magic.

What drew her attention most was what appeared to be an ordinary stained-glass window high on the wall—the aptura discerna, a window that looked inward instead of outward. In Kyja's case, it allowed her to see Marcus's world. It was one of the only magical items that worked for Kyja because, as the wizard explained it, the aptura discerna didn't try to change people or affect them in any way. It was merely a window into what they cared about most.

If she could just get a little peek . . .

"I'd let you use it if I thought it would help."

Kyja turned toward the voice and smiled at the sight of a large gray wolf with a pair of silver spectacles balanced on its nose, leaning over a scroll. The wolf waved its paw and changed into an old man in a long blue robe. He took the glasses off and polished them on his sleeve. "Wolves' eyes are sharper than a man's. But even wolves get old."

Kyja glanced at Riph Raph, who was perched high on a shelf. The skyte was never completely comfortable here, although Kyja wasn't sure whether it was the wolf or the magic that bothered him more. She turned back to the wizard. "I, um, just came to tell you that I've been studying some old maps."

The wizard put his glasses back on. "And?"

"I didn't find anything about the location of Air Keep," Kyja admitted. "I might as well be looking for a three-headed dragon."

"Now *that* I could help you with," Master Therapass said. "Unfortunately, I'm not surprised with your lack of success. Of all the elementals, air is possibly the most elusive. Other than the fact that they control the skies and are said to have a rather unique sense of humor, precious little is known about them."

"Then how are we supposed to get their help?" Kyja grabbed a cane-backed chair and held on before sitting. Items in Master Therapass's study tended to move about without warning, and Kyja had gone to sit on a chair more than once, only to have it run across the room, dumping her rudely on the ground.

The wizard tugged at the tip of his long beard. "Perhaps when Marcus gets here, we will figure that out."

Kyja gave Riph Raph a *see-I-didn't-bring-it-up* look and casually said, "Speaking of Marcus, have you made any progress?"

"Magic is not a science of progress as much as it is one of discovery," the wizard said. It was just like him to answer without giving any information.

"What have you *discovered* then?" Kyja asked, knowing she sounded cranky.

The wizard glanced at a murky gray liquid bubbling in a glass tube and chuckled. "I have discovered many things. But no protection from the realm of shadows just yet."

Kyja gave an exasperated huff. "Then there's no point in waiting any longer. Let me bring him here."

"On the contrary—we have all the more reason to wait. When one discovers that one drawer is locked, the logical answer is to try opening another drawer. Or one could look for a key. A key could very well unlock both drawers, assuming the second was locked as well. Of course, it might have a different lock entirely. In which case, one might need two keys."

"Who cares about keys?" Kyja shouted. "Can't you at least let me check to make sure he's all right?"

Master Therapass studied Kyja. "You seem out of sorts. When did you last have something to eat?" The next thing Kyja knew, the wizard was shuffling her out of his study. "I'll tell you as soon as I've discovered anything, child. Trust me; the boy is fine. Now go down and have some of Bella's cornbread and gravy. Oh, and the bacon is especially good today. You could bring me back a slice or two if you are so inclined."

"There *is* no cornbread or gravy. Bella doesn't have enough water to make it. And I don't want any bacon," Kyja muttered under her breath as she walked down the hall. She couldn't believe the wizard was worried about filling his belly when he should be trying to find a way to bring Marcus to Farworld safely.

When Kyja started up the staircase again, Riph Raph said, "I thought we were heading to the kitchen."

"I'm going to my room," she snapped.

"What about the bacon?"

"Get it yourself. Food is all any of you seems to think about anyway." She stomped up the stairs until she reached a small wooden door that led to an even smaller room. Since the Goodnuffs' farm had been destroyed, this was her new home. It was stiflingly hot in the summer and drafty in the winter—and barely big enough to hold a bed, a chair, and a dresser. The only thing good about it was the tiny balcony that overlooked nearly all of Terra ne Staric.

But Kyja didn't care about the view now. All she wanted to do was go to sleep and forget about the fact that as far as she could tell, she was the only person in the entire city who cared about Marcus.

As she dropped onto the bed, something crinkled under her back. Curious, she sat up and pulled out a piece of parchment that must have been lying on her blanket. Where had it come from? It hadn't been here when she left. Four lines were written in a small, neat handwriting.

PURSUE ME AND I FLEE
RUN FROM ME, AND I FOLLOW
AT MORN AND AFTERNOON I AM HERE
AT DARKEST NIGHT AND BRIGHTEST DAY, I DISAPPEAR

There was no signature of any kind. She turned the parchment over. Nothing on the back either. Who was it from? What did it mean? It seemed to be a riddle. For the moment, at least, her thoughts were pulled away from worrying about Marcus as she focused on the riddle.

What disappeared at night? The sun. It was there in the morning and afternoon. And depending on which way you walked, it could appear to follow you or go away. But it definitely didn't disappear at the brightest part of the day.

What else came in the morning and afternoon? Hunger, if you asked Riph Raph. But hunger couldn't follow you or run away. A person could follow you or run away. But what kind of person disappeared in the middle of the day and at night?

Trying to work out the puzzle, she looked at the floor, where sunlight shined through the balcony. There was the answer, on the floor in front of her. Something that ran if you chased it and followed you wherever you went. It disappeared at night when the sun was gone and also when the sun was directly overhead.

A shadow.

CHAPTER 2

A Change of Plans

MARCUS SLAMMED HIS BOOK to the patio stones in frustration. It made a bang that sounded thunderous in the quiet of the Arizona morning. A monk, startled from his work digging in a nearby flower garden, looked up quickly.

"Sorry," Marcus said, feeling his face growing hot. "Where is that scroll?" he whispered to himself, reshuffling the small stack of books and papers in his lap. He'd been looking at it just a few minutes before, and now he couldn't find it anywhere. It wasn't like he could have misplaced it. He was sitting in his wheelchair in the middle of an open stone courtyard. And because he was in a monastery surrounded by monks, the odds of someone taking it were fairly slim.

But that didn't change the fact that the scroll was gone.

This seemed to be the way everything had gone over the past few weeks. His land and water spells, ones he'd been getting really good at, were suddenly either so weak as to be useless, or not working at all. His body felt like a wet washcloth someone had begun wringing every night. He'd gone months without a word from Kyja or Master Therapass. And now, every day seemed to have at least one instance of him losing or misplacing something.

The only good news at all was that things couldn't get any worse.

"You dropped this?" Father Shaun picked up the book and handed it to Marcus with an uneasy frown.

"Um, thanks," Marcus said, taking the volume and turning it over so the cover faced down. He hadn't heard the monk's approach and wasn't thrilled to see him there. Most of the fathers either seemed to enjoy Marcus's company or at least tolerated his presence in their monastery. Of all of them, only Father Shaun appeared actively uncomfortable with their long-term guest.

Although the monk had never said so, Marcus suspected Father Shaun's discomfort was due to the books and papers Master Therapass had sent with him to study. Marcus tried not to do magic in the presence of anyone at the monastery, but more than once he'd been in the middle of an incantation when a father showed up unexpectedly. With Father Shaun's habit of routinely arriving with catlike stealth, he was often the one who witnessed the spells.

"How are your studies progressing?" the monk asked.

"Good." Marcus patted his stack of papers. "Just working on my, uh . . . algebra. Then some U.S. history. Gotta love the Industrial Revolution."

Father Shaun tugged at the sleeve of his raso, the long, black garment worn by all of the monks there. "I have some news that should make your studies go even better."

Marcus waited silently, seriously doubting that whatever news Father Shaun had would be good.

When Father Shaun realized Marcus wasn't going to say

anything, he coughed into his fist and said, "We've received notification from the state. They have requested that we return you to the custody of Principal Teagarden at the Philo T. Justice School for Boys."

"Terrible Teagarden?" Marcus's throat tightened. Had he just been thinking things couldn't get any worse? "You can't do that. Elder Benson said I was welcome to stay at the monastery as long as I wanted."

If the monk was disturbed by the outburst, he didn't show it. Instead he smiled sadly. "We will miss you. But we have no choice. The state says this is not the proper place for a young boy. The monastery is not an orphanage."

Marcus couldn't believe what he was hearing. Master Therapass had told him he could stay with the monks. He'd said the monastery was a place of safety, protected somehow from the reach of the Dark Circle. Then again, Master Therapass had also said it would only be a few weeks before Marcus could return to Farworld, and look how that had worked out—six months without a word of what was going on. "How did they even find out I was here?"

The monk looked quickly away before raising his hands. "I'm afraid I don't have an answer to that."

It wasn't like Marcus had been able to talk to anyone outside the monastery. No phone. No Internet. Not even a TV. He'd been completely out of touch. Every day for the first few weeks, he'd waited for a message. Better yet, for the disorienting tug in the pit of his stomach that meant Kyja was starting to pull him to Farworld. But the tug never came. He was beginning to wonder if it ever would.

What if Kyja and Master Therapass had decided to find the other elementals without him? He couldn't imagine Kyja going along with something like that. But he couldn't have imagined her leaving him here so long either. Maybe she'd forgotten about him completely.

Or . . . what if something had happened to Kyja? The thought made Marcus sick to his stomach. He slammed his fist on his lap and immediately regretted it when a bolt of pain lanced through his bad leg. "If Elder Ephraim were alive, he would never allow this. I won't go."

Elder Ephraim, founder of the monastery, was the one who had found Marcus as a baby. The one who had raised him and stayed in contact with Marcus until the old man's death.

Father Shaun straightened his raso again. "You'll need to hurry and get your things packed," he said in the same calm voice. "A van will be here soon to pick you up. The school would like you to be ready to go with them when they arrive."

The heavy book Marcus had thrown earlier slipped out of his withered left hand and dropped to the stones again, flipping open to a complex diagram showing how to combine the flows of air and land magic. Marcus barely noticed it. "They're coming *today?*"

Father Shaun glanced briefly at the pages of the book before averting his eyes. Is *that* why this was happening? Had the monk contacted the state because of Marcus's magic?

"Principal Teagarden said to expect him and a few of the boys from your school by lunchtime," the monk said.

Lunchtime! That was only a few hours away. "Please," Marcus begged. "You can't do this. Tell them to wait. Just a day or two." He wanted to tell the father how dangerous it was for him outside the monastery, about the Dark Circle waiting for him. But if the monk had a problem with Marcus studying magic, he could just imagine how Father Shaun would respond to the idea of dark wizards who could change into huge black snakes anytime they wanted.

"I'm sorry," Father Shaun said. "We really don't have any choice."

As Marcus watched the monk turn and walk away, drops of sweat trickled down his back—ice cold despite the harsh Arizona heat. He could deal with Principal Teagarden. Even the boys' school held no fear for him now that he'd discovered his magic. The Dark Circle was another matter, though. With six months to plan, there was no doubt in his mind that they were just waiting for him to get back within their reach.

He had to get out of here—now. But how? And where would he go? Kyja had all of their money. And even if he *had* money, what could he do with it? The monastery was located on a few acres along the edge of the Sonoran Desert. Miles of sandy emptiness stood between him and the nearest city.

He could wheel himself out to the road. And then what, head into the desert? Try to hitch a ride on a remote road that might see two or three cars pass by in a day, if that? Even if he did get a ride, with no money, no food, and no place to stay, the Dark Circle would have no problem catching up with him.

He spun his wheelchair around and headed back to his room, passing a group of monks walking sedately into the chapel. A few of them glanced in his direction. Did they know he was being thrown out? That it was putting his life in danger? If so, none of them did anything about it. No more than Kyja was doing, or Master Therapass.

Fine. He was on his own then. He'd been on his own most of his life anyway, before there was Kyja, and Therapass, and all of the other people he'd met over the last year. He'd managed to survive before. He'd have to do it again now.

He raced down the hallway leading to his room, rubber wheels whirring against the polished floor.

It wouldn't take him long to gather his things. He didn't have much in the way of possessions, and his room was so barren it looked more like a jail cell. He tucked his staff into a Velcro strap on the back of his chair, hung his leather pack on a handle, and began gathering Master Therapass's scrolls and books, along with his clothes and personal items.

At least there was one thing he had going for him: the motorcycle he and Kyja had driven across the country was still here. He didn't know how much gas it had in the tank, and managing to start it and drive it the few miles to the monastery after his last jump from Farworld had been an ordeal to say the least. But it was his only chance. He couldn't stay here and wait to be taken away.

Marcus turned to put his things into his backpack, but it was gone. He looked under his chair, assuming it must have slipped off the handle. It wasn't there. He looked on his bed, thinking he might have put it there. But he distinctly remembered hanging it on the back of his wheelchair.

He wheeled his chair in a circle, already knowing what he would find. As impossible as it seemed, his backpack was gone. He looked at the door. Could Father Shaun have slipped in and silently taken the pack to keep Marcus from leaving?

Marcus wheeled himself to the door and whipped it open, ready to confront the monk. But there was no one in the entire fifty-foot length of the hall. But something *was* lying on the floor at the far end. Marcus wheeled down the corridor to the intersection of the guest quarters and the wing of the monastery with the monks' rooms. There, lying neatly on the stone floor, was his pack.

He glanced down the hallway leading into the monks' quarters and craned his neck to check the way he'd just come. Was this a trick? A joke? If so, who was playing it, and why?

With his pack on his lap, he returned to his room. Whatever kind of trick the monk was playing on him, Marcus would not let it throw off his plans. As soon as he packed his things, he would locate the motorcycle keys, check for gas, and . . .

When Marcus opened the door to his room, all of his books and papers were gone. His mouth dropped open. This was impossible. No way could anyone have come into his room without him seeing. He stretched to look under his bed, but the floor was as bare as the rest of the room.

Cautiously he turned back to the open door and wheeled out. Something fluttered across the far end of the hall where his pack had been, flipping end over end despite the fact that the air in the hallway was still.

Air magic?

But he hadn't felt anything, hadn't sensed the flows of magic required to ask an elemental for its help. Biting the inside of his cheek, Marcus wheeled to the end of the hall and picked up one of the scrolls the wizard had given him.

He looked down the hall leading into the monks' quarters and saw a neat line of his books and papers spread evenly down the corridor. There was something very odd going on here and the only explanation Marcus could think of was magic. But as far as he knew, he was the only one on Earth who could use magic—because he was the only person on Earth who was from Farworld.

Except for members of the Dark Circle.

Were they here? Had they somehow breached the monastery's security?

A cold chill ran across his skull and down his back as he hurried along the hall, gathering his books and papers. If the Dark Circle *was* here, the Thrathkin S'Bae could be hiding anywhere. But why would the dark wizards resort to silly tricks? Why not attack him?

After reaching the end of the corridor, he picked up the last of his papers and saw something in front of the final door. Something that could not possibly be there. He shifted the papers on his lap, looking for the backpack he'd piled them on top of, but it was no longer there.

Instead, somehow, it was lying on the floor in front of the one door in the entire monastery that was forbidden to him. The door that was always kept locked. The door to the room Elder Ephraim had stayed in until his death.

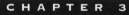

CHAPTER 3

DROPPING IN

"THIS IS A REALLY, REALLY, *really,* bad idea," Riph Raph said, his voice cracking.

"I told you—you don't have to come," Kyja whispered back. The two of them crept slowly down the tower stairs, keeping an eye out for wizards, who were unlikely to be moving around at that time of night, and guards, who were *quite* likely to be about.

"Oh, that makes it *much* better. Maybe Turnip Head would let you go sneaking around the tower by yourself, but I won't."

"I told you to stop calling him that." Kyja paused at the corner where the staircase intersected the level she needed to reach. She peeked around a corner, spotting a guard resplendent in full battle armor, trying to get the last drops out of his waterskin. "Besides, Marcus would be far more likely to do this kind of thing than either of us. Now, do you want to stand here talking all night, or do something about that guard?"

The skyte poked one large yellow eye around the wall. "What I should do is shout, 'Hey, you big galoot. Get that thing out of your mouth and keep this girl out of more trouble than she's already in!'"

Kyja stuck out her tongue. "Do, and I'll tell everyone we meet that you're my pet flying lizard."

Riph Raph shot an evil look in her direction. There was nothing he hated more than being called a lizard. "All right. But don't blame me if you get caught anyway. We skytes are known for our good looks and winning personalities, not our stealth."

Kyja pointed silently to a spot just above the guard's head. Riph Raph gulped, his Adam's apple bobbing, and launched himself into the air. Flapping his small wings as silently as he could, he flew around the corner and into the landing.

The guard, with his head tilted straight up, never noticed the skyte.

I probably could have walked up to him and pinched him on the behind without him seeing me, Kyja thought.

It wasn't until a tiny ball of blue flame bounced off the guard's helm, that the waterskin dropped from his hand and he grabbed the hilt of his sword.

With the guard's attention focused on him, Riph Raph darted toward the window. Unfortunately, the guard stepped directly into his flight path, long sword flashing. Narrowly avoiding the blade, the skyte looped in the air, bounced off the ceiling, screeched in surprise, and shot out another fireball.

"Help!" the guard shouted. He swung his sword wildly back and forth as Riph Raph dodged and circled.

Kyja, unsure whether she should continue sneaking past the guard or come to Riph Raph's aid, stood halfway between the stairs and the hall, completely unnoticed. She could hear the guards' armor clanking as they raced up the stairs, but she couldn't leave her friend alone. It wasn't until the skyte made an awkward circle, ricocheted off the wall, and flew straight out the window that she hurried out of sight.

As she sneaked down the hallway, she heard the guard shout to his companions something about two, possibly three, full-size wyverns.

Kyja placed a hand over her mouth, stifling a laugh. Reaching the end of the corridor, she rushed to where Riph Raph sat preening on a windowsill. "Are you all right?" she asked, searching his wings for any nicks or cuts.

Riph Raph tossed back his head and flapped his ears. "Are you joking? That fool might as well have been using a dust mop instead of a sword. Skytes are known in the animal world as the kings of the sky."

Kyja grinned. "I thought you were known for your good looks and personalities."

"As well as for our superb acrobatic flying skills. And daring."

Kyja rubbed the skyte's back scales and listened to him purr. "But maybe not for your humility. Now come on. Let's finish what we came here for together, before your head gets too big to fit through the doorway."

"Speaking of that," Riph Raph said, hopping from the windowsill to her shoulder. "Could you please explain again exactly what it is we're doing? Other than sneaking around and nearly getting ourselves thrown in the dungeon?"

Kyja sighed. "I knew you weren't listening before. Now pay attention. It's obvious that the note on my bed was left by someone who wants Marcus to get back to Farworld."

"Like all those people trying to kill him?"

"Of course not." Kyja reached a spot where two hallways joined, checked to make sure all four directions were clear, and turned right. A stone gargoyle statue watched her go past with sleepy eyes. "Why would someone who wanted to kill Marcus help us?"

Riph Raph blinked, clearly not convinced.

Kyja tiptoed by a slightly open door through which came a loud, wet snoring sound. "Whoever gave us that note was also giving us a clue about how to get Marcus safely through the realm of shadows."

"That's where I'm unclear," the skyte said. "How does a riddle get Marcus past the shadow creatures? Even Master Therapass hasn't found a way to do that."

"I'll tell you when I know for sure. But first we need to make sure Marcus is okay." Kyja stopped outside a familiar door; Riph Raph stiffened on her shoulder.

"And how do you mean to do that?"

Ever so gently, Kyja pushed open the door to Master Therapass's study. She peered through the opening to where a large gray wolf lay sleeping in front of the fireplace. His yellow eyes were cracked open just enough that they reflected the glow of the embers. But Kyja knew that was how the wizard slept. "That's where you come in."

Riph Raph immediately leaped off of her shoulder and flapped halfway down the corridor to a chandelier lit with magical flames. During the day, the flames were bright yellow, but at night they dimmed to a deep blue. "No. No, no, no. I said I'd help you get here. But I am not breaking into that wolf's den so you can steal his *aptura discerna*. Have you seen those jaws? He could eat a dozen of me in one sitting and not be full."

Kyja eased the door shut and caught up with him. "Master Therapass wouldn't eat you. And we aren't breaking in. You saw for yourself—the door isn't even locked. And it's not stealing, it's just *. . . borrowing.*"

"Then we can go back to our room, sleep—which you don't seem to be doing enough lately—and in the morning, ask Master Therapass to *borrow* it."

Kyja stomped her foot. The skyte could be so infuriating at times. "You know very well he won't give me permission. Besides, I need to check on Marcus tonight. There has to be a reason we got that note when we did. Are you going to help me or not?"

"Not," Riph Raph said at once, refusing to budge from his perch.

"Fine." Kyja turned around and started down the hall.

"At last she sees reason." The skyte flew to her shoulder. "Trust me. You'll feel much better about this in the morning."

"I *will* feel better," Kyja said, easing the wizard's door the rest of the way open. "Because I'll have checked on Marcus. If I see anything suspicious at all, I'll bring him to Farworld at once."

"How are you going to do that?" Riph Raph dug his talons into Kyja's shoulder, clearly upset. "The aptura discerna is at the top of the wall—nearly to the ceiling."

Kyja winced as the skyte's talons bit into her flesh. "Then it's a good thing I can climb." She stretched her arms over her head and stared up at the aptura discerna glowing dimly in the dark room as she took off her slippers.

Riph Raph looked from her face to the circle on the wall. "Stop," he hissed softly when it was clear she meant to go through with her plan. "Let's talk about this some more."

"I'm finished talking," Kyja whispered. "Keep an eye on the wizard and let me know if he wakes up." She tiptoed into the study, watching for traps and alarms.

"You'll know if he wakes up, because he'll be crunching our

bones for a midnight snack," the skyte said, waiting just outside the door.

The good thing about being immune to magic was that there were almost no traps that worked on Kyja. Motion or heat-sensing alarms, on the other hand, were another thing completely. The best of those had been stolen when the wizard was locked in the dungeon, and he hadn't gotten around to replacing them yet. But Kyja knew of at least two that were still active.

The first sensor looked like an ordinary teapot—unless you noticed the way the spout rotated 360 degrees, checking for anyone other than the wizard in the room. If it spotted an intruder, steam shot out of the spout in an ear-splitting whistle. Kyja might never have figured it out if it hadn't been for the fact that Master Therapass despised tea.

The trick to avoiding the teapot was staying low enough to keep out of its line of sight and sticking close to large objects that tended to throw it off. Kyja slithered across the room—stomach pressed against the cool stone floor—until she was just below the pot. Then, when it was looking in the other direction, she jumped up and slipped a blue wool tea cozy over it.

"You won't be doing any tattling tonight," she whispered.

The second alarm, a magical flying cookie tin, though far more obvious, was not nearly as easy to trick. It swooped around the room on tiny silver wings, watching for anything airborne. Had Riph Raph not been such a coward, the tin would have spotted him flying in the room at once. Getting up to the aptura discerna would put Kyja right in its sights, setting off a raucous clanging and rattling, which would immediately wake the sleeping wolf.

Fortunately Kyja had come prepared. She reached into her robe pocket and pulled out a thick brown bar wrapped in cloth. Careful not to let the cookie bar touch her skin or clothing, she unwrapped the cloth and waited for the tin to swoop into range. When the flying spy was almost directly over her head, she tossed the cookie into the air.

Instantly, the tin swooped down, opened its lid, and chomped the molasses treat. Gooey brown liquid oozed onto the lid, gluing it shut. Eventually the tin would dislodge the cookie, but by then Kyja would be gone, and hopefully Master Therapass would assume his scout had been indulging in a late-night kitchen run.

She looked over her shoulder and smirked at Riph Raph. Teach him to underestimate her. The skyte rolled his eyes and flapped his wings, urging her to hurry up.

Now that the alarms were disabled, the trick was reaching the window itself. Despite her earlier claim, Kyja wasn't sure she could climb up to it. The stone wall had a few cracks and crannies she could lodge her fingers and toes into, but looking from the floor to the top of the wall, she couldn't find a clear path all the way up.

A tall set of shelves provided a way to get nearly as high as she needed, but from the highest shelf, she'd have to stretch almost two arm lengths sideways. She'd made tougher climbs, exploring nearby cliffs as a little girl, but back then, she'd had ropes and climbing hooks. And a sleeping wizard hadn't been nearly at her feet, ready to wake up at the first noise.

It wasn't like the aptura discerna would come to her, though. The longer she waited, the better the chance of Master Therapass waking up. As though warning her of that very thing, the wolf yawned—his dagger-like teeth glittering—and shifted a little closer to the fire.

Riph Raph let out a strangled squawk; Kyja pressed a finger to her lips.

Taking a deep breath, she gripped a shelf at eye level and pulled herself up. Her toes found the ledge of a shelf below, and she began climbing. Working her way up was like scaling an avalanche-prone ravine. Bottles and knick-knacks balanced precariously close to her hands. She found herself watching the unstable trinkets, checking on Master Therapass, and trying to ignore Riph Raph's anxious signals, all while scaling high enough that a fall would not only wake the wolf, but quite possibly cause her serious harm.

When at last she pulled herself onto the top shelf—securing a glass owl with her right foot and blowing on a precariously tilted scroll to keep it from rolling off—she released a relieved breath and tried not to look down.

Outside the door, Riph Raph hopped from one foot to the other, his ears flapping nervously. Kyja vowed that the next time she attempted something like this, she'd bring a less high-strung companion.

She eyed the glowing circle, so temptingly close, yet just far enough away that reaching it would require her to lean farther out than was safe. Clamping the side of the bookshelf between her knees, she stretched until her shoulder felt ready to pop from its socket. Her fingers were so close to the aptura discerna that its colors reflected on the back of her hand, but she still couldn't quite reach it.

Holding her breath, she moved one leg a few inches away from the shelf. Her body wavered on the edge of losing its balance. The shelf groaned. With a desperate lunge, she grabbed for the edge of the circle. As her fingers closed around it, something slammed into the back of her head.

Kyja turned to see the cookie tin circling around for another attack. The bookshelf shifted under her weight, and then she was falling. With a cry of dismay, she spun and grabbed for support. But she was too far out; there was nothing to hold. Her arms flailed as the hard stone floor raced to meet her.

At the sound of her voice, the wolf's yellow eyes flew open. Silently, it bent its legs and leaped across the room. In midair it transformed into a human. With incredible grace for a man his age, Master Therapass leaned forward and wrapped his arms around Kyja right before she hit the ground.

The wizard's stern eyes darkened and his lips drew tight as he spotted the colored circle in Kyja's hand.

Riph Raph backed slowly away from the door, his ears nearly disappearing under his chin. "Er," he squeaked, "he's awake."

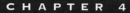

CHAPTER 4

MISSING
REFLECTIONS

MARCUS LOOKED FROM HIS PACK to the door. A coincidence? He didn't think so. Whoever, or whatever, had taken his things had clearly led him here, to his old guardian's room. The question was, what was he going to do about it?

He reached for the door and froze. What if a giant black snake waited for him on the other side? He didn't know of anyone other than the Thrathkin S'Bae—and himself—who could do magic on Earth. And there was no doubt in his mind that whatever was happening involved some sort of magic.

Glancing down the hallway to make sure no one was coming, he reached for the power of water. One of the first things he'd learned from Cascade, the water elemental who'd agreed to join him and Kyja on their quest to open a doorway between Earth and Farworld, was that water magic held the power of seeing.

The Fontasian with the blue skin and white hair could literally see through forests and mountains for miles in any direction. Marcus wasn't *that* good with water magic, but he should be able to

41

see through a door. That was assuming he could tap into the power of water at all. For whatever reason, using water magic had become harder and harder over the last few months—almost as though the elementals controlling it were trying to cut him off from their power.

"Help me see," he muttered, summoning the help of the Fontasians.

Unlike how most people on Earth viewed magic, it wasn't just waving a wand or saying a bunch of random words. Casting a spell had two parts. The first was knowing which magic to use—water, land, air, fire, or some combination—and what to do with it.

The second part was asking the elements who controlled that magic to do what you wanted. Black magic, the kind used by the Dark Circle, involved forcing the elements to obey your commands. That kind of magic could not be used without ultimately corrupting the caster, and it was most effective for spells that were inherently evil. The kind of magic Master Therapass used required the willing help of the elements.

Marcus closed his eyes, picturing the flow of water that would let him see through the solid surface of the door, while focusing on the importance of his need. For a minute, he didn't think the spell would work, like picking up a phone and hearing no dial tone.

Then, as he was about to give up, something tickled the backs of his eyes, and he got the briefest glimpse of a room much like his own. A bed. A desk. And something else, which he didn't recognize.

He was almost positive no one was in the room. But there *was* something. Some kind of power he didn't recognize bounced back at him like a voice echoing in a mountain pass.

Was it possible that this was the work of Master Therapass? He knew for a fact the wizard couldn't cross from Farworld to Earth.

Kyja and Marcus were the only humans who had ever made the leap without the use of dark magic. But maybe it was some kind of message. Marcus had to get into the room.

He tried the door and wasn't surprised when the brass knob turned barely a quarter of an inch before stopping. The monks had been very clear that this room was off limits. He'd never thought to question why a simple bedroom should be forbidden—until now.

Marcus peered into the small keyhole. Changing the state of things—hot to cold, on to off, or, in this case, locked to unlocked —required the power of air. He wasn't nearly as familiar with that magic, but one of the few air-magic scrolls Master Therapass had given him had a spell that might be able to disengage the inner workings of a lock. The scroll was in his bag, but he'd read it so many times, he nearly had it memorized.

Gripping the knob in both hands, he focused on changing the lock from closed to open. Magic didn't require words, but he'd found that he could focus his powers if he used little poems.

"Currents of air, wind, and sky," he said quietly. "Through this keyhole quickly fly. The way I must go has been blocked. Help me to undo this lock."

It wasn't much of a poem, but he could feel it working. A soft breeze brushed by his cheek. The doorknob rattled, started to turn, then stopped. He reached up and tried the knob. Still locked.

Had the elements rejected his request? He'd managed to lock and unlock the door to his own room before. But maybe because he was trying to break into a room the monks had forbidden him to enter, the air elementals had refused his request.

Somehow he needed to communicate the importance of his need. Focusing his thoughts again, he tried to convey how important it was that he open this door. Surely the elementals would understand why he had to break into a room if it was the only way he could escape the Dark Circle.

"My need is great; I ask once more. Help me to unlock this door."

The power of air magic swirled around him, and, for a quick second, he felt something else. It seemed to be a response to his magic—coming not from inside the lock, but from behind the door. Almost an echo of his request bouncing back at him, reflecting his magic in a way he'd never experienced.

The knob rattled ever so slightly, followed by a soft click. Somewhere behind him, footsteps echoed; Marcus glanced over his shoulder. Someone was coming. Quickly, he turned the knob. He pushed the door open, wheeled inside, and swung the door shut behind him.

Inside the room, he pressed his ear to the closed door. Had he been seen? Or heard? When several minutes had passed, and no one came to check the door, he breathed a sigh of relief. Now to see what was in here.

He turned around, but was disappointed to find the room almost empty. It was a tiny cell, as barren as his own. The only furnishings were a bed—stripped of its blankets and sheets—a tall standing mirror, and a plain wooden desk. Nothing that could have accounted for the power he'd felt.

He wheeled over to the desk and tried one of the drawers, expecting them to be locked. Instead, they slid open, and inside were all his missing things—scrolls, papers, a pair of smelly socks. Everything he'd thought he'd misplaced over the last few weeks was tucked neatly into the drawers of the desk.

How did all of his things end up here? He looked around the room, searching for a clue. Other than his socks and scrolls, there was nothing out of the ordinary here. It was just an empty room with an old desk, the standing mirror, and a plain bed. But then why would someone go to all the trouble of locking it up? He glanced at the mirror—the only thing that looked out of place. Monks weren't exactly known for their vanity, so there weren't many mirrors in the monastery. Maybe something was hidden behind it.

His hopes were quickly dashed when he realized there was no place behind it to hide anything. Even the mirror was useless. At some point, the glass inside the ornate frame had been removed. He peered through the empty oval and found only a dusty baseboard. There was nothing here. Nothing at all.

With a sigh, he spun his chair around. One of the wheels bumped the mirror, and it started to tilt forward. Afraid someone would hear the crash, Marcus reached out to catch it. His palm met the edge of the frame, steadying it.

As his fingers wrapped around where the glass should have been, he felt something he thought he never would again. It was a jerk, deep in his stomach—like a hook caught somewhere in the middle of his gut, pulling until it seemed like he was turning inside out. Marcus gasped as the world spun. A giddy excitement raced through him.

He was jumping!

CHAPTER 5

WINDOW TO THE SOUL

MASTER THERAPASS RELEASED KYJA so quickly, she barely had time to get her feet under her before hitting the ground.

"I . . . I can explain," she said, straightening and smoothing her robe.

"It was my fault," Riph Raph blurted. "I told her to do it."

Master Therapass flicked his right hand, and suddenly Riph Raph was lying on his back in the center of the room, his legs bound with silver string and an apple stuffed in his beak like a pig ready to be cooked. "I have no time for stories," the wizard said sharply. He glared at Kyja. "And no patience for thieves."

He held out his hand, and Kyja meekly returned the glowing circle. She opened her mouth to explain, but realized there *was* no explanation. Riph Raph had been right; she should have shown the wizard the note as soon as she found it and asked for his help. She wondered if she'd lost his trust for good. Looking at the ground, she reached into her pocket, took out the note, and handed it to him.

"What's this?" Master Therapass drew his glasses from the sleeve of his robe and balanced them on the end of his nose as he studied the scrap of parchment. He read the message, turned it over and examined the back. "Where did you get this?"

"I found it on my bed yesterday morning, after you told me I couldn't . . ." Kyja chewed her lower lip. "After you told me I couldn't use the aptura discerna."

"Do you have any idea who put it there?"

Kyja shook her head. "It's just . . . I thought it was a riddle. I figured out that it's talking about a shadow, and I thought—I thought . . ." She wiped a tear from her eyes, trying hard not to cry. She wanted to be strong. She wanted to do the right thing. But lately she didn't seem to know what the right thing was anymore. "I'm so sorry." She sniffed.

The wizard's eyes softened. He placed a hand on Kyja's shoulder. "Now, now, there's no need for tears. I know you were only worried about Marcus."

Kyja bunched up the front of her robe and dabbed at her eyes with it.

The wizard lifted the parchment to his nose and sniffed. "Odd."

"What?" Kyja asked

"The ink. It has a strange aroma I've never smelled before."

Kyja hadn't noticed. "I thought maybe the note was a clue about how to get Marcus safely through the realm of shadows."

"I'm not sure I understand," the wizard said.

"The riddle talks about shadows disappearing at noon and in the middle of the night." Kyja swallowed. It had all made sense to her at the time. Now, as she tried to put it into words, the whole thing seemed sort of silly.

But Master Therapass was tugging at the tip of his beard, his eyes thoughtful. "Go on."

"I thought that maybe the riddle meant that if those are the times shadows are at their weakest, maybe they're also when the realm of shadows is the least dangerous. I thought I could try pulling Marcus over at midnight. To see if it worked."

Master Therapass frowned. "Making guesses like that is far too dangerous. You could have put Marcus's life in danger because you had a simple hunch."

Kyja pressed her lips together, her eyes feeling hot again.

The wizard sighed. "Would it help if I let you see for yourself that Marcus is safe?"

Kyja nodded. "Oh, yes!"

"Very well. I had thought it would be easier if you could keep your mind on other things, focus on something other than the boy. But it's clear I was mistaken." He laid the aptura discerna flat on a nearby table.

Still trussed nearby, Riph Raph mumbled around the apple in his mouth, his yellow eyes bulging. "Grprut turhurg ribe bor."

Master Therapass glanced at him and snapped his fingers, releasing Riph Raph from his bonds. "Try to stay out of trouble."

The skyte flew to Kyja's side and pouted.

As soon as she looked into the aptura discerna, Kyja's heart began to pound. Was Master Therapass right? Would she be better off not seeing Marcus? Maybe seeing him *would* make it harder to wait until he could be brought safely over. Maybe she was being selfish.

But the wizard didn't understand. Kyja had always had a special connection with Marcus. Sometimes she could almost think his thoughts, feel his feelings. She knew how frustrated he had to be by now. And she *did* have a strong feeling that he needed her help.

As she looked into the window, the colors began to mix and blur, taking on a hazy pink hue. She tried to remember everything

Master Therapass had taught her about using the aptura discerna. First, she had to clear her mind. She had to push aside all negative emotions—fear, anger, disappointment. She wasn't angry, and disappointment wasn't a problem. But to let the window look inside her, she'd have to get rid of her fear. That would be harder. If she hadn't been afraid for Marcus, she wouldn't be here in the first place.

Instinctively, her hand went to Riph Raph. They argued sometimes, but ever since she'd rescued him as a baby, the skyte had been her best and most loyal companion. "I'm sorry I got you into trouble."

Riph Raph rubbed his head under her chin. "It's all right."

She tried thinking of happy things. Riding the motorcycle across the roads of Earth while Riph Raph cowered in terror. Floating down the Noble River with Cascade. Watching the skyte catch fish. Finding Marcus safe in Land Keep. A little at a time, her breathing evened and slowed.

Riph Raph edged around to look into the window, where the pink haze was slowly clearing. "Let him be all right," Kyja whispered under her breath.

As the pink disappeared, Kyja made out a small room. Marcus's? She saw a bed, a desk, and a mirror. There, beside the mirror, Marcus's wheelchair was turned on its side. But where was Marcus? Her breathing sped up, and as it did, pink began to swirl back into the window, clouding her view.

"Relax," Master Therapass said. "Clear your mind."

But she couldn't. Where was Marcus? She'd come to the window looking for him. The aptura discerna had found his room. Why not him? Her heart thudded. Why wasn't the window working? The image began to fade.

"Show me Marcus," she demanded, reaching for the aptura discerna. "Show him to me."

But the room disappeared and a terrible certainty filled her chest. Something had happened to Marcus. Something horrible.

CHAPTER 6

THE *IS*

WHEN MARCUS WAS THREE OR FOUR, he'd dreamed of going to the ocean one day. Cold wind blowing in his face, waves crashing on the shore. He'd never made it to the ocean, but he thought he must be there now.

A rhythmic roaring filled his ears like waves pounding against a rocky beach, and a bitterly cold gray fog swirled around him. He shivered so hard the back of his head repeatedly knocked against the icy ground.

"K-Kyja?" he groaned, opening his eyes. "Where are you?"

Where are you?

Where? Where?

Are? Are?

You?

His words echoed back from all directions at once. Only they didn't sound like his voice, more like someone repeating what he'd said. He tried pushing himself to a sitting position, but the smooth stone beneath him was so bitterly cold, it numbed his fingers as soon as he touched it.

He yanked his hand back and blew into his cupped palms, trying to warm them. Where was he? And how long had he been there? He could remember reaching for the mirror. The tug in his stomach. After that . . . he wasn't sure. Kyja must have pulled him over to Farworld. If she did, though, where was she?

He tried to peer through the thick clouds swirling around him, and for a moment thought he caught a glimpse of blue eyes to his left. But the mist closed in again too quickly for him to be sure. "Hello?" he whispered, fear tightening like a belt across his stomach.

"A seeker," a papery voice said from somewhere to his left.

A voice that sounded exactly the same spoke from his right. "A finder."

The fog in front of Marcus danced, and he briefly caught sight of a face staring back at him. It was hard to tell what the face looked like; the features were . . . fuzzy.

"A wise man."

"A fool."

The voices came from all around him.

Marcus hugged his arms across his chest, trying to stave off the icy gray curtain leeching the heat from his body. His teeth chattered so violently, he could hardly speak. "W-who's th-there?"

"I am a supplicant," said the voice behind him.

"I am a prophet."

"I am a stranger."

"I am a friend."

A terrifying thought occurred to him. What if this wasn't Farworld at all? Could he somehow have launched himself into the realm of shadows? He tried to stand before realizing he'd left his staff in Elder Ephraim's room along with his wheelchair.

With each breath, clouds puffed from his mouth and nose; he was amazed to see tiny crystals of ice forming on the hairs of his arms. "I have to get out of here."

Four different voices shouted at once. Or was it the same voice coming from four different directions? "Leave as you wish! You have been given a gift! Use it wisely! Spend it carefully!"

"What gift?" This was crazy. He had no idea where he was or who was talking to him. Something jingled in his hand. He looked down to see four gold coins in his palm. Where had they come from? He hadn't been holding them before.

At the same time, the roaring stopped, and the mist cleared. Marcus looked up to see that he was in the bottom of a deep, round pit. The walls were solid ice, so high he could barely make out a small gray opening hundreds of feet overhead. A frigid wind whistled down on him as if he were in the middle of an arctic wilderness.

The walls looked like waterfalls had flowed down them once, but now they were frozen solid. The silence was so complete that he could still hear the roaring, which had been abruptly cut off, echoing in his ears.

No one else was in the pit with him, and he saw no way for anyone to get in or out. So whose were the voices he'd heard? Then he saw them. Trapped in the waterfalls were four old men, their penetrating blue eyes locked open behind clear ice. Each wore a long, gray robe and had a beard to his waist. It was impossible to tell for sure, but from where he sat, they looked identical. It was as if they had all stepped into the water right before it froze. They all stared at him.

Marcus ran his tongue across his upper lip, and the cold made it stick for a moment. He looked down at the coins. "What am I supposed to do with these?"

None of the men said anything. How could they? They were obviously dead.

He turned the first coin over. Something was engraved in the center of it: two letters, *I* and *S*.

"Is?" he whispered.

At the sound of his voice, the waterfall to his left came to life. The previously frozen water crashed into a small pool at its base. Mist flowed from the pool. The roar of the falling water buffeted his eardrums. A hand reached through the mist, and before Marcus could think to pull away, it dragged him into the water.

———◇———

Marcus was in his wheelchair again, sitting in Elder Ephraim's room. Everything looked the same. The desk. The bed. The glassless mirror. His backpack lay in his lap as though he'd never been pulled into the mirror at all.

Had he? Or had it been an illusion caused by whatever magic had moved his things?

"Good choice," a voice said.

Marcus spun around to see a boy about his own age, leaning against the wall by the door.

"The wisest people choose the *Is*," the boy said with a smile.

"Who are you?" Marcus asked, wheeling his chair backward. "How did you get in here?"

The boy shook back a lock of blond hair and laughed, his amazingly blue eyes sparkling. "I'm your guide. You brought me here."

Marcus stared at his own arms and legs. He wasn't wet. And

despite the fact that he could clearly remember almost freezing to death, he wasn't cold. Could the boy have made him believe that he was in that place with the frozen old men? Marcus had nearly convinced himself he'd never gone through the mirror at all, when he realized he was still gripping the gold coins.

"I'll take that," the boy said, reaching out a hand.

Marcus looked at the four glittering circles. The one reading *Is* still lay on top of the others. "The *Is*," he whispered. "You said the wisest people choose the *Is*."

"Of course. No worry what might or might not happen down the road. No regrets over what took place before. The here and now is the best place, I think."

Marcus didn't understand, but he thought he was beginning to. "Are we in the . . . *Is?*"

The boy laughed delightedly and nodded like a proud parent seeing a baby take its first steps.

Marcus looked around the room. It looked like Elder Ephraim's quarters, but maybe that was part of the magic. "You said you were my guide. Did you bring me here?"

The boy laughed again, but this time shook his head. "No one can bring you to the *Is*. You've always been here. Once you pay me, I can make sure you stay forever."

Now Marcus was confused all over again. "If I've been here all along, why would I have to pay you to stay?"

Footsteps sounded from outside in the hallway. "Marcus?" a voice called. They'd found him. Was Principle Teagarden here already?

He was trapped. He had no way to get to his motorcycle. No way to escape. He turned to the boy. "Can you get me out of here?" He jingled the coins in his hand. "I'll pay you."

The boy stretched out his fingers eagerly, and Marcus nearly handed him all the coins. But something in the boy's eyes made him hesitate.

Someone pounded on the outside of the door. "Marcus," a man's voice called. "What are you doing? Come out of there at once."

"Give me your gift. You must spend it," the boy hissed. He seemed too eager to take the money, almost greedy.

"Get me away from here first," Marcus said. "Then I'll pay you."

The doorknob jiggled, and Marcus heard someone whisper something about a key.

"Why would you want to leave?" asked the boy, his lower lip pushing out in a pout. "You can stay here forever. Never growing older. Never losing loved ones." His eyes shined. "Never experiencing death."

A key rattled in the lock. The knob started to turn.

"Give me your coin!" the boy cried, snatching at Marcus's hand.

"No!" Marcus screamed. He threw the coin to the ground and felt something pull in his stomach.

CHAPTER 7

THE WAS

COLD AIR BIT AT MARCUS'S EXPOSED SKIN. His fingers were numb, and his face felt frost-bitten, as if he'd been in the pit the whole time instead of back in the monastery. He no longer knew what was real and what wasn't. The only clue that something had changed was the fact that now he held only three coins.

"What do you want?" he shouted at the four old men, all of them once again frozen in their icy tombs. He got no answer. No sign that anyone had heard him at all, even though he had a clear sense he was being watched by the four sets of eyes.

He turned over the next coin in his hand. The letters *W-A-S* were engraved on the front. *Was,* he thought, careful not to say the word out loud. He wanted to fling the coins to the ground—tell whoever was playing this game that he refused to take part.

But what if he did that, and the coins disappeared? How would he get out? The walls were far too steep to climb, even if he'd had two good legs and arms.

"Is this some kind of test?" he asked. "If it is, I don't understand what it means." His muscles ached, and his teeth chattered.

"F-fine," he said, when it was clear he had no other choice. He closed his fingers around the coin along with the other two and said, "Was."

Water roared behind him, and before he could turn, a hand was pulling him into the mist.

———◆———

Marcus stood at one end of a hallway so long it appeared to go on forever. The floor was a bright red stone, the walls so yellow he couldn't look at them for long without blinking. Every few yards, a door opened to the right or left. Between the doors were paintings set in elaborate gold frames. He started to crawl toward the first painting before realizing he was standing—without pain. Without even the aid of a staff.

Marcus flexed his right leg. It was strong and straight—no longer withered. His left arm was normal too. How could that be? He looked for the boy he'd seen before—the one who had called himself a guide—but there didn't appear to be anyone else in the hallway.

"Hello?" His voice echoed in the long empty corridor.

What was he supposed to do? He walked to the nearest picture frame and stared. It was a painting of himself lying on his back in the middle of the icy pit. He was looking at the coins in his hand. The image was realistic enough that it could have been a photograph if not for the brush strokes, their textures clear against the canvas. How could there be a painting of something that had taken place only minutes before? Who could have painted it? And why?

The air had a faint musty smell to it, as though no one had been here for years. That couldn't be true.

Was this another illusion? A trick? He slapped himself across the

face with the hand that, in the past, he could hardly move. He felt a
tingle in his cheek and palm, but no pain.

"It *is* a trick," he said.

The first door down the hall swung open, and a boy no older
than seven or eight skipped out. "There is no pain in the *Was*," he
sang. "No pain. No pain. No pain."

The boy looked like the guide from Elder Ephraim's room. He
had the same shockingly blue eyes. Same blond hair. Only he was
younger.

"Are you the other one's brother?" Marcus asked.

The child only giggled and skipped around the hallway.

The door the boy had come through hung partway open. Marcus
peeked in, expecting something amazing, or frightening, or dangerous. What he saw instead was so unexpected, he could only gape.

It was the exact same image as in the painting—himself, lying
on the ground in the pit, studying his coins. He turned to the little
boy, who was watching him with a slight smile.

"You can go in if you like," the boy said.

"No." Marcus shook his head. He wasn't going back to the pit.
Instead he started down the hallway. There were plenty of other
doors. He stopped at the next one and opened it. He saw himself
again, this time sitting in his wheelchair. Father Shaun stood in
front of him.

"He's funny," the boy said, peering through the doorway beside
Marcus and pointing at the monk.

Marcus glanced at the little boy. "Father Shaun?"

The child clapped his hands over his mouth and nodded.
"That's not who he really is."

Marcus stared at the monk. "Of course it is. Who else would he
be?"

The blond boy only giggled and began skipping in a circle. "Ice worm, mud worm, piece of pie."

Marcus had heard those words somewhere before. He spun around. "Where did you learn that?"

The boy ignored him, hopping across the hall on his hands and feet like a frog. "Ice worm, mud worm, piece of cake."

Marcus looked back through the door again. Looking at himself and Father Shaun was like opening a window to a moment in the past. Everything was accurate, down to the smallest detail—Father Shaun, the book on the ground, the monk weeding in the flower bed—as if he could snap his fingers and everyone would start moving. He could nearly smell the flowers growing in the garden and the arid scent of the Arizona desert beyond.

What would the Marcus inside the door do if he turned around and saw his double watching him?

Marcus turned to look at the hopping boy. He wasn't very old, but he seemed to understand what was happening, which was more than Marcus did. "Are you my guide?"

"I guess so," the boy said.

Marcus pointed through the door. "Is that . . . are they . . . real?"

"To you."

Maybe if Marcus went through the door, he could warn himself not to go into Elder Ephraim's room—to go straight to the motorcycle. Then he'd never get sucked into the mirror and be in this . . . whatever it was he was in.

"Hey!" he shouted. Nothing happened.

"They can't hear you," the child said, making faces at himself in the shiny red floor.

"You said I can go in, right?" Marcus asked.

The boy nodded, then went back to making faces.

Marcus swallowed. What would the monk do if he saw two Marcuses? "Can I get out if I go in?"

The boy nodded again.

Marcus tried to think it all through. If he went in and warned himself, he wouldn't go through the mirror, which would mean that he wouldn't be here to come out of the door again. Only if he wasn't here, how could he warn himself? The whole thing was too confusing. He could spend all day worrying about the consequences, or he could just do it.

He took a deep breath, checked on the boy, who didn't appear to be paying any attention to him, and stepped through the door.

He was back in his wheelchair again.

"You dropped this?" Father Shaun picked up the book and handed it to Marcus with an uneasy frown.

"Um, thanks," Marcus said, taking the volume and turning it over so the cover was facing down.

What was happening? He tried to turn and look behind him, but his body didn't seem to be under his control.

"How are your studies progressing?" the monk asked.

He tried to say, "I'm not going back to the school." Instead he said, "Good," and patted his stack of papers. "Just working on my, uh . . . algebra. Then some U.S. history. Gotta love the Industrial Revolution." The words forced themselves out of his mouth as though he had no control over his body, as if he had to repeat exactly what had happened the first time.

Father Shaun tugged at the sleeve of his raso. "I have some news that should make your studies go even better," he said.

Marcus wanted to scream, *No, you don't! You have terrible news.* But his mouth wouldn't move.

Their conversation continued exactly the way it had before, and

Marcus began to fear that he'd walked into a trap. Would he be stuck here forever, looking through his own eyes, but unable to act?

The little boy walked around from behind Father Shaun, as though he'd been hiding there all along. "It's more fun if you watch from outside yourself."

The monk smiled sadly. "We will miss you. But we have no choice. The state says this is not the proper place for a young boy. The monastery is not an orphanage."

"Not a monk. Not a monk. Not a monk." The little boy stuck his fingers in his ears, made a face at Father Shaun, and laughed. "Come play," he said to Marcus, reaching out a hand.

Suddenly, Marcus was standing beside Father Shaun, watching a copy of himself struggle with the news he'd just received. "How did you do that?" he asked at the same time the Marcus in the wheelchair asked, "How did they even find out I was here?"

"Being *in* the *Was* is boring," the guide said. "But when you watch it, you can do anything you want." He ran around the back of the chair and pretended to mess up the other Marcus's hair.

Marcus watched himself slam his fist on his lap and wince in pain. "If Elder Ephraim were alive, he would never allow this. I won't go," his duplicate said.

"Can't they see us?" Marcus asked. "Or hear us?"

The little boy shook his head as Father Shaun spoke. "Can't see, can't hear," the boy chanted.

The other Marcus dropped his book. "They're coming *today?*"

The last time he'd been here, Marcus had seen Father Shaun look away from the magic diagram. He'd assumed the monk was either embarrassed or offended. But this time, watching more closely, he noticed a mischievous grin on the father's face. Why would the monk smile about a book of magic spells?

The monk's smile disappeared as quickly as it had come. "Principal Teagarden said to expect him and a few of the boys from your school by lunchtime."

Marcus watched himself beg and the monk turn him down.

"You said Father Shaun isn't really a monk," he said to the guide, who was dancing among the flowers. "Who is he?"

"Another one. The one who took your things." The child knelt to smell a blossom.

"Father Shaun took my things?" That didn't make any sense. Why would the monk want Marcus's belongings? "How could he do that?"

But the boy seemed to have lost interest in the conversation. He stood up and wriggled his toes in the dirt. "Are you ready to go?"

The Marcus in the wheelchair turned and rolled toward the monastery. At the same time, the courtyard and garden began to grow dark.

"What's happening?" Marcus spun around. The color was fading out of everything as though the sun had disappeared from the sky. But he could still see it overhead, a sphere as gray as everything else.

"It's time to go," the boy said.

For the first time Marcus noticed the doorway—a rectangle of light in a world quickly turning black.

"I don't understand," Marcus said. Everything was disappearing. The flowers, the monastery, even the ground under his feet appeared to be losing substance. It was like he was floating in the middle of a black, empty space. A hand grabbed him and yanked him through the door.

CHAPTER 8

GOOD ADVICE

KYJA! KYJA, CONTROL YOURSELF." Master Therapass placed his wrinkled hands on Kyja's shoulders, and she realized she'd been banging her fists on the aptura discerna, willing it to show her Marcus.

"You said he was all right. You said he was safe." Kyja gripped the edge of the table to keep her hands from shaking. "Where is he?" she demanded, her heart pounding.

"Just because you cannot see Marcus does not mean he's in danger."

"Sure," Riph Raph said. "Maybe Turnip Head just knocked over his wheelchair, spread his things around on the floor and, um, took a nap . . . where you can't find him."

Master Therapass and Kyja glared at Riph Raph, and the skyte tucked his head under one wing. "I'll just let the two of you work this out."

Kyja took several deep breaths, trying to get herself under control. "What does it mean that I can't see him? He's not . . ."

"Dead?" The wizard shook his head, his long gray beard waggling. "No. If something had happened to the boy, you would see him anyway. This is odd. Most odd." He drummed his fingers on the table, and a series of scrolls and books marched in front of him, opening to certain sections or uncurling to reveal a few lines of text. The wizard looked at each one, then shook his head. The document moved on, and another took its place.

"You said the aptura discerna shows what's inside me, what I care about most," Kyja said. "What I care about is knowing that Marcus is safe. So why is the window showing me his things, but not him? Did I do something wrong?"

Master Therapass took off his glasses and looked down at her with his gentle brown eyes. "No, child. The all-seeing eye is not a wishing well. I have studied it for years and yet I still know but a small part of its power. There are many things I don't completely understand. Why it shows us some things and not others. Why it only works when our minds are calm. How it works on someone like you, who is immune to traditional magic."

Kyja shivered. Her entire life she'd dreamed of having magic. It wasn't until the wizard explained that she was from another world— a world that didn't use spells, wands, and potions—that she'd understood why she was different from everyone else on Farworld. But that didn't mean the desire for having magic had gone away.

"What we *do* know is that the aptura discerna is a window into the soul," Master Therapass continued. "What we see in it is a reflection of not only our desires, but our thoughts, our beliefs. To some extent, even our memories." He touched her shoulder. "The thing to do now is get some sleep. I will give the situation further study, and we can try again—"

"No!" Kyja blurted, cutting him off.

Master Therapass blinked.

"Marcus is in trouble." Kyja jumped up from the table, knocking her chair across the floor. "We don't have time to study. We need to help him."

"What are you suggesting?" the wizard asked. His face tensed, but she didn't care.

"I need to pull him over. Something's wrong." She put a hand to her chest. "I can feel it."

"Please sit down." Master Therapass pointed to her chair. It jumped up and hurried back to the table beside her. But Kyja didn't want to sit. She couldn't. Fear and anger fueled a desperate energy that forced her to keep moving.

"I understand your worry," the wizard said as Kyja paced the room. "But there are things you don't know. Things I probably should have told you before now. For one thing, Marcus *is* safe."

Kyja stopped pacing. "How can you know that?"

Master Therapass coughed into his fists. "I told you that I sent Marcus to Earth. That you are from there as well. What I didn't tell you was that just as there is a link between you and Marcus, there is a link between Earth and Farworld. I've known this for some time.

"What kind of link?" Kyja asked.

"I don't understand it completely. No one on Farworld does. When I first sent Marcus to Earth, I sent him to a person I'd been in communication with for some time."

Was he talking about Elder Ephraim, the man who found Marcus? "How could you communicate with someone on Earth? I thought the only way that was possible was by opening a drift."

The wizard held up a hand. "Now is not the time. Suffice it to say that when the time is right, I will explain more to you. You know that Marcus is destined to save Farworld. But you've never asked about *your* destiny. About how you will save Earth."

Kyja was speechless. She licked her lips. A day ago, this conversation would have fascinated her. But now she was worried about Marcus. "What does any of this have to do with keeping him safe?"

"There are places on Earth," Master Therapass explained. "Places of safety created by others who also understand the link between our worlds. The monastery is not as it seems. Elder Ephraim was a great religious leader. But he was more than that. As long as Marcus stays within the monastery, the Dark Circle cannot reach him."

"But he isn't there!" Kyja stamped her foot. "I would have seen him if he was. He must have left."

Master Therapass ran a finger across the aptura discerna, and the colors of the window swirled. "That is not possible. People are watching him, making sure he does not leave the grounds. I would have been alerted by one of them if he had."

Kyja ran her fingers through her long dark hair. "So we're supposed to just wait? I'm sorry; I can't do that. I know you don't believe the note. But I do. It's almost exactly the middle of the night. I can bring him over now. We can talk to him. See where he went."

"It is too great of a risk," Master Therapass said. "I have been studying Marcus's link to the shadow realm, and I fear it is an even greater threat to him that I had first thought. Believe that I am making progress. I've uncovered a way to keep him in Farworld longer than normal so he doesn't have to pass through the shadow realm as often. But I need more time to find a way to protect him when he does pass through."

Kyja wanted to tell him that if he wanted to protect Marcus, the best way to do it was to bring him here. But she bit back the words, knowing what he'd say.

The wizard smiled as though reading her thoughts. "If you care about him as much as you say you do, you will go back to bed while I think over what I've learned tonight. I will study the note. It may mean exactly what you think it does. If so, it will provide the solution we have been looking for. If not, we will avoid making what could be a terrible mistake. Tomorrow we can try the aptura discerna again."

It made sense. Kyja had known she was being rash. Maybe her feeling was wrong. She believed the wizard when he said the monastery was safe. Still . . .

"All right," she said. "I'll go back to my room."

The wizard studied her, clearly suspicious. "You give me your word that you will wait before doing anything?"

Kyja nodded. "I give you my word."

Master Therapass nodded. "At times you must choose logic over feelings. Wisdom comes with experience."

"I know." Kyja ran a hand longingly over the colored window, then walked to the door. "Good night."

"Good night," the wizard said and went back to studying.

As soon as they were in the hallway, Riph Raph landed on Kyja's shoulder, and she walked quickly to the stairs. The guard there gave the skyte a suspicious frown and touched the hilt of his sword.

"Tell me you aren't going to do what I think you are," Riph Raph said, digging his talons into Kyja's arm.

She set her jaw. "There are times to trust your feelings. Times when logic is a bunch of hogwash, no matter what experience and wisdom might say."

Riph Raph huffed. "You promised the wizard you'd wait."

"And I will." Kyja broke into a run, and the skyte had to flap his wings to keep from falling off. "Right until I get to my room."

CHAPTER 9

THE WILL BE

MARCUS WAS IN THE HALL AGAIN. "This way!" the little boy called, running deeper into the corridor. "It's more fun the farther you go."

Marcus followed the boy, noticing how the paintings he passed continued to go back in time. There was one of him studying in his quarters. Him in the desert. He jogged past a couple of doors and stopped at a painting of Kyja, Riph Raph, and himself riding the motorcycle. He ran his fingers across the image, realizing just how much he missed Kyja, and looked at the closed door beside it.

"If I go in, I'll be . . . ?"

"With the *girl?*" The little boy giggled. "As long as you want."

"Back there, it ended," Marcus said, remembering how everything had turned black inside the previous door.

The guide shook his head. "Didn't end," he said, closing his eyes and trying to touch the tip of his nose with his finger. "Memory just went away when the other Marcus left. Have to stay with him if you want to stay in the memory."

That made sense. If this was his past, he couldn't see things he hadn't experienced. A thought occurred to him. "How far back can I go?"

"How far do you want to go?"

"Could I see my . . ." Marcus rubbed a hand across his mouth. "When I was a baby?"

"Your parents?" The boy grinned as though he and Marcus had shared an especially good joke.

Marcus had never known his mother or his father. Even his name wasn't real. Elder Ephraim had given it to him when he was discovered as a baby. *Marcus,* after a famous bishop. And *Kanenas* because it was the Greek word for *nobody.*

The boy held out his pint-sized fingers. "Pay me, and I'll show you."

Marcus gripped the coin, his hand trembling. This might be his only chance to discover who he really was. "If I go, I can come back?"

The guide's smile faltered ever so slightly. "Won't want to."

He wasn't sure he'd heard right. "Of course I would."

"Nope." The boy shook his head. "People who live in the past never want to leave it. The past is safe. It's known. You can visit only the good parts. Skip the bad."

For a moment, Marcus was tempted. If he stayed in the past, he could relive all the happiest experiences of his life. He could see his family. Maybe, even more importantly, the pressure of saving a world—something he was still struggling to even comprehend— would be removed from his shoulders. *If I stay here, I can't fail.*

"*You can't succeed either.*" Kyja's voice was so clear, Marcus looked around, sure she had to be somewhere nearby.

But it was only in his head. Yet the voice was right. If he stayed here, there was no chance he and Kyja could open the drift. He would be dooming them and their worlds to destruction. He couldn't do that.

"Sorry, kid." He tossed the coin, sending it rolling down the corridor. As the boy raced after it, Marcus turned and ran in the other direction.

At the end of the hallway, he thought he'd smash face-first into the yellow wall. Instead he found himself back in the icy pit. His hands were so numb he could hardly feel the last two coins in his palm. He turned the top one over and read, "Will be."

<hr>

Marcus floated in a swirling mist. Not the one from the pit. This was warm and slightly damp. He tried to wave it away, but his hands seemed as insubstantial as the fog around him. He looked at his arms and legs, realizing he could see right through them. Was he dead? A ghost?

"I give you this one chance to go back," a soft voice said.

Marcus turned to see a man watching him. The face was lined, the blond hair thinning, but he recognized the boy from the *Is* and the *Was*. Like Marcus, he appeared to be little more than a spirit floating among clouds of dark smoke.

"Why would I turn back?" Marcus asked. The *Is* had been a dead end, forcing him to leave the monks. The *Was*, no more than memories disguised as reality. But, assuming this swirling smoke was the *Will Be*, he might actually be able to learn something here— to get a glimpse of his future.

The transparent guide frowned, his blue eyes stern in a way neither of his earlier selves had been—as if life had taught him things he would rather not know. "The future is a fickle thing, shifting and prone to change. But go any farther, and you lock it permanently in place."

"That's not possible," Marcus said. "If I don't like what I see, I'll do something different. I'll change the future." He could feel his tongue and lips forming the words, his breath pushing them out of his mouth. But they were barely loud enough for him to hear.

The guide stared at him wordlessly.

Marcus squinted, trying to see through the fog. He could almost glimpse what was on the other side, but just as he started to focus, the images changed. He tried to chew on the tip of his thumb, but his teeth went right through it. Seeing even a small amount into the future might help him figure out a way out of his current mess. Besides, what was the worst that could happen?

"Take me to the *Will Be*," he said.

The guide nodded.

Marcus found himself in a familiar room—Master Therapass's study. It looked even more disorganized than usual. Marcus reached out to pick up a fallen book and only when his hand moved through it did he realize he was still a ghost.

"You are in a world yet to come," the guide said. "Your presence is insubstantial."

"Where is everyone?" Marcus asked.

The guide led him out of the room and down a hallway to a window. Marcus looked out and gasped. Terra ne Staric looked like it had been through a war. Huge chunks of the tower lay scattered on the ground. The outer wall was damaged almost everywhere, and the surrounding countryside was shredded, as if some giant dragon had raked its claws from one end to the other.

"What happened here?" he whispered.

The guide pressed his lips together. "The future."

Outside the western gate, a large group of people gathered around something that glittered in the sun. If Marcus could get down to them, maybe he could find out what had happened and come up with a way to prevent it.

"What are they doing?" he asked.

In a blink, he and his guide were inside the crowd. Most of the people were crying or had been recently. Marcus recognized some of them.

"I can't believe it," sobbed Bella the cook, pressing a handkerchief to her mouth.

A one-armed man with a scraggly gray beard put his arm around the cook's shoulders. "I don't understand how this could have happened."

Maybe this hadn't been such a good idea after all. Something terrible had happened. He moved forward to see what they were all looking at and passed a pair of children pressing their faces into their mother's dress.

"Hush, my babies, hush," the woman whispered, patting her children's heads. But she was crying as hard as they were. It took Marcus a moment to recognize the mother as Char, the wife of Rhaidnan—the man who had given his life to save Marcus and Kyja from the zentan.

Thinking of Kyja made Marcus realize he hadn't seen her yet. "Where is she?" he tried to shout, but his voice barely made a peep. "Tell me Kyja's all right."

The guide took his arm and pulled him through the crowd. Suddenly, Marcus didn't want to see whatever it was the people were crying over. "No," he tried to say, tearing at the guide's hand. But the word wouldn't come, and the man's grip was too strong.

They stood at the edge of an open hole. The leaders of the city surrounded a glittering glass box suspended above the hole. Master Therapass stood at the head of the group, looking older than Marcus had ever seen him. His eyes were dark red holes.

Marcus didn't want to look at the box, but he couldn't help himself. His gaze traveled from the gold handles carved like leaves to the white satin blanket inside. To still, pale arms inside. Black hair braided with flowers around a girl's head. And finally, the face that he knew so well. The lips that had kissed him what felt like yesterday. Her eyes were closed, but that didn't stop him from remembering what they looked like.

"No!" he screamed. "No. Take me back. I changed my mind."

The guide only looked at him.

Kyja couldn't be dead. She couldn't. He wouldn't let her be. He'd die himself before he let anything happen to her. He had to know how this had happened so he could stop whatever had done this to her. He *had* to stop it.

"Show me," he sobbed, tears burning his cheeks.

Now they stood in a dark, foul-smelling dungeon, in front of a barred cell. Water dripped slowly from the ceiling in a steady pat, pat, pat.

A man knelt before the cell. It was Breslek Broomhead, the new High Lord of Terra ne Staric. "Did you do it?" the High Lord asked, his hands gripping the iron bars of the prison cell. "Did you kill her?"

A figure sat hunched in the back of the cell, head down, face lost in shadows. Marcus lunged toward the bars. He had to know who had done this. No matter what it took, he would see that this coward would never get anywhere near Kyja.

As Marcus reached the cell, the figure whispered, "Yes." He looked up and Marcus fell backward.

"No," he said, his mouth dry. It wasn't possible. Of all the people who might harm Kyja this one couldn't.

"I did it," the person in the back of the cell said. "I murdered her."

Marcus felt his mind snapping. The person who had killed Kyja—the one he had to stop—was himself.

The coin dropped from his numb fingers and rang on the dungeon floor.

CHAPTER 10

THE TIME OF SHADOWS

MAYBE YOU SHOULD THINK about this a little more," Riph Raph said, hopping from the chair to Kyja's bed and back again. "Master Therapass seemed pretty sure that bringing Marcus to Farworld was a bad idea."

"Master Therapass thinks *everything's* a bad idea." Kyja walked to the balcony and looked out at the night sky. Two of the three moons were visible—an almost completely full pink circle and a green fingernail. Should she wait to pull Marcus over? She definitely didn't want to put him in danger. But what if he was already in danger, and she did nothing about it?

She ran her fingers along the worn surface of the stone railing. Should she try to help Marcus but risk hurting him or leave him to something that might be even worse? There *was* no good choice.

Riph Raph flapped over to the balcony. "What if you can't find him?"

Kyja chewed the inside of her cheeks. The first time she'd found Marcus, she wasn't even sure he existed—or if he did, where he was.

She'd never heard of Earth, but she'd found him then. "It wouldn't hurt to look for him."

The skyte clucked. "Why do I think I'll regret agreeing to this?"

"You're not agreeing," Kyja snapped. "You're not doing anything."

Riph Raph cringed at her tone, making her feel worse than she already did. Things were happening on Farworld—none of them good. The strange weather patterns were drying up every body of water. Land and water magic had lost most of their potency. Cascade and Lanctrus-Darnoc hadn't been seen or heard from in months. None of it spelled anything good, and yet, as far as she could see, no one was doing anything about it. They were waiting, studying, planning. It was enough to make her scream.

"Keep an eye on the door," she said, crossing to her bed. "I promise, if anything seems wrong, I'll stop."

"It doesn't matter to me." Riph Raph flicked his tail. "I'm not doing anything."

She'd soothe the skyte's feelings later. Now it was time to act. It was either the middle of the night or slightly past. Kyja settled herself on the center of her bed, legs crossed.

Closing her eyes, she let her mind wander. In the past, when she wanted to bring Marcus to Farworld, she'd reached for a golden rope. She didn't know if the rope was real or imaginary, but it had always worked. Now, as she reached to find it, there was nothing.

"Where are you?" she whispered. She pictured herself floating off the bed, through the balcony, and into the night, letting herself drift farther and farther away. She felt like a fisherman casting out her net for one certain fish. Only she had no idea where the fish was, so her net had to be extra big.

Still nothing.

Sweat rolled down her forehead as she reached into the dark

void before her. Where was he? She'd never worked this hard to find Marcus before, never stretched so far. Little by little, she felt herself losing touch with the room she was sitting in. The sound of Riph Raph scratching anxiously at the stone floor disappeared, replaced by the smell of the outside air. The rough feel of the wool blankets against her fingers dissolved as if she was no longer in her room at all, but floating in space.

"Marcus!" she called inside her head. "Where are you?"

If I go, I can come back?

The voice was so faint, she wasn't sure she'd heard it at all. It might have been her own voice, questioning whether she was stretching too far in her search.

Won't want to, another voice said.

"Marcus?" she murmured.

A feeling came to her—one she was almost sure hadn't come from herself. Someone was thinking . . . thinking . . . thinking what? The voice was so far away, so hard to make out. She pressed her hands to the sides of her head, trying to concentrate.

The words came to her distantly, like the sound of an Earth radio. *If I stay here, I can't fail.*

"You can't succeed either," she said at once, not sure why she was saying it or who she was saying it to.

"Who are you talking to?" Riph Raph's words pulled her back to the room, and Kyja looked around. How long had she been sitting there? It felt like hours, but outside the balcony, the moons seemed to be in about the same positions as before.

"I think Marcus is lost," Kyja said. "Even he doesn't know where he is. And I have the strongest feeling that if he doesn't get back soon, he might never find his way out."

Riph Raph licked his beak and nodded. "Then go get him."

———◆———

Marcus lay on the floor of the pit, beyond cold and exhausted. His mind ached in a way he'd never known it could—as if someone had reached into his head and torn his brain to pieces. Tears dripped down his face and froze to his cheeks.

Let me freeze to death. Let me die here and now. It was better than the future he'd seen.

"I won't," he whispered to himself. "I won't let that happen."

Dully, he glanced at the last coin in his hand. It was blank. He turned it over with the tip of his thumb. The other side was blank too. Mist rolled over him—although he hadn't heard the falls start up—and a figure in black stepped out of the fog and lifted him. He felt a blanket being wrapped around him.

"Leave me," he managed to get out between chattering teeth.

"Shh," the figure whispered.

He felt himself being eased onto a soft bed, and he opened his eyes, expecting to see the boy again. Instead he found a woman watching him. At least, he thought it was a woman. She wore a long black robe, and her face was almost completely hidden behind a gauzy black veil. The only visible parts of her were her white hands and beautiful blue eyes.

He was in a dark room with a shiny black floor glittering with specks of silver and gold. He rolled onto his side but saw no walls or ceiling.

The woman leaned over him. "You didn't choose to come here," she said—her words a tickling breeze against his ear.

He shook his head.

"Yet here you are."

Marcus felt blood returning to his hands and feet in a painful rush. "Who are you?"

"I thought you would have guessed." It was impossible to read anything from the woman's voice or eyes. "I am *Time*."

Marcus shook his head and coughed. His lungs burned. "I know. The *Was*. The *Is*. The *Will Be*. But *when* are *you?*"

Instead of answering, the woman pointed a finger as white as death toward the mist they'd come through. "You can still choose any of them."

"The guide said I couldn't change the future."

The woman nodded. "Your visit to the *Will Be* has set your path in stone."

Marcus clenched his eyes and buried his face in the pillow. "Put me back in the pit. Let me die."

———◄◆►———

Kyja closed her eyes and reached out again. She could sense Marcus now, feel the direction he was in. But it was so far away she wasn't sure she could reach him without losing her grip on where she was. If only she could get him to come to her.

"Marcus!" she shouted. "It's me, Kyja."

No! No. Take me back. The words exploded inside her head so forcefully they seemed to rock her backward. *I changed my mind.* He sounded like he was sitting on the bed next to her, screaming into her ear.

What would make Marcus scream like that?

A tidal wave of dark emotions rushed over her. Fear. Terror. Self-loathing. She felt her stomach heave, and it was all she could do to keep from pulling away. What was happening to Marcus? Where was he?

"Come to me!" she cried, holding out her hands.

———◆———

The woman rolled Marcus over, her fingers neither warm nor cold. "You choose not to return to the *Is,* the *Was,* or the *Will Be?*"

"Yes," Marcus groaned. "Leave me in the pit." He couldn't take any chance of hurting Kyja.

"Time can only be frozen for so long," the woman said, her voice showing no hint of emotion. "You cannot stay in the pit. But there is another way."

"Will it keep me from the future?" Marcus asked. The frozen moisture on his cheeks began to melt, and salty tears dripped to his lips.

"Yes," the veiled woman said.

"How?" Marcus asked. "Whatever it is, I accept it."

"The *Never Was.*" The woman pointed to a swirling darkness Marcus hadn't noticed. It looked as if the floor of the room itself was being sucked into a vast whirlpool. The longer he looked at it, the more the darkness pulled at him. He thought he could see worlds spinning in it. Worlds that had never been, choices not made, chances untaken. Mistakes erased.

"The Void of Unbecoming," the woman whispered. She held out her thin fingers.

Marcus reached up and dropped the coin into her palm.

———◆———

Let me die.

The words rang in Kyja's ears.

What was happening to Marcus? The feelings, so strong only a moment before, had dissolved into almost complete nothingness.

She stretched her mind, desperately searching, reaching. She had no doubt that Marcus was in terrible danger. But she didn't know how to help him.

"Marcus!" she screamed again and again. "Where are you?"

The only thing she felt was black despair. In all the time she'd known Marcus, he'd never given up; she didn't think it was in him. They had both faced the possibility of death several times. But what she felt now was even worse than that. It was as if Marcus stood on the edge of a cliff to nowhere—a precipice that went on and on and on forever.

Whatever it is, I accept it. His tone was one of failure. Of complete and total surrender.

"I won't let you give up!" she cried. Tears flooded her eyes and ran down her cheeks. Her brain seemed on fire. She couldn't find the golden rope, but that didn't matter. She wouldn't let Marcus die. Releasing her hold on Farworld, she dove over the cliff into the darkness, wrapped her arms around something only she could feel, and pulled with all her might.

———◄◆►———

As the coin slipped through Marcus's fingers, a million images raced through his mind—everything he'd ever done, seen, or felt. Like bits of wood pulled into a whirlpool, the memories swirled into dark emptiness.

The woman's fingers reached out to accept his payment.

Marcus felt himself swirl into the void along with his past, and a sense of relief came with it. He was falling, disappearing. But at least he wouldn't ever—

Something more powerful than he ever could have imagined reached into the darkness and snatched him out.

For the first time, the blue eyes behind the veil showed an emotion: shock.

Marcus felt a tug at his stomach. He seemed to turn inside out. Then he was lying on a cool, stone floor. He looked up to find Kyja staring down at him—face pale with fear and desperation. In that moment, he saw her face as he'd seen it inside the glass coffin.

Marcus screamed.

PAIN

DEEP BENEATH THE BOWELS of the Dark Circle's fortress, the pain never stopped. It only changed in texture, flavor, color, intensity. Bonesplinter's mind lasted much longer than he thought was possible, registering each new atrocity inflicted upon him with a sense of horror and wonder, always hoping that *this* would be the pain that killed him at last. Day by day, hour by unending hour, what little sanity remained was leeched away by the continual torment heaped upon him. Until it all ran together, so that he could no longer tell one pain from another and his brain shut off completely.

It wasn't that the pain stopped; his mind just quit recognizing it as such. Then, just as he had decided the torture would never end, it did.

"Wake up."

It—no longer *he*, for he no longer remembered who he was— opened its eyes and stared down from a black stone pedestal. It was in a smoke-filled room so large the ceiling and far walls disappeared in the blackness. Standing below, dozens of black-cloaked wizards watched with mingled awe and terror.

"How do you feel?" asked a papery voice.

Something flashed in the darkest recesses of its brain—some vague and hazy memory. Had it once been like the creatures below? Frail and weak? Anger poured through it, as steady as the blood pulsing in its body. The creature spread its great red wings wide and screamed in fury. It lunged out at the figures below, and they fell back before its wrath. Thick links of hardened steel caught at its neck, jerking it backward. It strained against the chain, screaming, tearing, gouging the platform on which it stood.

"Yessss." Another cloaked figure stepped out of the smoke. "You are so lovely." The figure held out a wrinkled hand and the Summoner lashed out, fangs gnashing. At the same moment, a force stronger than any chains jerked the Summoner around, slamming its jaws closed and flattening it to the pedestal. It tried to raise its head but couldn't move. The wizard was human, like the others, but something was different. Power flowed through this one greater than all the others combined—as though he drew magic directly from a limitless source. The Summoner stopped struggling, recognizing its master.

A dark chuckle floated from inside the black cowl and the master stooped to lay a limp shape on the ground.

The Summoner sniffed at the shape. A thick snarl emerged from the back of its long throat, past the row of its double fangs. It was the corpse of a two-headed dog. A stench rose from the body, and the Summoner felt a tug in its gut. Dark power flowed through its veins, heating them until it thought its blood would boil.

Power more terrible than anything it could imagine coiled like a snake beneath its scales. It spoke in a language only it understood, making the dead dog jerk. For a second—less than a second—a tiny voice inside the Summoner cried out in disgust and revulsion. But the voice was stamped out immediately. A single spark of terror crushed by an ocean of rage, and an unquenchable desire for violence.

The Summoner spoke again, its tongue pronouncing garbled syllables no human mouth could produce. The dog lurched to its feet, dragging itself forward until it stood directly in front of the Summoner, waiting to be commanded.

The Summoner unfurled its massive wings, stretched its fang-filled jaws, and howled. Below, the army of Thrathkin S'Bae raised their two-pronged staffs in salute.

The master nodded his approval and, with a gesture, sent the undead dog stumbling out of the room. He turned to address the multitude, raised his arms, and shouted. "The boy is here!"

The crowd roared, and the Summoner roared with them, its claws digging into the stone. Its red eyes blazed, and the smoke began to swirl.

"He and the girl do not know it yet, but they have stepped directly into our trap." The master pointed a gnarled gray finger, his gold ring flashing. "To the east are floods. To the west is drought. To the north, ice."

The dark wizards slammed their staffs on the ground. Blue fire jetted into the air, sparking off the walls and turning the smoke into a thundercloud of dark magic.

The master lowered his arms, and the room grew quiet. "Terra ne Staric will soon be destroyed. Its people are weak from thirst. They are afraid. They will crumble before my army of golems." He pointed across the room at the wizards. "You will hound the children night and day, forcing them deeper and deeper into my web."

"Yes!" the wizards cried.

He turned to the Summoner. "And you, my pretty. You will fly north with a force of my most powerful servants to wait for them where they must end up. When they arrive . . ." He laughed his papery laugh again. "You will kill them and raise them up to serve me."

The master nodded silently to himself, and in a voice only he and the Summoner could hear whispered, "Then Farworld will be mine. And perhaps more, much more."

PART 2

Air Keep

CHAPTER 11

RETURN

FOR A MOMENT KYJA didn't know where she was. Her head spun, and her limbs seemed loose and wobbly. She felt as if she'd been flung far into space then yanked back, like one of those toys Earth kids played with—the ones that spun up and down on the end of a string. Bo-bos or no-nos or something.

Someone screamed, and she jerked, nearly falling off the bed.

"Good to see you too," Riph Raph said to the boy trembling on the floor.

"Marcus!" Kyja dove off the bed, wrapping her arms around him. "I thought you were . . ." She couldn't say it.

Marcus jerked in her arms. His teeth chattered.

"You're freezing." Kyja tore a blanket from her bed and moved to wrap it around him, but Marcus pulled away from her. "What's wrong?" A terrible thought occurred to her. What if Master Therapass was right? What if *she* had done this to him? "Was it the shadow realm?" she whispered, terrified to hear the answer.

Marcus shook his head, and Kyja dropped to the edge of the bed, her legs weak with relief.

A tall, long-haired man holding a slim, silvery stick stepped into the room. He took in Marcus and Kyja then rubbed his pointy chin. "You *do* know how to make an entrance."

"S-s-sc-Screech," Marcus said, his body shaking uncontrollably.

"He's freezing," Kyja said. "I don't know what's wrong with him."

"Let's get him to Therapass," said Graehl, the tall man who, until six months earlier, had been transformed into a trulloch named Screech. He placed the stick into his robe pocket and scooped Marcus into his arms. Kyja handed him the blanket.

"How did he get here?" Graehl asked, taking the tower steps two at a time.

"I brought him." Kyja said it defiantly. She didn't know what was wrong with Marcus, but if it hadn't been caused by her pulling him from Earth, then she'd done the right thing. Clearly something terrible had happened to him wherever he'd been.

"Maybe we should take him to the kitchen," Riph Raph said. "You know, get him some nice, warm food. No need to wake the wizard twice in one night."

Graehl arched a questioning eyebrow.

"I was trying to *borrow* his aptura discerna," Kyja explained quickly. "I wanted to check on Marcus. I had a feeling something was wrong. And I was right."

For the third time that night, they passed the guard Riph Raph had dive-bombed. He gave them all a wary look as they passed. At least he didn't try to stop them.

Marcus groaned, and Graehl pulled the blanket more tightly

around him. "Master Therapass gave you permission to bring him here?" he asked Kyja.

Kyja ducked her head stubbornly and didn't respond. If the wizard was mad, so be it. She'd do it again if given the chance.

"I think his exact words," Riph Raph chirped, "were 'wait before doing anything.'"

"Ahh." Graehl nodded.

At least Master Therapass hadn't gone to sleep again. As soon as they entered his study, the wizard looked up from his books and jumped to his feet. His gaze went from Marcus, shivering in Graehl's arms, to Kyja—who tried to meet his dark eyes but failed miserably.

The wizard clapped his hands, and a pile of blankets and rugs flapped across the room, forming a bed on the nearest table. "Stand back," he ordered Kyja as Graehl set Marcus gently on the makeshift bed.

Kyja moved back far enough to be out of the way, but close enough to see what was happening. She wanted to explain, but now wasn't the time.

The wizard placed a hand on Marcus's forehead. "Ice cold." He pointed at the shelves on one side of the room, speaking words Kyja didn't understand. Beakers started pouring liquids into a wooden bowl, while boxes sprinkled powders and other ingredients into it. The teapot Kyja had successfully avoided earlier that night hopped across the table, and the bowl emptied its contents inside.

By the time the teapot had returned to the wizard, thick, green smoke steamed from its spout. The smoke smelled like rotten fruit. "This may taste rather nasty," the wizard said. "Unless you've developed a taste for gooey goblin slime, as I have, in which case, it will be a pleasant treat."

Master Therapass poured a small amount of the hot liquid

into Marcus's mouth. Based on the face Marcus made as the liquid touched his lips, Kyja didn't think he considered it a pleasant treat. He coughed and choked a little, but stopped shivering almost immediately.

Master Therapass looked up at Kyja, his old face stern. "Didn't I warn you that bringing him through the realm of shadows could have disastrous results?"

"Not the . . . realm of shadows," Marcus said. He looked a little better. His cheeks had some color, and he appeared to be breathing easier.

Master Therapass rubbed a hand across his face. "Eh?"

"It wasn't the shadows." Marcus sat up a little, resting on one elbow. "I didn't feel them at all. I was—"

Marcus's words were cut off abruptly as Master Therapass poured more liquid into Marcus's mouth. The wizard had moved so quickly that Kyja hadn't even seen him pick up the teapot.

"Enough." Marcus coughed, pushing the pot away from his mouth. "That tastes disgusting."

Master Therapass gave a puzzled glance at the pot and set it on the table again. "You were saying?"

Marcus wiped his mouth with the back of his hand and hacked. "I said, I don't think it was the realm of shadows. When Kyja pulled me over, I was—"

Somehow the wizard had the teapot back in his hands with the spout placed firmly between Marcus's lips.

"Gah!" Marcus spat a mouthful of green goop on the floor and knocked the teapot away with his good hand.

"I'm pretty sure he does *not* have a taste for gooey goblin slime," Riph Raph said with a chuckle.

Master Therapass frowned briefly at the skyte before gazing slowly around the room. "This is very odd." He snapped his fingers, and the teapot blinked out of existence. "Tell me one more time exactly where you were and what you were doing when Kyja pulled you over."

Marcus coughed again, pounding his chest, then put a hand protectively over his mouth. "I was at the monastery when I found out that the boys' school was coming to take me away."

"I knew it," Kyja couldn't help saying. So much for Master Therapass making sure Marcus didn't leave the monastery.

"Go on," the wizard said, his thick gray eyebrows bunched low over his eyes.

"I went back to my room, and some of my things were missing," Marcus said, still covering his mouth as if he expected the wizard to try to force more goblin slime down his throat. "I found my things inside Elder Ephraim's quarters. When I went in, I saw a—"

Kyja was watching everything closely this time. She was sure no one had moved. But as soon as Marcus said, "I saw a," the flying cookie tin was on the table next to him, and the molasses cookie Kyja had used to glue its top closed was shoved into his mouth.

Riph Raph snorted as Marcus pulled the sticky brown substance, trying to pry it from his teeth. Even Kyja couldn't help smiling a little. Something very strange was going on.

Marcus was furious. He yanked the cookie out of his mouth, brown crumbs clinging to his lips and chin. "If you don't want me to tell you what happened, just say so!"

Master Therapass's eyes darted around the room, and his lip pulled up in a snarl. "This is not my doing. Something—or someone—clearly does not want you to tell us where you have been." He pointed to the door. "Graehl, check the hall."

The tall man hurried to the door and looked outside in both

directions. "Nothing," he said, blocking the doorway with his broad shoulders.

The wizard turned to Kyja. "Tell me what you saw when you pulled him over."

Kyja gulped. "I didn't exactly *see* anything. I *felt* something, though." She tried hard to remember. "It was almost as if—"

The room went dark, and her mouth was suddenly full. Something pulled tight across her eyes. She tugged at it with both hands and pulled off Master Therapass's hat—which was what had been shoved over her head.

Dozens of moist, round objects filled her mouth until her cheeks bulged. "Yuck!" she grimaced, spitting them into her hands. "Blueberries. I hate blueberries."

Now it was Marcus's turn to hide a smile.

"It could have been worse," Riph Raph said. "It could have been beetles. I'm not fond of berries, but I hate to see good insects go to waste."

Kyja wiped her mouth with the sleeve of her robe. "This isn't funny."

"No, it isn't," the wizard agreed. "I have dozens of protections placed in this room to warn me of outside magic. But it's clear some sort of conjuring is at work here."

Graehl pulled a glittering dagger from his belt. "The Dark Circle?"

"I think not," the wizard said. "But until I know what has breached my security, I want the two of them watched over day and night." He pointed a finger to the door. "There is a windowless room across the hall. Place both of them inside with a dozen guards outside the door. And I want two wizards in the room with them at all times."

Marcus met Kyja's eyes, then looked quickly away. "I don't want to be in the same room with her."

CHAPTER 12

WHO'S AT THE DOOR?

MARCUS LAY ON A BED in a dark room down the hall from where Kyja had been taken. Guards were posted outside, and two wizards—a man with spotted hands and a woman with extremely large ears—stood inside the room to either side of the door. Both held long staffs covered in complex runes.

After six months of waiting to come to Farworld—of wanting so much to see Kyja, Master Therapass, and even Riph Raph—how could everything have gone so wrong so quickly now that he was here?

He tried to convince himself everything would work out all right—that the future wasn't set in stone, no matter what the guide had told him. But how could he take that chance? He couldn't even imagine what Kyja must be thinking. The look she'd given him when he said that he didn't want to be in the same room with her was worse than any physical pain he'd felt. And the most terrible part was that he couldn't tell her why.

Someone knocked on the door, and the two wizards tensed.

Marcus looked up quickly as the door opened. It was only Master Therapass. The old wizard crossed the room and took a seat by Marcus's bed.

"How's Kyja doing?" Marcus asked.

Master Therapass pinched his lower lip, his eyes thoughtful. "Hurt. Confused. Are you angry at her for bringing you here?"

"No!" Marcus said, his voice too loud. The woman with the big ears glanced in his direction. "No," he repeated softly. "I'm not mad at her at all."

Master Therapass sat quietly, waiting.

"I just think it might be better if we spent some time apart." He couldn't say any more than that.

The wizard nodded thoughtfully. "The last two hundred days apart haven't been enough?"

Marcus squirmed.

Master Therapass pulled a green trill stone from one of his sleeves. The game piece rolled out of his hand, up his arm, and around the back of his neck.

Marcus admired the wizard's easy use of magic. He'd worked on his magic for over a year, but he still couldn't pull off anything that smooth. "I think Kyja might have saved my life," Marcus said at last. "Maybe it's better not to talk about it. I don't think I can stand any more of that green stuff."

The truth was, getting a mouthful of goblin goop was only a small part of his worry. How could he tell Master Therapass—or anyone, for that matter—that the reason he was afraid to be alone with Kyja was because he was terrified he might kill her? He definitely couldn't tell that to *Kyja*. Just the idea made him so ashamed, he wanted to bury himself under the nearest mountain and never come out.

Kyja had saved him from what he was pretty sure was something

even worse than death—having never been born at all. And by doing so, she had come one step closer to being killed, if the man in
the *Will Be* and the woman in the *Never Was* were telling the truth.
Marcus had no idea when it would happen or what—if anything—
he could do to stop it.

He could tell Master Therapass wanted to dig deeper, but the
wizard only nodded. The trill stone rolled out from behind his neck
again, but this time it was red. "You said the boys' school was going
to take you from the monastery?"

"Yeah," Marcus said. "They were coming this afternoon. I
mean yesterday afternoon, I guess. I'm not even sure what day it is.
Terrible Teagarden himself was on his way."

The trill stone jumped off the wizard's shoulder as though making a break for it, and he snatched it out of the air. "That's not
possible. The monks would never have let you leave the monastery
without contacting me first."

"It is, though," Marcus insisted. "Father Shaun said so himself."

The wizard's eyes narrowed. "There is no Father Shaun at the
monastery."

Of course there was. Marcus had met him within days of arriving. But then he thought back to what the boy in the *Was* had
been singing. *Not a monk. Not a monk.* The boy had also said Father
Shaun was the one who took Marcus's things. He opened his mouth
to tell Master Therapass, before remembering what had happened
every other time he tried to talk about the pit or the mirror. Maybe
there was a way to approach the topic without mentioning the pit.

"Do you think he could be a fake? Someone from the Dark
Circle? And that was why he was trying to make me leave the monastery?"

"I think we're missing something," Master Therapass said,

steepling his fingers in front of his face. "I must consider this. Try to get some rest. We will speak more in the morning." The wizard stood up. He seemed much older than he had six months before. He patted Marcus on the shoulder. "And think about talking to Kyja."

Marcus nodded. He knew he had to give Kyja some kind of explanation. The easiest thing would be to make up a story. But Kyja knew him so well it would be hard to hide the truth from her. And the idea of lying to his best friend made him almost as sick as the thought of telling her the truth.

He closed his eyes and tried to put the pieces together. If Father Shaun wasn't really a monk, who was he? The Dark Circle wanted Marcus to leave the monastery. But if that's what they were trying to accomplish, why hide his things?

Unless the reason for lying to him about the boys' school wasn't to get him to leave the grounds at all. What if the whole point was to force him to—

"Marcus," a voice called softly.

Marcus opened his eyes and rolled over. He looked at the two wizards standing on either side of the door. Had one of them called him?

"Marcus," the voice called again. "Out here." The voice was coming from the hallway.

"Kyja?" Marcus whispered back. What was she doing outside his door? She was supposed to be locked in her room.

"Hurry up," she called.

Marcus sat up and rubbed his face. What did she want? The man and woman watching over him must have heard Kyja calling him, but they didn't so much as blink an eye. He cleared his throat and looked at the wizards. "I, um, I think Kyja wants to talk to me. Do you mind if I open the door for just a second?"

Neither of the wizards said a thing. They didn't move or look in his direction. There was something strange about this whole situation.

"Are you coming or not?" Kyja called. "I don't have all day."

"Okay . . ." Marcus eased himself out of the bed. He balanced his weight on his good leg—which wasn't feeling all that good—and, using the wall for support, hopped to the door. He kept waiting for his guards to stop him, but they both looked straight ahead as though they hadn't noticed a thing. They might as well have been statues for as still as they were standing. Were they giving him their permission without actually saying so?

"Stop messing around," Kyja hissed. "This is important."

"Fine!" Marcus grabbed the door and pulled it open, feeling a little cranky. "What do you want?"

——◆——

Kyja balled her fists and slammed them against her thighs. "Did you hear what he said to me back there?"

Riph Raph flipped his tail. "For the third time, yes."

"What did he *mean,* he didn't want to be in the same room with me?"

"Maybe the green stuff gave him dragon breath, and he was embarrassed to have you smell it?"

Kyja paused for a moment before realizing the skyte was teasing. She ground her teeth. "You think this is funny? I should send you to stay with him so the two of you can be rude to each other."

Riph Raph clung to the bed's headboard with his right claw and scratched himself with his left. "If you're going to be this way all night, staying with him might not be such a bad idea. At least I could get some sleep."

"Ohhh," Kyja growled. "It's just . . . I don't understand. Why is he mad at me? What did I do?" She knew the wizards standing at her door were listening, but she didn't care. She thought she and Marcus were friends, maybe even more than that. All their time being apart, she'd assumed he'd missed her as much as she'd missed him. Now she wondered if that was true. Maybe he was glad to be away from her. Maybe he didn't want to come back at all.

"You could try asking him," Riph Raph said, searching the room for any tasty bugs.

Kyja thought about that. She *did* want to talk to Marcus. Tell him what she'd discovered about the air elementals. Find out what was happening on Earth, and what he'd been doing when she pulled him to Farworld.

But what if he didn't want to talk to her? What if—

"Kyja," a voice called from outside her room. "Are you in there?"

She looked toward the door. "Marcus?"

"Come out here, quickly. We need to talk." It was definitely Marcus. But what was he doing out of his room?

She looked at Riph Raph. The skyte flapped his ears. "He found some mints to cure his dragon breath?"

He was no help. She got out of bed, wondering if the wizards at the door would try to stop her. Neither of them even looked at her as she approached.

"Hurry up!" Marcus called. He sounded urgent. Was he in trouble?

"I'm sorry. I have to leave," Kyja said, determined to get past the guards whether they tried to stop her or not. But they didn't move as she turned the knob, opened the door, and stepped into the hallway.

Marcus was standing just down the hall. Before she could say a word, he looked at her and said, "What do you want?"

CHAPTER 13.

NO TIME LIKE THE PRESENT

WHAT DO YOU MEAN, 'What do I want'?" Kyja looked at Marcus with a confused expression.

"You called me," Marcus said. "What do you want?"

Kyja blinked. "I didn't call you. You called me."

Marcus shook his head. Was she playing some kind of game? "No, I didn't. I was just sitting on my bed, thinking about . . . well, it doesn't matter what I was thinking about, when you told me to come out into the hall. You said it was important. So what do you want?"

"I did nothing of the kind," Kyja said. "If you changed your mind and don't want to talk to me, just say so."

"I didn't say I didn't want to talk to you," Marcus said. "I mean I did—before. But not just now. *You* said you wanted to talk to *me.*"

Kyja opened her mouth to argue, when Riph Raph flew out of her room. "I could listen to the two of you go on like this all night.

In fact, it feels like I already have. But I think we may have bigger things to worry about."

Kyja whirled on the skyte. "What things?"

Riph Raph flapped his wings until he was right above the nearest of the guards stationed in the hallway. The guard didn't move as the skyte landed on his plumed helm and pecked at the metal visor. Twelve guards were posted in the hall, and all stood perfectly still.

Clinging to the doorjamb to stay standing, Marcus moved to study the man nearest him—a short guard with a bushy mustache and a crooked nose. "Hello?"

The man didn't blink. He didn't twitch. He wasn't even breathing, as far as Marcus could tell.

"What's wrong with them?" Kyja asked, waving her hand in front of the eyes of the guard Riph Raph had landed on.

"It's like they're frozen or something." Marcus looked back at the wizards inside his room. They were frozen too.

"Listen," Kyja said.

Marcus stood and listened. The only thing he could hear was the sound of his own breathing. "I don't hear anything."

"That's what I mean," Kyja said. "It's never this quiet in the tower."

"It's night. Everyone's probably asleep."

"Turnip Head's been gone too long," Riph Raph said.

Marcus frowned. "What did you call me?"

"Forget him," Kyja said. "There's always someone up doing something. People cooking, guards patrolling, dogs barking. It's never this quiet."

Marcus glanced up at a chandelier and gaped. "Look," he said, pointing to the flames.

Kyja looked up and stared as well. "They aren't flickering. It's like the fire is . . ."

"Frozen," Marcus finished, and an odd feeling tightened his stomach. What was it the woman in the *Never Was* said? Something about time being frozen. But this couldn't have anything to do with that. "We need to tell Master Therapass," he said. "This could have something to do with whatever was going on in his study."

Riph Raph squawked. "That might be the most intelligent thing I've ever heard him say. Not that he's ever said anything really intelligent to compare it to."

Marcus rolled his eyes. "Quiet, birdbrain." He limped toward Kyja, leaning against the wall. "You'll need to help me walk." On Farworld, his leg and arm weren't quite as weak as they were on Earth. Somehow his health was tied to the health of Farworld. But even at the best of times, he couldn't walk here without some kind of assistance. And tonight, he felt especially weak.

"You can use your staff," Kyja said.

Marcus shook his head. "I can't. I left it in . . ." But there it was, leaning against the wall. It couldn't be here. The last time he'd seen it, it was with his wheelchair in Elder Ephraim's room. He grabbed the stick and ran his hands over the polished surface. "This is impossible," he muttered. But there was no question that this was his staff.

"Something really weird is going on here," he said, moving slowly down the corridor.

Kyja walked by his side. "Usually the halls are drafty at night. But I don't feel any breeze."

Marcus nodded. It was like everything but the three of them had somehow just stopped in time. He glanced at Kyja. "About what I said before. I didn't . . . I mean, I wasn't . . ." He wasn't sure how to finish the sentence.

"Are you mad at me?" Kyja asked softly.

"No," he said. "I just . . ." What could he say? He couldn't tell her the truth.

"Tell her you had dragon breath," Riph Raph whispered.

"What?" Had he actually thought he'd missed the annoying skyte and his sarcastic comments? "Why did you leave me on Earth for so long?" he asked, hoping to change the subject.

"I didn't want to," Kyja said. "Master Therapass said it was too dangerous to bring you back. He was trying to find a way to protect you from the realm of shadows."

Master Therapass had explained that when Marcus or Kyja jumped from their own worlds to the other's, they weren't completely in the world they jumped to. Part of them remained trapped in a gray area between Earth and Farworld, called the realm of shadows, which was why they couldn't stay in the other world for more than a few days without getting sick. The wizard believed that one of Marcus's parents was actually a creature of shadows, making it especially dangerous for him to jump.

"But you *did* pull me over," he said.

Kyja brushed back a lock of hair. "I kind of disobeyed Master Therapass," she said with a smile. Marcus had missed that smile.

They passed two more guards and a girl carrying a pot of hot soup, frozen in mid-step. The steam rising from the soup was locked in a motionless cloud just above the pot. Marcus passed his hand through the cloud and felt moisture on his fingers. But except for the spot where he'd put his hand, none of the steam blew away.

"When I looked for you in the aptura discerna, I saw your wheelchair and your things," Kyja said. "But when I couldn't find you, I panicked." She looked over at him, the question of where he'd been clear in her eyes.

Marcus leaned heavily on his staff. Based on how much his arm and leg ached, Farworld had to be in pretty bad shape. "I'm not sure where I was or what happened to me," he said. Kyja had saved his life. He owed her as much of the truth as he could tell her without revealing what he'd seen in the *Will Be*.

"There was this mirror, except it wasn't really a mirror. And when I touched it . . ." He waited for something to stop him from speaking, hoping he wouldn't have to go on. But it didn't.

Kyja watched him expectantly.

"When I touched it, I got pulled somewhere else."

Kyja gasped. "Into the realm of shadows?"

"I don't know," Marcus said. "But I don't think so. There were no shadow creatures. Only a little boy who showed me a bunch of weird stuff." Why was it that whatever had stopped him from telling Master Therapass about the mirror and the things he saw was letting him tell Kyja?

They rounded a corner and reached the wizard's study. Marcus had been secretly afraid that whatever had frozen the guards had frozen Master Therapass as well. He was relieved to see the wizard studying a large book.

"Something's wrong," he said, limping through the door. "Everyone's frozen and . . ." His words died away as the wizard continued to stare down at his book.

"He's frozen too," Kyja whispered.

Everything in the room was frozen as well. The cookie tin with wings hung in midair. The fire in the fireplace didn't crackle or move, although it still felt hot. Marcus limped across the room as quickly as he could and touched the old man's shoulder. He felt normal. Warm. Human. He definitely hadn't been turned into a statue, and Marcus didn't think he was dead.

"What's this?" Kyja knelt and reached toward a thin silvery line on the floor that started just inside the wizard's door and led out into the hallway.

"Careful," Marcus said, unsure why he was warning her. "Don't touch it."

Kyja pulled back her hand. "What's wrong? It's just some kind of paint, I think."

"I'm not sure," Marcus said. He knelt beside Kyja and studied the silvery line. It didn't look like paint to him. It looked more like . . . he couldn't think of exactly what. Every time he tried to remember, he kept seeing the flower gardens outside the monastery. "Was this here when we came in? I didn't notice it."

"It had to be," Kyja said. "We just didn't see it because we were focused on Master Therapass."

"I guess so." Marcus looked at Kyja and she looked back. She had to be thinking the same thing.

"Should we follow it?" she asked.

"Definitely not," Riph Raph, said, eyes wide. "In fact, let's stay as far away from it as possible."

Marcus grinned at the skyte. "You can stay here if you want, lizard breath, but we're going."

CHAPTER 14

ON THE TRAIL

"THIS IS WHY I DON'T LIKE Turnip Head," Riph Raph said, hopping along the floor behind Marcus and Kyja as they followed the thin silvery trail down the hallway. "Before he comes, things are dull, just the way I like them—eating bugs, catching fish, reading books. Then he shows up, and suddenly everyone gets frozen."

Marcus laughed. "Was it *really* boring while I was gone?"

Kyja felt her face grow warm. "Maybe a little." She knew she should be frightened. Obviously, something strange was going on. But to tell the truth, it felt sort of like old times. She'd discovered that she liked adventure. "What about you?" she asked. "Were you bored?"

"You have no idea." Marcus rolled his eyes. "Imagine no TV. No Internet. No phones." He suddenly realized what he'd just said and burst into laughter. "Okay. I guess you can imagine that. But it was *so* boring. Nothing to do. No place to go. No one to talk to."

Kyja grinned. She liked that he missed talking to her.

Marcus stopped and turned around. "That's weird."

"Hmm?" Kyja looked back at the line they'd been following and realized it was gone. She looked forward; the line was still there.

"It's disappearing as we follow it," Marcus said.

"Maybe we just brushed it off with our feet." Kyja nudged the toe of her slipper cautiously across the line. It didn't even blur. She rubbed harder. Still nothing.

Riph Raph poked his beak between the two of them. "Who's up for forgetting this whole thing and heading down to the kitchen for hot scones?"

Kyja ignored him. "There has to be a reason we're the only ones who don't seem to be frozen. Someone wants us to follow the line."

"I agree," Marcus said. "But who and to where?"

Suddenly, Kyja remembered the letter she'd found on her bed. Could the same person be behind this? Quickly she told Marcus about what the note said. "I realized it was talking about shadows, and I thought maybe it was a clue about how to get you here safely."

"Of course," Marcus said. "That totally makes sense."

"It does?" Kyja felt a satisfaction she hadn't experienced in a long time. Not since she and Marcus had defeated the zentan at the top of the tower. "Master Therapass thought I was being too impulsive."

"Master Therapass would tell a glacier it was too impulsive. What was he going to do, wait another six months to bring me back?"

Kyja giggled. "Probably."

Marcus leaned on his staff. "You know, I had kind of a message too, at the monastery. A bunch of my stuff was taken out of my room and spread down the hall. That's how I found the mirror that took me to . . . the other place."

Kyja had a feeling Marcus was hiding something from her. "Do you think the same person who moved your things made this trail?"

"I don't see how," Marcus said. "We're the only ones who can cross between Earth and Farworld. Except for . . ."

"The Dark Circle," they said at the same time. Suddenly things didn't seem quite so funny anymore.

Kyja followed the line with her eyes to where it disappeared around the next bend in the hallway. With no guards or wizards to protect them, they would be on their own if the Thrathkin S'Bae had managed to find a way past the protections of the tower. Kyja had been practicing sword fighting and archery for months. But here she was without a weapon of any kind.

"Do you want to go back?" Marcus asked.

Riph Raph bobbed his head up and down so enthusiastically his ears flapped like wings.

Kyja licked her lips. "No. But let's be careful. I'll watch behind us, and you watch ahead. And please tell me you've been practicing your magic."

"I have," he said, his voice low.

Together they followed the line as it led up one hallway and down another, always in the center of the corridor. Every time Kyja checked behind them, the line was gone, yet she never once saw it actually disappear.

Her head was turned when Marcus stopped and pointed. "Look!"

Kyja spun around, bracing for some kind of attack.

Marcus pointed to where the line finally left the center of the hallway and turned into an open door. Kyja hadn't been paying attention to which way they'd been walking, but now she recognized where they were.

She looked back the way they'd come—the line was gone—and ahead. "This isn't possible."

"What's inside that door?"

Riph Raph hopped up onto Kyja's shoulder, tilted his head and said, "Someone has a twisted sense of humor."

———◆———

Marcus looked from Kyja to Riph Raph. "What does he mean?"

Kyja walked up to the doorway and pointed inside. "See for yourself."

Marcus's leg was hurting and his back throbbed. All he wanted to do was rest somewhere, but even so, he tensed as he approached the door. The silver trail didn't come back out, so whatever had made it must still be inside.

Pressing his back against the wall, Marcus inched forward until he could see into the room. His jaw dropped, and he looked at Kyja, unable to believe what he was seeing.

Kyja nodded. "We're back where we started—it's Master Therapass's study."

Marcus stepped into the study and looked cautiously around. Everything looked exactly the same. The wizard hadn't moved. The books and papers all appeared to be in the same places. The fire was still frozen in the fireplace.

"This doesn't make any sense," Marcus said. "Who would want to lead us back to where we started?"

Kyja tugged on a strand of hair. "*Why* is the more important question. Either someone wanted us out of the way, or they wanted to get us frustrated."

Riph Raph gave a wide, jaw-cracking yawn. "We could always

sleep on it and see how things look in the morning. If time stays frozen, we won't have to worry about waking up late."

Marcus found a large brown shell in the corner of the room and dropped onto it, stretching out his sore leg. He looked at the last bit of the silver trail that led in through the study door. Something about the way it glistened looked familiar. Why? Was it supposed to mean something to him?

He closed his eyes and tried to concentrate. He was almost positive he'd seen something like the trail before. Only not quite as big. More like—

The shell he was sitting on shifted. Marcus rolled off it with a yelp.

"What's wrong?" Kyja cried, rushing to his side.

Marcus sat up and looked at the shell. It was moving. Almost too slowly to tell, but it *was* moving. It wasn't just a shell. It was . . . "A snail!" he shouted. "That's what made the silver line. It's a snail trail."

Kyja walked around to the other side of the snail and squatted down. "You're right," she said. "I can see its head. I've never seen a snail so big before."

Riph Raph flew over and licked his beak. "Looks juicy."

"You're not eating it." Marcus left his staff lying on the ground where he'd dropped it and scooted along beside the snail. "Something doesn't make sense. Look how slowly it's moving. No way could it make that loop in one night. And if it was here earlier, someone would have noticed."

"It's the only thing besides us that's not frozen," Kyja said. "Maybe it's magic. It might be some kind of message." She knocked on the snail's thick brown shell. "Hello? Anybody in there?"

Marcus couldn't keep from laughing; Kyja scowled at him.

"Laugh if you want to," she said. "But there are much stranger things than talking snails in Farworld."

"I know." He'd seen quite a few of them himself—a giant scorpion thing that could look like anything it wanted, a flying ice-dragon, farm animals that told jokes, and a creature that was half fox and half boar. From what he'd heard, that wasn't even the smallest part of what was out there. He hiccupped and covered his mouth. "It's just that when you were talking about snails, it made me think of . . ." He paused, an idea forming.

"Made you think of what?"

Marcus frowned and slowly looked around the room. He'd seen snails once before in Farworld. But it had to be a coincidence. The other snails were small and quite possibly even dead. Nothing like this beast at all. Only with so many weird things happening, it almost seemed to fit.

"Look!" he shouted, pointing to a shelf a few feet above the snail. He reached out and picked up a tiny golden horn no bigger than his little finger.

Kyja's eyes went wide. "You think that belongs to . . . ?"

Marcus nodded. "It makes as much sense as anything else that's happened today." He wet his lips, put the tiny horn to his mouth, and blew. It created a surprisingly loud *rooo-oop*. Before he could take the horn from his lips, the air in front of the fireplace went sort of hazy and a small man appeared lying on the rug before the frozen fire.

The man, who was barely half as tall as Kyja, was dressed in a long black coat, purple velvet vest, and baggy green pants that barely came past his knees. A battered top hat covered his eyes.

"Mr. Z?" Kyja said.

At the sound of her voice, the man sat up. The top hat tumbled from his head and looked like it was going to hit the ground. But somehow, he managed to catch it with the toe of his boot and kick it into the air. With one hand, he grabbed the hat and slapped it onto his thin gray hair while the other hand caught a pair of silver spectacles that fell out of the hat.

He rubbed his bulbous red nose, put on the glasses, and looked from Marcus to Kyja.

"Um hum, um hmm," he coughed, clearing his throat, and in a squeaky voice called, "Let the games begin!"

CHAPTER 15

An Unexpected Ride

WELL," THE LITTLE MAN DEMANDED. "What are you waiting for?" He pulled an old shoe out of his coat pocket, tossed it to his snail, took out a half-eaten loaf of bread, stuck that back in his coat, and finally found a pocket watch that seemed far too big for his puny hands. "We don't have all day." He opened the watch and rubbed his nose. "Although technically, I suppose we do."

"Who's the dwarf with the weird clothes?" asked Riph Raph.

Mr. Z gave Riph Raph a scathing look. "One of the many reason I prefer snails to flying reptilians—they're almost never rude. And when they are, it is always called for. And entertaining."

Kyja could only stare. The last time she'd seen Mr. Z, he'd sent them on quests to become land elementals. She was sure they'd never run into him again.

"What are you doing here?" Marcus asked, clearly as flabbergasted as she was.

"Until you blew that horn, I was sleeping."

"Did you do all this?" Kyja finally managed to ask. "The trail? Freezing everyone?"

Mr. Z clucked and shook his head, threatening to knock off his top hat again. "Dear girl, do I look like I leave a trail of silvery, slimy, snaily goodness everywhere I go? Why, if I could do that, I would be a star, a celebrity, a . . . well, a *snail*. No, I'm afraid I only leave footprints. Just like the rest of us unfortunate enough not to be born gastropods."

Marcus shook his head like a man who'd taken one too many punches. "But you *did* freeze everyone."

"Freeze? No, lad. I didn't freeze anyone." He twiddled his fingers as if he were preparing to play the piano. "I simply slowed them down while speeding you up. I can speed them up again anytime you like. Observe."

Kyja waited for something to happen. When nothing appeared to have changed, she said, "Well?"

Mr. Z beamed. "All in the wrists, you see. And a bit in the ankles." He stuck out one of his stubby legs and examined it. "I ought to consider using the ankles a bit more. Who knows what might happen. Did you like it?"

"Like *what?*" Marcus asked.

The little man yanked the lapels of his coat. "You think you can do better? Go ahead and try. I've got all day." He glanced at his pocket watch. "Or rather, I've got all night."

Marcus looked to Kyja, but she had no idea what Mr. Z was talking about either. "It's not that I think I can do better," Marcus said. "I just . . . I don't know what you did."

Mr. Z's lips drooped. "You missed the performance of a lifetime?" He turned to Kyja. "You saw it, didn't you?"

Kyja felt terrible about shaking her head. The man seemed so dejected. "Sorry."

"I see." Mr. Z took a deep breath, tugged on the lapels of his coat, and seemed to pull himself together. "Never fear. What can be done once can be done twice." He pointed at his eyes with two fingers and then at Master Therapass. "Watch closely. You don't need glasses, do you? I've got spares."

Kyja shook her head. She watched Master Therapass, determined not to miss whatever was about to happen.

"This is going to be so amazing," Mr. Z said. He waggled his fingers.

If she hadn't been staring directly at Master Therapass, Kyja wouldn't have noticed anything. The wizard's hand twitched ever so slightly, his finger moving no more than an inch across the page. His chest also appeared to rise a little. Then he froze again.

"Ahhhh." Mr. Z grinned, rubbing his hands together with obvious glee. "To be completely honest, I wasn't sure I could repeat my last performance. Or at least not so well. Perfection is impossible to match and surprisingly difficult to top. Or is that the other way around? In any event, I'm only glad I could share this moment of unsurpassed glory with you—two of my closest friends. And your . . . *pet.* But we really must be going now."

Kyja, who had forgotten how annoying Mr. Z could be, grimaced. "You didn't do anything. His hand only moved a tiny bit."

Mr. Z seemed genuinely confused. "Well, of course. That was the point. Do you have any idea the degree of difficulty in moving time up only a fraction? What did you expect? An oafish parody of chronological manipulation? A remedial reign of ridiculosity? A . . . a . . ." He threw his hands up in despair, and everything started up again.

Master Therapass turned the page of his book. Kyja looked for Mr. Z, but he and his snail were gone. From outside in the hallway came a cry of alarm, and then another. Horns sounded. The wizard looked up. "Kyja? Marcus? What are you doing out of your rooms?" The old wizard's eyes went from Marcus to Kyja with growing distress. "Something has happened!"

"I, I mean we . . ." Kyja gulped, unsure how to explain, especially since she wasn't completely sure what had happened herself.

A guard raced down the hallway—his armor clanking—and hurried into the room. "Master, outside—"

Everything froze in place again. Mr. Z and his snail were back. "You see what happens," he said sadly, "when one uses heavy-handed chronology correction?"

Kyja tried to catch her breath. This was all completely confusing, almost as if Mr. Z was distracting them on purpose.

Marcus stomped toward the fireplace. Even bent and leaning on his staff, he towered over the small man. "What I see is you doing a bunch of tricks and not telling us why you're here. Are you the one who made me drink that goblin goo?"

"Are you the person who left me the note?" Kyja asked.

"It's time to stop messing around and give us answers," Marcus said.

"Any more lizard jokes," Riph Raph added from his perch high on a bookshelf, "and that snail of yours is going to be slug sautéed."

"I can see they were right when they said you would be difficult to work with." Mr. Z patted the top of his hat.

"*Who* said?" Kyja tried to ask. But something was wrong. She could barely move her lips. Her jaws felt like they were stuck in molasses, and when she tried to look at Marcus, her neck moved so slowly it would have taken fifteen minutes just to turn her head.

"I'm afraid we'll never get through this if you keep asking questions." Mr. Z's voice was much higher than its normal pitch, and his words came so quickly, it was hard to understand everything he said; it all seemed to run together.

"I've taken the liberty of slowing you both down I will try to speak clearly enough that you can understand but I must say this is rather difficult for me and for you I would imagine I have an important message that happens to be somewhat time sensitive it is one I believe you will be quite interested to hear and I have gone to extreme measures to deliver it if you think you can listen without interrupting blink your eyes otherwise I will be forced to keep you in a state of diminished chronological capacity."

Marcus and Kyja both blinked.

Mr. Z tugged at his ears. "—nopu etarobale rehtar ro nialpxe ot em wolla neht lleW" He quickly pulled his ears. "Sorry about that. Wrong direction. As I was saying, allow to me explain, or rather elaborate upon, why I am here."

He tucked the watch into a pocket of his vest and pulled out a small silver scroll. "I, the undersigned, having been procured by the first party, hereafter referred to as Aerisians, as their agent, emissary, intermediary, mediator, and negotiator, do hereby—"

"Wait," Marcus interrupted. "Are we supposed to be making sense of any of this?"

Kyja didn't understand most of it either, but she did recognize one word thanks to her studies. "*Aerisians*. The air elementals?"

"Indeed." Mr. Z put away his scroll. "As it so happens, they are willing to meet with you, and they have sent me to bring you to them."

The air elementals! Was it really going to be this easy to find them? "When?" Kyja blurted.

"Are we sure this is a good idea?" Riph Raph complained.

"How?" Marcus asked.

Mr. Z waved his hands over his head. "Why must you all speak when you should be listening? This is why I enjoy the presence of my spiral-shelled friends. Snails can go months without uttering a single word. And when they do speak, that single word may be so profound that they need say nothing more for another several months. Why, just last week, my good friend Helix looked me straight in the eye and said, 'Ubiquitous.' Scintillating, is it not?"

Kyja didn't dare say a word. Partly because she was afraid the little man would freeze her again. And partly because she had no idea what either *ubiquitous* or *scintillating* meant.

Marcus nodded half-heartedly. "Definitely, um, scintillating."

"Precisely," Mr. Z scratched his head. "Now then, how was I? Where was I? Who was I?"

"You were telling us about the air elementals?" Kyja suggested.

"They prefer to be called *Aerisians*. They feel it's more dignified. Which is rather amusing, considering . . ." He waved his hand and giggled. "But that's really not my place. To answer your earlier questions. Now. Most definitely. And Drymaios."

Marcus looked at Kyja. She raised her hands palms up. "I don't understand."

"I'm quite sure you do not," Mr. Z said. "But you will. Until then, yes, it is a good idea. We must leave now, if not sooner. And we shall get there on . . ." He pointed to the snail that Marcus had sat on earlier, which was now busily eating the old shoe Mr. Z had thrown it. "Drymaios."

CHAPTER 16

AT THE SPEED OF SNAIL

MARCUS COULDN'T HELP bursting into laughter. They were traveling to the air elementals on a *snail?* This had to be another one of Mr. Z's bizarre jokes.

"We'll need to get you packed," Mr. Z said. "You'll want warm clothing—it gets cold where we're going—food and water for the trip, and perhaps some comfortable slippers and worthwhile reading material. I favor free-verse poetry. But to each his own."

Marcus waited for the punch line. "I don't have any clothes except what I'm wearing. I left them all back on Earth."

Mr. Z squinted through his silver glasses, which Marcus was pretty sure didn't have any lenses. "No time for that anyway." He stepped into the fireplace, right through the flames, and a second later returned carrying the backpack Marcus had left in Elder Ephraim's room and a bag for Kyja.

"How did you do that?" Marcus asked.

Kyja looked through her bag. "These are all from my room upstairs."

"Make haste," Mr. Z said, ignoring their questions completely. He hurried into the hall, stepping around the guard, who was still frozen in mid-warning. "Come, come."

"Is he serious?" Marcus asked Kyja.

"Seems to be," she said.

It made absolutely no sense. The snail, which was not much taller than a large dog, hadn't moved more than twelve inches at most since they came into the room. Even if the three of them could all somehow fit on the shell, it would take a week just to get out of the tower.

"Not to be rude, but wouldn't we get there quicker if we rode something a little . . . faster?" Marcus asked as he and Kyja followed Mr. Z out the study door.

"*Faster?*" Mr. Z took off his glasses and polished the space where lenses would normally be. "My boy, apparently you didn't recognize that Drymaios here is a *racing* snail. Faster even than a jousting snail. If you've never ridden one, you are in for a treat. The thrill of pure speed, the wind blasting in your face, adrenaline pulsing through your veins as the countryside blurs past. Truly a once-in-a-lifetime experience."

"O-kay," Marcus said, still extremely doubtful.

"Maybe it really *is* fast," Kyja whispered. "It managed to stay ahead of us when we were following its trail."

"Or maybe the doorstop in a hat is nutty in the noggin," Riph Raph said. "I'm not riding any slimy snail."

"That might be for the best," Mr. Z said. "I wouldn't mind leaving you behind. You seem to be rather a nuisance."

Riph Raph hissed.

"All right then, gather 'round," Mr. Z said once they were all in the corridor. "There are a few rules to remember when riding a beast this powerful and fleet. First, no spitting, dribbling, or drooling. Nothing worse than getting a face full of high-speed saliva from your traveling companion. Second, keep your arms, feet, and hands upon your mount at all times. I once saw an unfortunate woman allow her foot to touch the ground while traveling at a speed which took one's breath away."

"What happened?" Kyja asked, clasping her hands to her chest.

"We had to go back for her shoe, of course," Mr. Z grumbled. "Took me completely out of my way." He took off his top hat, somehow managed to completely flatten it, and tucked it inside his long coat. "Shall we go?"

Kyja glanced toward the study, and whispered to Marcus. "Are we sure leaving without telling anyone is a good idea? Maybe we should talk to Master Therapass first."

Marcus knew exactly how she felt. Mr. Z had always been more than a little strange. Could they even be sure he was taking them to the air elementals? He turned to the little man. "How do we know we can trust you?"

"Funny you should ask," Mr. Z said with a laugh. "Now then, let's ride."

"That's not an answer," Kyja said.

Mr. Z nodded sagely. "I'm sorry. I didn't know it was an answer you were looking for. How about one of these? Red, forty-two, and the underside of a dribble fish's dorsal fin."

Marcus rolled his eyes. Talking to Mr. Z was like trying to have a discussion with a three-year-old, except that occasionally a three-year-old made sense.

"Ready to mount up?" Mr. Z asked, rolling the sleeves of his coat to his elbows.

Kyja sighed. "Fine."

Marcus looked toward the snail, who was still nibbling on the shoe back in the study. "Shouldn't he be out here?"

"*She,*" Mr. Z hissed. "Never, under any circumstances, allow a racing snail to hear you call her by the wrong gender." He folded his arms across his chest and shuddered. "They do not take it well."

"Sorry." Marcus thought of asking how you could tell a female snail from a male one, and decided he didn't really want to know. "So is *she* coming?" After everything Mr. Z had said, he found that he was actually kind of excited to see the snail move at more than a snail's pace.

"Stand back," Mr. Z said. "You don't want to step into the path of a racing snail. Not if you value your toes." He put two fingers in his mouth and gave a shrill whistle. "Drymaios. To me!"

Marcus and Kyja watched intently. But the snail kept eating the shoe.

"Impressive," Riph Raph said flatly. "I've got goose bumps."

Mr. Z brushed at the front of his vest and whispered, "They can be a bit temperamental." He whistled again. "Come, Drymaios! We have places to go."

This time the snail at least looked up. Then she pulled her head back inside her shell.

Kyja put her hand over her mouth, trying not to giggle. "I think she went to sleep."

"Poor beast is exhausted from all her travels," Mr. Z said. Marcus thought it was a lot more likely the snail was just full of shoe. "Would you mind lending me a hand?" Mr. Z asked Kyja, taking her by the arm.

"With what?" Kyja asked.

Mr. Z led her to the snail and leaned down to grab one side of the shell. "When I say three, lift."

They were going to carry the great racing snail out of the room? Marcus snorted.

"One, two, three." Mr. Z heaved up his side of the snail.

Kyja lifted hers, her arms straining. "Who knew snails were so heavy?" she said, as the two of them shuffled around the guard and toward the door.

"It's the foot muscle," Mr. Z grunted. "All that running builds it up."

"I think the only muscle is in his head," Riph Raph said, and for once, Marcus agreed with the skyte.

"There," Mr. Z, said, once they were outside the study. Carefully, he and Kyja lowered the snail to the floor. He turned and closed the door. "No need to mess the place up with the speed of a fast takeoff."

Marcus looked at the snail, which still had her head hidden inside her shell. "So we're going to ride her down the stairs?"

"You would prefer to go out the window?" Mr. Z patted the shell. "You first, young man. Mind you don't scratch her shell with your staff."

"There's no saddle or anything," Kyja said.

"Saddle?" Mr. Z roared with laughter. "Oh, you are a gem. Why, if you tried to put a saddle on a racing snail, it would buck you off so quickly, your head would spin."

Marcus tried to imagine a bucking snail but couldn't do it. "How do you steer?"

"Do you think this is a wagon? Or a beast of burden?" the little man said, sounding offended. "Snails are some of the most intelligent of all animals. You don't steer them. You ask them politely to take you where you want to go. *Steer.* Hah!"

Feeling extremely uncomfortable with the idea, Marcus pulled on his pack, tucked his staff under one arm, and slid onto the shell.

Kyja clamped her hands together in front of her chest. "What will Master Therapass say when he sees we're gone?"

"I would imagine something like, 'Where did they go?'" Mr. Z giggled.

"That's not funny," Marcus said. "Can't you be serious for one minute?"

The little man pressed his fingers to his temples as though his head ached. "If you do as I say and stop dillydallying, the wolf in wizard's clothing will never know you've left." He turned to Kyja and motioned her toward the snail. "Now you."

Kyja climbed onto the back of the snail—wrapping her arms around Marcus. "Don't let us fall off," she whispered.

"How?" he asked. "There's nothing to hang on to."

"This is nearly as bad as the time you almost killed us in that motor-thingy," Riph Raph said. He hopped onto the shell behind Kyja, and clamped his beak onto the back of her robe.

"Where are *you* going to sit?" Marcus asked. There was no more room on the shell.

"I prefer an inside seat," Mr. Z said. "The wind makes a mess of my hair, and I have to brush and comb it all day to get the tangles out."

"*What* inside seat?" Kyja asked.

Mr. Z got down on his hands and knees, crawled around to the front of the shell and said, "Move over now. Don't hog the entire shell to yourself, Drymaios." Then he disappeared inside.

Kyja leaned over, trying to get a better view. "I didn't think you could climb inside a snail."

"I didn't think you could *ride* one," Marcus said.

"Right then-en-en," Mr. Z called, his voice muted and echoing. "Everyone hang on tight-ight-ight."

Marcus tried to find something to hold on to with his good hand. But the best he could do was place it flat on the shell. If this snail actually went fast, he, Kyja, and Riph Raph would fall right off.

"I'm a little scared," Kyja whispered.

"Me too," Marcus whispered back. What if they fell? What if that was how he killed Kyja? "Maybe we should rethink this," he said.

But it was too late. "Ready or not, here we go-go-go!" Mr. Z called from inside the snail.

Kyja's arms tightened around Marcus's chest, and he could feel his heart pounding against her hands. He clamped his legs as tightly around the shell as he could and held his breath.

Nothing happened.

"Is she still asleep?" Kyja asked.

"I told you he was a whack job," Riph Raph said.

Marcus shrugged. "I don't know. Keep holding on just in case."

Seconds passed, but still nothing happened. The snail didn't move at all. Marcus's arms and legs began to cramp. Right when he was about to suggest they get off, Mr. Z came tumbling out of the snail shell, his face flushed.

"What happened?" Kyja said. "Why didn't it go?"

"What do you mean?" Mr. Z asked, wiping his forehead with a silk handkerchief. "We're there."

CHAPTER 17

Icehold

K YJA SLID OFF THE BACK OF THE SNAIL. "We didn't go any-where."

"Really?" Mr. Z looked around. He pulled off his glasses and replaced them with another pair he took from his pocket. "Are you sure?"

"Of course we're sure." Marcus climbed off the snail and slammed the end of his staff on the floor. "What was the point of all that?"

Mr. Z put a finger on the end of his nose and turned slowly around. "No. No, I'm quite positive we're here."

"Get this off me," Riph Raph squawked, tugging at a bright red knit cap with a pom-pom on the top that was tied under his chin.

Kyja suddenly realized that she and Marcus were wearing heavy coats. "Where did these come from?"

Mr. Z pointed to the door to Master Therapass's study. "What's through there?"

Kyja threw her hands into the air. This was ridiculous. "That's the door we just came out of." She turned the knob, pushed, and . . . dropped through the opening, landing on her knees in a bank of snow.

All at once, she was grateful for her coat. She was freezing, the air so bitterly cold it was hard to breathe. Snowflakes blew against her face, stinging her cheeks. A moment later, Marcus landed in the snow beside her. Then Riph Raph came flapping, flopping, and squawking.

Kyja looked around. They were in a snow bank that was piled at least twelve feet high above an icy street she'd never seen before. She raised her head in time to see Mr. Z leap through a rectangular doorway that floated in the middle of the air, three or four feet above her head. Through the opening she could just make out the hall where they'd been. Then the door slammed closed, and the opening disappeared.

Kyja got shakily to her feet. She handed Marcus his staff and helped him up. It was evening, and people were moving up and down the snow-crusted street—some walking, several on horses, and others in carts or wagons. A few wagons were pulled by horses as well, but most were propelled by invisible flows of air magic.

The people were dressed in furs or heavy, boiled leather. Many of them wore armor and carried weapons. They had broader shoulders than she was used to, and fatter faces, with wide noses and thick jaws. Everyone appeared to be in a hurry, as though anxious to get out of the cold. Kyja couldn't blame them; her cheeks were already beginning to ache, and her nose felt like an icicle.

Some of the people glanced in Marcus and Kyja's direction, but only in the way they might notice a stranger, not in the way they would gawk at a boy and girl who had just fallen out of the sky.

"Where are we?" Marcus asked, brushing snow off his pants.

"I have no idea," Kyja said. She cupped her hand to her face, trying to warm her nose. "I don't think I've ever been anywhere this cold before, except maybe the Windlash Mountains."

"We are in Valdemeer," Mr. Z said. "In the city of Icehold."

Riph Raph squawked. "Are you crazy?"

Kyja shook her head. "That's not possible. Valdemeer is two months' travel at least. And that's on a fast horse. It's in the far northern borderlands."

"Valdemeer," Marcus said. "Why does that name sound familiar?"

Mr. Z tapped his fingers against his lips.

"You said you were taking us to Air Keep," Kyja said.

Mr. Z nodded. "That I am, most definitely. But after a long day's journey, even the most intrepid traveler needs food and rest."

Kyja opened her mouth to say she wasn't hungry, and that they hadn't traveled at all, before realizing that it had been the middle of the night when she pulled Marcus to Farworld. Now the sun was beginning to set. And she *was* tired. It was all she could do to keep her eyes open. Obviously they had gone somewhere, even if she couldn't remember doing it.

Marcus's stomach rumbled, and he stifled a yawn.

"The Seven-Fingered Lady down the street serves the most scrumptious roast Lentus Beast with a fungus sauce to make the tongue sing. I've arranged rooms for the night," Mr. Z said, scampering down the snowbank as if it were a staircase.

Marcus and Kyja tried to follow but ended up slipping and falling most of the way down. As they stomped their feet and tried to clear the snow and ice from their faces, Mr. Z pulled his top hat over his ears. "Dinner isn't for another hour or so. Why don't the two of you toddle about until then?"

"Are you joking?" Riph Raph said, hopping from one foot to the other. "It's freezing out here. I think my tongue is stuck to my beak."

It *was* cold; if it hadn't been for their heavy coats, they'd probably have frostbite. And once the sun set all the way, it would get even colder.

"You might want to think about heading that way," the little man said, pointing toward a side street. "It could be . . . *informative.* And wear your scarves and hats. It's nippy out here if you hadn't noticed." With that, he turned and headed off in the other direction.

"Scarves?" Kyja reached into her coat pocket and found a long woolen scarf and a knit hat—both the same blinding red as Riph Raph's hat.

"I think he's trying to make us look like strawberries," Marcus said. But he still put on the hat, scarf, and a pair of bright red mittens he found in the other coat pocket.

Kyja did the same as they started down the street Mr. Z had suggested. They passed a shop that sold singing candies, a row of stands selling self-pounding nails, horseshoes that made your horse run faster, and a variety of other magical items, and not surprisingly a large number of places selling coats, hats, and various warming devices.

"Do you think we really traveled?" Kyja asked, her breath steaming in front of her eyes. "I mean all day?"

"It feels like we've been doing something. My back and legs are screaming. And if I don't eat something soon, I'm going to gnaw my own fingers off."

Until Marcus mentioned it, Kyja hadn't realized that she was stiff as well. Her rear felt like she'd been . . . like she'd been sitting on a hard snail shell for hours.

Marcus yawned again. "What I don't understand is how there can be a drought in Terra ne Staric while it's blizzarding here."

"Something's gone completely wrong with the weather," Kyja agreed.

Riph Raph blew out a line of blue flames, trying to warm his feet. "Something's going to go wrong with me if I don't get out of this cold. Skytes are not made for snow. I'm going to find someplace warm." He flew off into the snow-filled sky, pom-pom bouncing back and forth on either side of his head.

After exploring for several minutes, Kyja and Marcus reached the edge of the city, where a winding wooden staircase zigzagged up the side of a stone wall.

"Whoa!" Marcus said, looking up. "It's huge!"

Kyja craned her neck to see the top, but the staircase was lost in the swirling white flakes. The biggest city wall she'd ever seen was in Terra ne Staric, but this was at least three times taller. And while Terra ne Staric's walls were mostly made of wood, this was built from squares of stone so large she couldn't imagine where they'd all been found.

"Shouldn't the two of ye be getting indoors?" asked a mountain of a man with a beard that hid everything but his bright eyes and white teeth. He was so covered in furs that he looked almost like a bear, but a well-armed one, with swords on both hips and a round shield strapped to his back.

"We were just admiring your wall," Kyja said.

"Mined straight from the Altarian Mountains. Even the most powerful of magic cannot so much as put a scratch in them." The man had an odd accent Kyja wasn't familiar with. He eyed the two of them. "Ye be not from around here. Were ye hoping to scry the view?"

"Scry?" Kyja frowned. She'd heard the word before but usually it meant looking into a crystal ball or some other magical item.

"Aye." The man scratched at his beard. "It's terrible weather for looking about. But then again, when every day brings another storm, ye begin to think mayhap it not be so bad after all. Perhaps this *is* fair weather."

He laughed uproariously at his own joke and looked a little disappointed when neither Marcus nor Kyja laughed along with him. "If it's scrying ye want, it be best to get up the wall now, 'fore the sun goes down."

Marcus studied the icy staircase going up the side of the wall and shook his head. "I can't make it up that. Too bad you don't have elevators here."

Now it was the man's turn to frown. "Never have I heard of an eely-vaytor. But fear not, young master. Scry ye will." He took Kyja's hand and led her to the first stair, then helped Marcus up. As soon as they were all on the staircase, the steps began to move, rising slowly up the wall.

Kyja laughed with delight. "It's like those moving things you have on Earth."

"Escalators," Marcus agreed. "Never thought I'd see one on Farworld, though."

The man seemed to enjoy their delight. "'Tis far too difficult to get a man in full armor to the top of the wall otherwise. In case of attack." He held out his hand. "Freeman Arstel."

Marcus and Kyja each shook his hand. His fingers were thick and calloused.

"Do you get attacked much?" Marcus asked.

"Does a friddersnap sheer ferns?" The man chuckled.

Kyja assumed that meant yes.

"Ye be on the edge of the civilized world," the man said. "Beyond this fortress roam creatures both wee and great. Some be tame. But most be fearsome wicked." He scratched his beard. "'Course, some of them be more fierce in men's stories than in real life. Why, just the day 'fore last, a group of soldiers returned from patrol, telling of a beast so fearful even I couldn't stomach it."

Marcus and Kyja clung to the wooden rail that moved along with the stairs. The higher they climbed, the harder the wind blew, and the stairs wobbled and creaked. "Is that what you are? A soldier?" she asked.

The man roared with laughter. "Girly," he said, patting his long sword. "In Icehold, everyone be a soldier. Even ones as wee as ye and yer friend here."

"What kind of creature?" Marcus asked.

"Eh?"

"What kind of creature did the soldiers say they saw?"

"What kind of creature, indeed." The man held out his arms and bared his teeth. "They say it was a beast red as blood, with wings long as an inn and teeth as large as a man. Tall as a dozen houses. Spouting all manner of fire and magic."

Marcus's face went white, and Kyja felt her stomach roll over. "Did they say anything about an army of walking dead?"

The man laughed. "Ye *have* heard the story already. Why didn't ye be saying so?"

A Summoner and its army of Fallen Ones. Kyja and Marcus had seen a Summoner before. It had nearly killed Master Therapass and would have killed *them* if it hadn't been for the help of the water elementals. But what was it doing all the way out here?

The Dark Circle, Marcus mouthed silently. Kyja nodded. It was the only thing that made sense. The Dark Circle knew they were looking for the air and fire elementals. It must be hunting them as well.

At last, the stairs came to a shuddering halt. "Here ye be," the man said. "Look ye upon the edge of the world."

Kyja stepped onto the top of the wall and gasped. It was . . . *incredible.* The air was so clear that even with the icy wind and falling snow, it seemed like she could see forever. To the right was a forest of trees so big they made the Westland Woods look like saplings. They were probably at least a day's walk away from the forest, but even from this distance, she thought the trunks had to be as wide as ten men standing hand to hand.

"The Forest of Before Time," the man said. "'Tis rumored those trees were full grown long 'afore man set foot on this land."

To the left, the mountains rose straight out of the ground, soaring so high they made her dizzy. Snow covered their sides, even though it was still summer, and mist cloaked their peaks.

"Are those the Altarian Mountains?" Marcus asked.

"Aye. 'Tis whispered that fanciful creatures with a devilish sense of humor live in the clouds," the man said. "Don't see how anyone can be knowing that, though, as no one's ever climbed to the top."

"They're beautiful," Kyja said.

"Aye, but ye haven't seen it all." The man placed his palm on a small stone pillar, and Marcus sucked in his breath.

"How did you do that?" Marcus asked. "It's like I can see every detail, down to the smallest blade of grass."

"Water magic," the man said. "Lets us see the badduns afore they can see us, if you catch my meaning."

Magic again. Kyja looked down and scuffed her slippers across the stone surface of the wall. She should have expected it.

Marcus glanced over at her, his eyes glowing. "Isn't it—" He stopped. "You can't see it, can you?"

She shook her head, trying not to let her disappointment show.

"What's this?" Beneath his beard, the man's lips drew down. "How can ye no see it?"

"She's immune to magic," Marcus said. "It doesn't work on her."

The man looked at Kyja like he'd discovered she was about to die. "Ye can do no magic at all? Not even a wee little thing like scrying??"

Kyja shook her head again. What she could make out was a beautiful view anyway, and she was glad she'd come up to see it. But the night had lost something, and she was ready to get warm.

"Let's go," Marcus said, taking her hand.

"Aye." The man reached toward the pillar to undo the water magic, but Marcus stopped him.

"Wait," he said, pointing. "What's that? Right by the spot where the trees are smaller than the rest. There's a bunch of rocks—like there used to be some kind of buildings."

The man's face darkened. His eyes studied the deepening twilight. "'Tis all that remains of one of the greatest cities ever built. A fortress stronger even than Icehold."

"What happened to it?" Marcus asked.

"I'll nay speak of Windshold," the man said. Whatever friendliness he'd shown before was gone. He turned to the stairs. "'Tis late. Ye wee ones should be indoors."

Kyja saw Marcus's face go white at the name of the city. "*Windshold?* Isn't that . . . ?"

Marcus swallowed and nodded. "It's where . . . I was born."

The soldier who had been walking toward the stairs spun around—his face red. "Nay! Ye be mistaken."

"I'm not mistaken," Marcus said, so softly his voice could barely be heard above the wind. "I was born in Windshold. But I was too little too remember."

"I tell ye, that *no* be possible," the man growled. His huge hands were closed into fists, and Kyja realized the man was shaking with anger. "Just over fifteen seasons ago, that great city was destroyed by a horde of creatures so foul they overwhelmed the city in minutes. We heard the alarm and tried to come to their aid. But by the time we reached them, every man, woman and wee babe was dead."

Tears dripped down the big man's face, freezing to his ruddy cheeks. He reached inside his coat, tore out a bronze medallion, and shoved it in Marcus's face. "See this?" he shouted. "'Tis the flying weasel! My brother, Gralik, considered it his good-luck charm. It wasn't lucky for him. I pulled it off his dead body."

He swiped at his eyes and shoved the medallion back into his shirt. "Now ya understand why I say ye can no be from Windshold."

CHAPTER 18

FIRE AND ICE

MARCUS KNOCKED SOFTLY on Kyja's door. "Are you awake?" He waited for a moment before deciding she must be asleep. As he was turning away, a soft voice said, "Come in."

He opened the door and found Kyja lying on her bed, one arm thrown over her eyes. She was still completely dressed. "Can't sleep?" he asked.

She shook her head.

"Me neither."

Riph Raph had no such problem. The skyte was snoring like a diesel engine, muttering something about tasty beetles in his sleep.

"I'm sorry about what that man told you," Kyja said. "About your city."

Marcus sat on a stool by the small fireplace, the flames warming his back. "It's not anything I didn't know. Only . . . remember when you came to Earth for the first time and wanted to look for your parents?"

"In Salt Pond."

"Salt *Lake*." Marcus laughed. "That's how I feel now. My parents could be nearby. Only . . ." He couldn't bring himself to say it. If Windshold was completely destroyed, his family must be dead.

"We don't know that your parents were in the city when it happened," Kyja said. "Not for sure."

"Maybe."

Master Therapass had said one of his parents was from the realm of shadows. Marcus didn't know what to think, except that maybe it meant one of his parents could still be alive. "About the scrying," he said. "If that's what's bothering you, don't worry. The view wasn't that impressive anyway. Next time we go to Earth, I'll show you something called a telescope. It blows scrying away."

Kyja sighed. "It's not that. It's just . . ." she shook her head and pushed herself to a half-sitting position, resting on her elbows. "While I was waiting for you to come back from Earth, I imagined things differently."

"What do you mean?"

"I hoped if I could figure out where the air elementals were then you'd come back, and we'd set off for Air Keep—maybe with Cascade and Lanctrus-Darnoc. It would be like when we went looking for Water Keep."

"You mean when I almost got us killed by the Mimicker, and we nearly died in the desert, and you were frozen in a block of ice, and—"

"All right, all right." Kyja giggled. "So maybe it wasn't perfect. But we were working together. Figuring things out."

"Is this about what I said before?" Marcus asked, his mouth feeling suddenly dry. "About being apart from you?"

"A little," Kyja said, sitting all the way up. "It bothers me that you don't trust me enough to tell me whatever you're hiding."

Marcus gritted his teeth, torn between desperately wanting to tell Kyja the truth and being terrified of what she'd think if he did. He ran his fingers through the top of his hair, which had gotten way too long. "I do trust you," he said. "More than anyone I know."

"I wouldn't keep a secret from *you*," Kyja said. "But it's more than your secret. Did you know Master Therapass has been communicating with people on Earth?"

"Not until yesterday."

"I didn't either," Kyja said. "Because he didn't tell us. I think there's a lot more he hasn't told us—like *how* I'm supposed to save Earth, what's supposed to happen once we open the drift, what he knows about the shadow realm that makes it so dangerous."

"What are you saying? You don't trust him?"

Kyja shook her head so violently her hair flew back and forth. "I'm saying *he* doesn't trust *us*. No one seems to trust anyone. The water elementals don't trust the land elementals. The land elementals don't trust the air elementals. And what about Mr. Z? Why does he always talk in riddles? Why send him to us at all? If the air elementals wanted to talk to us, why didn't they come themselves?" Outside the window, the wind blew, and snowflakes danced like someone peeking into the room.

Kyja pulled a blanket around her shoulders. "The Dark Circle is more powerful than we are. They have bigger armies and stronger magic. They always seem to know where we are—they found us here and on Earth—while we have no idea what they're doing."

Marcus wanted to disagree, but she was right.

Kyja pounded a fist on her pillow, and Riph Raph grunted in his sleep. "How can we beat them if we don't work together?"

And there it was. She was speaking the truth. She wouldn't keep a secret from him. If he told her what he'd seen in the *Will Be*, she might run away from him in terror. He guessed he could live with that, somehow, some way, knowing he deserved it. But what if telling someone locked the future in place? By keeping it a secret, there was a chance it would never happen. The minute he told someone, though . . .

He closed his eyes. "If you want me to tell you, I will."

Kyja gave him a small smile. "Not until you're ready. I have to trust you too. To tell me. When the time is right."

"Okay," Marcus said. "That seems fair. I hadn't thought about Mr. Z, though. Why *did* the air elementals send him?"

"I've been thinking about that." Kyja turned to hang her legs off the side of the bed. "From what I've been able to learn, air elementals are curious and capricious." The wind swirled outside again.

"What does *capricious* mean?" Marcus asked. "It sounds like a word Mr. Z would use."

"Don't worry," Kyja said. "I had to look it up too. It means they're unpredictable. They have lots of mood swings."

"Sounds like Riph Raph," Marcus joked.

The skyte stopped snoring long enough to crack one eye open. "Don't think I didn't hear that."

Kyja laughed. "Anyway, I was thinking—what if they're testing us?"

"Trying to see what we'll do if Mr. Z keeps messing with us?"

"Something like that," Kyja said.

Marcus nodded. He could see that. "Do we let him know we're onto them?"

"I don't think so. We should watch him closely though, to see if we can figure out what exactly he's up to."

Outside, a bell began to clang. A moment later, a second one joined it.

Marcus went to the window, where he saw a bright glow in the distance. "I think something's burning."

Kyja jumped off the bed to look. At the same time, an explosion outside rattled the window, making the night even brighter.

Riph Raph woke up and blinked owlishly. "I smell smoke."

"Come on," Kyja said, "Let's see what's happening."

She ran to the door of the inn. Marcus hurried after her as quickly as he could. Outside, people were running and shouting. All of them seemed to be carrying weapons of one kind or another. Two boys raced by armed with bows and arrows, and a giant of a man loped down the street swinging a heavy mace in each hand.

The air was filled with a dark, gritty smoke, and ashes covered the snowy ground. New fires seemed to be igniting everywhere she looked. Bells continued to clang in the night. Marcus heard the crashes and screams of battle, but he couldn't tell where they were coming from. Should he and Kyja go back inside? He looked for Mr. Z, but the little man was nowhere to be found.

"What's going on?" Kyja asked, grabbing a woman by the sleeve of her coat.

"Attack!" the woman yelled before running down the street, a spear clutched in one gloved hand and a round wooden shield in the other.

Just behind them, the ground exploded, and Marcus spun around to see a cloud of dirt and ice billowing. A figure shuffled out of the snow. Marcus froze, shocked by the sudden appearance of the bony creature clad in bits of hanging flesh and torn clothing.

The Fallen Ones. If they were here, that meant a Summoner was here too.

The skeleton lunged toward Marcus and Kyja, a silver-handled short sword clutched in its bony fingers. Riph Raph dropped out of the sky, firing one blue fireball after another. The flames climbed the skeleton's ragged clothes, making it drop the sword. Kyja darted forward and grabbed it.

Marcus had forgotten how good Kyja was with a sword. She swung the blade with a quick, practiced swing, and the creature's burning arm dropped to the ground with a hiss. She spun around, reversing her swing, and its head went flying off as well.

"Behind you!" Riph Raph shouted. He blew a pair of bright blue fireballs at another undead figure lurching around the corner. The creature stumbled to one side of the road, its clothing and bones on fire. Three more were right behind. Two held swords, and another clutched a spiked mace in its bony fingers.

"Help me!" Kyja screamed, slashing at the first skeleton.

Marcus's mind was a blank. He needed to do something, but he couldn't think what. Every spell he'd studied had disappeared from his head.

The undead creature was taller than Kyja, its reach longer. Their blades met with a clang of steel. It brought its weapon, a curved sword with a jagged edge, down at Kyja. But she was quicker. She stepped inside the swing and stabbed the skeleton in the chest.

"Help her," Riph Raph shouted. He dove at the creatures, shooting fire, but it wasn't enough. The second creature raised its mace. The spiked metal ball came down at Kyja.

Marcus finally reacted. He cast the first thing that came into his head—a simple land magic spell to block the mace. But his land magic was weak, and the weapon missed Kyja by bare inches.

That could've hit her. I could've gotten her killed.

The thought finally broke Marcus out of his daze. He stretched out his hand and called on the power of air. A flock of birds swooped from the branches of a bare tree as a funnel of ice and snow began to spin and swirl in the air in front of Marcus.

Kyja chopped the legs out from under the creature, and it fell to the ground, still trying to reach her with its sword. The other two skeletons closed in.

Marcus pointed, and the funnel of air raced toward them. "Get back!" he yelled to Kyja as the miniature tornado lifted the first skeleton from the ground and slammed it into the one beside it. Bones crunched and weapons went flying.

Kyja backed away from the swirling vortex.

Four more skeletons charged, and Marcus knocked them over like bowling pins, his arms and hands tingling with power.

"Take that! Go back to your mossy graves," Riph Raph screamed, swirling and looping in a skyte victory dance. But the celebration was short-lived.

Creatures were filling the street from every direction. Not just undead humans, but dogs with two heads and lolling tongues, bears with gaping wounds and slavering teeth, and things Marcus couldn't recognize at all. He smashed them with his tornado, but for every creature he destroyed, two more appeared.

A pair of Thrathkin S'Bae appeared from behind the inn. The dark wizards looked in Marcus and Kyja's direction, and she grabbed his arm. "We have to go."

He didn't want to. The feeling of power raging through him was thrilling. He was no longer the boy with one good arm and leg; he was a wizard, a warrior. But Kyja continued to pull, screaming for him to stop, and only then did Marcus realize they were nearly surrounded.

"This way," Riph Raph called above the roar of the skirmishes all around them. He flew through an alley, and Marcus and Kyja followed as best they could, forcing their way through snow nearly up to their hips in some places. The entire city seemed to be on fire. Everywhere they went, buildings collapsed, hissing on the snowy ground. Living fought with undead. It was hard to see through the smoke and steam. Marcus's leg screamed with pain; he was having a hard time keeping up. They turned a corner and found themselves in a dead end. From one side of the road to the other, flaming debris and collapsed buildings blocked their way.

"Back," Kyja said. But when they turned, something huge plummeted out of the darkness. Wind knocked them backward as huge wings battered the air.

Marcus skidded to a halt as the Summoner landed in front of them. He searched for somewhere to run, but they were trapped. The creature clawed the ground, talons ripping furrows ten feet long in the frozen ground. Its mouth opened in an evil grin, revealing two sets of needle-sharp teeth—each one bigger than Marcus and Kyja combined.

Riph Raph shot balls of fire at the creature, trying to create a distraction, but they bounced harmlessly off its bloodred scales.

"I have longed for this moment," the Summoner snarled. Its voice was garbled and twisted—barely understandable. But Marcus knew it at once.

"Bonesplinter?" What had happened to the Thrathkin S'Bae to turn it into this monster?

The creature threw back its head, roared in triumph, and laughed. "Die, chosen ones!" It blasted them with a stream of killing fire they couldn't possibly survive.

CHAPTER 19

DECISIONS

KYJA STARED UP at the immense red beast. The sword dropped from her fingers. It was less than useless against the powerful magical creature.

"Die, chosen ones!" it roared again.

In that moment she realized that she and Marcus would both be killed—with too many things undone, too many words unsaid. As the Summoner opened its jaws wide, she reached out and took Marcus's hand—terrified of dying alone.

A stream of fire erupted from the creature's mouth, and Kyja clamped her eyes shut. She waited for the flames, knowing the heat would crisp her on contact.

Nothing happened. Everything went silent.

Kyja opened her eyes. The Summoner was still there, its jaws opened wide. The flames shooting from its mouth stopped only a few yards from her and Marcus. She could feel their heat baking her face. But she was still alive.

"Close my eyes for ten winks, and look what you two get your-selves into," a high-pitched voice said.

"Mr. Z!" Kyja's legs wobbled, and it was all she could do to keep from falling to the ground. Marcus appeared just as shaken.

She looked at the Summoner—frozen and defenseless—and re-alized that this was their chance to kill it. "Cast everything you can think of at it," she told Marcus, grabbing her sword off the ground.

"No, no!" Mr. Z said, raising a finger. Kyja felt her body drop into slow motion.

"You-must-not-attempt-to-harm-anyone-or-anything-or-time-restarts-immediately," the little man said, his words coming rapid fire. "Doyouunderstand?"

Kyja tried to answer, but couldn't until Mr. Z sped her back up.

"What are we going to do about this?" she asked as soon as she could speak again. Everything had stopped for the moment, but as soon as Mr. Z let time resume, the city would be burned to the ground.

"Nothing," Mr. Z said. "It's time to go. The Aerisians are wait-ing." He put his fingers between his lips to whistle.

"Stop," Marcus said, grabbing Mr. Z's hand. "We can't leave. The city will be destroyed. Like Windshold."

Mr. Z waved a handkerchief in front of his face, trying to clear away smoke. "But we can't interfere." He whistled again, and Drymaios was suddenly by his side.

Kyja clenched her jaw. "Why can't we interfere? Isn't that the point of finding the elementals—to stop the Dark Circle and to save people?" She waved her hands at the death and destruction frozen all around them. "The Aerisians could stop this."

"Which is why we must speak with them." Mr. Z gestured to the snail. "We must leave immediately."

Kyja turned to Marcus, anger and helplessness making her feel like crying. There were children in the city. Children who would die if she and Marcus didn't do something. But what could the two of them do? If they let time restart, the Summoner would kill them too.

Marcus gripped his staff. "We'll come back. As soon as we can."

By the time they returned, it would be too late for the city and its people. Kyja looked at the burning buildings, and a tear dripped down her cheek. Silently, the two of them climbed onto the snail.

As before, Mr. Z got inside. Sometime later, Kyja couldn't tell if it was a second or a day—she didn't remember any time passing, but she could feel that it had—the little man climbed out of the shell.

Remembering how they had traveled from Terra ne Staric to Icehold, Kyja looked for a door. Instead Mr. Z led them into a bank of especially thick smoke. With fires burning all around, the air was far too warm for her heavy coat. But a moment later, they had stepped out of the smoke into a snowy chasm, and she had her answer.

Wherever they were was cold, but not as frigid as it had been in Icehold. She looked up at the snow-covered cliffs to either side. "Is this Air Keep?" she asked. After Water Keep—which had been a strange mixture of air and water with buildings and fountains floating past, and Land Keep—a huge library shaped like a spiral tree—this place seemed ordinary.

Mr. Z pointed into a thick mist at the end of the chasm.

"We go through there?" Marcus asked, trying to keep his balance in the deep snow.

"Absolutely not," Riph Raph said. "Who knows what's in there?"

"Go or stay. Wait or play," Mr. Z said. He started to get back into the shell, but Kyja grabbed the sleeve of his coat.

"You're leaving?"

"I'm late already." Mr. Z checked his pocket watch. "Perilously late. Preposterously late. Perniciously late. Should have left days ago. In fact, I think I will."

And suddenly, he was gone. With no good-bye. No explanation. Not even a footprint to show where he'd stood. "Watch what you say-ay-ay!" a voice echoed.

"What's that supposed to mean?" Marcus asked.

"I have no idea." Kyja glanced toward the swirling mist. Why had Mr. Z left them here? Why not take them directly to Air Keep? The thick fog made her distinctly uncomfortable. "Should we go in?" she asked.

Marcus shifted from one foot to the other. "If we don't, we'll probably freeze to death."

Kyja slid her shoulder under Marcus's arm, helping him through the heavy snow. Riph Raph flew to her arm and latched onto her robe. "If we f-freeze to death, I want to say for the record that I never thought we should have left the tower in the first place."

"If it were up to you, we'd spend all our time sleeping and eating," Kyja said.

Riph Raph snuggled against her robe. "And you have a problem with that why?"

As they walked toward the mist, Kyja realized her sword was gone. Had she dropped it sometime during their trip here, or had Mr. Z taken it on purpose? She had no reason to think the air elementals were dangerous, but she would have felt far less anxious with a weapon of some kind.

Kyja and Marcus pressed against each other as they stepped into the thick cloud bank, which blocked all light. The air felt slightly warmer in the fog, but as the moisture froze to their skin and clothing, it made the cold twice as bad. Not being able to see anything was terrifying. "Can you feel ahead with your staff to make sure we aren't about to fall off a cliff?" Kyja asked Marcus, tugging him forward.

"I'm trying," Marcus said. "But the snow is so deep, I'm not sure I'd be able to tell I've hit a hole until we fall into it."

Riph Raph sneezed. "Maybe if we were to call Mr. Z and tell him we changed our minds, he'd take us back. I'd be willing to let him keep Turnip Head in exchange."

Marcus's staff made a *shushing* sound as he jabbed it into the snow ahead. "Or we could offer *you* to his snail. I've heard racing snails think skytes are a delicacy."

Kyja's robe hung heavy against her body, with ice weighing it down and cracking every time she moved. "D-do you th-think you can use m-m-magic to warm us?"

"I've b-been trying s-since we g-g-got here," Marcus said. They'd been walking for less than five minutes, but already he sounded exhausted. He leaned on her more and more with each step. "Something s-seems to be bl-blocking fire magic."

"Can you breathe fire?" Kyja asked Riph Raph.

The skyte coughed a blue flame no bigger than a grape, which winked out as soon as it left his mouth.

"It has to b-be the Air Eh-Elementals," Marcus gasped. "They've cr-created some k-kind of barrier." His staff clunked against something solid, and the two of them stopped.

"What is it?" Kyja asked.

"Not sure." Marcus jabbed his staff again. *Clunk-clunk.* "Feels like dirt or maybe rock."

Kyja squinted into the fog. Was it just her imagination, or could she see through the mist just a little? "I th-think we might be r-reaching the end," she said, keeping her voice low. "Let's be c-careful. We have no idea what's on the other s-side."

"Nothing good," Riph Raph muttered.

Kyja and Marcus moved slowly forward. The fog was definitely thinning.

"Does it feel warmer to you?" Marcus whispered.

"Yes," Kyja said, "and the snow isn't as deep."

Marcus's staff thudded regularly ahead of them now, and Kyja was almost sure she could see light ahead. A moment later, the fog disappeared completely.

"Ohhh," Kyja gasped as they stepped out onto a grassy meadow. "It's beautiful." Sunlight beat down on them from a clear blue sky, melting away the snow and ice. Hundreds of butterflies danced about multicolored wildflowers, which filled the meadow like a living rainbow.

"Look!" Marcus pointed to another meadow ahead and slightly above them. It was perhaps thirty paces across. Thick grass covered a base of solid rock. But what made the meadow so incredible was that the entire thing floated in the middle of the air.

"It's like an island," she murmured. "A floating island." But if nothing held it up, what about the meadow they were standing on? Her stomach leaped into her throat as she looked around the meadow and realized they were standing on an island as well. The only direction that didn't appear to drop completely away into thin air was back into the mist. "What's holding us up?"

"Air magic?" Marcus suggested.

"Get me out of this hat," Riph Raph said, the pom-pom above his head swinging wildly as he clawed at it.

"Here," Kyja said, untying the knot beneath his chin.

"Gah!" Riph Raph spat. "Who would put a hat on a skyte?" He flew to the edge of the island and flung it over the side.

Kyja laughed at the thought of someone seeing a skyte-sized hat falling out of the sky—although she wasn't exactly sure who or what was below them.

Marcus struggled out of his coat and mittens. "I'm sweating to death in this thing."

Kyja pulled her coat off as well. With the warm air and bright sunlight, even her robe felt too heavy. "Let's leave them here."

They piled the coats near the edge of the mist, and Marcus pointed to a rope bridge leading from their island to the next one. "I think we're supposed to walk up that."

At the same time they noticed the bridge, something leaped from the wood-and-rope structure, onto their island. As Kyja saw the creature, her hand reached for the sword that was no longer there.

"What *is* that thing?" Marcus asked, taking a step backward.

Kyja shook her head. She'd never seen anything like it. A giant set of teeth with no mouth or body, which appeared to be made completely of ice. The teeth took another hop toward them. They looked sharp, and big enough that one bite could take off an arm or a leg.

They jumped again, icy molars and incisors clicking against each other.

Riph Raph flapped his wings and launched himself into the air. "I hope they only have a taste for turnip."

CHAPTER 20

SOMETHING TO CHEW ON

THE GIANT ICE TEETH leaped toward them again and landed nearly halfway across the meadow. Kyja stumbled into Marcus. "Can you do something? Some kind of spell?"

"Right." Marcus tried to create a fireball. But there was no response to his request at all. He tried blasting rocks and earth at the teeth, with the exact same result. It was like he was completely cut off from all land and fire magic

"Use air," Kyja said, seeming to realize what was happening.

Marcus remembered the air spell he'd used against the undead creatures in Icehold and tried to conjure it. Nothing happened. "None of my magic is working," he said. The teeth jumped twice more. Sun glinted off their gleaming surface. "We have to go back."

They turned to retreat, but when they tried to go through the mist, they slammed against its cold surface.

"We're trapped!" Kyja yelled, pounding her fists against the gray wall that had closed in behind them.

Riph Raph dove toward the teeth, shooting fizzling bursts of flame. The teeth leaped incredibly high, nearly snatching the skyte from thin air. He flapped higher to get out of their reach.

Marcus ran his hands across the frozen fog, hoping to find a hidden entrance, but the wall was solid from one edge of the island to the other. He glanced over the grass and saw a vertical drop-off that went so far down, he couldn't find the ground below them.

The teeth turned and took two more quick leaps. Three or four more, and it would have them.

"We have to go around!" Marcus yelled.

Kyja took Marcus's arm, and the two of them raced along the edge of the meadow—Kyja nearly dragging Marcus as he limped behind her.

Marcus had no idea how the teeth even knew where they were. As far as he could tell, they had no eyes, ears, or nose. But as soon as the teeth realized what they were trying to do, it turned and cut off their path to the bridge.

Marcus's foot caught in a clump of grass, and he sprawled to the ground. The teeth attacked. Kyja grabbed Marcus's staff and jabbed at the creature. It chomped down on one end, gnashing the wood to splinters.

She jabbed again, managing to knock the teeth back a little, but it was a fight she couldn't win. Kyja held the teeth off the best she could, but little by little she and Marcus were forced to the edge of the meadow. Marcus found himself staring down at an endless drop.

The creature leaped at Marcus. Kyja stabbed at it, but the broken staff slid off the slippery teeth and they clipped the edge of Marcus's calf. Icy pain raced through his leg where the teeth had cut it. As the creature snapped at him again, Marcus tried to shield himself with his arm, but the teeth sank into his bicep.

"Leave him alone!" Kyja screamed, battering the teeth with her fists.

Riph Raph screeched, throwing what little fire he could at the ice teeth. None of it affected the creature at all.

Marcus looked at his arm. The skin from his bicep down had turned gray and hard. He couldn't feel anything. It was almost like he had—

"Frostbite," he muttered.

The teeth disappeared in a puff of white smoke, and a swarm of butterflies rose into the air in a kaleidoscope of colors.

Kyja turned left and right. "Where did it go?" she cried, holding out the shattered remains of Marcus's staff.

"I don't know." Marcus scanned the small island. The meadow was empty. Insects chirped and buzzed as though the giant teeth had never been there at all. Prepared for the worst, he looked at his arm. But it was fine—there wasn't a mark on his bicep. The skin that had turned icy and gray was pink and warm. He flexed his wrist. No pain at all. His leg was fine too. Except for the rip in his pants, he wouldn't have known he'd been bitten.

Kyja knelt by him in the grass. She turned his arm, looking at the front and back. "I was sure it got you."

"It *did*." Marcus had seen the teeth sink into him, felt their icy cold.

"Did you cast a spell?" Kyja asked.

Marcus tried to remember what happened. "I don't think so. I was trying to. But I couldn't find any magic. Then the teeth cut my leg." He pointed to the tear in his pants. "And it bit my arm. It was like it froze me or something. I thought I had frostbite."

Riph Raph landed on the ground. "I probably scared it away with my flames of death."

"More like flames of nothing," Marcus said. "And it didn't get scared away. It just . . . *poofed*. Into smoke."

Kyja tugged on a strand of hair. "What did you say it felt like?"

"Cold," Marcus said, remembering how he'd lost all feeling in his arm. "Like frostbite. You know, when part of your body gets so cold it actually freezes? We learned about it in Scouts one year."

"Frostbite," Kyja repeated, staring off in the distance. "We have that here too."

"What are you thinking?" Marcus asked.

Kyja turned to him. "Did you *say* the word *frostbite?* Out loud?"

Marcus thought. "I guess so. Yeah. I'm pretty sure I did. Why?"

"I'm not sure." Kyja plucked a flower that looked like a tiny orange snowflake and sniffed it. "Mr. Z said the air elementals have a strange sense of humor. I think he called it 'devilish.'"

"So?"

Kyja twirled the flower between her fingers. "I've never seen a creature like that before. I've never even heard of one."

"I never want to see one again," Riph Raph said. "It nearly used me for a toothbrush."

"It used my staff for a tooth*pick,*" Marcus said, picking up a piece of his walking stick.

Kyja dropped the flower, and it floated slowly to the ground, spinning as it fell. "What if it isn't even a real creature? What if the air elementals made it up?"

Marcus looked toward the bridge again. "That thing could have killed us. And for all we know, there could be more of them. Who cares if they're made up or not?"

"But if the Aerisians created the creature, they could have named it."

Marcus couldn't believe what he was hearing. He shook his hair out of his eyes. "We nearly got killed, and you're wondering what that thing's name was? When the next one comes across that bridge, maybe we can formally introduce ourselves. 'Hello, Mr. Jaws. Nice to meet you.'"

Kyja punched him lightly on the shoulder. "It's not that. It's just that Mr. Z told us to watch what we said. What if . . ." She shook her head. "It's probably nothing."

"No," Marcus said, pushing himself up onto his knees. "You're right." The little man's last words had been *Watch what you say.* "You think he was giving us some kind of clue? Or a warning?"

"Magic doesn't seem to work here," Kyja said. "And we don't have any weapons. Maybe all we have is our words. What we say."

Marcus thought through the idea. "What could we say that would make a difference? Go away? Leave us alone? I don't think those will help much. We didn't say anything to make the teeth disappear."

"Maybe you did. Accidentally." Kyja's eyes sparkled. "If you created a creature that was nothing but a set of giant teeth made of ice, what would you call it?"

Marcus scratched his head. "Ice fangs?"

"Canines of cold?" Riph Raph suggested. "Teeth of terror? Dentures of doom?"

"*Dentures of doom.*" Marcus couldn't help giggling. Riph Raph was a pain, but he did manage to get off a good one now and then. "What does it matter? I didn't say anything important. It bit my arm, and the only thing I could think of was that I was going to lose my hand because I had . . ." All at once he understood. "Frostbite. They named it Frostbite, didn't they?"

Kyja nodded. "And right after you said its name, it disappeared."

Marcus rubbed his palm across his mouth. "You think it's like a . . . a test or something?"

"A word puzzle. A joke."

"A pun," Marcus said. "That's what we call them on Earth anyway. Like, what do you get when you cross a snowman with a vampire? Frostbite. Or the joke about the guy who kept listening to a rubber band, waiting to hear music. "

"Rubber band?" Kyja asked, confused.

Apparently they didn't have rubber bands on Farworld. But that didn't matter. This place was starting to make a twisted kind of sense. It was exactly the kind of thing that elementals with a devilish sense of humor would do. "So we passed their test, and now we can cross the bridge."

"We might have." Kyja pointed to the next island, where Marcus could just make out another bridge leading up from that one. A swirling mist floated around the bridges. "Or maybe that test was just beginning."

CHAPTER 21

VERY PUNNY

YOU THINK THERE ARE MORE FROSTBITES?" Marcus asked as Kyja helped him to his feet. "If you're right, all we'd have to do is say their name, and *poof.*" He flicked the fingers of his right hand like a small explosion.

"Maybe," Kyja said. "But that would be too easy. There might be more joke creatures. What did you call them? *Pans?*"

"Puns."

"Pans or puns," Riph Raph said. "They aren't a joke. If you hadn't said the creature's name, it would have killed both of you."

"The Aerisians wouldn't have let it kill us," Marcus said. "They would have stopped it before that happened. Wouldn't they?"

Kyja stared at the next floating island. She was beginning to think the Aerisians' sense of humor might not be all that funny. "I don't think we can count on anything."

Together, the two of them walked toward the first bridge. Marcus had one arm wrapped around Kyja's shoulders for support, and she carried the broken end of his staff. They scanned the way ahead for any signs of attack. At the edge of the bridge, they paused. The air smelled of fresh flowers, damp grass, and morning sun. A flock of green and gold birds chased each other through the air, chirping what sounded like laughter.

"It looks so peaceful. It's hard to imagine anything bad happening here," Kyja said.

"That's exactly what I was thinking right before those teeth attacked." Marcus looked up at Riph Raph, who was circling a few feet above them. "Maybe you should fly ahead and check things out."

"What do I look like, monster bait?" Riph Raph yelped.

"I think we should stick together," Kyja said. "Three heads are better than two if we get attacked."

"Even if one of them is shaped like a turnip," Riph Raph said.

A step at a time, Marcus and Kyja crossed the bridge. Kyja wasn't especially scared of heights, but she thought crossing a rope bridge hanging in the middle of the sky would terrify her. That turned out not to be the case. Although the wooden steps swung gently from side to side, they felt solid. And when she looked down, she saw puffy white clouds instead of an endless drop.

"They look like big pillows," Marcus said.

"Pillows that send you plunging to your death if you fall through them," Riph Raph said cheerily.

"If you're going to keep talking like that, you can go wait back with our coats," Kyja said.

The skyte waggled his ears. "Sorry. I'm nervous."

"We all are," Marcus said. "Just keep an eye out."

The last creature had appeared shortly after they arrived on the first island. As the three of them stepped off the bridge onto the second island, they all anxiously searched. Every chirp of a bird or jump of an insect made Kyja flinch. They waited for several minutes on the edge of the meadow. When nothing happened, she allowed herself to relax a little.

"Maybe there *was* only one."

Marcus slowly unclenched his fist. "I don't see anything else."

With Kyja leading the way and Marcus limping beside her, they started across the meadow. "It is a *little* funny, when you think about it," he said. "Giant, icy teeth named Frostbite. What if they made a huge rolling foot called Football?"

Kyja giggled, feeling more and more relieved with every step. "Or a creature with no body because it quit while it was ahead?"

They were almost to the next bridge when Riph Raph shouted, "Incoming!"

Kyja looked up just in time to see something round and green plummet from the sky. It hit Marcus above the eyes, knocking him to the ground in a curtain of spraying bits. For a terrifying second, Kyja thought his head had exploded, before realizing that whatever had hit him had smashed itself open.

Marcus wiped his hand across his face, blinking. He sniffed his palm then cautiously licked one finger. "Tastes kind of like watermelon."

"Honey pot," Kyja said. "It's called a honey pot." She waited to see if the melon would disappear now that she'd said its name. Instead she was attacked with a spray of tiny pellets that spattered painfully against her face and chest.

Marcus gasped. "Are you hurt?"

Kyja looked down and saw her robe dripping with dark purple. "It's not blood," she said. "It's berry juice."

"Someone's throwing fruit at us?" Marcus asked, rubbing his forehead.

"Get away from me!" Riph Raph screeched. He flew through the sky, pursued by at least a dozen red apples. It was sort of funny, Kyja thought. But the skyte didn't look amused at all when one of them bounced off his head, splattering apple juice and pulp down his back.

"Look out!" Marcus yelled, rolling to one side.

Kyja ducked as a spiky green fruit narrowly missed hitting her shoulder and embedded its finger-length spines in the ground. If the pin fruit had hit her, those spines would have been stuck in *her* instead of the grass.

But there was no time to think about that. The air was filling with more and more fruit. Melons, berries, apples, plums, and many varieties she didn't even know, all pounded the ground around them as Kyja and Marcus ducked and rolled to avoid the attacks and Riph Raph winged furiously away from the island.

"What are they?" Marcus yelled as a spicy pear smacked his shoulder.

"Pin fruit," Kyja tried. "Honey pot, passion plum, sour apple, poke berries." She ducked a sugar fruit big enough to have knocked her sprawling, but she couldn't avoid a flock of flying cherries that spanged painfully off of her shins in quick succession. "It's not working. I know the names of some, but not others."

A bright yellow oval the size of Marcus's fist made a line drive toward his face, and Kyja swung the broken staff, sending it flying back where it came from.

"Thanks," Marcus said. "It's got to be another pun."

Kyja thought furiously. She was pretty good at word games; they were some of the few games she could play that didn't require magic. "Melon balls?" The fruit kept coming.

"Cherry bombs!" Marcus shouted. That didn't work either. "Jump!" he yelled, and Kyja leaped into the air, barely clearing a blue-and-gray striped fruit the size of a log, which rolled across the meadow and off the edge of the island.

"Apple heads!" Riph Raph called, his beak dripping with something orange. "Berry attacks. Plum bobs."

Kyja tried to concentrate, but it was hard to think when at any second, a flying piece of fruit could take your head off. If only . . .

Then she had it. "Fruit flies!" she screamed. "Fruit flies!" Immediately the attack stopped, and the remaining fruit disappeared.

"Whoa," Marcus sighed, trying to catch his breath. "Good one. How did you think of that?"

Kyja shrugged, embarrassed it had taken her so long. "I just wished the fruit would stop flying so I could think." Like most puzzles, once you figured out the answer, it seemed obvious.

"It was on the tip of my tongue," Riph Raph sputtered, dropping to the meadow.

"Pretty sure that was a grape." Marcus snickered.

"I didn't notice you thinking of it, Mr. Cherry Bomb," Riph Raph said.

"It doesn't matter who solved the puzzle," Kyja said. "The important thing is that we figured it out. I don't know how many islands there are. But it doesn't look like the tests are going to stop anytime soon." She pointed ahead, where she could see at least three more islands, connected by swinging bridges. They had to assume each was protected by a pun.

She reached down to grab Marcus's wrist, and he let her help him up. "It's a shame all the fruit disappeared after you solved the puzzle," he said. "Some of it looked pretty tasty."

"Don't say that." Kyja laughed. "The Aerisians might hear us and send more." Overhead, the green and gold birds, who had returned as soon as the fruit disappeared, spiraled and chirped.

On the third bridge, Kyja paused halfway across, wondering if it was possible to get a glimpse of what the next obstacle would be before they encountered it. But, as though the Aerisians had read her thoughts, as soon as they stopped, the ropes on the bridge erupted into flames.

"Back!" Kyja screamed, tugging on Marcus's arm. If they didn't get off the bridge before the ropes burned through, they would plunge to their deaths.

"No, we have to keep going," Marcus said, yanking her forward. "We have to get across."

But they couldn't go backward or forward. Flames raced across the ropes in front of and behind them, cutting off escape in both directions.

"Get off!" Riph Raph called, circling madly.

"We can't," Kyja yelled back. Thick, yellow smoke billowed from all around them, making it hard to breathe and impossible to see. "It has to be another riddle." She coughed, choking on the yellow clouds. "Cross fire?" she tried.

"Something about blaze or flames," Riph Raph called, hidden by the smoke.

"It has to have something to do with bridges." Marcus wrapped an arm across his mouth. "Bridge fire. Burn your bridges."

"The ropes." Kyja gagged, the heat scorching her legs. "They're the only things burning. Rope fire. Rope flame." Her lungs ached.

"Rope *burn*!" Marcus yelled. "It's rope burn!"

The flames disappeared, and Marcus and Kyja stumbled into the next meadow before falling to the ground. "I don't know if I can take any more of this," Kyja said, pressing her face into the cool grass.

Marcus coughed and spat. "I don't know if we have any choice."

CHAPTER 22

AIR KEEP

MARCUS WASN'T SURE how many bridges they crossed. After a while, the islands became a blur of attacks and word puzzles. Kyja solved most of them, like the "saw horse" that galloped around threatening to cut off their legs, and the "bee witch" that cast spells while attacking with a long, spear-like stinger.

Marcus guessed the solution to the "insti-gator" that appeared without warning, snapping its pointed teeth, and the "acro-bat," whose flying gymnastics even Riph Raph couldn't match.

But possibly the hardest one was solved by the skyte himself. Marcus and Kyja could hear the beast's ferocious growls and feel its claws raking at their backs, but every time they turned around, it somehow managed to move to their rear. They could very well have been eaten alive if Riph Raph hadn't figured out they were being at-tacked by a "bear behind." For the next two islands, he crowed over his success, "A bear behind. Do you get it? Like a bare behind only it was a bear."

Marcus and Kyja blushed furiously, trying not to look at each other.

Marcus had narrowly avoided getting a black eye from the punches of a pointed wizard's hat, which Kyja correctly identified as a "hat box," when Riph Raph circled around them and pointed ahead with one wing. "Look at that!"

Marcus had been so focused on facing each threat that he'd stopped looking ahead. Doing so seemed pointless when the only thing he could see was another bridge leading to yet another floating island. But now, as he glanced across the next bridge, he was stunned to discover a magnificent castle rising out of the clouds.

"I think it's made of glass," Kyja whispered, her eyes wide.

Marcus could only nod wordlessly. He'd never seen anything like the structure before them. Turrets and parapets glittered in the sunlight. Bridges and towers that seemed too fragile to hold up their own weight rose, fairy-like, into the sky. The entire castle appeared to be spun from fine glass threads with strands of silver and gold embedded in the glass.

"Is that it?" He swallowed, unwilling to believe they had finally found the home of the air elementals, which they'd worked so hard to reach.

"I think so," Kyja said, just as breathless.

"Air Keep," Riph Raph hooted.

As they stared, a gust of wind scooped up hundreds of petals from the flowers strewn across the meadow and sent them dancing and flying over the bridge. A dozen intoxicating aromas filled the air.

"I think they want us to come in," Marcus said.

Kyja glanced at her robe, which was ripped in several places, and at Marcus's pants, which were shredded from the knees down. "I'm not sure we're dressed for it."

"Who cares?" he cried. An incredible sense of joy and well-being flowed through his limbs, and he found himself limping across the bridge without Kyja's help.

Kyja hurried to catch up. "What do you think the Aerisians look like?" she asked as they reached the other side of the bridge. "I think they'll be fairies."

"I don't know." The water elementals had looked more or less like people, except that they were blue. But the land elementals had been bizarre combinations of animals he never would have expected. "Something beautiful. And majestic."

As Marcus and Kyja emerged from the fog floating over the last bridge and the full castle came into view, they both stopped, filled with wonder.

Even the grounds were incredible. Streams flowed along the transparent castle walls, dropping to the gardens below. But the waterfalls never hit the ground. Instead, the moisture turned into mists of pink, turquoise, gold, and every other color of the rainbow, beading on bushes shaped like dragons, unicorns, gnomes, and hundreds of other fanciful creations. Roses, vines, clovers, and grasses in colors Marcus could barely take in flourished beneath the great building's architecture.

"What's with the flowers?" Riph Raph asked. And for the first time, Marcus noticed daisies, tulips, and many flowers he didn't recognize, walking through the gardens on tiny green root-legs, digging and pruning.

Kyja clapped her hands and laughed. "Haven't you ever seen a flower *garden?*"

The blossoms, still spinning and twirling, blew along a perfectly manicured path of polished stone and over a drawbridge. As they followed, Marcus and Kyja looked down, through the glass bridge, to colored domes bobbing along a pink river. "Is that ice cream?" Marcus murmured. "Ice cream floats?" Air Keep was so perfect he thought he could stay here forever.

"I can see why no one has ever been allowed to find this place," Kyja said, as they crossed an immaculate lobby. The huge glass hallway was filled with sculptures made of tiny bits of colored glass and rock that flowed and turned in a constant stream of motion on unseen currents of air. "If they did, they'd never want to leave."

The flower petals danced ahead of them up a sweeping staircase. Marcus started to follow before realizing that nothing supported the steps. Each thin glass platform hung in midair.

"I think it's okay," Kyja said, taking his arm. "If they can make islands float, stairs should be easy." Together, the two of them climbed step after floating step.

Marcus craned his neck and was amazed to see that the rooms, walls, and passages overhead overlapped to create breathtaking geometric patterns. He couldn't fathom how such a thing was possible.

How could anyone have made all this? Why create such an elaborate home if no one but the Aerisians would see it? What kind of creatures combined the elegance and grace to create a castle so glorious and intricate, with the odd sense of humor to surround it with killer puns, flowers that cared for their gardens, and ice-cream float moats?

"Do you think they'll help us?" he asked Kyja. "I mean, if you had all of this, would you even care what the Dark Circle was doing? Would you leave this castle to help create a drift?"

Kyja squeezed his arm. "We have to convince them. It's not just humans that are in danger. It's all of Farworld—including the Aerisians." She glanced down at their ragged clothes again. "I just wish Mr. Z would have warned us so we could have brought something more appropriate to wear."

At the top of the staircase, a long hallway, with walls constructed completely out of precious gems, led to a pair of tall silver doors. The blossoms paused before the doors, swirled into the air, and then disappeared in all directions.

The three of them stopped at the end of the hall, and a sudden feeling of doubt filled Marcus's chest. What if the air elementals turned them down? Or worse, laughed at them? What if Mr. Z had been playing a trick all along, knowing the Aerisians' help was out of reach?

He ran his fingers through his hair. "So, I guess we just knock?"

Kyja brushed her hands across the front of her robe, trying to remove a few of the wrinkles. "I think so."

Marcus took a deep breath, approached the doors, and rapped three quick times.

From all around came the sounds of tiny bells chiming together. The floors and walls began to glow, and the air itself sparkled with energy. Part of Marcus was thrilled that he and Kyja were actually in Air Keep. But another part of him wanted to run screaming before they were forced to reveal themselves like ragged beggars at the feet of a powerful monarch.

When he glanced at Kyja, she looked just as terrified. Riph Raph licked his scales and brushed at his beak with his wings.

As seconds passed and no one answered the door, Marcus began to fidget. "Maybe we should come back another time. Maybe they're busy."

But it was too late. The tall silver doors swung open, revealing a long, golden carpet. At the other end of the room, the carpet led to a raised pedestal with a high-backed throne, which faced away from the doors. Although the throne was made of glass too, it was frosted so Marcus couldn't see who sat there.

Clasping hands, Marcus and Kyja stepped onto the carpet and walked toward the throne.

"Where is everyone?" Marcus whispered. Except for the throne, the room was completely empty. "Shouldn't there at least be guards or something?"

"Maybe they don't need guards here," Kyja whispered back. "We might be the first visitors . . . ever."

The thought made Marcus a little dizzy. Would they really be the first humans ever to see an Aerisian? It was like discovering an ancient city or a fantastic painting. He blew into his palm and sniffed, hoping his breath wasn't too bad.

At the end of the carpet, Kyja stopped and knelt. Favoring his bad leg, which was back to aching, Marcus lowered himself to the carpet beside her. It was thick and soft, yet the fibers glittered like real gold.

When they were both kneeling, the bells stopped chiming. Silently, the pedestal began to turn. Marcus leaned to his right, trying to catch a glimpse of the air elemental seated on the throne. As the side of it came into view, he blinked. There was no one there. The great chair was empty.

He was about to ask Kyja if this was some kind of joke. Or maybe the air elementals were invisible. Right then the throne finished turning, and he realized that there *was* someone—or at least some*thing*—there.

Seated in the center of the great glass throne was a creature not much bigger than a rabbit. It was white and furry like a rabbit too. But it had no face or ears; it was just a fuzzy white ball of fur with a golden crown on top. As the pedestal came to a halt, a pair of milky white eyes opened, and two long, pink feelers rose up through the crown.

"An ishkabiddle?" Riph Raph barked. "The air elementals are ishkabiddles?"

CHAPTER 23

ALL HAIL THE FUZZ BALL

WHAT'S AN ISHKABIDDLE?" Marcus asked under his breath.

Still kneeling, Kyja didn't know how to respond. Of course she knew what an ishkabiddle was. The furry white creatures could be found hiding in their burrows or nibbling clover nearly everywhere on Farworld. They were almost as common as cats and dogs on Earth. Some of her friends even had them as pets. But how could the air elementals be ishkabiddles?

Behind the throne, two small doors she hadn't noticed before swung open, and more ishkabiddles entered the room on their fuzzy little legs. Some of them wore long flowing cloaks of silver, red, gold, and dark blue. A few of them had glittering jewels clipped to their fur. At the end of the group, came ishkabiddle soldiers with golden armor covering their bodies and tiny swords strapped over their furry backs.

The soldiers stopped at either side of the throne, their white eyes blinking suspiciously. The rest of the ishkabiddles spread out along the carpet.

"Those fuzz balls are *not* air elementals," Riph Raph said. His voice echoed throughout the throne room.

Kyja frowned at him. "Hush," she whispered. Then, turning to the ishkabiddle on the throne, she cleared her throat. "Thank you for seeing us, Your Majesty."

The ishkabiddle in the crown stared back at her, and Kyja felt her throat begin to tighten. What if they'd already offended the Aerisians because of their surprise?

"We, uh, came here to ask for your help," Marcus began uncertainly. "Mr. Z sent us. Do you know Mr. Z?"

Several of the ishkabiddles who were lined up along the carpet shuffled about, and Kyja was pretty sure she saw the king (or was it the queen?) nod. Taking that for a yes, Kyja continued. "My name is Marcus and this is Kyja. Um, sorry." She tugged at her tattered robe. "I mean, my name is *Kyja,* and this is Marcus. We need your help to open a drift between here and Earth before the Dark Circle destroys Farworld."

The bells tinkled softly, and a flock of tiny, colorful birds flew through an open window and perched on the sill.

"Was that supposed to be an answer?" Marcus hissed at Kyja.

"How am I supposed to know?" she hissed back. She bowed as much as she could while still on her knees. "The water elementals and land elementals have sent us help. Now we only need you and the fire elementals."

Bells chimed again, and a gust of wind blew through the window, scattering leaves and flower petals across the floor.

"Do you think that was a yes?" Marcus asked.

Kyja could feel herself beginning to lose her temper and tried to control it. "Maybe?" It would have been nice if Mr. Z had mentioned that Aerisians didn't use words to communicate.

Riph Raph flapped his wings. "Maybe I can help." He turned to the air elemental on the throne. "Ding dong, ding ding. Ring-a-ling ting-ting."

"What are you doing?" Marcus whispered.

The skyte rolled his eyes. "Speaking *Bell*. What did you think?"

"Stop it!" Kyja said, speaking louder than she meant to. She turned to Marcus. "Show them your arm."

Marcus reached for his shirt, then hesitated. Kyja knew he was uncomfortable showing his scar. But it was the only sure proof they had that he was the child prophesied to save Farworld. She nodded, urging him on.

Slowly, he pulled up his right sleeve, revealing the hardened scar tissue on his shoulder. Kyja had seen the scar several times, but it still fascinated her. On it, two creatures were locked in battle. The first, she was almost sure, was a Summoner with a snake-like body, long teeth, and huge wings.

The Summoner had its talons closed on a creature she'd never seen or even heard of. It had the head of a boar, the tail of a fish, and a bird-like body with long, feathered wings. The bird-boar-fish's head had two horns sprouting from it, and a pair of human arms held a flaming sword high in the air. The creature's tusks were closed on the Summoner's body. Not for the first time, she wondered what kind of creature was powerful enough to fight a Summoner one-on-one.

"I've had this as long as I can remember," Marcus said. "It proves that I'm . . . I'm, you know, the child from the prophecy."

Kyja couldn't understand why he was so uncomfortable admitting who he was. If she were the person foretold to save Farworld, she'd shout it from the rooftops. She turned to the Aerisians, waiting for a response. But other than a soft chiming of bells, there was no reply.

"Will you help us?" she asked. "You must be able to talk at least a little."

On the window, birds fluttered and chirped, sounding almost like they were laughing, which made Kyja even more frustrated.

"Don't upset them," Marcus said, pulling down his sleeve. "We need their help."

Kyja knew he was right, but she was getting so angry at the little white eyes watching her, with no visible response. She had a sudden urge to pick one of them up and fling it across the room—its tiny red cape fluttering behind it like one of the superheroes she'd heard about in Marcus's world. What would the ishkabiddles do? Stab her ankles with their tiny swords?

She clenched her teeth, trying to control her temper. "If you don't speak our language, could you please bring someone here to translate?"

Another gust of wind sent the leaves and flower blossoms spinning into the air, and a handful of butterflies flew into the room.

Kyja wanted to shoo the birds away, slam the windows shut, and demand an answer from the fur ball on the throne. "Well?" she asked. "Is one of you going to say something?"

One of the soldier ishkabiddles sent a gray cloud of dust up from its feelers and the birds chirped louder, sounding even more like laughter.

Riph Raph flapped onto Kyja's shoulder and whispered, "I'm not sure if you noticed, but this doesn't seem to be going very well."

"You think you can do better?" Kyja snapped, her face getting hot.

The skyte flapped his ears.

Marcus tried talking to the ishkabiddles again. "Why don't we leave for a while, and you can discuss this among yourselves?"

The Aerisian on the throne wiggled a little and blinked again.

Kyja had had enough. "No! We left a city under attack to find you. We fought flying fruit, giant teeth, bears, bats, and saws, and a bunch of other things. We nearly got burned on your stupid bridge. We've spent I don't know how many days, riding a giant snail from one side of Farworld to the other. We came here for an answer, and we're going to get it *now*!"

The chiming of the bells grew louder, and the wind picked up, lifting petals, leaves, twigs, and butterflies in a whirling vortex.

Marcus grabbed Kyja's sleeve. "You're making them mad. We need to get out of here while we still can."

"I agree with the turnip head on this," Riph Raph said, his head darting left and right. "We've got to go. Now."

But Kyja wasn't done. She jumped to her feet. "Do you hear me? Do you?" She stomped toward the throne, Marcus's broken staff still clutched in one hand. She was determined to get an answer one way or another. And if it meant knocking the arrogant little ball of fur out of its precious throne, she would do just that.

Riph Raph flapped his wings, tugging on the back of her hair. "This is a really bad idea!"

"Wait!" Marcus scrambled to his feet, but Kyja was beyond caring. It was one thing to solve riddles, and to play games. Maybe those things kept casual intruders away. But to stay locked in a glass castle, ignoring the outside world, and then to act like Marcus and Kyja—who were sacrificing everything to save their worlds—weren't good enough to deserve an answer? That was too much.

Two soldier ishkabiddles hopped in her way, but Kyja kicked them with the side of her slipper, sending them rolling across the floor with squeaks of surprise and anger. High on its pedestal, the king of the air elementals cowered against the back of his throne, gray dust spewing from his feelers.

The bells were chiming so loudly, they seemed to be inside her skull, and the wind whipped her hair around her face. Kyja ignored it all. She raised her stick over her head, hoping she wouldn't have to use it, but willing to if that's what it took to get the creatures' respect.

She glared at the tiny white ball. "I. Want. An. Answer."

The wind shrieked, spinning birds, flowers, leaves, sticks, and even a few rocks into a whirling tornado. The ringing of the bells grew louder, louder, and suddenly crashed in one great orchestra of sound—then stopped.

Everything disappeared around them. The ishkabiddles, the throne, the carpet. The entire castle collapsed in a shatter of ringing glass. Kyja found herself standing in the middle of a meadow on one of the floating islands. Marcus pressed his hands to his ears, his eyes two great circles of fear and surprise. Riph Raph flapped midair, unsure of which way to go.

The spinning tornado split into two, then formed into what looked like a man and a woman created completely of birds, leaves, butterflies, twigs, rocks, grass, and hundreds of other bits and pieces.

The man, leaning against a spear jabbed into the ground, grinned widely. Beside him, the woman chuckled as if she'd heard an extremely funny joke. "Very well," she said, spreading arms in which birds chirped, butterflies flapped, and flowers bloomed. "An answer you shall have."

ULTIMATUM

THE LAND ELEMENTALS APPROACHED the room cautiously. The dimly lit tunnels didn't bother them. Land Keep was, after all, underground. Nor did the odd creatures they passed. When one dealt with a master of black magic, one expected certain . . . *oddities*. It was the smell that made them uneasy—a foul miasma of rotting corpses, spoiled meat, and something beneath it all, which they both preferred not to think about.

As they entered Fein Ter'er, the master's inner sanctum, they found him sitting in his throne, head lowered as though asleep or deep in thought, or—based on his chest, which seemed not to rise and fall with breath at all—dead.

"You called for us?" they asked.

For a moment he didn't look up. When he did, they shifted uneasily, gripping the silver scepter in their hands as if it might give them some protection from the thing seated in the throne before them.

"Did I?" From deep inside his dark hood, red eyes studied them unblinkingly. "Yes, I suppose I did."

The land elementals felt a little relief. They tried not to let the master see their unease, but they knew he probably sensed it anyway. "The land army grows stronger every day," the elementals said, fluttering their wings.

"Land *and* water." The master chuckled. "You must not try to take all the credit. And Land Keep?"

"Still trapped," the elementals said. "The water boy's river holds."

The red eyes glowed like embers. "Cascade can be very effective with the right motivation." He waved his hand. "Very well. Return and wait. I imagine the children will arrive soon enough. If they survive, I want you ready for them."

The land elementals bowed and dropped to their knees. "And when we catch them?"

"Bring them to me, of course. Alive or dead."

PART 3

Aerisians

CHAPTER 24

A DARK VISION

ARCUS COULD ONLY STARE at the people—or were they *creatures?*—standing before him. After everything he and Kyja had been through, he didn't know what to think. Did this mean the ishkabiddles had been . . . what? A joke? Another riddle? Or were these beings—who seemed to be nothing more than a crazy patchwork of other plants and animals—the joke?

Just before he found himself here, Marcus had seen the glass castle tearing itself apart. Was *that* real? Or had the whole thing— castles, gardens, and ishkabiddles—been some kind of elaborate illusion?

He had no idea. And he didn't think the man and woman before him would provide the answers.

"Are you . . ." He searched for the right word, but the best he could come up with was, "Real?"

The woman looked at the man to her left and giggled—a tinkling of bells, a splashing of water, and a whistle of wind through trees, all in one.

The man pulled his spear—a tree branch with green leaves still growing along its length—from the grass, drew back his arm and launched the spear into the air. It soared far above the island, circled back like a boomerang, and planted itself in the ground. A dark-green vine climbed the spear. Pink roses bloomed along the vine like a movie set to fast forward.

"Does *that* look real to you?" the man asked.

Marcus was almost positive the Aerisian's words hadn't been uttered by human vocal cords. Like the woman's laughter, the sound came from something else. The scream of a dragon, the clang of metal on rock, the roar of a rushing river. Somehow they all blended to form words he could understand. It reminded him a little of the electric pianos that let you play a song using dog barks or other random sounds.

"The ishkabiddles looked real too," Marcus said.

The woman laughed again. "They are." She had the same mixed-together voice as the man, except while his sounds were all growls, roars, and crashes, her voice was made of gentler sounds—chirping crickets, rustling leaves blown across the ground, and the tinkle of water tapping against a window pane. "I'm Divum and this is Caelum. Would you prefer to speak with the ishkabiddles? I rather think they looked quite splendid in their crowns and capes."

"We'd *prefer* to get some answers," Kyja said, her face stern. "Some *serious* answers."

Caelum chuckled, and Marcus thought their constant laughter was going to get old fast. "I'm afraid you've come to the wrong place for *serious* answers. Didn't you get enough of those from your water and land friends?" From the man's tone, it was clear what he thought of the land and water elementals.

Marcus snorted. "At least they didn't attack us and put us through a bunch of stupid riddles."

"Welcomed you right in, did they?" Caelum held out his hand, which was made of tiny frogs, each puffing up its throat and croaking softly. Marcus wondered what would happen if they leaped away at once. Would the man lose his hand? Or would something else take their place?

"Well . . ." Marcus hesitated. They'd had to pass several tests before they found the land elementals, and at least two of the tests could have killed them. When they'd tried to go through the wall around Water Keep, Marcus had been turned into a fish.

Kyja clutched Marcus's broken staff as if she was prepared to threaten these creatures the same way she'd threatened the ishkabiddles. "Are you air elementals? *Real* air elementals? This isn't another trick or joke or test?"

Divum nodded, and a cloud of butterflies flew from her hair. "We are."

Marcus remembered the birds on the windowsill—the ones that sounded like they were laughing. "Were you in the castle when we were trying to talk to the ishkabiddles?"

"We were."

"Then you know what we want," Kyja said. "You know we need your help to open a doorway between Earth and Farworld."

Caelum and Divum looked at each other, both still smiling.

"You think this is funny?" Marcus demanded. "Do you think it's a big joke that we came all this way to ask for your help?"

Caelum roared with laughter. He did a wild little jig, turning a circle as he danced. Inside his body, birds chirped and flew about, frogs jumped and croaked, flowers bloomed in wild profusion, sending their petals spinning into the air, before blooming again. "Of course it is." He slapped his arms together like an alligator's jaws. "Teeth of ice, racing snails, ishkabiddles on thrones. It's a fine joke."

"One of the best I've heard in ages," Divum agreed, covering her mouth.

"Come on," Kyja spun around. "Let's get out of here."

"Someone should lock them up in a deep, dark dungeon," Riph Raph said. "They're crazy as beetles in a brushfire."

Marcus turned away, the weight of failure dragging at his shoulders like a boulder. To have come all this way, to have passed all of their tests—for nothing—was worse than not having made it at all.

"Wait," the woman called. "Where are you going?"

Kyja threw her stick to the ground. "What do you care? You're not going to help us."

"We never said that." Caelum sounded as close to serious as either of them had. Then, as though the man couldn't stand to keep a straight face for long, he grinned and added, "Perhaps it was the ishkabiddle king who refused your request."

"I don't understand," Marcus said, turning back. He remembered how annoyed he'd been by Cascade's missing sense of humor. The water elemental took everything literally, with no trace of emotion. Now Marcus wished he could get one of the Fontasian's straight answers. "You laughed when we asked for your help. You said it was funny."

"But it is." Divum tittered. She spread her arms, and the air filled with falling snow. Unlike ordinary snow, each tiny flake had the face of a man, woman, or child on it. "*Life* is funny. The struggles, the accomplishments, the triumphs, the failures."

"You *laugh* at people's failures?" Kyja's face scrunched in anger. "That's horrible! What kind of monsters are you?"

The male air elemental ran his frog fingers through his twig and leaf-filled hair as the snowflakes disappeared. "To not laugh at your own misfortunes, and those of others, would be to weep continually. A life like that would be . . . *unbearable.*" He raised his hands into claws, did an incredibly accurate impression of a bear's growl, and chuckled.

Marcus couldn't understand these people—everything was a joke to them.

But Kyja leaned over and whispered in his ear, "I don't think they're trying to be rude. I think it's just the way they are. Their laughter is like the land elementals' thirst for knowledge." She turned to the Aerisians. "So *will* you help us?"

Caelum looked at Divum and grinned. "I'm afraid it's too late for that."

Marcus swept his hair out of his face. "What do you mean?"

"Show them," the man said.

This time, Divum didn't laugh. Instead, she puffed out her lower lip like a two-year-old who didn't get a slice of birthday cake. "Must I?" She grinned impishly. "I could show them the courting rituals of a three-eyed long toe instead. They would laugh for hours."

Caelum began to chuckle, then shook his head. "No. They must see to understand."

"Fine." The woman stomped her foot, making a blaze of colored flowers spread across the meadow around her.

Suddenly, Marcus found himself suspended high in the air. Clouds floated by, and the trees below looked like toothpicks. He reached for something to grab on to and found only empty space. Kyja gripped his hand in hers.

"What are you doing?" Marcus called to the air elementals floating beside them, wind blowing in his face. "Why did you bring us here?"

Caelum pointed to their left. Kyja turned, and her face went white.

Marcus looked down and felt his heart freeze in his chest. Terra ne Staric was laid out below them like a toy city. And it was under attack. Even from this distance, he could hear the muted crash of stone on stone and the rumble of timber being crushed. An army of brown giants pounded at the walls of the city, using tree trunks as battering rams and hurling boulders like baseballs.

A small army of stone warriors and wizards, and a larger group of humans, stood against the giants, but it was clear they wouldn't be able to hold the city for long. Even as Marcus watched, a distant trumpet sounded, and a city gate collapsed.

"Do something," Marcus said to the elementals. "We have to help them."

"It's not just this city," Caelum said. He turned to the woman floating beside him, and she reluctantly raised an arm.

The view changed. Now they were above a city on fire. From the thick stone walls, Marcus knew it had to be Icehold. Smoke billowed into the sky, turned bloodred by the fires. Black-cloaked wizards walked the streets, bringing carnage with every step, while undead creatures swarmed like ants. A great, red creature, which had to be Bonesplinter, screamed and rose into the sky. For a moment, Marcus was sure it looked straight at him. He felt the knot in his chest tighten, and he looked at Kyja. Tears were streaming down her face.

"Would you help them, too?" the man asked, no humor at all in his voice.

"Yes!" Marcus said at once. "Of course."

Divum raised her other arm, and they were floating above the Noble River. Except it was no longer the lazy brown snake Marcus and Kyja had floated down months earlier. Now it was a raging torrent that washed away villages and cities, flooding homes and carrying away those caught in its ruthless grip.

"And these?" Caelum asked, pointing to those caught in the flood.

Marcus wiped at his burning eyes.

"How can this be happening?" Kyja said. "There's a drought. There shouldn't be nearly enough water for floods."

Caelum motioned to Divum, and Marcus looked down on a range of snowy peaks that had to be the Windlash Mountains. On the side of the mountain, a group of humans fought against a swarm of what looked like winged octopuses. One of the humans cast a spell that knocked a monster from the air, and the people attacked it with their spears and swords.

"It's not completely hopeless," Marcus said. "They're winning."

The ground began to shake. Part of the mountain broke away, sending boulders rolling onto the humans. As they turned to flee, the mountain itself cracked open, and the tiny figures plunged into a black crevice that closed over them.

Marcus thought he could hear their screams; black despair filled him. How could things be this bad? How did the Dark Circle get so powerful? Farworld was being torn apart.

"Stop," Riph Raph said, turning away from the carnage.

Kyja clenched her eyes shut and pressed her hands to her ears. "Make it go away."

Divum nodded, and they were back on the island. The Aerisian wiped at her eyes and tried to smile.

"You see?" the man said. "Laughter is the only thing that keeps us from weeping."

CHAPTER 25

TRAITORS?

KYJA COULD ONLY STARE at the ground, tears running down her cheeks and blurring her vision. This wasn't the way things were supposed to happen. She and Marcus were supposed to get the four elements together, create the drift, and save their worlds. The Dark Circle was supposed to be defeated.

After that? She didn't know. But she knew it wasn't supposed to end like this. She'd seen what the Dark Circle was capable of, and she'd rather be dead than live in a world ruled by them.

"Would you like to turn into snow monkeys and belly slide down a glacier?" Divum asked. "That always cheers me up."

"No." Kyja wiped her face with her palms and took a deep, shuddering breath. "If you knew it was too late, why did you bring us here? You *did* bring us here, didn't you?"

"Technically, a snail brought you. Which seems shell-fishly slow," Caelum chuckled.

"No. Shellfish would be if they came by crab." The woman clicked her fingers together like claws, and her hands turned into dozens of tiny red and blue crabs snapping and clacking their pincers.

Kyja fumed. How could they laugh at a time like this? Did they have no sympathy at all?

Caelum sighed. "We brought you here because you were looking for us."

"And we grew tired of waiting," Divum added. She put out her arms and twirled like a child, her dress of leaves and butterflies poofing about her legs. "I hate waiting. It's so dull."

Riph Raph leaned close to Kyja's ear. "I still think they're crazy."

Marcus rubbed his bad leg. "I don't understand something. If all that terrible stuff is happening right now, why don't I feel it? My body always hurts when Farworld is in danger. But I feel better than ever."

"You aren't *in* Farworld." Divum laughed. "Those boring land elementals and stodgy water elementals are part of Farworld. But we are above it all. Just like the fire elementals are—"

Caelum looked at her, cutting off whatever she was about to say. "Air is a magic of time and place," he said. "You are not in the same place as what you saw happening to your world. Nor are you in that time."

"Then what time are we in?" Marcus got a strange look on his face, and Kyja thought she saw something pass between him and the Aerisian.

"Here you are in no time at all," Caelum said. "If you return to your when and where, you would arrive just before you began your journey here."

"Oh, but don't go!" Divum said. She spread her arms, and the group was in the glass castle again, which was restored completely to the way it had been. She sat on the throne, petting the crowned ishkabiddle. Caelum was now dressed in the same gold armor and sword the ishkabiddle soldiers had been wearing earlier. "It's been so long since we've had guests," Divum said. "We can play so many games together."

Kyja stepped forward. "You're saying that if we go back to Farworld, it will be *before* we saw the snail tracks?" she asked, trying to understand.

Caelum admired his armor and pulled his sword from its scabbard. "I *do* look dashing in gold, don't I?" He clapped, and suddenly his whole body was made of gold. "Do you think I look silly?"

"Only if it's *fool's* gold." Divum giggled and grinned. All at once, she was made of glittering diamonds, rubies, emeralds, and other precious stones. "Look, I am a gem *and* a jewel." She smiled at Kyja. "Would you like to be a gem too? You're not quite as polished as I am, but you could be a diamond in the rough."

"I don't want to be anything but me." Kyja fumed. "How long after we left Terra ne Staric will it be attacked?"

If the Aerisians were upset by her outburst, they didn't show it. "Two of your days. Maybe three," the man said. He pulled out his sword, which was as golden as the rest of him, and said, "I have three golden arms."

Kyja chewed on her lip, thinking. "Three days. That's enough time to warn the city of the attack and maybe even to stop it."

"But it's not just Terra ne Staric that's in trouble." Marcus shook his head. "The Dark Circle seems to be everywhere. The floods and earthquakes. How did they do it? And what were those giants?"

"I thought you'd never ask," Caelum said. "I hope you don't take offense, but humans seem a bit . . . *scattered* at times." His golden arms and legs separated themselves from his torso and wandered leisurely around the throne room, while his head floated several inches above his neck.

"Unfocused," the woman agreed, becoming suddenly so fuzzy it hurt Kyja's eyes to look at her.

Caelum's left arm returned to rub his chin. "How could mere humans harness such amazing powers?" his floating head asked. "It's a bit of a puzzle."

Divum's glittering gem body blew apart like the pieces of a jig-saw puzzle. "Oh, I love puzzles."

"I think I'm going to be sick," Riph Raph said.

"Would you stop fooling around?" Marcus demanded. "How are we supposed to think with you changing all the time?"

The golden arm rubbing the Aerisian's chin grabbed his head and offered it to Marcus. "Maybe another head would help?"

"No thanks," Marcus said, waving it away. "I think I'll just use my own."

Divum's body changed to a flock of birds. "Perhaps they need a hint," she chirped. "What do quakes, floods, and golems have in common?"

"Is that what those giants were?" Marcus asked. "Golems?"

Kyja tried to think. "They destroy things?"

Riph Raph shuddered. "They are all things we should stay as far away from as possible. Which goes double for these lunatics, if you want my opinion."

"We don't," Marcus snapped. He whispered to Kyja, "What's a golem?"

In her search for air elementals, she'd learned a lot more about Farworld's creatures than she ever imagined possible. "They're magic creatures made out of dirt and water mixed into . . . That's it!" She looked at the Aerisians with a grin. "They both have to do with land and water. Quakes come from land. Floods come from water. And golems come from land and water mixed together."

The birds making up the woman's body chirped excitedly.

"But what does that have to do with anything?" Marcus asked. "It doesn't explain how the Dark Circle is creating so much damage."

"He's slowwwww," the Caelum said, and his body snapped back together, changing from gold to tiny snails, slugs, and turtles. "I think I'll take a nap. Wake me up when he figures it out. At this rate, he'll be an old man."

Kyja frowned. "I guess you could use water magic to make floods. But you'd still need enough water to do it. And there hasn't been any rain for six months. Besides, all the wizards have been saying that water magic hasn't been working very well."

"What?" Marcus asked, his face suddenly intense. "What's that about water magic?"

"It hasn't been working," Kyja said. "Water and land magic both. The spells have all been weak or useless."

"Really?" Marcus asked. "I thought it was just me. Or maybe it was because I was on Earth. I haven't been able to cast almost any of the land or water spells Master Therapass gave me. And when I do, they're weak. It was like the elementals themselves didn't want me to use their magic."

The birds chirped louder, but the man just yawned. "Are they still here?"

"It doesn't make sense," Kyja said. "If no one is having much luck using land or water magic, the only ones who could do something that powerful would be . . ." She stared at Marcus, a terrible thought occurring to her.

Marcus must have had the same idea. His forehead wrinkled. "The elementals would never willingly help the Dark Circle."

"Absolutely not," Kyja agreed.

Marcus bit his lower lip. "Where are Cascade and Lanctrus-Darnoc? The last I heard, Master Therapass had sent them out on some quests."

"They haven't come back," Kyja said. "Lanctrus-Darnoc went with the stone wizards and warriors. No one knows where Cascade went. Master Therapass sent him out on a secret mission six months ago—the same time the army left. But neither of them has come back."

Marcus's eyes went dark. "Wait, how long did you say it's been since the last rain?"

"Six months. The drought started the same time the land began shaking." She put her hand to her mouth, understanding what Marcus was thinking. "Ever since Cascade and Lanctrus-Darnoc left."

"Put a rose on his nose," Caelum said, and a large red rose bloomed on the front of Marcus's face.

CHAPTER 26

FUN AND GAMES

I KNEW WE COULDN'T TRUST the blue-faced water-wielder," Riph Raph said. "Didn't I tell you there was something fishy about that boy? And any creature that can't decide whether it's a pig or a fox is no good as far as I'm concerned."

Marcus slapped the rose away from his face, the blossoms dropping into a pile at his feet. "I don't believe it. The elementals would never join the Dark Circle. Why would they? Do they want to see Farworld destroyed?"

Kyja turned to the Aerisians. "It's not true, is it?" she pleaded. "Tell me the water and land elementals haven't joined the Dark Circle."

"*The water and land elementals haven't joined the Dark Circle,*" the birds repeated, mimicking Kyja's voice. The woman reappeared. "I'll tell you that the sky is syrup, and grass is made of mint jelly, if you'd like. But that doesn't make it true."

"I like the sound of jelly grass," Caelum said. "It would squish

196

between your toes when you walked on it. And if we added a few bread trees, we could have all the sandwiches we wanted."

"Oh, and what about sausage shrubs?" Divum squealed. "I love sliced sausage and mint jelly sandwiches. Should we start now, do you think?"

"Stop it!" Marcus shouted, and the Aerisians stared at him like two children caught passing notes. "You said you'd answer our questions."

"Fine," the man huffed. "We will answer exactly three questions. Then I'm having a jelly-grass sandwich."

"With sausage," Divum added.

It was probably the best they were going to get, Marcus decided. "You first," he told Kyja.

"Do you know for a fact that the water and land elementals are helping the Dark Circle?"

"Yes," Caelum said, holding up one finger.

Marcus felt like someone had just punched him in the face. He wanted to tell the Aerisians that they were lying. That Cascade and Lanctrus-Darnoc were friends. That they'd fought against the Dark Circle side by side with the people of Terra ne Staric. How could they have turned their backs on them to join with evil?

Yet it all made too much sense. The only time he'd ever seen water and land magic this powerful was when Cascade and Lanctrus-Darnoc fought against the Keepers. "I guess that's how they knew we were in Icehold. The Fontasians must have been spying on us." He pressed his hands against the sides of his head, trying to push away a headache that felt like it would split his skull in two. "Are humans strong enough to stop them?"

Neither of the Aerisians bothered to answer. The man simply shook his head and ticked off his second finger.

"You have to help us." Kyja dropped to her knees. "You must fight against the Dark Circle. Please say you will."

Caelum shook his head. "We are not fighters."

"We are laughers," Divum said. "Jokesters and tricksters. Lovers of beauty and players of games."

"Then why not think of this as a game?" Marcus said. "The air elementals against the land and water elementals."

"A game." Caelum tapped his foot, which was currently made of wood chips and gray and brown moths. "With you as our partners?"

"Sure," Marcus said. "We're good at games. We got past your puns, didn't we?"

Kyja bobbed her head. "And if you go back with us, we'd have two or three days to prepare before the attacks."

"It's been ages since we left Air Keep," Divum said. "It might be fun."

Caelum grinned. "There would be lots of humans to play jokes on."

"I can think of several right now," Kyja said. "Will you do it?"

The man whispered to the woman. She giggled and whispered something back.

"We will," they said at the same time.

"Yes!" Marcus punched his fist in the air.

"I don't like it," Riph Raph grumped.

"On one condition," the Aerisians said, speaking as one.

Marcus got a tight feeling in his gut. Somehow he knew it couldn't be that easy. "What's the condition?"

Caelum and Divum glanced at each other and nodded. "That you prove yourselves worthy."

"I told you I didn't like it," Riph Raph groused. "You can't trust anything these bubble brains say."

"Hush," Kyja said. At least there was a chance the air elementals might help them, which was more than they'd had before. She brushed her hands over her hair, again wishing that she was wearing something more presentable than a ragged robe. "How do we prove we're worthy?"

"It's quite easy." Caelum laughed. "But rather difficult."

"Simple," Divum agreed. "But complicated."

"It can't be easy *and* hard," Marcus said. "And it's either complicated, or it's simple."

"On the contrary," the woman said. "Some of the best things in life are both."

"Well?" Kyja folded her arms across her chest. "What is it? Another riddle to solve?"

"No." Divum shook her head. "I'm tired of riddles."

"A game, then?" the man suggested. A look passed between him and the woman, and suddenly Kyja had a feeling that none of this was random. The air elementals seemed silly on their surface. So then why did she have a feeling they'd been planning this all along?

"What kind of game?" Marcus asked.

Both Aerisians appeared to consider the question.

"The box?" Caelum asked with a twinkle in his eyes.

"Yes." Divum clapped her hands and bounced. "The box." She gave a piercing whistle, and an ishkabiddle hurried into the room. On its back was a silver eight-sided box. The woman picked it up, balancing it in one hand as she ran the fingers of the other across it. Kyja recognized the symbol engraved on the top of the box: a loop with a curlicue on one end—the symbol for air.

The Aerisian handed Kyja the box. It was lighter than she

expected, but it felt solid. She turned it over in her hands. "What is it?"

"This is the game piece," the man said. "Next, we need a playing field. Come." He led them through the throne room, down the stairs, and out of the castle. When they reached the gardens, he waved a hand toward the sky.

Kyja looked up to see six or seven creatures circling in the air above them. She'd never seen anything like them before. They had curved bodies with graceful necks and long, flowing tails. Their clawed feet were tucked against the fronts and backs of their silvery purple bodies. They each had broad wings, but when the Aerisian summoned them, they moved by pumping their bodies in a swimming motion instead of flapping their wings.

"They look a little like seahorses with wings," Marcus whispered.

Kyja had no idea what a *seahorse* was, but she was awed by the sight of the magnificent creatures. "What are they?"

"Ciralati," Divum said. "Each ciralatus is born of the clouds and fed by the wind."

Four of the ciralati landed in the garden, somehow managing not to crush a single flower or bend so much as a blade of grass.

"Here," the woman said, handing Kyja and Marcus the coats they'd left on the first island. "You'll need these." The Aerisians lifted Marcus and Kyja onto the creatures' backs. Kyja had never seen the woman leave them; when did she get their coats?

Caelum glanced at Riph Raph. "Would you like to ride?"

The skyte shook his head. "I prefer my own wings."

"Do you think you can keep up?" Divum laughed.

"Are you kidding?" Riph Raph puffed out his chest. "Skytes are the kings of the sky." One of the ciralati glanced over with violet eyes, and Riph Raph coughed. "No offense."

"Where are we going?" Marcus asked as the Aerisians climbed onto their mounts.

The man grinned. "Somewhere you may be familiar with."

Marcus stiffened as his ciralatus lifted into the sky. Kyja tried to catch his eye, but for some reason, he wouldn't look at her.

Riding the ciralatus was like rafting on air. For the next few minutes, she forgot about all of their problems. The creatures bounced from one invisible current to another, climbing up and sliding down, like fish in a rushing river. Occasionally, out of the corner of her eye, she caught sight of other ciralati soaring through the clouds above them.

"Are those more Aerisians?" she asked.

"Yes," Caelum called back.

"How many are there?" Kyja wondered why she and Marcus had only come across these two.

Divum laughed. "How many leaves are in the trees, or flowers in the garden, or butterflies in the sky?" That wasn't much of an answer. Then again, the Aerisians didn't seem very informative about anything.

The ciralati climbed so high, it was hard to breathe and the air turned icy cold. But Kyja found that by leaning into the soft skin of her mount, she could stay warm. The Aerisians led them through clouds and swirls of bone-chilling fog, until, at last, a single mountain peak appeared. The creatures circled the top, and Kyja spotted a dark opening in the snow below. She glanced at Marcus; he was staring at the opening, eyes wide with what looked like horror.

"What's wrong?" she called as her ciralatus flew downward.

Marcus shook his head, his face white.

At the mouth of the dark opening, wind whistled around them. One by one, the ciralati folded their wings and dove inside. A circular chasm led down and down, until the last ciralatus came to a landing on the floor of the pit. Kyja gazed around her and realized that each side was a frozen waterfall.

"Look," she said, pointing to the nearest. "There's something inside the ice. I think it might be a man."

Marcus climbed off his mount and faced the Aerisians, eyes flaring. "No deal. We won't do it." Suddenly, his face went white, and he collapsed to the ground.

CHAPTER 27

FINDING THE TRUTH

EVER SINCE THE AIR ELEMENTALS had started talking about time, Marcus had had a bad feeling. He'd thought it was just nerves, but his recent experience with traveling through time had been too painful—what he had seen in the future was impossible to forget, even with everything that had happened since.

But as soon as the Aerisian mentioned going back to Marcus's *When*, his mind had flashed back to the *Is,* the *Was* and most importantly, the *Will Be.* Was it possible the Aerisians talking about magically returning to a different time was just a coincidence? After all, the air elementals were on Farworld. How could they know about something that had happened to him on Earth?

But he was almost sure that the freezing cavern Elder Ephraim's mirror had taken him to hadn't been on Earth. And could it be a coincidence that ever since he had decided to leave the monastery, everything strange thing that had happened to him revolved around time? The *Is,* the *Was,* and the *Will Be,* Terra ne Staric being frozen, and now the air elementals.

Things were beginning to add up. The monk who wasn't a monk. The way he was led to the mirror. The note Kyja found. Some unseen force keeping him from telling Master Therapass what he'd seen. Mr. Z stopping time and then bringing them to Air Keep. All of it seemed to point to one thing: whatever was happening here wasn't coincidence.

Were he and Kyja really convincing the air elementals to help them? Or were the elementals the ones doing the convincing? If so, what were they trying to accomplish?

When the Aerisian told him he might be familiar with where they were going, Marcus was almost certain. And as soon as he saw where they were flying to, there was no doubt left in his mind. This whole thing was a trick—possibly even a trap—but he wasn't going to get caught here again.

As soon as Marcus told them he refused to play their game, the pain that had disappeared from his body as they entered Air Keep returned with a sickening jolt. His right leg buckled in agony, and he fell to the ground.

"What's wrong?" Kyja jumped off of her ciralatus and ran to his side.

Groaning in pain, he felt like he was reliving his first time here. His body aching, the bitter cold, the tiny circle of gray sky far overhead. All that was missing was the roaring of the waterfalls, the fog, and the coins.

He pushed himself up so that he could look the Aerisians in the eye. "It's been you all along, hasn't it?"

"Who else would we be?" Caelum laughed. "It's far too much fun being ourselves."

"I've always wanted to be a tree," Divum said. "It might be fun to branch out." Her arms changed to sweeping pine branches.

But Marcus wasn't buying their act anymore. "You set this all up. You made me think I was in danger at the monastery. You made Kyja bring me over. How did you convince Mr. Z to help? I'll bet he knows all about your act."

"What are you talking about?" Kyja said.

Marcus noticed the box in her hand. "Is *that* what this is all about? What's in there that you need? And why do you need our help to open it?"

"The cold has frozen his brain," Divum said.

"You asked for our help. Are you getting cold feet now?" The man grinned, but Marcus sensed something behind his smile as he said, "If you don't think you can win the game, just say so."

Kyja looked down at her slippers. "My feet *and* my hands are cold. Does that have something to do with the game?"

Marcus glanced at Kyja and a thought occurred to him. He turned to the Aerisians. "Where did you learn the saying 'cold feet'?"

"It . . . it's a common expression here," Caelum's smile disappeared momentarily but quickly returned. "A play on words. Meaning 'to back out of a promise.'"

"Have you ever heard it?" Marcus asked Kyja.

She shook her head.

"That's because it's not from Farworld. It's from Earth." He glared at the man and woman. "Tell us who you really are—and why you brought us here—or the game's over. I quit."

—◆—

"You would let your world be destroyed?" Caelum asked, a grin still lurking at the corner of his mouth.

"No," Kyja said at once. Whatever Marcus was doing, he had

to stop it before this went too far. Without the Aerisians' help, Terra ne Staric would be destroyed—quite possibly with the rest of Farworld—and their chance of opening a drift would be doomed.

"It is *our* game," Divum said. "We set the rules."

"We're not playing your game anymore," Marcus said.

"Stop it!" Kyja hissed. Had he gone crazy? "Yes, we *are* playing."

Marcus held up one hand. "Do you notice they keep saying *your* world will be destroyed? As if Farworld doesn't matter to them one way or the other?"

"We're above your world." The woman giggled and waved her hands. "We don't care what happens down there."

Something about that didn't sound right. "If you don't care what happens outside Air Keep, why did it matter that we were searching for you?" Kyja asked.

"As we told you," Caelum said, "we grew bored waiting for your tiresome search to lead you to us."

"But if you don't care what happens on Farworld, it shouldn't have mattered whether we found you or not."

"There's something they aren't telling us," Marcus said. "They went to a lot of trouble to get us both here. Then they acted like they didn't care once we got here. The whole thing from the puns to the ishkabiddles was all a trick to make us think we were earning the right to see them. But if they didn't have a reason for needing us here, they never would have sent Mr. Z."

Kyja thought back to her feeling before that this whole thing had been orchestrated—that the silliness was at least partly an act.

"Give them back the box," Marcus said. "They were right; this place is familiar, and we're leaving."

Kyja glanced at him curiously. How could this place be familiar? There was no way Marcus could have been here before. She looked at the carved silver box in her hand. If they left now, and the Aerisians let them go . . . She just had to hope Marcus knew what he was talking about. Gritting her teeth, she held out her hand and offered them the box.

"This is your last chance," Caelum said. "If you choose to leave the game now, you will never return to Air Keep again. The Dark Circle will destroy your world."

Kyja looked at Marcus, her heart pounding. Unless he was absolutely positive, giving the box back now would be making a terrible mistake. He nodded.

"Take it!" Kyja raised the box over her shoulder like a ball, cocked her arm, and swung it forward, but before she could throw it, Divum cried out.

"Wait!"

The man grimaced.

"We have no choice," she said.

"There will be others," he snarled.

"No." Divum studied Marcus and Kyja and shook her head. "They are different. They are the ones."

"Are you going to tell us what's really going on here?" Marcus asked. "Or should we leave?" He pointed behind him. "I'm pretty sure this one will take us back to Terra ne Staric."

Kyja looked where he was pointing. There was nothing but a frozen waterfall, with what she was almost sure was an old man encased inside it. What did he mean by saying it would take them home? Obviously the Aerisians weren't the only ones keeping secrets. Could this have something to do with what he'd been hiding from her?

"Very well," the man said.

Kyja felt her body sag with relief.

"Who are you?" Marcus asked. "Are you part of the Dark Circle?"

Divum giggled, and Kyja's temper flared.

"I'm sorry," Divum said, putting a hand to her mouth. "It's just . . . do you really think any humans are powerful enough to do what you've seen us do? Do you think the ciralati would answer the call of a mortal?"

Caelum grinned. "In some ways, you appear so intelligent. And in others, your foolishness is beyond imagining."

"Then you really *are* air elementals," Kyja said. She didn't know what she would have done if they'd come all this way only to discover that the two of them were frauds.

"*See the Lords of Air—Above the clouds they creep,*" Divum said. "Isn't that how your poem goes?"

Kyja nodded.

"*Creep,*" Caelum said disdainfully. "Have you ever seen an Aerisian creep?"

Kyja had to admit she hadn't. And it really didn't seem in their nature to, now that she'd met them.

Riph Raph flicked his tail. "Maybe you should do a little more creeping and a little less dancing and twirling."

Caelum flipped his hands dismissively. "And perhaps as a creature who relies on flight, you should show more respect to the Lords of the Air."

The skyte gulped and ducked his head.

"Now that we know who and what you are, isn't it time you tell us why you brought us here and what you want from us?" Kyja asked.

Divum looked at Caelum. "That may take some time," she said.

Marcus, who was still lying on the ground, shivered and said, "In that c-case, how about if we go s-somewhere a little warmer?"

CHAPTER 28

THE REFEREE

MARCUS RECLINED ON A LARGE PILLOW inside the throne room, sipping a hot drink that tasted like a mix of caramel, nuts, honey, and peppermint. It was light and foamy, tickling his nose when he accidentally inhaled a little of it.

Kyja, who sat on a pillow beside him, rubbed her stomach and groaned with delight. "This is delicious. What is it?"

"You wouldn't be able to pronounce it without choking on your tongue," Divum said with a grin that left Marcus unsure if she was joking or not.

Marcus took another long swallow. "You know, if you'd just given us a drink of this first, you wouldn't have needed all those tricks."

"Who says your drink isn't a trick as well?" Caelum said with a straight face. It wasn't until Marcus jerked the cup away from his mouth that the Aerisian chuckled.

"Very funny." Marcus looked from one air elemental to the

other—if that was really what they were. "You've gone to all the trouble to get us here. Who wants to tell us the real reason?"

Divum, who sat on the throne again, tucked her feet under her, flowers and butterflies swirling about her legs. "You are here because you want our help."

Kyja turned the box in her fingers. "But what do *you* want?"

"Isn't it obvious?" Divum smiled. "We want to help you."

"Fine," Marcus said, sick of all the lies and half-truths. "Then agree to help us now, with no tricks or games or tests."

"You must prove yourselves worthy," Caelum said. "By winning our—"

"Stop it!" Kyja jumped off her pillow, spilling her drink. "Why do we have to prove anything? Why do we have to play your games or figure out your riddles? Why not help us because it's the right thing to do? Because we need you? Because *Farworld* needs you?"

Marcus could have hugged her.

Divum stuck out her lower lip. "Because we can't."

The room went totally silent. Kyja stared at the air elemental with a look of disbelief. Even Caelum seemed surprised.

"You mean you *won't*," Marcus said.

"No." Divum shook back her hair, colored leaves falling to her lap. "We *cannot* help you."

Caelum walked to the throne and placed a hand on the woman's shoulder. "Divum speaks the truth. We are unable to help you, no matter how much we may want to."

"Are you two going to listen to these lying leaf-bird-bug creatures?" Riph Raph said. "Don't you get it? They say the land and water elementals are working with the Dark Circle, but they're the ones who lured the two of you all the way up here while Farworld gets destroyed."

Marcus looked from Riph Raph to the Aerisians. For once he agreed with the skyte. They'd been so eager to find the air elementals and get their help that they never considered it might be a ploy to get the two of them out of the way.

Kyja stared into Divum's eyes. "I think she's telling the truth."

"How can she be?" Marcus stood—the pain he'd felt earlier was gone. "You've seen the kind of powers they have."

"Only here," Caelum said softly.

"Huh?" Marcus had no idea what that meant.

Divum waved her arms, sending swarms of black and yellow butterflies rising toward the ceiling. "The reason we fill our world with such elaborate creatures, plants, and buildings is because it's the only world we have. We are forbidden from leaving it."

Marcus opened his mouth, found he had nothing to say, and closed it.

Riph Raph sputtered.

It was Kyja who finally found her voice. "You can't leave Air Keep?"

The Aerisians shook their heads. "Water and land are of your world," Caelum said. "Air is above it. And fire . . . well, that is a discussion for another time."

Marcus couldn't believe it. All this time. All the puns. All of it was a total waste. "It really was just a game for you, wasn't it? You thought it was funny to see how far we'd go to get your help even though you knew it was pointless."

Caelum gave a deep, throaty laugh that made Marcus want to throw something at him. "It *was* funny. And it is a game. But that's not why we brought you here. At least, not the only reason."

It was Kyja—the one who was always so good at understanding

others—who finally figured it out. She held up the box. "This isn't just a game piece. It's the whole reason you brought us here, isn't it?"

Divum nodded.

"What's inside?" Marcus asked, still furious. "What's so important that you brought us here, lied to us, and tried to trick us into opening it for you?"

"A key," Caelum said. "The key to our freedom."

———◄•►———

In all of her studies, Kyja had been mystified about why no one had ever been able to see even a sign of an air elemental. Now she understood. The Aerisians couldn't leave Air Keep. They were trapped here, looking down on a world they couldn't reach.

And while a part of her was as angry as Marcus for the Aerisians' deception, another part of her understood their reasons completely. She knew how it felt to see a world you could never be a part of.

"Why didn't you just tell us?" she asked.

"We didn't think you'd help," Divum said.

"Why would you help us," Caeulm said, "unless you thought it was to your advantage?" He smiled in a way that made Kyja feel uncomfortable.

"That's the thing with all of you elementals," Marcus growled. "All you think of is yourselves. Did it ever occur to you we might help you because it's the right thing to do? Because we could?"

"I don't think it's their fault," Kyja said. "I don't think empathy is an emotion they understand." It was something she'd been thinking a lot about lately. Way back when Master Therapass first told them that the elementals wouldn't work with one another, she'd thought it was because they were stubborn. Or maybe because no one had ever asked them to. Now she was beginning to wonder if cooperation was something elementals were incapable of. Even if she and Marcus did manage to gather all four, it might not matter.

"I don't care what their problem is," Marcus said. "Before, we might have been willing to help you because we could. Now, you've lost that chance. If you want us to get your key, it's going to cost you."

Kyja pulled him close. "I don't think this is the way to handle them," she whispered in his ear.

"What do you mean?"

She backed him away from the Aerisians and kept her voice low. "Remember what the Augur Well told us?"

"Kind of." He squinted his eyes in concentration. "Um, three would join us. That was Screech, Tankum, and Rhaidnan."

Kyja nodded, her heart aching at the memory of the hunter's betrayal and ultimate sacrifice.

"Dreams and old enemies," Marcus scratched his head. "There was something else."

"It told us that one of us had family looking for us," Kyja said. That was something she'd been thinking a lot about too. "But it also said a *key* would bring great power and great danger."

"I thought that meant the gauntlet," Marcus whispered. "It was powerful and dangerous."

"But it wasn't a key," Kyja said. "What if the key that the oracle was prophesying about is inside this box?" The silver octagon, which had felt so light at first, seemed to have taken on a great weight. "I think we need to find out what's in here."

Marcus nodded. "I still don't trust them."

"I don't either," Kyja admitted. She especially had a strange feeling about Caelum—like he looked at humans as less than him. Play things.

"You spoke of a cost," Caelum said, as Marcus and Kyja returned to the throne. "Are you suggesting a bargain of some sort?"

"Not a bargain," Kyja said. "A promise. We promise to open the box, and you promise to help us fight the Dark Circle."

"And open a drift," Marcus said.

The Aerisians glanced at each other. "That seems like a high price for such a little thing as opening a box," the woman said.

Marcus sneered. "It's actually a pretty low price . . . for your freedom."

"Very well," Caelum said. "You open the box. Once we are free to leave Air Keep, we will send Aerisians to aid you in your quests."

Divum gave him a look Kyja didn't understand.

"Let us bring forth a witness to attest to our bargain," Caelum said.

"What kind of witness?" Kyja asked. "Aren't the five of us enough?"

Divum stood. "No agreement is complete without a judge to certify the arrangements. What do you call someone in your world who witnesses a contest, handing down impartial rulings?"

"A referee?" Marcus said, clearly dubious.

"Who could we use that we would both trust?" Kyja asked.

"Not another one of your creatures," Riph Raph said. "I don't trust any of them."

Caelum grinned. "I believe I know just such an individual." The Aerisian waved his hands, and a figure tumbled into the room, arms and legs flying like a windmill. A top hat flipped off his head, and a pair of large, white dice dropped out of his hand, clattering across the floor to land in front of the throne.

"What's this?" the little man sputtered, leaping to his feet and reaching for his hat. "Who summoned me? I was in the middle of a very important . . ." He looked up at Caelum, who was smiling, and Marcus, who was not, and shoved his hands in his coat pockets. "Oh."

"Mr. Z!" Marcus shouted. "You think Mr. Z is an impartial judge?"

"*We* trust him," Divum said.

"Of course you do." Marcus's face was scarlet with fury. "He's been working for you all along."

Divum giggled. "That's how we know he's trustworthy."

Caelum clapped Mr. Z on the shoulder. "We must have someone who can witness anything that might take place whether on Farworld or on Earth. He's the only one capable of following the two of you."

"Wait, you can go to Earth?" Marcus stared at Mr. Z, his mouth hanging open. "It was *you*, wasn't it? You were the one who tricked me into entering the mirror."

"What do you mean?" Kyja asked.

Marcus jabbed a finger toward Mr. Z. "All along I've been thinking the air elementals were the ones who moved my papers in the monastery. But they can't go to Earth. You did it, didn't you? And . . ." His mouth dropped open. "Were you Father Shaun?"

Mr. Z rubbed his glasses furiously on the lapel of his coat, his nose bright red. "I might have spent a little time pretending to be a certain monk."

"Did you leave the note on my bed?" Kyja asked.

The little man cleared his throat noisily.

Divum grinned. "He shall be our—what did you call it—referee?"

"He is not going to be the referee," Marcus sputtered. "No way is he impartial."

"The boy's quite right." Mr. Z scurried across the room and picked up his dice. "I have very important business to attend to. Big things going on. Far too busy to referee anything. If you'll excuse me, I'll—"

Kyja stepped forward and wrapped her arms around him in a bear hug that squeezed the air from the little man's lungs in an audible whoosh. "We'll take him," she said.

CHAPTER 29

EXSALUSENTIA

"ARE YOU CRAZY?" MARCUS WHISPERED. "That sneaky little guy has been lying to us ever since we met him. We can't trust him."

"I don't think he's ever actually lied," Kyja said. "He just didn't always tell us everything."

"He didn't tell us *anything*," Riph Raph said. "I don't trust him. And I *definitely* don't trust his snail."

The three of them stood on the other side of the throne room while the Aerisians watched and Mr. Z fidgeted.

"He's strange," Kyja admitted. "But I've had a good feeling about him ever since we met him in Land Keep. There's something about him. I don't understand what exactly, but I think he can help us."

Marcus rolled his eyes. "Okay, but I still don't like it." They walked back to the throne, Marcus leaning only a little on Kyja for support. "Let's go over the rules again. Just so there are no *misunderstandings* down the road. We open the box, and you help us fight the Dark Circle and open a drift. No tricks."

"No tricks." Caelum smiled as though Marcus had told an especially good joke. "A fair game."

Kyja examined the box, but she couldn't locate a keyhole, lid, button, or latch of any kind. "How do we open it?"

Divum gave a startled laugh. Caelum blinked, as though unsure if Kyja was serious, then clutched his stomach, doubling over as he guffawed. Even Mr. Z chuckled into his silk handkerchief.

Kyja looked at Marcus, wondering how she had missed the joke, but he seemed as confused as she was. "What's so funny?"

Caelum wiped his eyes and laughed even harder. Mr. Z honked his big red nose.

"What's wrong with you people?" Marcus scowled. "We agreed to your rules. So tell us what we're supposed to do. Is it another riddle? A quest? Do we have to defeat a dragon?"

Divum dropped into her throne and rested her chin in her palm. "Your question is just so silly. If we knew how to open it, we would have done it long ago ourselves."

It took a moment for their words to sink in. When they did, Kyja felt all her confidence that things would work out slipping away. "You mean *you* don't know how to open it?"

Caelum hiccupped and tried to control his laughter. "Of course not."

Marcus collapsed onto his pillow as though his strength had suddenly left him. "You must have some idea. I mean, it's your box, isn't it? Is it magic? Does it have a key? Whoever gave it to you must have given instructions."

Caelum paced the room, his spear in his hand. "It has been with us always. It is called Exsalusentia."

"That's a mouthful," Riph Raph said. "Sounds like something you'd drink for an upset stomach."

The Aerisians frowned. "It means salvation, destruction, and freedom," Caelum said. "It is the most sacred of all items in Air Keep. It is said that in the day it is opened, all Aerisians shall be freed from the chains which bind us here, to choose their destiny— be it salvation or destruction."

Kyja wasn't sure she'd want to open something that could cause her own destruction. "But if you don't know how to open it, what makes you think *we* can?"

For the first time, Kyja saw an Aerisian look truly angry. Caelum spun around to face Mr. Z, his spear clenched in one hand. "You said they were the ones!"

Mr. Z coughed, backing away as the Aerisian stalked after him. "I believe I said they *might* . . . that is, based on thoroughly verified, but not entirely substantiated . . . which is to say, the likelihood is that . . . yes, I believe they are the ones who can open your box."

Marcus shook his head at the Aerisians. "You mean to tell me that you took the word of a man who spends his time watching snails joust?" This time, he was the one laughing, while the Aerisians looked confused. "Oh, that's just great. Well, now you know what it feels like to have the joke on you. You've just wasted your time." He got up from his pillow and turned to Kyja. "Let's go. Maybe they'll introduce Mr. Z to their puns. I hope you like fruit!"

Caelum reached down to grab Mr. Z by the arm. He lifted the little man, squirming, into the air. "If you have lied to us, your debt is still unpaid. We will—"

Mr. Z tried to wriggle away, but the Aerisian's grip was too tight. Caelum tilted him upside down, and a profusion of items fell from his pockets. Glasses, coins, dice, cards, snails, old shoes, mismatched socks, wands, silverware, and even a large green soup bowl clattered to the floor.

"Help!" he shouted to Kyja and Marcus. "Tell him to unhand me!"

"Put him down." Kyja ran to Mr. Z, grabbing him around the waist. For a moment, she and Caelum both tugged at the little man, in different directions, and Kyja was afraid the Aerisian would pick them both up and fling them across the room. Finally, he released his grip. She stumbled backward—barely managing to set Mr. Z down before the two of them fell over.

"Why did you think we could open the box?" she asked him, trying to catch her breath.

Mr. Z gave an anxious glance toward Caelum, his face pale. "You passed the land elementals' tests, didn't you?" His voice was a little more shrill than normal. "And you entered the walls of Water Keep, which no human has ever done. You can't open a drift without all four elementals, and the Aerisians can't leave Air Keep until the box is opened. So, if A equals B, and B equals C, *ideo non constat . . .*"

"Cut the garbage," Marcus said. "You made this whole thing up to save yourself. What was that about you paying a debt?"

The little man straightened his hat, eyes twitching. "There might have been a small wager involving a certain snail and a certain winged creature." Caelum growled, and Mr. Z jumped. "And I might have made certain promises I am not currently able to deliver upon. But that does not change the fact that the Aerisians are in need of a key. And you are in need of an Aerisian."

Kyja was disappointed in the little man. She'd been so sure his motives were nobler than settling a bet. And it did appear that he'd stretched the truth more than once. But that didn't change the fact that he was right. "We'll do it," she said. "We'll open the box."

Mr. Z let out a breath so loud it sounded like a balloon being released, and a little of the color returned to his face.

Caelum looked at Kyja. "You can do this?"

Marcus shook his head. "We have no idea how to open your box. And we need to go. We should be fighting the Dark Circle."

"And opening a drift," Kyja reminded him. "Which we can't do without their help." She turned to the Aerisians. "What was that place with the waterfalls? Why did you take us there?"

Marcus's body stiffened. He was breathing rapidly, like he'd just finished a race, and sweat beaded his forehead. "Fine. We'll open your stupid box. But we're not going back into the pit."

Kyja stared at him. Clearly he was scared of the place. But why?

"The Abyss of Time is the home of Exsalusentia," Divum explained. "It is a place of power—the spindle upon which time and space revolve. Although we do not know how, we believe that it is vital to opening the box."

"I don't care what it is," Marcus said, his hands balled so tightly his arms were actually shaking. "We're not going in there again."

Kyja pulled him aside. "What do you know about that Abyss of Time?"

Marcus shot an annoyed look at Mr. Z, then whispered, "Remember when I told you about that mirror?"

Kyja nodded. "The one you touched when I couldn't find you on Earth."

"Yeah, well . . ." Marcus's jaws strained. He swallowed. "When I touched it, I went to that place."

Kyja stared at him. "You've been in the Abyss?"

Marcus nodded. "It's a kind of magic doorway that takes you to different places. And different times. And it's really bad. Maybe even dangerous. No matter what they say, you have to promise me you won't go in there. We'll find another way to open the box."

Kyja looked into his eyes. She was almost positive he wasn't telling her everything, but it was enough to know that whatever had happened in the Abyss left him terrified. She squeezed his arm. "All right. We'll find another way."

She turned back to the Aerisians. "We'll open the box. But we won't go into the Abyss."

"You must," Caelum said. "It is the *only* way."

Kyja dropped her eyes. "The Abyss wouldn't work for me anyway. I'm immune to magic."

She expected the air elementals to be shocked, maybe even repulsed, by her confession, but neither seemed surprised. It was as if they already knew. "We have considered this," Divum said. "It is one of the reasons we chose Mr. Z, as you call him, to join you. He is a creature of pure magic. As long as you hold his hand, you may enter the *Is,* the *Was,* the—"

"Didn't you hear us?" Marcus shouted. "We're not going through those doors!"

Divum smiled, eyes bright with hidden knowledge. "If you do not return through the Abyss of Time, you will have no city to return to. It will already have been destroyed by the time you get back."

CHAPTER 30

ONE WAY BACK

HOW COULD TERRA NE STARIC be destroyed?" Marcus asked, an icy ball in the pit of his stomach. "You said we could go back to our time, to just before Mr. Z brought us here on the snail."

"That is only if you go back through the Abyss of Time," Divum said. "To aid you in your travels here, we locked time in place before you left. Think of it as a sort of shortcut—a doorway you can return through. If you go back using the Abyss, no time will have passed since you left. Terra ne Staric will not have been attacked by the golems, Icehold will be untouched by the Summoner. But if you try to return by means other than the Abyss, that doorway will close, time will have passed, and . . ." Her dress of birds flapped and tweeted, but Marcus only watched her eyes—tiny spinning flowers that seemed to be trying to hypnotize him. Was this a trick to force him and Kyja into the pit? He had no way to know.

"Is it true?" he asked Mr. Z, unsure he could trust the little man any more than he could trust the Aerisians, but desperate to find some way of avoiding the Abyss. "Do you swear that the Abyss is the only way back to where we started?"

Mr. Z scratched his head. "Well, I suppose . . . I mean . . . considering . . ." He tugged his ear. "Yes, I'm afraid it's true."

"What's so bad about the Abyss?" Kyja whispered. "What makes you think it's dangerous?"

How could he tell her that if she went through the wrong door, she'd discover that he was going to kill her? He ran his hands through his hair, trying to think. "Okay. We'll go through the Abyss. But only to get back to Terra ne Staric. Only through the *Is*."

"Where you go after leaving here is up to you," Caelum said. "Just as what we do when we leave Air Keep is up to us."

"Except that you promised to help us."

Divum looked at Caelum and he nodded. "The Aerisians keep their word."

"It'll be okay," Kyja said. But Marcus wasn't sure. He felt like he was being drawn step by step into the future he'd seen, no matter how much he fought against it. Maybe it would have been better if Kyja hadn't pulled him out of the *Never Was*. One thing he was certain of: if he came to a point where he was about to do anything to hurt Kyja, he wouldn't hesitate to return through the door and hurl himself into the Void of Unbecoming.

The Aerisians led them out of the castle again and summoned the ciralati. On the ride to the Abyss, Marcus clutched his coat tightly around him, a million questions swirling through his head. Where should they start looking for a clue to opening the box? And could they find it before Terra ne Staric and Icehold were destroyed? If they only had two or three days, should they spend them trying to stop the attack or finding a way to open the box?

Above all, how could he find a way to change the future?

When they landed inside the pit, all of his previous pains returned. His left arm throbbed, and his right leg felt like it was on fire.

Divum helped Marcus off his mount. "You may need this." She handed Marcus his staff, which looked completely undamaged—just as it had before the Frostbite. Marcus started to ask the air elemental how she'd fixed it, before deciding it didn't matter.

"Is this still part of Air Keep?" Kyja asked, running a hand across the back of her ciralatus.

In the cold, Divum's body had changed from birds, leaves, and butterflies, to snowflakes, icicles, and what looked to Marcus like white ferrets. "This is the border," she said. "It is as far as we can go. The doors of the Abyss of Time are not open to us."

"Until we open the Exsalusentia," Kyja said.

Caelum shook his head. "The Abyss of Time may not be used by elementals.

Marcus leaned on his staff, looking forlornly at the frozen faces inside each of the ice-blocked falls. "What now? Do you give us the coins?"

"You have no need of coins," Divum said. "Tokens are for those who wish to spend their days . . . elsewhere—people who long for the past, or can't wait for the future. As long as Mr. Z is with you, you may freely enter and leave any of the doors of the Abyss."

"But beware," Caelum said, his eyes as hard as the ice around him. "There is one more difference from the last time you entered these portals. With a being of pure magic, you cannot only view what is through each portal, but you can change it as well. You must be extremely careful not to do so."

Marcus felt his heart race. "We can change what's through the doors?"

"You *can*," Divum said. "But you must not. The danger is too great. The spindle upon which time and space spin is a fragile thing. The smallest changes may upset the balance and destroy the Abyss completely, trapping you permanently, if you are inside it."

But Marcus wasn't listening. For the first time since entering the *Will Be,* he knew there was a chance to change what he'd seen in the future. No matter the danger, he was determined to save Kyja.

"Know also," Divum said, "that anything sent into the Void of Unbecoming in the *Never Was* cannot be brought back by any means."

"What are they talking about?" Kyja asked. "What are the *Never Was* and the *Void of Unbecoming*?"

"Don't worry," Marcus said. "I'll tell you all about it." Despite his pain, he felt like singing. "Well," he said, turning to Mr. Z, "are you ready for more fun and adventure with your three best friends?"

"I'm no friend of his," Riph Raph said. "And I'm not even sure I'm a friend of yours, Turnip Head."

"Riph Raph!" Kyja scolded. But even the skyte couldn't dampen Marcus's spirits.

Mr. Z took off his top hat, rubbed it on the sleeve of his coat, and asked, "Where would you like to go?" with far less enthusiasm than he'd had on their first trip.

Marcus's first thought was to go straight to the *Will Be* to change what he'd seen there. But if they went now, Kyja would find out what he'd nearly done. Besides, they had to focus on opening the Exsalusentia and on stopping the Dark Circle. He'd have to find a way to sneak to the *Will Be*—alone.

"Take us to the *Is*," Marcus said. The waterfall to their left roared to life, filling the Abyss with an icy mist.

"Oh!" Kyja gasped, backing away from the pounding water.

"Don't worry," Marcus said. "You won't even get wet."

Kyja took Marcus's arm in one hand and Mr. Z's in the other. The three of them walked side by side into the mist and stepped out into Master Therapass's study.

"Master, outside . . ." a guard shouted. "There's a . . ." The man stopped in midsentence, staring at Marcus and Kyja.

Marcus realized they were standing in a different part of the room than they'd been before. Not to mention that they suddenly wore heavy coats and probably looked like they'd been through a hurricane. He looked around for Mr. Z, but the little man had disappeared again.

The guard rubbed his eyes before returning his attention to Master Therapass. "There's a messenger here with news from the field."

The wizard ignored the guard, studying Marcus and Kyja with a concerned look. "What's going on here? How did you get out of your rooms? And what are you wearing?"

Marcus shook his head. "It'll take longer to explain than we've got time for. And I think you're going to want to hear what that messenger has to say."

"Yes. Of course." The wizard nodded. "Come with me," he said, following the guard into the hallway.

Kyja put one arm around Marcus, helping him walk. As they passed the room where Marcus had been resting before Mr. Z came for him, the door flew open.

"The boy has disappeared!" the woman with big ears shouted.

At the same time, the door to Kyja's room swung outward, and both wizards tried to shove through at the same time. "Kyja is gone!" they yelled.

"Yes, yes," Therapass muttered. "We'll discuss your dereliction of duty later."

The wizards gaped as Marcus and Kyja hurried down the hall. Marcus heard one of them mumble, "Not possible," as he disappeared around the corner.

The guard led them to the staircase, where they hurried down three levels. "Where's Mr. Z?" Kyja whispered as she helped Marcus down the steps.

He looked around, but the little man was nowhere to be seen. "If he skipped out on us, I'm gonna kill him."

Kyja pulled the silver box from her robe pocket. "As long as we've got the Exsalusentia, I don't think he'll go far. I think the Aerisians would have something to say about it."

The guard led them off the staircase and down a hall that opened into a large circular meeting room. The room was already nearly full of wizards.

As they entered, Master Therapass stopped to speak with Terra ne Staric's High Lord, Breslek Broomhead. "What is it?" he asked. "What's the news?"

Breslek shook his head, long beard wagging. "I was only just pulled out of bed myself. But from what I hear, it's not good."

Just then, a woman walked through the door. She was at least six inches shorter than Marcus or Kyja, with flowing red hair. Dressed in shining chain armor and mail gloves, she marched to the center of the room.

"Who's that?" Marcus whispered to Kyja.

"Eden," Kyja whispered back. "The captain of the guards."

"Captain?" Marcus knew there were female warriors. He'd seen them fight as valiantly as any man. But this woman didn't look any taller than a child, and not much older.

"She's never been defeated in battle," Kyja whispered back. "They call her the Unquenchable Fire."

The captain gripped her sword and stared around the room, green eyes cold and serious. "Take your seats. We have urgent news."

Master Therapass motioned Marcus and Kyja to sit near the back of the room. The captain waved two guards through the door. They supported a young boy who looked half dead. His dark hair was wet with sweat and matted to his forehead. Cuts and bruises covered nearly every exposed part of his body, and dried blood was crusted on his face.

"Someone needs to get the lad medical attention," a wizard near the front exclaimed.

"We will," the captain said. "But the news he brings is vital."

"Couldn't this wait until morning?" complained a cranky little man in the corner. His hair stuck straight up in crazy swirls, and his beard looked like a bird's nest. "I was sleeping."

"No!" the captain roared, her voice booming, and the little man ducked out of sight. The captain turned to the boy. "Can you speak?"

"Yes," the boy croaked in a hoarse, trembling voice, which sounded like it should have come from someone much older.

As the boy looked up, Kyja gasped. "Jaklah."

"Who?" Marcus asked, thinking the name sounded familiar.

"It's Jaklah. Don't you remember? The boy from Land Keep."

Marcus studied the boy more closely. It was hard to believe the battered figure standing at the front of the room was the same boy he'd met after he'd been captured by the harbingers. But he was almost sure Kyja was right. What was *he* doing here?

"Sent . . . by . . . Tankum," the boy wheezed. Around the room, the wizards drew in a collective breath.

"What is it, lad?" the captain urged.

"Golems." Jaklah coughed, and a line of red dripped down his lip. He swayed on his feet.

"Get him some water," High Lord Broomhead called, but the boy seemed to regain a little strength.

"Golems," he said, his eyes wide with fear. "As tall as . . . three men. Coming fast. Tried to . . . stop, but . . . for every one destroyed . . . two more rise from . . . ground. Too strong. Army retreating."

All around the room, men began to talk, but the captain silenced them, slamming a mailed fist against the table in front of her. "How far away?"

"Three . . . days," the boy gasped and passed out.

CHAPTER 31

GOLEMS AND GALLONS

A T JAKLAH'S WORDS, the room exploded in a storm of confused shouts and demands.

"Close the gates."

"Erect barricades."

"We have no choice but to leave the city."

"Surrender is our only option."

"Stop!" High Lord Broomhead raised his hands. "We are not surrendering, and we are *not* leaving the city. We will spend the next three days fortifying our defenses and preparing to withstand any assault. This is not the first time Terra ne Staric has been attacked, and it won't be the last."

The captain of the guard raised a hand to her mouth and coughed loudly into it.

Breslek turned to face the green-eyed woman, his irritation obvious. "What is it? Do you have a better plan?"

"No, High Lord," the captain said. "It's only . . ." She leaned close and whispered something.

The High Lord's eyes widened, and the skin on his forehead crinkled into a tight little mountain range.

"Well?" shouted the wizard who'd complained about being awakened. "Speak up! If you have something to say, share it with the rest of us. It's not like we aren't all in the same kettle of stew."

Kyja leaned forward as the captain looked over at High Lord Broomhead. He nodded. "Go ahead," he murmured. "He's right. They might as well know."

Eden clenched her fists, biceps bulging beneath her mail armor. "It doesn't matter how strong our defenses are. They will all be for nothing."

"You're saying we have no hope?" a woman asked.

"Coward!" a man shouted.

The crowd of wizards went wild, standing and shouting until the room was in complete chaos.

"What does she mean?" Marcus yelled, cupping his hands to his mouth so Kyja could hear.

"I have no idea," Kyja yelled back. She knew the golem army was strong. But it made no sense for the captain herself to give up before the enemy was even within striking distance.

A deafening explosion rocked the room, and red and white sparks lit the ceiling and walls. Master Therapass held his staff sideways above his head. His eyes burned. "The next man who says one word must deal with me!"

Instantly, the room went silent.

"Now then." The wizard turned to Breslek and the captain of the guard. "How can you two be so sure these creatures will defeat our best wizards and warriors?"

"I will fight with the last drop of blood in my veins to see that it doesn't happen," Eden said, her face grim. "But it is not defeat that will be our undoing."

Master Therapass lowered his staff slowly. "I'm afraid I don't understand. If you don't fear defeat at the hands of the golems, what *do* you fear?"

The captain licked her chapped lips, hand tight on her sword as though wishing she could be out fighting something instead of standing in the center of this room. "We are down to our last twenty barrels of water for the entire city. By the time the golems arrive, it will be completely gone. The golems won't need to break through our defenses. We'll die of thirst before that."

For a third time, the room erupted. As Master Therapass and High Lord Broomhead tried to restore order, Kyja tugged on Marcus's sleeve. "Let's find somewhere to talk," Kyja said. With everyone arguing, it was easy to slip out of the room and into the hallway unnoticed.

Together they walked down the stairs until they reached the tower entrance. Riph Raph glided along behind them, blinking sleepily.

"Just a minute," Marcus wheezed, leaning against a wall and trying to catch his breath. "Is it true? Can the city be out of water?"

Kyja thought back to what she'd overheard in the kitchen. To her, it felt like several days since Bella complained about the single barrel of water she'd received. But to the rest of the city, it had been less than twenty-four hours. Outside, the morning sun was still hidden behind the mountains—the sky just beginning to turn pink.

"I think it might run out," she admitted. "There hasn't been any rain in months, and the wells have all dried up. Even the Two Prongs River is nothing but brown mud, no matter how deep you dig."

"It doesn't make any sense," Marcus said. "Icehold is waist-deep in snow. The Noble River is flooding. How can the weather be so screwed up?"

Kyja sighed and started down the path that wound around the hill from the tower. Once, the grass had been green and lush, filled with stone statues of the city's greatest wizards and warriors. Now the area was totally different. The statues were gone—the stone figures were out fighting the golems. And the grass was dead and brown.

"You don't really think Cascade has something to do with this, do you?" Marcus asked, limping beside her.

Riph Raph circled above their heads. "Floods, blizzards, and droughts don't just occur all at the same time."

Kyja ran her hand along a cold, empty pedestal. She wasn't sure what she thought. "If Cascade doesn't have anything to do with the weather, why is he letting it happen? It can't be a coincidence that all of the weather problems have to do with one form of water or another."

They walked silently down the path until they reached a small grove of trees—the leaves were shriveled and brittle. Riph Raph flapped onto a branch, tucked his head under one wing, and instantly fell asleep. Kyja felt like sleeping herself, but she didn't think there was going to be much time for that over the next few days.

"Maybe Cascade isn't fixing the weather, because he *can't*," Marcus said. "Maybe someone or something is stopping him."

The thought was chilling. What was powerful enough to keep a water elemental from controlling water? But the only alternative was just as scary. If Cascade had turned against them, like the Aerisians had suggested he had, they'd never be able to open a drift between their worlds.

Somewhere nearby, a branch cracked. Kyja peered into the shadows but couldn't see anyone.

"Probably just an animal," Marcus said, but they moved a little deeper into the trees anyway, to stay out of sight.

Marcus leaned against a trunk and lowered himself to the ground, wincing in pain.

"Is it bad?" Kyja asked.

"Not *too* bad." But the way his hand kept returning to his leg made Kyja suspect the pain was worse than he let on.

Kyja took out the Exsalusentia, hoping some part of it might look different now that they were back in Terra ne Staric. But from what she could see, it appeared exactly the same. "We've only got three days to figure this out before the golems arrive. Do you have any ideas?"

"It would have been nice if all we had to do was take it outside Air Keep and it just popped open," Marcus said. "Can I see it?"

Kyja handed him the box. He turned it over slowly, mumbling under his breath as he poked, twisted, and tapped. Nothing he did made any difference. "Can you try magic?" she asked.

"Just did." Marcus sighed. "Didn't do a thing. It was like trying to do magic in Air Keep."

Overhead, a branch creaked; Kyja and Marcus looked quickly around. But it was only Riph Raph shifting in his sleep.

Marcus handed the Exsalusentia back. "We could spend all three days trying to figure out how to open this thing, and we still wouldn't be any closer than we are now."

Kyja had been thinking the exact same thing. "I want to search around in the library for any mention of the box. But if we don't find some way to get Terra ne Staric some water, everyone here is going to die."

"Everywhere we go people are about to die," Marcus said. "And we can't do a thing about it. It's like that game with the colored rocks."

"Trill Stones?"

"Right. It's like we're playing Trill Stones with the Dark Circle. Only they're eight moves ahead before we even start playing. No matter what move we make, they already—"

Something moved in the dry leaves. Kyja began to turn—her hand reaching for the sword no longer at her side. Strong coils wrapped around her legs and arms, pinning them in place. As her hands touched cold scales, she yelled, "Run!"

Marcus began to cast a spell, but a huge black head appeared directly in front of him.

"Not s-s-s-o quickly," the snake hissed, black tongue flicking between its dripping fangs. "Try any magic, any magic at all, and I will crush every bone in your friend's body."

Marcus's eyes darted toward Kyja; she thought she heard him mutter something like, "Is this how it happens?" The snake's coils tightened around Kyja's chest, and she gasped for air.

"Okay." Marcus raised his hands slowly. "I won't cast anything. Just let her go."

"S-s-smart boy." The snake blinked its yellow eyes. It glanced up at Riph Raph, who'd woken up and was creeping silently through the treetops. "That goes-s-s-s for you as-s-s well, *li-z-z-ard.* One flame ball from you, and you'll be prying the girl from the tree bark."

Riph Raph hissed but stopped where he was.

How had this happened? How had a Thrathkin S'Bae made it past the city's guards? From inside the snake's coils, the only thing

Kyja could think of was that thirst and the shaking ground had made the guards less attentive than usual.

"What do you want?" Marcus asked.

"Jus-s-s-t you." The snake darted its head closer to Marcus, its mouth opening wide. Venom dripped from its twin curved fangs. "I bring you back to the master, and she goes free."

"Don't believe it," Kyja tried to tell Marcus, but she couldn't get enough air to speak.

Marcus stiffened. One hand started to come down. Kyja was sure he was about to try a spell, but then he glanced at her and stopped. What was he waiting for? Didn't he understand that the Dark Circle wouldn't rest until it had killed both of them?

"Don't move now," the snake said, weaving its head to and fro. "I'll use jus-s-s-t enough venom to s-s-s-end you into a nice, comfy s-s-s-leep."

"Kill it!" Kyja tried to scream. But all that came out was a muf-fled, "Kkkkk—"

The Thrathkin S'Bae opened its jaws impossibly wide. A drop of venom slipped from its left fang and sizzled on the ground. Marcus clenched his jaws and closed his eyes. The snake lowered its head. Kyja couldn't stand to watch, but she didn't dare look away.

Just as the fangs reached Marcus's neck, a tall figure with long, dark hair stepped out from behind the tree Marcus was leaning against. Seeing the movement, the snake tried to attack, but the fig-ure was too quick. A glimmering blade blurred through the air. Like a nail, it plunged into the snake's head and pinned it to the ground.

CHAPTER 32

GRAEHL'S RETURN

WELL, THAT WAS EXCITING." The tall man checked to make sure the snake was dead before pulling the silver blade from its head, and the Thrathkin S'Bae reverted to human form. Its body shuddered one last time then lay still on the ground.

Marcus frowned. "*Screech.*"

"The very same," the man said. He wiped his sword on a handful of dead leaves.

Kyja, finally able to get enough breath to talk, hurried over and took his hand in both of hers. "Thank you, Graehl. That was amazing."

Marcus grabbed his staff and pushed himself to his feet. He studied the tall man with obvious suspicion. "What are you doing out here?"

"Snake hunting, it would seem." Graehl grinned and slid his sword into its scabbard. "But you don't seem particularly grateful." He looked around. "There could be more of them out here. Let's find someplace a little more secure."

They left the grove of trees and entered a part of the city filled with closed shops and darkened stables.

"Took long enough," Marcus snarled as Graehl led them down a row of buildings.

Kyja couldn't believe the way he was acting. "What's wrong with you? He just saved our lives."

"A second later, and he wouldn't have," Marcus said. Graehl stopped in front of a small feed shop. He fiddled with the lock, and a moment later, the door swung open. They walked behind the counter into a small storage room filled with crates and boxes. Riph Raph found a comfy-looking bale of hay and curled up on it.

Marcus sat on a crate of dried corn, and slammed his fist on the splintery wood. "If you were back there all the time, what were you waiting for?"

"To be perfectly honest, I was sort of hoping you were going to do something yourself. A little magic to distract the dark wizard would have made attacking much easier."

Marcus balled his fist and stared at his feet.

Kyja shook her head. Marcus didn't trust Graehl, and in some ways she could understand that. As a cave trulloch, he had frozen Kyja in a block of ice, allowed Marcus to be tortured in ways she couldn't even imagine, and nearly gotten them both killed by the Unmakers. Although he'd explained about the curse placed on him by the Keepers, Marcus wasn't ready to forgive him so easily. Kyja, on the other hand, believed him when he said he was sorry and wanted to help.

"Aren't you even going to say thank you?" she asked.

Marcus pressed his lips together before muttering, "Thanks."

Graehl gave a small bow. "That wasn't as bad as say, poking your eye out with a red hot cinder, was it?"

"It was close."

"Get used to it," Riph Raph said from his hay pile. "He never thanks me either."

"Maybe I would if you ever did anything to be thanked for," Marcus said.

Kyja wanted to knock both of their heads together, but she turned to Graehl instead. "How did you happen to be there?" she asked. "I thought you were still up in the tower, arguing with everyone else."

"I was spying on you," Graehl said in a perfectly ordinary tone.

"I knew it," Marcus barked. "You're still working for the Dark Circle. You probably led that Thrathkin S'Bae straight to us." He held out his hand as though preparing a counter spell for an attack.

Graehl pulled out a knife, but instead of attacking, he took a long stick of silvery wood from his pocket and began carving it. "If I *am* working for the Dark Circle, I can't imagine they'd be too happy with me leading one of their wizards to you and then stabbing him in the head."

"Don't be silly," Kyja said. "We know you aren't working for them. Were you *really* spying on us?"

The tall man turned the stick left and right before carving something into the tip. "As a matter of fact, I was. Have been ever since you got here. After all, I promised to help you with your search. I wanted to make sure you didn't go anywhere without me. From the looks of you two, though, I think you did. What I can't figure out is how."

"We don't need your help," Marcus said.

"Marcus," Kyja cried, embarrassed by his outburst. "Stop being such a . . . what's that word you use? Oh, yeah. Stop being such a *jerk*."

Marcus looked down. "We're doing fine on our own,"

"That's not quite what you were saying a moment ago." Graehl laughed. "Didn't I overhear you say something about being in a game of Trill Stones, eight moves behind the Dark Circle?"

"As if one more person will make any difference," Marcus said. "Now it's three against the Dark Circle, the water elementals, and the land elementals. Four if you count Spaz, the snoring skyte."

"Wha? Huh?" Riph Raph, who had fallen back asleep, opened his eyes briefly, blinked, and went back to snoring.

"What makes you think the elementals are helping the Dark Circle?" Graehl asked.

Kyja considered mentioning what the Aerisians had told them, before deciding it might be better to keep at least some secrets. Instead, she mentioned the floods, the quakes, and the creatures of land and water. "And then there are Cascade and Lanctrus-Darnoc. No one knows where they've gone or what they're doing. And all the weather problems began right after they left."

"That's not entirely true. I know a certain wizard who knows exactly where they went. But he's not telling anyone." Graehl sliced off a narrow sliver of wood, which floated feather-like to the wooden floor. "You know, I actually chanced upon him speaking with the two of them out by the stables just before they left. It's a shame I couldn't have arrived a little sooner. I might have been able to over-hear something useful."

"Great," Marcus said. "Now you're spying on Master Therapass too."

"Not spying so much as *watching*," Graehl said. "A lot can be said for keeping your eyes and ears open. And trust me, there's a lot you can pick up around here if you pay attention."

"*Pay attention*," Kyja murmured softly.

"What?" Marcus asked, still cranky.

"You said this felt like playing Trill Stones. Only the Dark Circle was eight moves ahead of us."

"It does," Marcus said. "It's like they've set this trap, and no matter which way we turn, we're going to get caught in it."

Kyja suddenly grinned. "A trap. Yes. That's exactly what it is."

Graehl chuckled. "Smart girl."

Marcus slammed the tip of his staff on the wooden floor. "Does someone want to tell me what's going on? Why are you both grinning? The Dark Circle is everywhere, and all we have is a locked bo—" He clamped his jaws shut, obviously not willing to tell Graehl about the Exsalusentia. Although if Graehl had been spying on them, Kyja suspected the man had already overheard them discussing it.

Graehl arched an eyebrow and looked at Kyja. "You're thinking about Y'sdine's Feint, aren't you?"

"Remember that time when we were trapped in the Westland Woods and Master Therapass played Trill Stones with you?" Kyja asked Marcus. "You thought you had him beat until he used Y'sdine's Feint on you."

Marcus nodded. "Sure. He waited for me to reveal my strategy—get him completely surrounded—and then he used it against me. I lost in, like, two turns."

"That's what we need to do against the Dark Circle," Kyja said. "We've seen their strategy. Now we have to find a way to use it against them."

Marcus laughed and Kyja gave him a dirty look. "Sorry," he said. "It's not that I don't agree. It's just . . . how are two kids—one who can barely walk, and one who can't do magic, plus a whining skyte and an ex-cave trulloch, going to stop an army of giant clay monsters, a Summoner, and the entire Dark Circle?"

Kyja pressed her lips together for a moment before fixing him with a determined gaze. "The same way we defeated the Summoner that attacked us at Water Keep, the harbingers, and the Keepers of the Balance."

Marcus stopped laughing. "That was hard. But this . . . It's too much. It seems impossible."

"It does," Kyja said. "But opening a drift was supposed to be impossible too. Finding the elementals was supposed to be impossible. We're only kids, and I have no idea how anyone could expect us to save our worlds." She held out her hands. "There are more reasons to quit than I can count. But only one reason to keep going. If we don't try, who will?"

Graehl paused in his carving. "What's this about a Summoner? I think it's time you two told me what's going on."

Ignoring Graehl completely, Marcus nodded at Kyja. "You're right. We have to do this. I guess we can start with the Dark Circle's strategy. That seems pretty clear. They've taken away any chance of getting help from the outside by hitting every part of Farworld with terrible weather. More Thrathkin S'Bae are probably looking for us, so we can't stay anywhere for long. Both Terra ne Staric and Icehold are going to be wiped out in three days. But how do we take advantage of all that?"

Kyja pinched her lower lip, thinking. The problem did seem overwhelming. What would she do if this were a game of Trill Stones? "The biggest advantage they have is the weather. If only we knew where Cascade is."

Suddenly an idea occurred to her. She turned to Graehl. "Do

you remember exactly when you saw Master Therapass talking to Cascade and Lanctrus-Darnoc?"

"Of course," he said. "I was talking with the blacksmith when I saw the three of them gather by the stables. It seemed to be a rather serious conversation, so I headed over to listen. By the time I got there, they were finishing up. All I heard was the wizard telling them to be careful."

"But if you'd been there earlier, you might have overheard the whole conversation?"

Graehl tapped his knife blade against the wood. "I suppose."

Kyja leaned over to Marcus. "Tell me more about the Abyss of Time," she whispered. "How does it work?"

Marcus gave her an odd look, almost like he was scared of her. "There are four doorways," he whispered back. "The first is called the *Is*. That's how we got here. The second one is called the *Was*. It takes you back in time."

"How far back?"

"I think as far back as you want," Marcus said.

Kyja's mind raced. "We could go into the past, return to where Master Therapass is speaking to Cascade and Lanctrus-Darnoc, and listen in to what he says?"

Marcus started to nod, then shook his head. "No, it doesn't work that way. You can only return to places you've actually been. If you try to go outside the area of your own memories, everything turns dark."

Kyja chewed on the tip of her thumb, thinking. There had to be some way. Finding out what Master Therapass had told the elementals might be vital to figuring out where they were now. And in turn, learning what the water and land elementals had to do with the Dark Circle.

"Does someone want to tell me what's going on?" Graehl asked. "I might be able to help."

"No," Marcus said. "Go find someone else to spy on."

"Actually," Kyja said. "Maybe you can." She turned to Marcus. "What if we took someone with us? Could we visit places *they've* been?"

"I don't know," Marcus said. "I've only . . ." He looked from Kyja to Graehl, and shook his head. "We're not taking him with us. I totally don't trust him. We don't even know if his story is true. For all we know, he could be lying about the whole thing."

"Why would he lie?"

Marcus shifted his leg and grimaced. "Who knows why he does anything? Besides, he didn't hear the conversation back then. So we probably won't be able to hear it in his memory."

"There's one way to find out," Kyja said. She turned toward the door and called, "Mr. Z! Mr. Z, where are you?"

At her call, Mr. Z appeared. His legs were bent, as though he'd been sitting on a chair, and in his hands he held a group of cards. With nothing to support him, he fell over backwards, spraying cards everywhere.

"Who's this?" Graehl asked, clearly shocked by the little man's sudden appearance.

"No one," Marcus said. He shook his head at Kyja. "I don't think we should do this."

"Give a body a little more notice," Mr. Z piped, dusting himself off and grabbing his cards. "I had the seven of giblets, the four of tarts, and the queen of abnormality."

"There's no time for games," Kyja said. "We want to go back to the *Was*. Right away. All four of us."

"Four?" Mr. Z shoved his cards into his coat. "That is highly irregular. Extremely unusual. I'm not sure I'm allowed—"

Graehl had reached for his sword, but now he seemed more curious than concerned. "What is this *was*? And why are we going there? Does the wizard know about this? I don't think—"

Kyja pulled out the Exsalusentia just enough so that the little man could see its silver edge. "If you don't want to help us, I'm sure . . ."

"Fine," he squeaked. "I'll do it."

CHAPTER 33

MEMORIES AND MESSAGES

THE GROUP OF FOUR STEPPED out of the mist and into the *Was*. Riph Raph clung to Kyja's shoulder, looking about nervously. The hallway was exactly as Marcus remembered it—the same bright yellow walls, same red floor, even the same gold-framed paintings. He looked around for the little boy but didn't see him anywhere. Maybe he was scared off by such a big group, or maybe his absence had something to do with Mr. Z being with them.

"Where are we?" Graehl turned quickly around, his eyes darting every direction. His hand was back on his sword. "Is this some kind of Dark Circle trap?" He looked at a painting. "This is me just a few minutes ago." He reached for the frame.

"Eh, eh, eh," Mr. Z squeaked holding up a finger. "That would be unwise. Unless you are the kind of person that pokes his head into a fire dragon's mouth to test the heat, it's best not to disturb one's past."

Graehl pulled back his hand and stepped away from the wall.

"It's okay," Kyja said. "The air elementals sent us here. It's safe." She glanced at Marcus. "At least I think it is."

"Look," Riph Raph said, standing by the other wall. "It's us."

Marcus looked at a painting showing him and Kyja flying above Air Keep on the backs of the ciralati. Riph Raph was a little way behind, struggling to keep up. Apparently the hall was now divided into two sides—one for Graehl and one for him and Kyja. He turned back to the other wall with Graehl's painting, but found himself looking at another painting of Kyja and himself. This one showed him and Kyja listening to Jaklah's report.

He turned back to Kyja's wall; there was the picture of Graehl. "Who keeps moving the paintings?"

"Don't be obstreperous," Mr. Z said. "The paintings are *not* moving."

Marcus had no idea what *obstreperous* meant, although he was pretty sure it wasn't a compliment. But the paintings were definitely moving. He pointed to the left. "That wall's Graehl." He looked right. "And that's Kyja and me." He looked left again. "But now this wall has a different painting of Kyja and me."

"He's right," Kyja said. "They keep moving."

Mr. Z gave an exasperated sigh. "Use your eyes, lad. That side is Graehl. That side is Kyja. And that side is you. Simple arithmetic."

Marcus opened his mouth to argue that there couldn't be three sides to a hall, before realizing that Mr. Z was right. There *were* three walls. He didn't notice when looking at one wall. But if he let his eyes relax, not focusing on anything specific, he could see three walls at the same time—like one of those optical illusions, where the stairs always went up in a square. It made him feel a little sick to his stomach.

Riph Raph looked from one wall to another and made a gagging sound. "Simple arithmetic, my beak. More like *sickening* arithmetic."

"Do I dare ask what's behind the doors?" Graehl asked, not coming close to touching anything after Mr. Z's last warning.

"This is called the *Was*," Marcus said, trying not to look at the paintings as he walked. Just like before, he had no pain in his leg or arm; he walked easily. He would have to try not to get used to the feeling, remembering how much worse the pain felt when he left the *Was*. "The paintings are like bits of memories, and the doors open into those memories. Except you can only visit places you've been. And if you try to leave your memories, you can't. The farther we walk, the further back in time we go. "

"Yes, yes," Mr. Z said, skipping impatiently ahead of them. "Memories, doorways. All well and good. Let's move along, shall we? Time is wasting. Important things to be about. Mustn't take all day."

"But it's *not* wasting, is it?" Kyja asked, hurrying to catch up. "I mean, time isn't moving while we're here."

"Don't be silly," Mr. Z said. "Well, be silly if you'd like. Just do it more quickly." He hurried them down the hallway like a dog herding sheep. "Of course time moves. Can't stop it any more than you could stop a rampaging nerite. Just runs more slowly *there* when we're *here*. Runs backwards *here* when we're *there*. Runs sideways if you're *here* and *there*, and the *other place*, which makes for delightful racing conditi—" He looked up as though realizing what he was saying, and quickly closed his mouth.

Marcus caught up with him. "Back in Air Keep you talked about losing a race."

The little man gave him a sideways glance.

"Is that the *only* reason you tricked me into leaving the monastery? And left Kyja the note? Just to settle a bet?"

Mr. Z gave him a crafty look and rattled a pair of dice in his hand. "There are more ways than one to win a wager. And not all wagers are created equal."

Like that answered anything. Marcus didn't know why he even bothered asking the little man questions.

"How did you two discover this *Was*?" Graehl asked, his long legs covering twice as much distance as Marcus and Kyja with each step. "And who's your little friend with the interesting taste in clothes?"

"Ask him yourself sometime when we're not around," Marcus muttered. "But make sure you have nothing else to do for a while."

Kyja ran a hand along a wall with paintings of her poring over scrolls and practicing sword fighting. "This doesn't seem so bad. In fact, it's kind of fun." She looked at Marcus. "Why were you so scared of coming here?"

"I wasn't *scared*." Marcus hesitated. "There's just more to the Abyss than you think. It's like this place is all one big trap."

Kyja studied him, but Marcus couldn't meet her eyes for fear she'd read what he was thinking. What if she realized he was trying to keep her out of the *Will Be* and decided they should visit the future? He could imagine her expression when she saw the glass coffin being lowered into the ground and realized who was inside it. He wiped his palms on his pants.

"This is it," Graehl said, stopping by a painting.

Marcus—who still had serious doubts that the man he continued to think of as a cave trulloch had witnessed any conversation between Master Therapass and the elementals—examined the painting. In it, Graehl was talking to a broad-shouldered man in a leather apron, but there was no sign of Master Therapass.

"That's Graham, the blacksmith," Kyja said, looking over Marcus's shoulder. She pointed to someone in the top left-hand corner of the painting, nearly out of sight. "Look, that's Master Therapass."

Marcus squinted, managing to make out a figure in a blue robe. He guessed it could be the wizard. But that still didn't mean he'd spoken to the elementals, neither of which was in the painting.

Graehl pointed to the door. "Shall we? Or would you rather stay here and continue to doubt my story?"

Marcus grunted. "Let's go."

Graehl, Kyja, and Marcus opened the door, but Mr. Z stayed in the hallway. "Aren't you coming?" Marcus asked.

"You paid me to bring you here," the little man said, rattling his dice. "That's exactly what I have done. No more. No less."

"Actually, we didn't pay you at all," Kyja said.

Mr. Z tapped his nose. "Of that, my girl, I am all too aware."

"Whatever," Marcus said, wondering how Kyja managed to surround herself with such an untrustworthy bunch—Riph Raph, who whined and complained all the time; Graehl, who up until a few months ago had spent his time feeding people to the Unmakers; and Mr. Z, who was plain nuts. He almost said something about her choice of companions, before remembering what he'd seen in the *Will Be*. What he'd seen there—what he'd done—made him by far the worst of the group.

They stepped through the door, and Kyja looked around, filled with wonder. "It's like we're back in Terra ne Staric all over again. Except right before you left. I think you're in the arena, practicing fencing with Tankum."

"Is that before or after you embarrassed Turnip Head?" Riph Raph asked.

Marcus felt his face go hot, remembering how Kyja had stepped into the practice arena and made his pathetic attempts at sword fighting look childish.

Kyja glanced around. "Where's Graehl?" She checked the door-way still open behind them. He'd been right there, but now he was gone.

"Probably freaking out," Marcus said, remembering how he got stuck in his old body the first time he'd entered a door in the *Was*. He crossed the open plaza to where Graehl and Graham seemed to be discussing swords. "You want an angular cut," the brawny black-smith said, making a chopping motion with one calloused hand.

"No." The Graehl from before shook his head, long hair flap-ping on his shoulders. "Stabbing. Light yet supple."

"How do you like the past?" Marcus asked the tall man. "Is it everything you hoped it would be?" He knew Graehl couldn't re-spond while he was inside the copy of himself, but he enjoyed the thought of him panicking when he realized he couldn't change his actions or words as long as he was locked in the other body.

Kyja walked cautiously up behind him. "Can't they hear you?"

"The blacksmith can't. And the Graehl from back then can't. They can't see or hear us." Marcus walked up behind the brawny man and pretended to pat him on the shoulder. "Blacksmith, any-one ever tell you your face looks just like your anvil? I hope that sulfur smell is coming from the forge."

Kyja glanced toward Master Therapass. "Hurry. Here comes Cascade."

"Fine." Marcus walked directly in front of Graehl, who was ex-plaining exactly the kind of blade he was looking for. He waved his hands before Graehl, like an eye doctor giving a checkup. "You know, you can come out of your body anytime you want. Unless you *like* being stuck in there."

For a moment, nothing happened. Then the Graehl from now stepped out of the Graehl from then. It was actually kind of cool to see it happen from the outside. The long-haired man turned to look at himself. He stared into his own eyes and shook his head. "Well," he said, rubbing the back of his neck. "That wasn't quite what I expected." He looked at Marcus, one side of his mouth rising in a wry smile. "Thanks for the warning, friend."

Marcus chuckled. "Any time."

"Come on," Kyja said, trotting toward the stables. "Here comes Lanctrus-Darnoc."

Marcus and Graehl ran after her, Graehl glancing over his shoulder as though he couldn't believe what he had just experienced.

As they reached the stables, Master Therapass was pulling the two elementals out of sight around the corner of the building. Things appeared a little grainier the farther they got from the blacksmith shop, as if Graehl's memory wasn't quite as clear. Marcus was afraid they wouldn't be able to hear anything, since Graehl hadn't heard anything in his memory. But apparently the past didn't work that way.

"You got my *megrsshktes?*" the wizard said.

"What did he say?" Graehl asked.

Marcus shrugged. "I couldn't make out the last word."

"Yes," Cascade said, and both the fox and boar heads of Lanctrus-Darnoc nodded.

"I think he said *messages,*" Kyja whispered, moving closer.

"Then you know there *culdghts* be spies *anywhqrts.*" The wizard's voice faded in and out like a poorly tuned radio. He glanced toward the blacksmith shop then turned his head to look straight at Kyja, Marcus, and Graehl.

Kyja—who had been sliding along the edge of the stables—froze at the wizard's gaze. But Marcus walked straight into the group. "They can't see or hear you."

Therapass turned back to the elementals, his expression grave. "I had hoped I was *wlkirths* about the *vhareticl,* Cascade. But it is clear that at least one elemental has *shytuu wintf* the Dark Circle."

Kyja frowned. "I can't understand everything he's saying. Some of his words are garbled."

"I think it's because we're near the edge of Graehl's memory," Marcus whispered. "But it sounds like Master Therapass knew there was a traitor all along."

Graehl shook his head. "If the land and water elementals are involved, there's more than one traitor."

Cascade's nostrils flared as he spoke to Lanctrus-Darnoc. "If *hy-ryb* is a betrayer, *jih rix* not a Fontasian."

"No *land* elementals *yehytrup* stoop to *slurger* thing," the fox head said.

"It *graunch* the stink of water," the boar snarled.

Kyja shook her head. "Listen to them, arguing like selfish children—and within days of fighting against the same enemy."

Master Therapass ignored their bickering and placed a hand on the water elemental's shoulder. "Someone has *hrkstn* relaying *inshteuyion* to the enemy. Information that *kratch ligert* come from the vision of a water *edbygdhgky* or the *jyuifthet* of land elementals. I need you to find the informer and *fghurling* back to me."

Marcus strained, trying to decipher what the wizard was saying.

"Why not us?" Lanctrus-Darnoc said. "Whether the *elietery* be land or water, we *axthir hornetrgbind* to see it stopped."

Master Therapass looked around the corner of the stables, where the Graehl of the past had finished speaking with Graham and was now walking in their direction. The wizard turned to Lanctrus-Darnoc and spoke quickly. "I have another *trighur* for you. I am sending you *erg* with Tankum's forces. As far as they *clegert* you are going to *sirght* for the Keepers."

As Graehl approached, everything looked less grainy, but the wizard's words were just as difficult to understand. Maybe because Graehl hadn't actually heard them?

"When you *ritdge* the Windlash Mountains," Therapass told Lanctrus-Darnoc. "I need you to explore the *caburts* of the Unmakers. I fear a *prectigggkle* has been *ophurter* there. A passage directly to the *shaflowerg ruleffs.*"

"What did he say?" Graehl asked. "What about the cavern of the Unmakers?" As the tall man pushed closer, his hip brushed against a shovel leaning against the wall.

Both Therapass and the elementals spun around as the tool clanged to the ground. Marcus froze in shock.

Mr. Z was suddenly at their sides, jumping around like his pockets were full of bees. "What are you doing? Didn't you listen to the Aerisian's warnings? You must leave at once."

Graehl brushed back his hair. "I'm sorry." He reached to pick up the shovel, but Mr. Z grabbed his wrist. "No," he piped. "You've done enough!"

"We have to hear the rest of what Master Therapass told them," Kyja said.

But Mr. Z was grabbing them, pushing them together toward the door.

Master Therapass reached a hand toward the current-day Graehl, his eyes dark with worry. Marcus and Kyja froze with fear, but the wizard's hand went straight through Graehl's body—as if he was a ghost.

Master Therapass turned back to Cascade and Lanctrus-Darnoc. "You must both go now. Cascade *grig* to Land Keep first. As a water elemental, *yig* cannot enter. Only observe. Lanctrus-Darnoc, be wary. There may be powers beyond *gygrun infin*. Both of you, be careful."

Marcus felt a tug in his stomach, and they were back in the Abyss of Time. Something felt different, though. The frozen ground was slightly tilted, and when he looked up, he saw a crack in the ice of the *Was*. A trickle of water leaked down the face of the frozen waterfall. Mr. Z shoved Marcus from the back, into the *Is*, and they were in the storage room again.

CHAPTER 34

THE TRILL STONES STRATEGY

WHAT HAPPENED?" Kyja asked. "Why did you make us leave?"

"Klutz!" Mr. Z howled, wringing his small hands together. "Bungler, lummox, lard-fingers . . ."

"I knocked over a shovel," Graehl said. "It was an accident. I don't see why you're so upset."

"*Upset?*" Mr. Z pulled off his hat, flung it to the ground, and stomped on it like a child throwing a temper tantrum. "Do I look *upset* to you?"

He looked rather upset to Kyja.

"You look bonkers," Riph Raph said. "That's what you look like."

Mr. Z clasped his head in his hands. "Didn't any of you pay attention to what the Aerisians said? Do *not* touch anything inside the portals of the Abyss of Time, they told you. Do *not* change anything."

"That's why the waterfall cracked, isn't it?" Marcus asked.

"I don't understand," Kyja said. "How could such a little thing as knocking over a shovel be all that bad?"

257

Mr. Z reached into his pocket and pulled out a top. With a flick of his finger, he set it spinning on the lid of a crate. He looked at Kyja and Marcus. "A little thing," he said, tapping the edge of the top lightly with his finger. Instantly, the top began to wobble. The longer it spun, the worse the wobble became until, at last, it lost its balance completely and flew off the crate. "Any change, any change at all, has effects that you cannot begin to fathom."

His message was clear. "Did we break the spindle of time?" Kyja asked.

"If you had," he said, snatching up the top, "you would not be here."

"We get it," Marcus said. "It was an accident, okay? We'll be more careful next time."

"There won't be a next time." Mr. Z picked up his hat, brushed it off, and pushed it back onto his head. "I'm returning to my . . . previous engagement while you . . . do whatever it is you do."

"You can't leave." Kyja grabbed him by the sleeve of his coat. "We need your help."

"Which is precisely what I have given you," the little man said. He stared at Kyja's hand. "If you will kindly remove your fingers from my person, I will be on my way."

"We have to go to Land Keep," Marcus said. "That's where Master Therapass sent Cascade."

"Are you out of your turnip-shaped noggin?" Riph Raph said. "If the land elementals are working with the Dark Circle, what do you think they'll do when you show up on their doorstep?"

Kyja knew that Marcus was right. If the elementals were somehow behind this, Land Keep and Water Keep were where they'd learn the most. But Riph Raph was right too. What would they do if they reached Land Keep and discovered the land elementals were now the enemy? Without the help of air elementals, they would be helpless. If only she could find a way to open the box.

"We need to get the Aerisians' help." She pulled the Exsalusentia from her pocket. "Tell me the truth," she said to Mr. Z. "Do you have any idea how to open this?"

Mr. Z reached toward the box, nearly touched it with one finger, but then pulled his hand back quickly. "Find the key, I would imagine."

"What key?" Marcus demanded. "We don't even know how to start looking for it."

Mr. Z shoved his hands in his pockets, a grumpy look on his face. "That is beyond my area of speciality. I *trust* you'll work it out on your own. Now, if you'll allow me to leave."

"We don't have time for this," Marcus complained. He turned to Kyja. "We have to go to Land Keep. We don't have any choice."

Graehl shook his head. "If the boy from Tankum's army was telling the truth tonight, an army stands between you and your destination. Besides, you'd never make it there before they attack Terra ne Staric."

Kyja looked at Mr. Z, an idea forming. "You said your snail is fast."

"A *snail*?" Graehl chuckled. "Somehow I think you might do better with a horse or—"

Mr. Z bristled. "Drymaios makes the fastest steed look like a tortoise. Why, I once raced her against a six-winged . . ." His words faded as he realized what Kyja was suggesting. "Out of the question," he squeaked. "I agreed to take you into the Abyss—which you nearly destroyed. But I said nothing about putting some of the finest snail flesh ever seen by man or beast in harm's way."

"You promised the Aerisians you'd help us," Marcus said. "Should we go back and tell them you broke your word?"

"Balderdash." Mr. Z pulled out a handkerchief and blotted the back of his neck. "Who said anything about breaking my word? I hauled you to Air Keep. Rescued you from the jaws of certain death. Brought you back. Took you through the *Was*— where I was nearly killed, I might add. It's enough, I say. More than enough. It's a travesty. A disgrace. A misguided, wrong-headed, pernicious—"

Kyja leaned down and hugged him. "Thank you."

Mr. Z's face turned red. He wiped his forehead, opened his mouth, and sputtered, "I . . . that is . . . well . . . you're welcome."

"Will you please take us to Land Keep?" she asked, staring down at him with her big, green eyes.

Mr. Z turned to Marcus.

Marcus grinned. "You might as well give up now."

Two minutes later, they were standing beside the door of the storage room. Mr. Z—who didn't seem entirely sure how he'd been talked into this—ran his handkerchief over Drymaios's gleaming brown shell, muttering about sweet-talking girls and green eyes.

"Will you come with us?" Kyja asked Graehl.

"I can't," he said. "I've got somewhere else I need to be."

Marcus sneered, leaning on his staff. "Running away when things get dangerous?"

Graehl's brow furrowed for a moment, then he broke into laughter. "You know, maybe I should have let the Unmakers keep you."

"Not that you didn't try," Marcus said.

Graehl ran a hand through his hair. "As a matter of fact, I am going back to the cavern of the Unmakers."

"Why?" Kyja asked, her throat tightening. The cavern, high in the Windlash Mountains—where she'd been imprisoned in ice and where Marcus had been tortured by the Unmakers—was a terrible place. Even with the creatures gone, the idea of going back there was horrifying.

"It's where Therapass sent Lanctrus-Darnoc," Graehl said. "I didn't understand everything the wizard told them, but it's clear he thought the cavern was still dangerous. I don't imagine anyone knows those caves better than I do."

"But if even the land elementals didn't return from the mountains . . ." Kyja said.

"It means Therapass was right." Graehl nodded. "If you succeed, and I don't come back, send help. Right now I don't think anyone can be spared from defending the city."

He was right, but Kyja didn't like it.

"I've got something for you," Graehl told her. "Actually, it's what I was talking to the blacksmith about in the *Was*. He finished it the day before yesterday." He unbuckled his scabbard and took out the sword he'd used to stab the Thrathkin S'Bae. Kyja hadn't been paying close attention before, but now she realized the red and gold hilt had the image of a skyte on it. The blade was silver metal that looked almost blue.

"It's belinium," Graehl said. "Not the strongest metal for one-on-one combat, but light and very flexible. Almost impossible to break, no matter how much stress you put it under—like someone I know."

Kyja took the sword. It was so light she nearly dropped it. "Look," she told Riph Raph, showing him the carving. "It's you." There was something engraved on the blade as well. She turned it and read, *The Most Powerful Magic Is Inside You.*

"I can't take this from you," she said, tears welling up in her eyes.

"It's the least I can do," he said. "After all, if it wasn't for you believing in me, I'd still be a monster."

Kyja wrapped her arms around Graehl, hugging him until Marcus coughed. The tall man helped Kyja strap on the leather scabbard, then turned to Marcus. "I've got something for you too." He reached into his cloak and took out the piece of silver wood he'd been carving.

Marcus waved his hand. "I don't need anything."

Graehl laughed again. "Once a trulloch, always a trulloch, huh?"

"It's not that. I just . . ." Marcus tried to refuse the gift, but Graehl forced the stick into his hands. "What is it?" Marcus asked, looking at the elaborately carved runes and figures.

"It's a wand. Shadow wood. Extremely rare. I discovered it in the caves. I haven't tested it, but I've been told that being from neither Earth nor Farworld, it works equally well in both."

Marcus looked down at the wand. "It's . . . well . . . thanks." He held out his hand to shake Graehl's, but the man pulled him into a rough embrace, pounding him on the back.

"Don't let her talk you into giving up that cynicism entirely. Not everyone is completely trustworthy. Not even me."

"Well," Mr. Z said, pulling out his pocket watch, "are you coming? I don't have all day."

Kyja and Marcus climbed onto Drymaios, Kyja with one hand on her sword, Marcus clutching his staff and wand. Mr. Z clambered inside. "Make sure you don't scratch that shell!" his voice echoed.

"Be careful," Kyja told Graehl.

"And you the same."

"I just wanted to say—" Marcus began.

Before he could complete the sentence, Mr. Z shouted, "Run, Drymaios!" and the storage room was empty.

Mr. Z tumbled out of the snail's shell, his hat tilted back on his head, gray hair standing up in wild tangles and swirls. "What a ride!" He grinned, patting Drymaios. "Even I didn't know she was capable of such lightning-quick speed."

Kyja looked to the door that led outside. "Through there?"

"Where else?" Mr. Z said, as though it was perfectly normal to travel long distances without ever leaving the place where you started.

"I don't get it," Marcus said, easing himself painfully off Drymaios's shell. "If we've already traveled all that way, how can we still be next to this door?"

Mr. Z pressed his lips together and looked at the ceiling as though he'd never heard such a foolish question. "This wonderful steed takes you all the way except for the first step and the last, and you complain about having to open a door?"

Marcus looked at Kyja; she raised her hands. She didn't understand it any more than he did. But if it worked, who were they to complain? "How long did it take us to get here?" she asked.

"A little over a day," Mr. Z said. "I do believe it's a new land speed record."

"Are you all right?" Kyja asked Marcus as he limped toward the door. He looked like he was in a lot of pain.

He gritted his teeth. "I'm fine. Let's get this over with."

"All right," Kyja said. They had less than two days left. Hopefully Land Keep would provide the answers they were looking for.

She pulled open the door and was plunged into icy water. Something slammed against her back, and she turned to find Marcus flailing behind her. She just had time to see bubbles stream from his mouth before the door slammed shut, leaving them in total darkness.

CHAPTER 35

A WET RETURN

MARCUS WATCHED KYJA pull the doorknob. At the last second, he realized she was walking into what could be terrible danger. He reached for her arm, but she was already through. It was hard to see what was on the other side of the door; everything looked dark. Afraid she'd entered into a trap, he jumped through the doorway behind her.

Cold water encased his body. Gasping in shock, he turned for the door, but before he could reach it, it slammed shut. Panic flooded his brain as everything went black. He kicked and swung his good arm, but he'd never learned to swim, and he could feel his body sinking.

Where was he? Where was *Kyja?* In the pitch black, he couldn't see a thing. The door was supposed to lead to *Land Keep.* Had Mr. Z sent them to this place on purpose? He coughed, and water filled his nose and mouth. Cold liquid ran down his throat, gagging him.

A hand closed on his arm, and he nearly screamed before realizing it had to be Kyja. The hand worked its way down his arms until the fingers closed around his wrist, his fingers, and . . . his wand. He was still holding his wand.

Kyja squeezed his hand twice. It was a message. He needed to cast a spell. But it was hard to think with his mouth full of water and his lungs burning. His brain seemed trapped in a fog. He had to have . . . *air*. Air. He needed to cast *air* magic.

Fighting against the cold that sucked all the energy from his aching body, and the lack of oxygen that turned his thoughts to mush, he tried to remember the spells Master Therapass had taught him. Was there one that would give him air?

His lungs screamed, and his arms and legs felt like lead. But Kyja still held tight to his wrist. He had to find a way to save them. Then he remembered: the umbrella spell he'd used to shield them from heat in the desert the first time they went to Earth, and later from the snow in the Windlash Mountains. If he changed the spell a little, he might be able to create a bubble of oxygen that he and Kyja could breathe.

He tried to think of a rhyme to help, but his brain wouldn't cooperate. Red and yellow lights flashed before his eyes. In desperation, he held out his wand and called out in his head, *Help me. Help us breathe.*

Something warm and dry pushed the water away from his face, and he gasped. Precious air filled his lungs. He coughed, sucked in another mouthful, and pulled Kyja beside him. He couldn't see her face, didn't even know if she was conscious.

"Breathe!" he screamed. "Breathe!"

He heard a gasp beside him. And another. "I . . . thought . . . I . . . was . . . drowning," Kyja managed to say, choking and wheezing.

"Sorry," Marcus said. "I was trying to think of a spell."

"Don't be sorry." Kyja's voice sounded a little better. "You saved my life and . . ." There was a panicked splashing sound. "Riph Raph?" Kyja cried. "Riph Raph, where are you?"

"Right behind you," came the skyte's voice. "Freezing my scales off. And if you don't mind me saying so, one of you has breath that smells like dead mice."

Marcus couldn't believe the skyte was complaining about bad breath at a time like this.

"It's probably me," Kyja said. "I haven't brushed my teeth in what feels like forever."

"Actually, it's not too bad," Riph Raph said. "I kind of like dead mice."

Marcus and Kyja clung to each other, laughing in relief. Marcus felt his feet touch something hard. "I think I just reached the floor."

"Me too," Kyja said. "But I'm freezing. Do you know where we are?"

Marcus shook his head before realizing Kyja couldn't see it. "Mr. Z said he was taking us to Land Keep. But he must have made some kind of mistake."

"Unless they installed an extra-large swimming pool without telling anyone," Riph Raph said.

Kyja squealed. "Ouch! Watch your claws."

"Sorry," Riph Raph said. "Skytes do *not* like water."

Marcus tried moving his feet. He was definitely standing on some kind of hard, flat surface. "I'm not sure how long our air will last. Maybe we should call Mr. Z. I'm almost positive he didn't come through the door with us."

"I'm not s-sure that's a g-good idea," Kyja said, her teeth chattering. "If we summon him into this, he and his snail might drown."

Marcus wasn't sure if a creature of pure magic *could* drown. But she had a point. They should probably figure out where they were and what had happened to Mr. Z before deciding what to do.

"We need some kind of light," Kyja said. "And heat, if you can manage it."

"I can do that," Riph Raph said, drawing in a breath.

"No!" Marcus shouted. "No fireballs."

"All right. All right," the skyte said. "Some people are so touchy."

"Let me try to cast fire magic." Marcus remembered a spell on one of the scrolls he'd studied. "Flame and fire, ember gray," he murmured. "Give us light to show the way."

The end of his wand began to glow. He still wasn't sure how he felt about Graehl, but the shadow wood wand was great. It felt like the strength of his magic had doubled, or even tripled. The wand also seemed to warm the water around them to make it almost bearable.

"Look," Kyja said, pointing through the murky darkness. "Aren't those doors?"

Clinging to each other, Marcus and Kyja half walked, half swam to a large pair of stone doors. Marcus held up his wand, and a symbol came into view—a gold loop on one end, and a square within a square on the other. "This *is* Land Keep," he said, barely able to believe what he was seeing.

"We come seeking knowledge," Kyja said.

Marcus had completely forgotten the password they'd used to get into Land Keep the first time, but it worked; the doors swung open at her words. Inside, everything was filled with water too. He could just make out the base of the tree of knowledge—its golden leaves glinting dully from the light of his wand.

"It's flooded," Kyja whispered. "All of Land Keep is flooded. How could this happen?"

"I don't know about you two, but this place is giving me the creeps," Riph Raph said, clinging to Kyja's shoulder.

Marcus looked up at the shadowy tree. "He's right. Something is really wrong here. We need to get out."

Quickly the two of them went out the door and through the tunnel beyond. Marcus didn't want to think about it, but the thought wouldn't go away. "Do you think Cascade could have done this?" he asked as they turned a corner. "He does control moving water, and the Noble River isn't far from here."

"No," Kyja said at once. "He wouldn't."

"I wouldn't put anything past those water breathers," Riph Raph said. "How can you trust someone with no emotions?"

Marcus tried to convince himself that Kyja was right. Cascade was their friend. He'd saved their lives outside Water Keep. How could he join the Dark Circle now? But he'd never really gotten along with Lanctrus-Darnoc. Maybe this was his way of getting back at the land elementals for some argument.

He looked over his shoulder as they started up the ramp that led out of Land Keep. "Why aren't the land elementals doing anything about this? Why don't they just block the river?"

"Maybe they can't," Kyja said. "Maybe the water is keeping them trapped in here."

"Is that light up ahead?" Marcus extinguished his wand, and a dim glow illuminated the water-filled corridor. "I think it's the end."

"Good thing," Riph Raph said. "If I have to smell turnip breath much longer, I think I'll puke."

"Oh, yeah," Marcus said. "Like bug breath is anything to write home about."

At last, they reached the end of the tunnel. Golden sunlight filtered through the water. Kyja climbed out onto land and pulled Marcus up behind her. He flopped onto the muddy bank, taking deep breaths of fresh air. "No swamp ever smelled so good," he said.

"Not to mention warmth." Kyja sighed. They stretched out on the ground, sunlight shining onto their faces. "I don't want to touch water again for a month. Even if it means stinking like a pig."

"You'll be lucky," a voice said.

"To live that long," another added.

Marcus sat up to see a pair of lizard heads watching him with glittering black eyes. One of the heads was deep purple. The other was black with green stripes. The lizards were connected to each other at the waist, and they shared a pair of green and brown wings, like a misshapen butterfly.

"I know you," Kyja said, sitting up. "You're land elementals."

"*King* of the land elementals," the purple lizard hissed, its pink tongue flickering.

"No," Marcus said. "We saw your king. He was half dragon, half lion."

"Silence!" The land elementals held up a silver scepter. The last time Marcus had seen it was in the paws of the land elemental king. "Do you recognize this?"

"*I* do," Riph Raph said. "And it doesn't belong to you."

"Fools!" The black and purple heads laughed together. "The scepter belongs to those who wield it. And with it comes all power. All control."

"Where are the rest of the land elementals?" Kyja asked.

One of the lizard heads laughed—a buzzing, papery sound, like wasps trying to get through a window screen. "Trapped," the other said. "And they won't get out. Land magic belongs to us alone. Farworld is ours. You will understand better when we deliver you to the Master of the Dark Circle."

"Never," Kyja said, drawing her sword.

Marcus raised his wand, but before he could cast a spell, the lizards swung the scepter, sending him flying through the air. Pain like he'd never imagined filled his body. It felt as if every bone had been lit on fire at once. He tried to raise his hand but found he could barely move.

"Marcus!" Kyja screamed.

She took a step toward him, but the lizards raised the scepter again. "Do you want a taste of what he got?" the one on the right asked. Their slit tongues licked their scaly lips.

"Go ahead and try," Kyja said. She ran at the lizards, blade raised.

The lizards swung the scepter as before, but nothing happened. Kyja jabbed her blade forward, its tip biting deep into the pebbly skin of the land elementals' right arm. Dark green blood seeped from the wound.

"Imbecile," the black head said to the purple head. "Don't you remember what the Fontasian told us? She's immune to magic."

Kyja stabbed again, but the land elementals knocked her away with a flap of their powerful wings. They swung the scepter again, and this time, a nearby tree ripped itself from the ground. Its roots reached out, wrapping themselves tightly around Kyja.

"Leave her alone!" Marcus cried as she struggled against the wood, which bit into her arms and legs.

"Immune to *magic*," the purple head said with a whispery

chuckle. "But not to pain." It looked down, where dark blood pooled on the ground at its feet. "You will pay for this."

Marcus looked from the lizards to the bloody puddle. Something about the ground gave him an idea. He looked up. The sun was directly overhead, so while the land elementals' blood dripped onto the ground, they didn't cast a shadow.

"It's midday!" he shouted. "There's no shadow."

One of the lizards turned to glare at him. The other hissed at Kyja as it raised the scepter over its head.

Kyja looked from Marcus to the sky.

Would she remember the note and understand?

Comprehension flashed in her eyes. She clasped her hand to the amulet around her neck—the amulet with the same symbol burned into Marcus's arm. But it was too late. The land elementals swung their scepter at Kyja's face, using it like a club. Kyja turned her head and Marcus instinctively closed his eyes, unable to look at what was about to happen.

Instead of Kyja screaming in pain, Marcus heard the land elementals howling in fear and surprise. Marcus's eyes snapped open. The elementals' silver scepter was lying on the ground behind them. They turned to grab it, and a familiar inside-out sensation tugged in Marcus's stomach.

The muddy ground he'd been lying on turned to cool asphalt. The bright sky went black. Marcus reached out with his mind and found Kyja and Riph Raph. He pulled, and suddenly Kyja was lying on the street beside him.

A pair of headlights flashed in front of them and brakes squealed. "Get out of the road, you punks!" a man shouted, driving his truck around them.

Beside them, a green bullfrog puffed up its throat. "*Ree-deep*. I really hate this. *Ree-deep*."

Marcus burst into laughter. He'd never been in so much pain in his life. He had no wheelchair. And they'd nearly been run over by a fast-food delivery truck. But they were on Earth. And they were safe. He didn't think he'd ever felt better.

CHAPTER 36

FLYING HOT DOGS

A STROLLER?" MARCUS SAID. "That's the best you could do? Couldn't you at least get a wagon or something? Even the grocery cart was better than this."

"It's all I could find," Kyja said. "I didn't want to steal anything, and this was abandoned in the middle of an empty field."

That wasn't surprising. After all, who would want a baby stroller with pink and blue-flowered upholstery peeling off in several places, a rusted handle, and one wheel looking like it might fall off at any minute? Not even a newborn would want to be seen in it.

"This is humiliating," Marcus said, as Kyja helped him climb into the seat. His legs hung over the front, nearly dragging on the ground and his rear could barely squeeze into the seat.

"Not as humiliating as being turned into a green sack of skin with a tongue long enough to fly a kite," Riph Raph croaked from the basket in the back.

From what Marcus had been able to determine, they were in

Gulfport, Mississippi. Not exactly a roaring metropolis, but at least it had a bus station. "Did you get directions?" he asked.

With her sword and scabbard carefully hidden beneath her coat, Kyja began pushing the stroller along the cracked and lumpy sidewalk. "According to the man in the grass station, it's on 13th Street."

"*Gas* station. Not grass station." Marcus sighed. If they were heading for 13th Street that meant ten more blocks of embarrassment. The loose wheel had a flat spot that made a *whup-whup-whup* sound as they rolled along. He just hoped it wouldn't come off. The only thing more embarrassing than being a teenage boy pushed in a baby stroller would be being a teenage boy falling out of a baby stroller into the street.

They'd considered calling Mr. Z. After all, he'd come to Earth before. But even if the little man came, Marcus was pretty sure his racing snail couldn't come to Earth with him. Besides, what had happened at Land Keep? Had Mr. Z known he was sending them into a trap that nearly drowned them? For now, Marcus wanted to do everything he could on his own.

The good news was that it was nearly two a.m., and almost no one was around at this hour.

"What happened back there?" Marcus asked. "The last thing I saw, they were about to hit you with that scepter. Then it was on the ground."

Kyja paused beneath a streetlight to catch her breath. "I don't know. I was looking away. Didn't you use some kind of magic?"

Did I? Marcus didn't think so. He'd been so out of it from being thrown across the field that he'd barely been able to see straight. He must have cast a spell, though. It was the only thing that could explain what happened. "Maybe."

Kyja started pushing again, the stroller wheel wobbling worse with each step. "Where do we go now?"

Marcus scratched his head. "Water Keep, I guess. If Cascade isn't at Land Keep, it's the only place I can think to look for him."

Kyja nodded and continued to push. Neither of them said anything more, but Marcus was pretty sure they both had the same thoughts. Land Keep had been flooded by the Noble River. Cascade controlled all moving water—including rivers. If the Fontasians had flooded Land Keep, what might that mean for Water Keep? It was entirely possible they could be walking into a trap there as well. But where else could they go?

"How will we pay for the bus ride?" Kyja asked. "All our money is back in Farworld. Along with all of our trill stones."

Money would have made the trip a lot easier. But they'd have to find a way to get to Water Keep without it. In a little over a day, the golem army would reach Terra ne Staric. They had to get to Water Keep before then and find a way to stop the attack. "I'll figure something out."

"*Ree-deep,*" Riph Raph croaked, his eyes bulging. "As I recall, the last time you arranged a bus ride, we ended up captured by the Unmakers."

"That's not fair." Kyja pushed the stroller off a curb, and the bad wheel gave an ominous *fa-wang* sound.

Marcus braced himself, waiting for the stroller to fall apart. Somehow it managed to hold together as they crossed the street and rolled onto the next sidewalk. It hadn't been his fault that the Dark Circle had set up roadblocks the last time they rode a bus. At least, not entirely. At the time, he hadn't known any Thrathkin S'Bae were on Earth, or how good they were at tracking him and Kyja.

If the land elementals reported seeing them, the Dark Circle's agents could already be on the way. The only thing he could hope for was that with attacks on so many fronts, they were spread too thin to pay close attention. He ran a hand along his silver wand, vowing that this time, he'd be ready for the Thrathkin S'Bae if they did show up.

Kyja pushed the stroller over an especially big crack, and a flare of pain shot up Marcus's leg and into his hip. "Sorry," Kyja said, as he hissed. "Is it bad?"

"It's been worse," Marcus said. That was true, but the problem was the pain was getting worse every hour—a sure sign that Farworld wasn't doing well. He slid around so his leg wasn't shoved against the stroller's frame.

Ten minutes later, they arrived at the Gulfport bus station. By then, the stroller was swaying back and forth like a ship in a rolling sea. Much more of this ride, and Marcus was pretty sure he'd throw up. He glanced around the small building: a bored-looking clerk sitting behind the ticket window, two vending machines—one selling sodas, the other candy and chips, a fuzzy TV showing what appeared to be a Spanish-language soap opera, and a hot dog cooker slowly turning leathery Polish sausages that looked like they'd been on their metal spikes for weeks.

The station was more crowded than he would have expected for the early hour. Two men in Army uniforms were snoring in their plastic chairs, heads thrown back. An old man who looked like he might have two healthy teeth was reading a battered paperback book. And a couple of young families were reading picture books and playing with toys to keep their kids entertained.

Kyja stopped the stroller near a group of three women playing cards and helped Marcus climb out of the stroller. Two of the women, who looked to be in their mid-fifties—and could possibly

have been sisters—glanced over at Marcus and smiled sympatheti-
cally.

"That doesn't look very comfortable," one of them said.

"Tell me about it." Marcus rubbed his legs and tried to stretch
his back.

"Isn't there a song about a baby stroller?" the second woman
said. She hummed a tune while the first woman tried to remember
the lyrics.

"Something, something, pram. Riding along with gram."

The third woman, who looked about twenty years older than
the other two, slapped down a card and grinned. "Skip Vicki."

"That's the third time," the first woman, who must have been
Vicki, complained. "Why don't you ever skip Anne?"

The older woman just laughed.

Marcus leaned toward Kyja. "Why don't you check and see
when the next bus to Chicago is due?"

A few minutes later, she returned from the ticket counter and
sat beside Marcus. "The next bus is in forty-five minutes. But the
fare is over a hundred dollars a ticket."

"They get you right in the old keister," the oldest woman said,
pointing to her back pocket.

"Barbara!" Anne said.

"What? It's highway robbery, is what it is. Why, when I was a
girl, you could ride across the country and back for twenty dollars
and have enough left over for Coney dogs."

Vicki glanced over at Kyja. "Did I hear you say you're going to
Chicago?"

Marcus nodded, unsure of how much he dared tell. The women
seemed nice enough. But adults tended to be suspicious of children
traveling alone.

"We're going to Chicago too," Vicki said.

"'Take me back to Chicago,'" the woman next to her sang.

"What are we going to do?" Kyja asked under her breath.

Marcus rubbed his hands on his pants and tried to smile. "We'll figure something out."

Barbara played another card, said, "Skip Vicki," and chuckled. She leaned toward Marcus and Kyja. "You know," she whispered, "I probably shouldn't say anything. But after the driver collects the tickets, he usually stops to have a smoke around the corner of the building. If there was some sort of diversion, a couple of quick children might be able to slip past the ticket taker onto the back of the bus without being noticed."

Anne looked shocked. "That's illegal."

"It's not like the bus isn't going there anyway, is it?" Barbara said.

Vicki smiled and nodded toward the older woman. "Mom always was a bit of a rebel. But she's right. Do you think you could create a diversion?"

Marcus grinned and ran a finger along his wand. "I think I might be able to."

Almost exactly forty-five minutes later, the bus pulled up in front of the station. "Express 474, with stops in Jackson, Memphis, and Chicago," the ticket taker called over the speakers.

The three women gathered their cards. "Go get 'em," Barbara said.

Vicki gave Marcus a smile that made him wish she were his mother. "Good luck."

"What now?" Kyja asked. The ticket taker glanced in their direction.

"Walk out the door, like you're waiting for someone," Marcus said. "Don't get close enough to the bus to make him suspicious. But be ready to move."

Kyja picked up Riph Raph and stuck him in her coat pocket. "Ew," he said. "It's still wet in here."

"You should like that," Marcus said evilly. "Frogs like wet places."

Sure enough, as soon as the bus driver checked the women's tickets, he took a quick look about the station, unzipped his jacket, and disappeared around the corner. As soon as he did, Marcus checked the ticket counter. The clerk was completely focused on a portable TV. Marcus was just thinking he might be able to sneak by without any diversion at all, when the two soldiers walked toward the bus, and the ticket clerk looked up from his TV.

Marcus pointed his wand at the soda machine. The big metal box rumbled, clunked, and a soda popped out of the bottom, rolling halfway across the station floor. The clerk glanced at the old man first, then at Marcus.

The old man eyed the soda. Marcus held up his hands and shook his head as if to say, *Weird, but I didn't have anything to do with it.*

When the clerk didn't do anything about the soda machine, Marcus waved his wand again. This time, the candy machine buzzed. Its lights blinked on and off. The clerk turned off his television, opened the door to his office, and came out. As the man approached the vending machines, Marcus waved his wand again. Another soda can flew out, and the clerk had to dodge to avoid getting hit. The candy machine buzzed even louder. Two candy bars dropped from their slots, and a bag of chips exploded, sending Cool Ranch Doritos everywhere.

The clerk peered through the glass and banged the machine. At the same time, Kyja peeked around the front of the bus.

Marcus started toward the door, but at that moment, the driver returned. He took the tickets from the three women, who climbed aboard with a concerned look back. The soldiers went next, and one of the young families.

By then the clerk had cleaned up the vending machines and was returning to his office. Kyja pointed toward the bus. If they didn't do something quickly, it would leave without them. The driver glanced at Kyja, "You getting on?"

"Um, not—not right now," Kyja stammered.

"Now or never." The driver started toward the bus. If Marcus was going to do something, it had to be now. And it had to be big.

Marcus pointed his wand at the hot dog machine. The motor turning the hot dogs suddenly sped up. At first it was only a little. But soon it was spinning so fast, the sausages began to slip off their metal spikes. The clerk—who was walking back from the vending machine—didn't notice what was happening until a shriveled sausage flew past his left ear like a guided missile. He looked up just in time to see another sausage soar over his head, hitting the actress on the TV in the face.

Marcus waved his wand at the drink machine. It clunked three times in quick succession, and boom, boom, boom, three sodas launched themselves across the bus station. The driver stepped away from the bus to see what was going on, and Marcus used air magic on the hot dogs, the drink machine, and the candy machines all at once.

It was like some kind of crazy video game. Hot dogs flew through the air. Sodas popped open, spraying their contents like geysers, the candy machine buzzed and rocked as though it might break into dance moves at any moment. Completely spooked, the clerk raced into his office and slammed the door behind him. He popped up just long enough to grab the phone off the counter, then disappeared from sight.

"Hello?" his panicked voice shouted from inside the office. "Police?"

The bus driver looked over at the ticket clerk. "What's going on, bud? You want me to grab a fire extinguisher or something?"

Marcus climbed off his chair. Scooting across the floor on the seat of his pants, he raced passed the nearly toothless old man, who was helping himself to a hot dog and a soda, and hurried to the bus. Kyja was waiting for him. She helped him up the steps, and by the time the driver returned, they were ducked down behind the ladies in the back.

"That was quite a diversion," Vicki said.

Marcus only shrugged. "Weird."

ATTACK

Tankum had never admitted defeat. Not in his mortal life, and not as a creature of stone. Not until now. Nothing he'd tried had worked. Not brute force. Not strategy. Not even trickery. With a mortal enemy, he could have worn them out. With a fixed count, even a count that far outnumbered his forces, he could have pared them down, changed terrain, improved his odds.

Even in Windshold, knowing he was outnumbered and overmatched, he had believed he could still win until the very last blade had taken his life.

But these creatures were like nothing he'd ever faced. For every one he destroyed, two took their place. Strategy didn't matter. If he flanked them, they simply turned to face the new threat with the same mindless ferocity.

When he tricked them into meeting his forces in the narrow mountain pass, he thought he might be able to hold them back. Or at least slow them down. But they simply ripped away the side of the mountain until it was wide enough for them to overwhelm his army.

His men were exhausted and dispirited. Most of the humans had been cut down or had fled. He couldn't blame them, although he'd never run from a battle and never would. But now, even the stone warriors and wizards were lagging. It wasn't because of their bodies growing weary; they no longer needed rest. But even a *stone* soldier's mind could only take so much before it began to break.

He could only hope the boy had reached Terra ne Staric in time to warn them.

Turning back to the fight, he raised his swords, charged against the overwhelming force, and shouted the battle cry he had lived by all his life. "To the death!"

PART 4

Battle at
Terra ne Staric

CHAPTER 37

AN OLD FRIEND

THE BUS RIDE TOOK LONGER than they would have liked, but at least they didn't go hungry. It turned out that Vicki, Anne, and Barbara had brought twice as much food as they could possibly eat. Kyja and Marcus, who hadn't had a meal since Icehold, gladly helped them finish off the sandwiches, cookies, and fruit. The women also taught them several card games, including Skip-Bo, Phase Ten, and Rook.

Riph Raph napped, caught the occasional fly buzzing around the bus window, and complained about being warty and squishy, when the women weren't close enough to overhear him.

Kyja was worried the ticket clerk might get in trouble and made Marcus promise to send money to the bus station to cover the costs of the sodas, candy, and hot dogs—even though Marcus argued that no one in his right mind would actually pay money for the disgusting Polish sausages. She also made him promise to send money to cover the cost of their tickets, although they didn't tell Barbara that.

The old woman seemed to be enjoying their prank far too much, and they didn't want to spoil her fun.

By the time the bus pulled into the terminal, it was a little after seven that night.

"Can we give you a lift somewhere?" Vicki asked. "My daughter is picking us up."

"No, thanks," Kyja said. "Our ride should be coming any minute." She and Marcus had discussed the possibility that the women might offer help once they reached Chicago. They both agreed that, although the women were very nice, the fewer people who noticed a boy and a girl traveling alone, the better it would be—just in case the Dark Circle came around asking questions.

As they left the bus station, Marcus said, "It's kind of strange."

"The city?" Kyja asked. Even though she'd been to Chicago once before, the size of it still amazed her. She could probably put every man, woman, and child in Farworld here, and not fill it up. And still, she found herself searching the face of every adult they passed, wondering if one of them might be her mother or father from Earth.

"Not the city," Marcus said. "The way people always help you."

Kyja paused. "What do you mean?"

Marcus scratched his head. "Every time we come to Earth, you do things for people, and they do things for you. Like those ladies on the bus. If I'd been here by myself, they might have been nice. They might even have felt sorry for me. But they never would have helped me sneak onto the bus or given me food. It's like you have a strange effect on everyone around you."

"That's crazy," Kyja said. If people were kind to her, it was just because she was kind to them. What was so special about that?

Marcus didn't say anything. But she could tell by his expression that he didn't agree.

"Which way?" Kyja asked as they exited the building.

Marcus pointed to the left. "The place we jumped from is about seven blocks that way."

"Can you make it?" Kyja asked. She'd tried not to say anything to Marcus about his pain, but it was clear he was suffering. Whenever he thought no one was watching, he squeezed the muscles in his bad leg, his eyes wincing, his teeth clenched.

"Sure," Marcus said. "It may just take me a little longer."

But they hadn't gone more than a few hundred feet when he had to stop to rest. Kyja glanced around. This wasn't the best part of town, and the sun was beginning to set. At this rate, it would be dark well before they reached the jumping point.

"Maybe I could carry you for a little bit," she suggested, although she wasn't even sure she could lift him.

"I'm fine." Marcus grimaced and forced himself to go almost another block before he collapsed against a chain-link fence, sweat beading on his face and arms.

Kyja looked through the fence to where a group of boys was playing a game she remembered from the last time they were here— *basselball*. Even though there were a million other things she and Marcus needed to be doing, a part of her longed to run onto the court and join kids her age in a game that didn't require any magic.

"Hey," a voice said from behind them. "Don't I know you?"

Kyja turned to look at the boy standing by the fence. At first she didn't recognize him. He was much taller than her or Marcus, with broad shoulders and long legs.

"You're the chicken girl, aren't cha?"

"Ty?" Kyja shouted. She couldn't believe it. What were the

chances of seeing the boy who'd helped them through the city over a year ago? And what had happened to him? He was so *big*.

Ty grinned, resting his basselball on his hip. "Thought that was you." He looked over at Marcus, who was still trying to catch his breath. "What's happening, little brother? You look like you've been working up a sweat."

Marcus wiped his forehead. "A little."

Ty glanced around curiously. "You get away from those dudes who was chasing you last time you was here?"

"Actually," Kyja said, "now we're chasing *them*."

"That's cool." He bounced his basselball. "Need me to drive you somewhere?"

Kyja's mouth dropped open. "You have a driving machine? Did you get your humbler?"

Ty laughed. "No. I ain't got no Hummer yet. But I got a real sweet ride."

Marcus frowned. "You're old enough to have a car?"

Ty suddenly lost control of the ball, bouncing it off his foot. "Well, it's sort of my car. Mostly it's my brother's. And I ain't exactly got a license yet. But he lets me drive it anyway. I'm just as good a driver as he is."

"Yes, please," Kyja said. "We would like a ride in your driving machine."

Ty grinned. "'Kay. I'll be back." He turned and disappeared down the street, bouncing his basselball as he went.

Marcus gave Kyja a knowing look. "See?"

"See what?" Kyja asked.

"What are the chances that in a city the size of Chicago, we'd run into the one person we know? And even more, that he would offer a ride at the very moment we need one? Doesn't that seem the least bit odd to you?"

"He's just nice," Kyja said.

"That's what you think," Riph Raph said, peeking out of her pocket. "He called me a chicken."

"Well you *were* a chicken the last time he saw you," Kyja said.

"I was nothing of the sort. I might look like a frog or a chicken or a . . . a *lizard* here on Earth. But once a skyte, always a skyte. There is no way to hide the noble race inside."

"'Noble race.'" Marcus chuckled, licking his cracked lips. "Maybe when you're racing away from danger."

Riph Raph scowled, but it was hard to look menacing as a frog.

"I'm telling you," Marcus said to Kyja, "something is going on with you, and it has been since the first time we came here. I'll bet Master Therapass knows about it too." He closed his eyes and rested his head against the fence.

Kyja was worried about him. His breathing was shallow, and even while he was resting, perspiration coated his face and soaked his shirt. She knew what it meant: Farworld was in danger. Maybe in the greatest danger it had ever faced. And Marcus's health was a reflection of that. The only way to help him was to find a way to stop—or at least slow down—the Dark Circle.

Several minutes later, a dark blue driving machine rolled down the street, its paint glittering under the setting sun as though bits of metal were embedded in it. Music like Kyja had never heard blared from its open windows as it pulled to the side of the street. The music had a rhythm that made Kyja tap her feet, although she couldn't understand most of the words.

Ty parked the driving machine, which was so close to the

ground that its sides nearly dragged on the street, and jumped out. "What you think?" he asked. "Is she fine looking or what?"

"'She'?" Kyja asked, not realizing that driving machines could be male or female. "Yes. *She's* beautiful."

Ty beamed.

Together they helped Marcus into what Ty called his *sweet ride,* and slid him to the middle of the front seat.

"He's not looking too good," Ty said when the three of them were in the car.

"I know," Kyja said. "But he'll get better when we arrive where we're going."

"Where are you going? The doctor? Or maybe the mall? Burger and a shake might make him feel better." Ty put his hand on the wheel that steered his driving machine and moved it away from the curb with a jerk that knocked Kyja back in her seat. "Sorry 'bout that. She got a lot of power."

Kyja could feel the machine vibrating through her body—or maybe it was the music. "We need to go back to the place you took us before."

Ty peeked at her out of the corner of his eye. "You gonna disappear again, ain't cha?"

"We have to," Kyja admitted. "It's the only way to help Marcus."

Ty stopped for a red light, and his hands tapped along with the music. "You some kind of magician or something?"

Kyja couldn't help laughing at that. He was the first person who had ever called her that. "No. I'm just a girl."

"Uh huh," Ty said, clearly not believing her. They passed building after building, each taller than anything in Farworld—even taller than the Aerisians' castle—and Kyja considered telling Ty the truth.

How would he react if she explained that she and Marcus were on a quest to gather four elementals to help them open a doorway between two worlds? Probably exactly as she would have responded if someone had told her about Earth before she met Marcus.

As they turned a corner, Kyja leaned over to check on Marcus, who seemed to be sleeping.

"Whoa!" Ty said, nearly running his driving machine off the road as he stared in her direction. "That thing real?"

Kyja looked down and realized that the pommel of her sword was poking out of her coat. She tried to push it back, but it was too late; Ty had already seen it.

"That's a *real* sword," Ty said. He stopped in front of the old, peeling building from where Kyja and Marcus had jumped into Water Keep before. "Can I look at it?"

Kyja didn't see the harm. He had brought them here; it was the least she could do. She took the sword out of her coat. The leather scabbard was warped and discolored after being soaked in water for so long. But as she drew the blade, it still gleamed.

"Holy smoking steel," Ty said, his eyes wide. "You know how to use it?"

Kyja couldn't help swelling a little with pride. "I'm as good with this as you are with your basselball. Maybe even better."

"You may be a girl," Ty said. "But you ain't *just* anything." He turned his head to read the writing on the blade. "'*The most powerful magic is inside you.*' What's that supposed to mean?"

"I'm not really sure," Kyja said, putting the sword back into its scabbard and sliding it inside her coat. "It's something a man told me once. A man who *is* a real magician. He said everyone has magic inside them. You just need to find it."

Ty thought about that for a minute before nodding. "I get that.

I always known I got something inside me. Maybe it's basketball. Maybe it's something else. But I'm gonna do something one day. Ain't gonna end up no bum sleeping in a cardboard box. Ain't gonna be doing no drugs neither. Not like my brother."

"I believe you," Kyja said.

Ty tapped his hands on his legs. "You gonna do something too. Something big. Knew it first time I seen you."

Kyja thought about what Marcus had said. Was it possible that there was something special about her? She didn't feel special. She turned to Ty. "When you ran into Marcus and me, it was just an accident, wasn't it?"

Ty blinked. "It's weird you ask. Tonight I was just hanging out, you know? Watching some TV. When all of a sudden, I get this feeling I need to head down to the court. Almost like I was *supposed* to find you. That sound crazy?"

Kyja began to nod, but then stopped. Maybe it wasn't crazy. Master Therapass had said she was supposed to save her world. She didn't know what she was supposed to do on Earth—how a girl could save such a huge and unimaginable world. But every time she came here, she got the feeling something was missing from this world. Something only she could give it.

"No," she said. "It doesn't sound crazy to me."

"Me neither." Ty looked out the window, where the sky had turned black and the streetlights were turning on. "So, you gonna do it now? You gonna disappear?"

"Not yet," Kyja said. "We have to wait until midnight. It's safer for Marcus that way." She reached for the door handle, but Ty stopped her.

"What cha doing? It's only nine. You ain't waiting out there for three hours."

"Don't you need to get your driving machine back to your brother?" Kyja asked.

Ty shrugged and gave her a shy smile. "Didn't exactly ask for permission to take her. So I don't guess it matters when I bring her back."

For the next three hours—while Marcus slept and Riph Raph squirmed in her coat pocket—Kyja asked Ty everything she could think of about Earth. For his part, Ty seemed to enjoy answering her questions, although he acted surprised by some of the things she didn't know and laughed when she mispronounced words.

He taught her about different kinds of music, scrolling through various "radio stations." "This is rap; it's def. That's rock. This is violins, and horns, and junk. That's cowboy garbage. Makes my ears hurt to listen to it."

He explained the game he liked to play—which was actually called *basket*ball, not *bassel*ball, as well as games called *football* and *baseball*.

"There's also some other games like soccer and tennis and stuff. But I don't know nothing 'bout them."

When midnight arrived, Kyja was actually sad to leave. She wanted to learn so much more. And hopefully, one day, she might be able to teach Ty about Farworld.

"We'd better go," she said.

"Yeah."

She gently shook Marcus, wishing she didn't have to wake him up.

"Is it time?" He reached up to rub his eyes and moaned in pain.

"Thank you for everything," she told Ty. "Maybe we'll see you again sometime."

"Maybe." Ty ran his hands across the top of the steering wheel. "That thing the magician told you, about having magic inside you?"

"Yes?"

"The dude was right. You got so much magic inside, I think it rubs off on other people just from being around 'em."

Kyja smiled and squeezed his hand. "Thank you." She took a breath and looked at Marcus. "Are you ready?"

He nodded. "As ready as I'll ever be."

"Good-bye," she told Ty. Then, closing her eyes, she found herself floating in the gray place between Earth and Farworld, and pushed. A moment later, she found herself floating in the strange half air, half water atmosphere of Water Keep.

But something was wrong. The blue city was dark, almost black, even though it was the middle of the day there. The sky that should have been blue-green was a sludgy brown, and the water on which buildings, statues, and trees normally floated in a constant parade of movement was still. The air had an odd stale smell to it.

A little girl with long, green hair turned around. She put a hand to her mouth—eyes wide. "You shouldn't have come here."

CHAPTER 38

THE TRAP

SITTING IN THE GREAT HALL, with all the water elementals but Tide, Marcus stretched out his leg, enjoying the weightlessness that made his pain almost bearable. Above him—or was it below him? It was hard to tell—Riph Raph flapped his wings crazily, trying to keep from spinning in a slow circle.

Cascade hunched on a sandstone bench, head resting in his hands. "Does Master Therapass know you're here?"

"No," Marcus said, realizing it had been a mistake not to tell the wizard where they were going. He had to be panicked by now.

"Can you see what's happening at Terra ne Staric?" Kyja asked.

"We can't see anything," said Mist, a thin woman with a silvery sparkle that now looked gray and dull. Every Fontasian in the room appeared defeated, their bodies slumped and heads hanging. Even Morning Dew, the little girl who was always laughing and playing, barely cracked a smile.

Marcus couldn't imagine how anything could keep the water elementals from seeing; their vision had always been so incredible, they could stare right through mountains. "I thought you could see out of anything that had water."

"Not anymore," Cascade said. "Ever since Nizgar-Gharat encased us in this land barrier, we can't leave Water Keep or see anything outside of it."

Nizgar-Gharat had to be the land elementals who had attacked them outside Land Keep.

"Can't you wash it away?" Kyja asked. "It looks like dirt."

"It's not just dirt," said Raindrop, a chubby woman whose color-changing robe was washed out and lifeless. "It's pure land magic—a prison we can't escape."

"But *we* can," Marcus said. "Kyja and I can jump to Earth, go outside the city walls, jump back, and—"

Cascade sighed. "You don't understand. The barrier was made using the land elementals' scepter of permanence. Anything created with it is unchangeable. You three can leave anytime you want, but we're locked in here forever."

"No!" Kyja jumped up too quickly and began floating away until Raindrop reached out and pulled her back. "We'll find a way to get the scepter and reverse the spell," Kyja said. "And if that doesn't work, we'll destroy the scepter."

"That's one of the things I find most interesting about you humans," Cascade said with a sad smile. "Your unwillingness to admit defeat in the face of impossible odds. Even if you could defeat Nizgar-Gharat and wrest away the scepter—which you can't—you could not undo this magic. You cannot break the spell without destroying the scepter first, and the scepter is indestructible."

Marcus hung his head. Then their quest was over. Even if they found a way to stop the Dark Circle's attacks, they couldn't open a drift without a water elemental.

"How did this happen?" Kyja asked.

"Tide," Mist said, her face contorted with anger. "He's been working with the Dark Circle all along."

"He's the one who pushed me outside the wall the first time you came here," Dew said, stomping her foot.

"It's my fault," Cascade said. "When Master Therapass sent me to find the traitor, I was so convinced it was the land elementals, I never considered it might be one of us. When I discovered Nizgar-Gharat's treachery, I came straight to our king. Not once did it cross my mind that he might be working side by side with the foul land elementals. He convinced me he had a plan to catch Nizgar-Gharat and any other land elementals cooperating with the Dark Circle.

"When I flooded Land Keep, I thought I was trapping the traitors, when, in fact, what I was doing was giving them a chance to steal the scepter and lock us in here. Now the only land or water elementals not trapped are Nizgar-Gharat, Tide, and Lanctrus-Darnoc."

Marcus slammed his fist against his leg. Pain flared in his knee and hip. If there was any way out of this, he couldn't see it.

"There has to be *something* we can do," Kyja said. "The Aerisians have given us the ability to go back in time. What if we went into the past and warned you about Tide?"

"Time travel? Interesting." Cascade thought for a minute before sighing. "No. That won't work either. It's hard to explain. You see, magic done with the scepter of permanence is impervious to time. If you went back in time, you would still find all of us trapped in Water Keep, even though the spell hadn't yet been cast."

Marcus shook his head in frustration. "What I don't understand is why Tide would agree to work with the Dark Circle in the first place. Doesn't he realize their goal is to destroy Farworld?"

"We are creatures of logic," Cascade said. "For Tide to choose an action this extreme, he must have been promised something of great value—although I can't imagine what."

"You're giving up?" Riph Raph squawked at the Fontasians. "I told Kyja we shouldn't expect anything from a bunch of fish farmers."

"What choice do we have?" Cascade pounded his fist on the bench, cracking the sandstone slab.

Marcus racked his brain, trying to come up with a solution. Whatever they did, the Dark Circle got there first. At least they'd been able to say they'd gathered half the elementals they needed to open the drift. But now even that accomplishment had been negated.

Kyja smiled sadly at Cascade. "It almost makes me wish we'd never started this quest in the first place. At least then you wouldn't be stuck here."

Something about Kyja's words struck a chord in Marcus's head, as if a flame had just been lit—burning, but so far away he couldn't make it out. He tried to follow the feeling through by talking it out. "Sure, if we hadn't started this quest, the Dark Circle wouldn't have trapped you here. And it's too late to go back and change it, because it wouldn't make any difference."

"No matter what you do, the barrier will still be there," Cascade agreed.

"Because it was created with the scepter. And the scepter can't be destroyed." It sounded completely hopeless. So why did he suddenly feel hope? He sat up straight. "We saw Nizgar-Gharat with the scepter only a few hours ago. When we swam out of Land Keep. If only . . ."

"What are you thinking?" Kyja asked.

"I'm not sure." Marcus rubbed his temples. A solution was there.

He knew it was. Something he had missed. If only he could see it. He went through all the facts he knew one more time. "The spell can't be broken as long as the scepter exists. And the scepter can't be destroyed. But even if we went back in time, the barrier would still be in place. So the only way to get rid of the barrier would be . . ."

Marcus jumped up, ignoring the pain in his body. That was it. The only way to break the spell was to get rid of the scepter. And there was only one way he knew of to get rid of the scepter. He turned to Cascade, "If we can take away the barrier, how quickly can you clear the water from Land Keep?"

"There would still be Tide to deal with, but we'd have him out-numbered. However, Nizgar-Gharat is all but invincible with the scepter. It's pointless though because removing the barrier is impossible."

"Isn't that what you said you liked about humans—that we don't understand impossible odds?" Marcus looked around at the Fontasians. "Kyja and I are going away for a few minutes. If nothing goes wrong, the barrier should disappear a few minutes after we leave. As soon as it does, free Land Keep. Then get to Terra ne Staric as quickly as you can. They're going to need your help against the golems. It might be too late already."

For the first time, Cascade lost his defeated look. "I don't know how you're going to do it. But, if you manage to free us, I will do everything in my power to save your people."

"We'll need to return to Terra ne Staric too," Marcus said. "How fast can we get there by frost pinnois?"

Cascade shook his head. "Zhethar is fast. But perhaps not fast enough."

"He would be if I created a storm," Raindrop said. "I could make a hurricane that would get you there in no time."

"What are you thinking?" Kyja asked Marcus.

"I'm thinking it's time to call Mr. Z again," Marcus said. "Where are you, you lovable little snail jockey?" he shouted.

Mr. Z appeared in front of them, holding a half-eaten sandwich. He was about to take another bite when he looked around and realized where he was. "What is this?" he cried. "I thought we agreed that you were done with my help."

"*We* didn't agree to that," Kyja said.

"Besides," Marcus said, clapping him on the back and sending the little man's sandwich flying. "You have to make up for nearly drowning us in Land Keep."

"Drowning? What is this about drowning? Preposterous. I only did what you asked. How was I to know that . . ." He eyed his sandwich as it slowly floated away. "Fine. Where do you want to go?"

"To the Abyss of Time," Marcus said.

"Too dangerous!" Mr. Z squeaked. He grabbed his glasses and rubbed them furiously with a handkerchief. "The spindle. The cracks. The whole thing could come down on our heads."

Marcus gave the little man a menacing look. "Do we need to talk to the Aerisians about this?"

Mr. Z rolled his eyes, but a moment later, the three of them stood on the tilted floor of the Abyss. As soon as he returned to normal gravity, Marcus's legs collapsed, and he slammed to the hard stone floor.

He had been hoping that the waterfall of the *Was* had frozen over again. But if anything, it looked even worse than before. A steady stream of water ran from the crack and down its face.

"I thought we decided going back in time wouldn't help," Kyja said, helping Marcus up.

"I'm going into the *Was*," Marcus said. "But I need *you* to go somewhere else." He took her hand. "This might be dangerous, so listen carefully. You're going into another portal. It's called the *Never Was*. It's extremely dangerous. No matter what happens, do not look at or talk to the woman in black. And don't go anywhere near the void."

"The Void of Unbecoming?" Kyja asked. "The one the air elementals told us about?"

"Yes. Stay far away from it." He turned to Mr. Z. "You stay with Kyja in the *Never Was*. Don't leave her, or I swear I'll make sure the air elementals hang you from your heels for the rest of your life."

"What are you going to do in the *Was*?" Kyja asked.

"I'm getting the scepter," Marcus said. "As soon as I do, I need you to pull me into the *Never Was*, just like you pulled me out of it before."

"No!" Mr. Z grabbed his gray hair and yanked so hard a tuft of it came out in his hand. "Are you crazy? Demented? Mad? Didn't you see what happened when you knocked over a shovel? This—this could bring the whole thing down on our heads."

"I know," Marcus said. "But there's no other way. Which is why, as soon as Kyja pulls me into the *Never Was*, you're going to get her out of there."

"I'm not leaving the Abyss without you," Kyja said.

"Maybe you should rethink this," Riph Raph said. "Larry the leprechaun here seems to be pretty sure this whole place is going to go *kaboom*!"

"No. I won't go without him." She turned to Marcus. "How will I know when you have the scepter?"

Marcus squeezed her hand. "If Mr. Z is right, I'm pretty sure you'll know."

CHAPTER 39

THE NEVER WAS

GOOD LUCK," MARCUS SAID. "Don't forget—do *not* listen to the woman. Don't even *look* at her if you can help it."

"I won't. You be careful too." Kyja watched as Marcus dropped to the floor and scooted toward the *Was*. The waterfall roared to life, startling her, and Marcus disappeared into the mist.

"Most irresponsible," Mr. Z muttered under his breath. "No idea of consequences. No consideration of repercussions. No respect for laws of time and space."

"Which way is the *Never Was?*" she asked.

Mr. Z trembled, and for a moment, she thought the little man was going to run. Instead he pointed a shaking finger at the waterfall to their right. Kyja glanced around the Abyss. The *Is,* the *Was,* the *Never Was.* Her eyes stopped on the fourth wall—the one Marcus had never named. Is that what he was so afraid of? For the tiniest moment, she considered seeing what was behind it before going into the *Never Was.* If she knew what was scaring Marcus, she could help him deal with it.

Just a peek.

But they didn't have time for that now. "Take me into the *Never Was,*" she told Mr. Z.

He pulled his hat down until it nearly covered his eyes, gave a deep sigh, and led her into the mist.

The first thing she noticed was the woman in black, sitting near an empty fireplace. The second thing was the intense feeling of despair which filled the room. If one could collect every failed plan, every shattered dream, every lost love, and put them all in one place, this was what it would feel like.

"You are alone," the woman said, without getting up.

"No, I—" Kyja began, before remembering she wasn't supposed to talk. Instead she studied the floor, shiny black, speckled with flecks of gold and silver.

"No parents. No brothers. No sisters. It must be very lonely."

Kyja glanced quickly at the woman, expecting some kind of monster. Instead, she saw the most astonishing blue eyes. Eyes that seemed to understand everything she'd ever been through.

"It must have been hard having no friends," the woman whispered. "Growing up as an outcast."

Kyja trembled. "I had Riph Raph. And Master Therapass. And the Goodnuffs."

"'Parents' who had *real* children who slept in their house. While you slept in the barn with the livestock. An old wizard who made you painfully aware of your own lack of magic. No children who would play with you, and your only friend a flying lizard."

"He's not a lizard." Kyja managed to pull her eyes away from the woman's gaze, feeling a small flame of anger.

But the woman quickly doused the anger, like a burbling stream putting out a fire. "You must have felt so alone. So unloved." Her words flowed into every crack of doubt and insecurity Kyja had, leaving her feeling cold and bleak. Why had Marcus sent her here, knowing what this woman could do?

Suddenly, the woman was at her side. "He's deserted you, like everyone else."

"I . . ."

Cold fingers traced her cheek. "The old man knew you were incapable of magic. He despised you. Your parents never wanted you in the first place. They were glad to see you go. And the boy sent you here—the home of lost souls, broken hearts, and miserable endings."

"No . . ." Kyja said. But could it be true? Marcus had told her not to listen to the woman. But maybe that was because he was afraid of her learning the truth.

Icy hands turned her head until she was looking at a swirling black pool. "He's not coming back. He left you here. But *I* understand. *I* know what you need."

———◆———

Marcus stepped into the *Was*, and water roared as mist filled his vision. Was this a mistake? Things had reached the point where almost any decision he made could be something that caused Kyja to get killed. But waiting and doing nothing could be even worse. He just had to hope that he was doing the right thing and try not to second-guess himself.

A second later, he entered the hallway—this time with only two walls, thank goodness. The last time, the three walls had made him a little queasy. He rubbed his sweaty hands on the front of his shirt.

"You're back!" a cheerful voice called.

Marcus turned to see the little boy from the first time he'd entered the *Was*, hopping on one foot toward him. Ignoring the boy, Marcus gripped his staff in one hand and raced down the hallway, his two legs whole again.

He didn't want to leave Kyja in the *Never Was* any longer than he had to. She didn't have the reason for wanting to throw herself into the void like he'd had. But he could still remember the way the place had made him feel—the way he'd been so convinced that unmaking himself was the only answer.

"You didn't bring the gunky man with you this time," the boy said, skipping beside him.

Marcus glanced at the paintings on the wall. They showed him and Kyja getting on the bus; he was nearly to the door he was looking for. "The *gunky* man?"

"The gunky man, the gunky man. The gunky man, the gunky man," the boy sang, still skipping. "I don't like him."

"Why not?" Marcus asked. He hadn't liked Mr. Z at first either, but he was getting used to little man's odd behavior.

"He's *different*." The boy shuddered and stopped skipping. "He can see more. Do more."

Marcus remembered the Aerisians saying that Mr. Z was a creature of pure magic. What did that mean, exactly? "Is that why you didn't show up when I was here before?"

The boy nodded. "Gunky."

Marcus reached the painting of him and Kyja standing in front of Nizgar-Gharat, the land elementals. Even in the painting, the land elementals looked terrifyingly strong. He hadn't given his plan much thought past this point. He knew what he needed to do, but not how to do it.

"You don't want to go in *there*," the little boy said, hopping from one foot to the other. "Let's go somewhere fun."

"I'd like to," Marcus admitted with a mouth that suddenly felt far too dry. "But I don't have any choice." Clutching his staff, he gave the boy a final glance and went through the door.

Given his choice, he would not have entered his past self at the exact moment he did. He just had time to see Kyja pull her sword and watch himself raise his wand before the land elementals flung his previous self through the air, slamming him abruptly to the ground.

"Ouch," the little boy said with a grin. "I told you not to come here."

Marcus stepped out of his body as Kyja screamed his name.

"I thought you said you couldn't feel pain in the *Was*," Marcus said to the boy.

As soon as he stepped out of his body, the pain disappeared. But he'd definitely felt it when he'd been thrown.

"You can't." The boy laughed. "Unless you're silly enough to choose to."

Nizgar-Gharat had just asked Kyja if she wanted a taste of what they'd given Marcus, and she was charging them with her sword. Marcus had to move quickly.

He raced across the field, leaping over a log as the land elementals swung their scepter, trying to use magic on Kyja. He jumped into the air, reaching. But he was too short. His fingers swung a good foot below the scepter.

Kyja stabbed Nizgar-Gharat, and Marcus tried for the scepter again as the land elementals cast their magic on a tree. But he still couldn't reach it.

Roots wrapped around Kyja, cutting into her skin.

"Leave her alone!" Marcus and his copy cried at the same time.

"Immune to *magic*. But not to pain," the purple lizard head said. "You will pay for this."

Marcus heard himself shout, "It's midday! There's no shadow."

Kyja reached for her amulet as Nizgar-Gharat raised the scepter. Suddenly Marcus understood what he had to do. As the land elementals smashed the scepter toward Kyja's face, she turned her head away. The Marcus on the ground closed his eyes.

Marcus raised his staff and swung it with all his might. He'd never held a baseball bat before—had never felt the power of putting your whole body into a swing and feeling the jolt of wood connecting with ball as you hit a home run. But when his staff caught the land elementals perfectly on the arm, knocking the scepter from their grip, he thought he knew what it must feel like.

At the same moment the scepter hit the ground, Kyja murmured something. An instant later, both she and Marcus disappeared.

As Marcus dove to the dirt and grabbed the scepter, the ground began to shake.

"That might not be the best idea," the boy said.

"What do you mean?" Marcus asked, just before something grabbed him by the back of the shirt, jerking him into the air. He turned to find both of Nizgar-Gharat's heads glaring at him.

"How did you do that?" one of the heads growled.

"Give us the scepter," the other hissed.

Marcus turned to the little boy. "I thought they couldn't see me," he yelped as clawed fingers dug into the flesh of his arm.

The boy shrugged. "They can't unless you're touching *them* or something from the past."

That would have been good to know. "Kyja!" he screamed as the shaking around him became worse. The land elementals reached for the scepter; Marcus yanked it away just in time. Claws slashed at his arm, drawing three angry red scratches down his wrist.

"Give it to us!" Nizgar-Gharat howled, shaking Marcus until his head rattled back and forth.

The land elementals reached for the scepter again. Marcus called up the strongest air magic he could think of. A blast of wind knocked the elementals backward at the same time he twisted in their scaly grip. The combined effect was enough to free him from their grasp, and he thumped to the ground, his head ringing.

"Drop the scepter!" the boy shouted. "Then they won't be able to see you."

But Marcus refused to.

"Kyja!" he screamed again. "Where are you?" He had the scepter in his hand; why wasn't she pulling him into the *Never Was*? A terrible thought occurred to him. What if she wasn't pulling him over because she couldn't? What if she'd already been lured into the Void of Unbecoming?

The land elementals charged at him, howling. Their sharp teeth gnashed, and their eyes blazed with hatred. "Give it to us!"

A blast of rocks, dirt, and sticks slammed against him, tearing his arms and face. A tree root wrapped around his ankles. He stumbled backward, calling on every spell he could think of. His wand was jammed in his pants pocket, but hot magic flowed through him anyway. Fire burned the roots around his feet. Air blasted away rocks and dirt.

But it wasn't enough. Nizgar-Gharat came at him with a fury of land magic he couldn't hope to hold off. The ground buckled under his feet. Boulders ripped themselves from the dirt. Entire trees tore up their roots, lunging at him.

"Drop it!" the little boy screamed.

"No!" he screamed back.

A fist-sized rock hit him in the side of the head, and he collapsed to the ground. Nizgar-Gharat towered over him, tongues hissing, wings flapping. They reached for the scepter clutched against his chest.

"Kyja!" he cried, not sure if she was even still alive. "Help me!"

CHAPTER 40

A Gold Ride

THE WOMAN TOOK KYJA'S HAND, guiding her toward the spinning darkness. "Look into its depths. See it take away your pain, your fear. You need never be alone again."

Kyja looked into the vortex and thought she saw stars in its depth. It was like staring up at the sky on a clear night. She could watch it forever, letting all her cares slip away in its whirling depths. "Yes, I . . ."

Something tugged at her arm, and she tried to shake it off. There was a sharp sting on the top of her head. Another on her arm. Something pecked at her toe. How was she supposed to stare into the pool with all of these annoyances?

She spun around to find Riph Raph yanking her hair, while flapping both wings. Mr. Z had his tiny arms wrapped around her legs.

"Would you two stop it?" she snarled. "I'm trying to . . ." But what *was* she trying to do? What was happening? How did she get here? She turned and realized she had somehow crossed the room. She was standing at the edge of the vortex.

"Kyja, get back!" Riph Raph screeched.

"Kyja, wake up!" Mr. Z shouted—and bit her toe.

The woman in black sat by the empty fireplace as though she'd never moved. But all around her, the room shook. Pieces of the black floor were shattered and tilted. A roaring filled the air.

Riph Raph and Mr. Z weren't the only ones calling her name. As if from the other side of a chasm, she heard a voice scream, "Kyja, where are you?"

Marcus. Suddenly she realized what was happening. He had the scepter. The Abyss was falling apart while she'd been in some kind of trance. How long had she been out?

"Kyja!" Marcus screamed. "Help me!"

She reached out with her mind, found the golden rope, and pulled so hard she nearly fell backward into the vortex. If it hadn't been for Riph Raph and Mr. Z, she would have.

Marcus slammed to the floor, his face a mess of cuts and bruises. One of his fingers was bent back so far it had to be broken.

"What happened?" Kyja cried, tears filling her eyes.

Marcus reached out to her with his bad hand, studying her face. "I was so afraid. I thought . . ."

"No time!" Mr. Z shouted. "We have to leave at once!"

In his good hand, Marcus grasped the scepter. "They didn't want to let it go. But when you pulled me, they couldn't hold on."

With a shout of triumph, he raised the silver scepter and flung it into the swirling vortex. The ground shook harder than ever, knocking Kyja to her knees.

Mr. Z grabbed both of them with a strength Kyja had no idea the little man possessed, and dragged them across the room.

Halfway to the door, she managed to get to her feet, and together, she and Mr. Z lifted Marcus and pulled him into the Abyss, where every waterfall was now cracked, with running water spilling from multiple spots.

The floor was tilted so far to one side that Kyja could barely stay on her feet. As they dragged Marcus toward the *Is,* a huge chunk of ice broke from the *Was,* sending deadly shards flying through the air.

"Get out!" Riph Raph screamed, flying straight for the mist of the *Is.*

Kyja stepped into the mist, and they were back in Water Keep. This time, it was the Water Keep she remembered. Blue-green light filled the air. Trees and fountains floated past in a profusion of color and sound.

"You did it!" Morning Dew shouted, throwing handfuls of golden balls into the air.

Kyja turned to Mr. Z, expecting him to be livid. But the little man was dancing a jig, black boots a blur as he spun around the room. "I'm alive!" he sang. "Alive, alive, alive." He threw his hat up, caught it in his mouth, and, to Kyja's amazement, bit a huge chunk out of the brim. "I thought we were goners for sure." He laughed, ramming the hat back on his head, and twirled Morning Dew until her long hair whirled around her like an umbrella.

"That's right!" Riph Raph whooped, looping crazily above their heads. "Take that, Nizgar-Stinkrat."

Marcus was the only one who didn't seem to be celebrating. "Cascade?" he croaked.

"He's on his way to Land Keep," Mist said, the silver clouds around her as sparkly as ever.

Kyja knelt by Marcus's side. He looked terrible. She mopped

some of the blood from his face with the hem of her robe. "Are you all right?"

"Fine," he said, his voice hoarse. "What about the golems?"

"There's no time to lose," Raindrop said. She scooped Marcus and Kyja up in her pudgy arms and raced for the nearest portal. Kyja just managed to grab the tip of Riph Raph's wing as they hurried past, or they would have left him behind. The skyte gave an outraged yelp anyway.

Raindrop plunged through a colored blob that transported them outside the city walls, then ran to a waiting Zhethar.

"Didn't think I'd see the three of you again," the frost pinnois said as Raindrop tucked them into a thick stack of blankets.

"You're still going to freeze your noses off. But at least these should help," she said.

Zhethar flapped his large blue wings, icicle-feathers tinkling like glass, and Raindrop raised her arms. A blast of wind hit so hard, it nearly knocked them from the frost pinnois. Kyja pulled the blankets tighter around them, burrowing into Zhethar's broad back.

"Stay on top of the clouuudddddssssss!" Raindrop called, her words snatched away by the storm.

Zhethar dove straight into the hurricane, forcing Kyja to duck beneath the blankets or risk being sucked away.

"Let's see a dragon try that!" the frost pinnois shouted, and they were off.

CHAPTER 41

THE TIME FOR TRUTH

MARCUS KNEW THEY WERE TOO LATE the moment they arrived at Terra ne Staric. The golem army was already there, smashing the city walls with powerful fists and hurling boulders over it. Tankum and his army fought to block the east gate while a group of human wizards and warriors protected the west. But even before they were close enough for the frost pinnois to land, it was clear the city wouldn't be able to hold out for long.

"Where's Cascade?" Kyja said, searching the battlefield.

"He's not here." Marcus shook his head. "Neither are the land elementals."

A ball of fire was hurled from the top of the tower, engulfing four of the golems at the west gate, turning them into dust.

"Master Therapass!" Marcus shouted.

A cheer arose from the men and women fighting there. But even before the flames had died away, six more golems rose out of the ground where the four had been destroyed. It was hopeless. Even with the scepter gone, it was clear that the army Tide and Nizgar-Gharat had created was too powerful.

"Take us to the tower," Marcus said.

Zhethar glided down to the balcony.

Master Therapass turned as Kyja slid off the frost pinnois's back and helped Marcus down. "There you two are," the wizard said. "I've been so worried."

Marcus had never seen the old man look as exhausted as he did now. Deep lines cut into his face, and his eyes seemed to be staring up from the bottom of a pair of dark wells. "Is there any hope at all?" Marcus asked, leaning against the wall to rest his bad leg.

The wizard frowned. "As long as there are people willing to stand up against evil, there is always hope." But just as he said that, a section of the south wall collapsed beneath an onslaught of golems. "To the south!" the wizard shouted. "Fill the gap!"

He raised his staff and cast a spell Marcus didn't recognize. Whatever it was, it didn't do much. A small pile of dirt filled the space where the wall had fallen, but it was barely enough to make the golems have to step over it. "Blasted land magic," the wizard muttered.

If land magic still wasn't working, that might mean Cascade hadn't managed to free Land Keep after all.

The wizard swung his staff again, and a lightning bolt fried the golems trying to get through the opening.

Marcus waved his wand, and a blast of air knocked a golem off its feet.

"Where did you get that?" Master Therapass asked, studying the silver wand.

"Graehl gave it to me," Marcus said. "It's shadow wood."

The wizard nodded. "Tell me where you've been and what's happened."

Fighting side by side with Master Therapass, Marcus recounted everything he and Kyja had done over the last few days.

Down below, the citizens of Terra ne Staric were putting up an incredible effort, but piece by piece, the walls gave way until, at last, a horn sounded.

"To the tower!" Master Therapass shouted. "Retreat to the tower!"

In the city, the cry was repeated as warriors and wizards gave up their positions and raced for the hill where the tower stood. Hundreds of golems followed like a brown sea.

Master Therapass collapsed against the wall. "I think you and Kyja should jump to Earth now. It's only a matter of time before the tower falls as well." As if to emphasize his point, a boulder slammed into the tower below them, ripping a hole in the stone wall. "Stay on Earth, for a few days, until the battle is over. Then return to whatever is left. Perhaps you can still find a way to free the Aerisians."

Marcus nodded. It was just like he'd seen in the *Will Be.*

The *Will Be.* He'd forgotten all about that. "Kyja!" he called, turning around.

She was gone.

"She went below," Zhethar said. "With the skyte."

Of course she had. She wouldn't stand around while a battle went on around her. She'd gone to fight. Marcus shoved his wand into his pocket and crawled to the stairs. What had he been thinking? If the city was being destroyed the same way he'd seen it would be in his vision, it meant that Kyja's death was close. Maybe that's how he killed her—he'd been focused on other things while she went to her death.

"Find Kyja and get her to Earth!" the wizard shouted, casting spells at the golems charging the base of the tower.

Marcus didn't have enough breath to answer. His arms and legs screamed in pain, but he wouldn't let himself think about that. Scooting on the seat of his pants, he slid down one step of the tower after another.

"Kyja!" he screamed "Riph Raph!"

Inside the tower, people ran into one another in a mass of confusion. Children cried while their mothers looked for places to hide them. Warriors with blood streaming from open wounds charged down the stairs and retreated up them in equal numbers. Explosions rocked the walls, and screams filled the air. Wafting through it all was the thick stink of mud.

How had he been so stupid? Why hadn't he made Kyja stay with him? He knew she was a good fighter, but she had no chance against creatures as powerful as the golems.

Taking turns cursing himself and screaming Kyja's name, Marcus hurried down the steps. But it wasn't fast enough. He was less than a third of the way down the staircase when the air began filling with smoke. The golems had set fire to the base of the tower. There would be no way for anyone to escape.

Marcus realized what he had to do. At the next landing, he crawled from the stairs into the hallway, checking each door until he found an empty room. He had to go back into the Abyss of Time and enter the *Will Be*. He had to discover how Kyja would die and find a way to stop it from happening. If it was already too late—he could barely stand to think about the possibility—if she was already dead, he'd go into the *Was* and change the past.

The guide in the *Will Be* had told him that the future couldn't be changed, but now that he could change the past, everything was different.

"Mr. Z!" he shouted. "Mr. Z!"

The little man didn't come. What if he *wouldn't* come? What if what happened with the scepter had been too much for him? Marcus tasted blood and realized he'd bit through his lip.

He screamed as loud as he could. "Mr. Z, come here now! I command you!"

"*Command?*"

Marcus turned to find the little man standing behind him, his face a mask of anger. "*You* command *me?*" He ripped off his coat, tore it down the middle, and threw it to the floor. "Enough. More than enough. This is too much, I say. You. Do. Not. Command. Me."

Marcus had never seen Mr. Z so angry. "I'm sorry," he said. "I didn't mean to say that. It's just . . . I didn't think you were going to come, and I have to go back into the Abyss one last time."

"No." Mr. Z folded his arms across his chest.

"What do you mean, 'no'?"

"I won't take you." Mr. Z picked up his coat, folded the torn pieces, and wrapped them in a bundle. "We're done. Finished. Complete. Kaput."

"Please," Marcus begged, fighting the panic rising inside him. "One last time. I *have* to go back."

"Don't you understand, lad? Have you been hit on the head too many times? If you enter the Abyss now, you will never come out."

"I don't care. It doesn't matter if I come back. You don't even have to go with me. Just get me to the pit, and I'll do the rest myself."

"I'm sorry." Mr. Z turned to walk away, but Marcus dove toward him, tackling the little man to the floor.

"You *will* take me," he snarled, jabbing his wand into Mr. Z's chest. "Or I swear . . ."

"Marcus!" Kyja cried, stepping into the room. "What are you doing?"

A weight lifted from Marcus's chest. "You're okay," he sobbed. "You're not . . ."

"What are you doing to Mr. Z?" Kyja pulled him off.

"The lad's gone crazy," Mr. Z said, his voice high and squeaky. "He wanted me to take him into the Abyss again. I said it would kill him. But he didn't care. He attacked me."

"Is that true?" Kyja asked.

Marcus turned away, but she walked around him, forcing him to look at her. "Why did you want to go back into the Abyss? What haven't you been telling me? It's about whatever is behind the last portal, isn't it?"

Marcus tried to speak, but his throat was locked. After all of their time together, he couldn't lie to Kyja. But he also couldn't stand for her to know the truth—to know what a terrible person he really was. Tears dripped down his face.

Kyja sat beside him and took his hand. "The one thing we have over the elementals is trust. With all of our mistakes and flaws, we still have that. If you don't trust me enough to tell me whatever it is that you've been hiding, what do we have left?"

Marcus looked into her eyes for a moment, unable to stand what he saw there. She *did* trust him, and how was he going to repay her? He had to let her see what he really was.

He turned to Mr. Z. "Show her."

"Eh?" Mr. Z cupped his ear. "Afraid I didn't hear you."

Marcus swallowed, the salty taste of tears thick in his throat. "You're a creature of pure magic. If you won't take me into the Abyss, show her what I saw in the *Will Be*. Can you do that?"

Mr. Z took off his glasses and turned them between his fingers. "Well, I . . ."

"Please," Marcus begged. "Do this one last thing, and I promise I won't ask you for anything ever again. Show her what's going to happen. Show her what I really am, and your bargain with the Aerisians will be fulfilled."

The little man placed his glasses on his big red bulb of a nose and sighed. "Very well."

CHAPTER 42

TRUST

K YJA FOUND HERSELF STANDING in a heavy, swirling mist. All sounds of the battle outside the tower were gone. Marcus was standing beside her. "Where are we?"

"In the future," Marcus said, his voice thick with emotion. "When I went through the mirror in Elder Ephraim's office, I entered into the *Is,* the *Was,* and then the *Will Be.* There was a man there who warned me that if I went any further, I would lock my future in place. But I didn't listen." He swallowed. "I wish I had."

For a moment Kyja thought about turning back. Did she really want to see what had terrified Marcus so much? But if she turned away now, how could she help him face whatever he was afraid of? She reached out to take his hand, but her fingers went through his. Apparently neither of them was really there. "Show me," she said. "Whatever it is, I'm ready."

Together they stepped out of the fog and into a room she recognized immediately. She'd spent countless hours there studying magic, trying to understand why she was different from all her friends.

The tower seemed oddly quiet. "Where is everyone?"

Marcus turned and led her out of the study and down the hall, to a window that looked out over the city. Kyja sucked in her breath. It seemed even worse now than it had during the battle. Terra ne Staric was in ruins—walls crushed, gates burned, farms and houses destroyed. The thought of how many lives must have been lost made her sick.

Turning to the west, she saw a large group of people gathered together. "It looks like most of the town. What are they doing?"

Marcus's face was as white as the bedding Kyja used to hang on the Goodnuffs' line at the beginning of every week.

"It might be better if you didn't know."

Kyja's stomach churned. There was something she was missing here. "Whatever it is, I want to know."

Marcus sighed. "All right."

Suddenly, they stood outside the west gate—one of the few areas where grass still grew and the ground wasn't torn up by the golems' attack. Kyja moved through the crowd. Every face was someone she knew. All of them were weeping. This had to be a funeral.

Of course, many lives had been lost in the battle. There would be many funerals. But who was loved enough—cherished enough— to bring the entire town out like this? Suddenly, she knew, and a ball of ice lodged in her throat. There was only one person who had affected this many lives for good.

"Master Therapass!" she screamed, racing through the crowd. She ran to the glass coffin as they prepared to lower it into the ground. She skidded to a halt. Master Therapass stood at the edge of the grave, openly weeping.

If he wasn't being buried, who was?

On wooden legs, she walked to the coffin and looked inside. Her mouth went dry as she saw who lay on the white satin pillow.

"No," she whispered, feeling dizzy. She turned to Marcus just behind her. His head hung, hair covering his face. Tears streamed down his cheeks, dripping from his lips and chin. She felt numb.

"How? How did I . . ." She couldn't seem to form the words. "Was it the battle? An accident?"

———◦———

Marcus couldn't take it anymore. He pulled himself out of the vision, knowing what Kyja would see—what she would discover about him—unable to see the vision again. That made him a coward as well as a murderer. Outside, he still heard the sounds of the battle going on, but none of that seemed to matter anymore.

Pacing the small tower room, he imagined Kyja going to the dungeon, discovering the cell holding her murderer. Learning who it was. What would her reaction be when she realized the truth?

First shock, then revulsion, and finally, horror.

Mr. Z watched him silently, but Marcus couldn't bear to meet the little man's eyes.

When Kyja finally returned, he buried his face in his hands, sobbing. "I'm sorry," he cried, his body shaking. "I'm so sorry."

———◦———

When Kyja returned, Marcus was shaking in the center of the room. A hundred questions filled her mind, but the first thing she did was hurry to him and put her arms around his trembling shoulders.

She held him close. "It's all right."

"Don't you understand?" he cried, jerking away from her. "You're going to die, and it's going to be my fault. I murder you."

Kyja searched her heart for anger or a sense of betrayal. But despite all her questions, none of her feelings for Marcus had changed.

"Now can you see why I couldn't tell you?" Marcus asked, his voice muffled. "I wanted to change the future, but I can't. It's too late. You must hate me."

She drew him back into her arms, squeezing so tightly he couldn't pull away. "I don't hate you. I love you."

Marcus looked up at her, his eyes red. "How can you say that after what you just saw?"

Kyja struggled to find the right words. "I don't want to die. But if I have to, I'd want it to be with the person I trust most. And that's you." She wiped her eyes. "You trusted me enough to show me the worst part of you. And I trust that whatever you do will be for the right reasons. You're the person I care about most in my entire life. That's not going to change."

Something clicked in Kyja's pocket. She reached into it, trying to remember what was there, and pulled out the silver box. "The Exsalusentia," she murmured. "It's open."

Marcus stared at it as Kyja lifted the lid. A pearly blue light rose from inside the box and disappeared. "How?" he asked, turning to Mr. Z.

The little man was grinning. "I trusted you'd find the key eventually."

"Trust," Kyja said. "That was the key to open the box. It's why the air elementals could never open it—because they don't have trust."

Marcus ran a finger across the symbol for air. "But if the box is open, that means . . ."

From outside of the tower came a rushing sound Kyja didn't recognize. She helped Marcus up, and the two of them hurried to the window.

"Look!" she cried, pointing upward. The sky was filled with hundreds of sleek, silver-gray creatures. On the back of each one was a figure. Kyja couldn't tell for sure, but she was almost positive the first two were Caelum and Divum.

"It's the air elementals!" she shouted. "They've come to help us."

Kyja turned to find Mr. Z climbing back into his snail. "Are you leaving?"

Mr. Z examined his coat, which was still ripped completely down the middle, and his hat, which had a large chunk missing from the brim. "I'm afraid I'll be spending some time with my tailor. Frightful fellows, tailors. Always keeping me on pins and needles."

"Thanks for your help," Marcus said. "Will we see you again?"

Mr. Z rattled a pair of dice in his hand. "I wouldn't bet on it." He opened his fingers, looked at the dice, and smiled just a little. "Then again, I wouldn't bet against it either."

CHAPTER 43

THE BATTLE

"COME ON," KYJA SAID, wrapping Marcus's arm around her shoulder. "Let's go help."

As they started down the spiral staircase, he felt a new sense of optimism in the tower—a new energy.

"Take up your swords!" someone shouted.

"Drive them back!" a skinny man yelled, and Marcus recognized the cranky little wizard who had complained about being woken up by Jaklah's message.

"Did you hear?" Jaklah called, racing past them. "Help has arrived. From the air. I hear it might be angels!"

Marcus grinned. The Aerisians were definitely their saving angels. Outside, the battle still raged at the base of the tower. Wizards of all ages fired blasts of light, fire, and air into the golem army. At the same time, unseen hands from above sent them reeling.

The golems seemed confused, unsure whether to concentrate on the fight in front or above them. One of the giants grabbed a stone that had fallen from the tower wall and lifted it over his head, taking aim at the nearest air elemental.

"Put that down, big boy!" Tankum charged at the golem, twin blades glinting in the sun. "You won't be needing that!" His right blade flashed, and the golem's leg separated from his body just above the knee. His left blade swung, and the arm holding the rock dropped to the ground.

"I'll be back!" Kyja yelled. She lowered Marcus to the grass on the side of the hill, then ran straight into the middle of the fray. "No one takes our city!" she shouted, her silver-blue sword a blur of motion. Dirt flew about her head in a dark brown cloud as she stabbed and slashed.

"You heard the lady!" Riph Raph screeched, raining blue fireballs that did little but looked impressive.

"Wait!" Marcus called, afraid that she'd get hurt. But Kyja seemed to be having so much fun that he couldn't bear to call her back. Instead he pulled out his wand and attacked the closest golems with all the spells he knew. It felt great to have the hot power of magic flowing through him again. He discovered that he was just as good as the older, more experienced wizards.

From the top of the tower, Master Therapass rained down fire while calling out directions and encouragement. "To your right, Graham!" he called to a blacksmith swinging a heavy axe. "Behind you!" he yelled to a pair of soldiers wielding swords that burned with a bright red fire. "Good work."

A huge black caldron bounced down the hill, passed Marcus, and knocked a golem flying like a bowling pin. "That's for trying to burn down my kitchen!" Bella shouted. "And believe me, there's more where that came from!"

Slowly, the golems were driven back outside the city wall.

Encouraged by their success, the citizens pressed their attack to the edge of the Two Prongs River.

Reaching the muddy banks, the golems seemed on the edge of defeat. But almost as though their goal had been the river all along, dozens of new golems rose from the mud. Injured golems grew new limbs and healed their wounds.

With a sick feeling, Marcus watched the army grow and re-group. Repaired, and with greater numbers, the golems drove their attackers back again, forcing them toward the city walls.

"Not so fast," a voice called.

Marcus craned his neck to see Divum flying straight over his head. The rest of the Aerisians formed a V behind her. "Wind!" she screamed. "All the wind you have!"

At her words, a huge gust of air blew across the battlefield, then another, and another. Wizards and warriors were thrown from their feet. Wands blew away, and staffs flew through the air like toothpicks.

"No!" Marcus screamed. Didn't the Aerisans realize what they were doing? The wind was knocking down the humans, but the golems were too big to be affected by it—too strong. Heads low-ered, they marched into the tornado.

The Aerisians had just guaranteed Terra ne Staric's defeat.

Then he saw something that didn't make sense. One of the golems' arms cracked and blew right off its body. Another golem took a step, and its leg crumbled. One of the monsters tried to turn, and the top half of its torso broke away from the lower half, crash-ing to the ground in a cloud of dust.

The golems were drying out. The wind was so strong that it was drying the clay, making it weak and brittle.

Seeing what was happening, the humans got to their feet. With the wind at their backs, they charged toward the weakened golems.

Kyja and Tankum fought side by side, raining blows that shred-ded the creatures.

"You've learned a thing or two, girly!" the warrior called.

"You're not too bad yourself!" Kyja yelled back. "I'll teach you a few things when this is over."

"Get 'em!" Marcus whooped from his spot on the hill.

Once again the golems were backed to the edge of the shallow river. With the muddy riverbed to draw on, they withstood the Aerisians' attack. Slowly, their forces rehydrated. The battle was a standoff. As long as the golems had water, they were unbeatable. The Aerisians managed to keep them from advancing toward the city. But how long could they keep it up?

A deep rumbling sound filled the air. Marcus looked to the north. Lightning flashed, and clouds were filling the horizon so thickly they looked like a solid gray wall. Rain was the last thing they needed. In a storm, the golems would have all the moisture they needed.

As if the thought of a storm had rejuvenated them, the golems gave one last surge. Air elementals and humans fought in a desper-ate battle at the edge of the river. But it couldn't last. Already, the human forces were tiring, while the golems didn't seem to need any rest at all.

Thunder roared again, the rumbling growing louder. He couldn't tell what was making the sound. Then he saw it. Racing down the bed of the Two Prongs River came a wall of churning water at least fifty feet high. Perched at the very top was a figure in a blue robe. Cascade!

"Get back!" the Fontasian shouted, his white hair rippling in the wind.

Just above Cascade, Raindrop flew, her robe snapping behind her in a rainbow of color. The storm boiled at her heels. Rain so heavy that it seemed to fall in blankets instead of drops pounded the ground.

"Get away from the river!" Marcus screamed, cupping his hands to his mouth.

Tankum recognized the danger and drove his forces back, carrying those who were too injured to move.

The golems saw what was coming. But either they were too stupid to understand the danger, or they were too slow to avoid it. As the wall of water came roaring down the riverbed, the golems turned into it, raising their fists as if they could fight the water itself.

Cascade pumped his fists in the air, shouting, "This is for you, Tide!" It was the most emotion Marcus had ever seen from him.

The wall of water lifted the golems like toys, ripping them limb from limb as they tried to attack it. Chunks of brown mud swirled in the melee, then disappeared.

Two minutes later, the flood was gone, and so were the golems.

For a moment, no one seemed to understand what had happened. Then a cheer went up.

"Victory!" Tankum yelled, raising his fists in the pounding rain. "Victory!"

Soldiers pulled off their helms and held them in front of them to catch the water. Townspeople celebrated—husbands and wives kissing each other as they slipped in the mud, parents picking up their sopping wet children and spinning them around.

Marcus found an abandoned staff and limped to the overflowing riverbank. His body felt better already. Not completely healed, but some.

"We did it!" Kyja screamed, throwing her arms around Marcus's neck and kissing him on the cheek.

Cascade rose up out of the river, his expression serious again. "I apologize for my late arrival," he said. "I was not aware of how long it would take to empty Land Keep. Nor did I account for the small amount of water available in local tributaries for the flow I wished to create in the Two Prongs River."

"You made it," Marcus said. "That's what counts." He held his hand up in the air, palm forward. "Give me five."

Cascade examined Marcus's hand. "Five what?"

Divum landed her ciralatus beside them. "Have you seen Caelum?"

Kyja shook back her wet hair. "I thought he was with you."

"Who cares?" Marcus said. "We won!" He was exhausted, but at least it was over. They'd opened the box, freed the Aerisians, and protected the city. Now, all he wanted to do was curl up into a ball and sleep.

"The battle is not yet over," Divum said.

Marcus looked around. "What do you mean? The golems are gone."

"We won." Kyja wiped her hands across her face, leaving muddy streaks. She looked as exhausted as he felt. "Thank you for your help."

"The battle *here* is over," the Aerisian said. "But another begins tonight."

Cascade cupped his hands to his eyes and stared into a distance none of the rest of them could see. "The air elemental is right. The Summoner's army will reach Icehold shortly after sunset."

Icehold! Marcus had forgotten all about that. A sick feeling of despair filled him. Hadn't they done enough? Wouldn't the Dark Circle ever leave them alone? "Can you get there in time?" he asked Cascade.

The Fontasian nodded. "Yes. But I would be no match for a Summoner by myself."

"What about you?" Kyja asked Divum.

"We can reach Icehold," Divum said. "But our mounts need rest first. We used them up getting here. Someone must arrive first and warn them."

Cascade could go, but would the people of Icehold believe a blue boy with white hair and no sense of humor? Or would they assume he was just another monster from the other side of the Forest of Before Time and attack him?

Kyja rubbed her eyes. Blood dripped from a dozen nicks and cuts on her arms and legs.

It isn't fair, Marcus thought. *Can't we get a single moment to celebrate any of our victories?*

"We have to go to them," Kyja said. "We promised."

Marcus nodded. "But how? There's no way we can make it in time."

"Am I correct in understanding that someone is in need of transportation?"

Marcus turned to see Zhethar basking in the rain. Drops hit his icy scales and froze in a glittering sheen.

"Can you take us to Icehold before the Summoner arrives?" Kyja asked. "On Mr. Z's racing snail, it took at least a day."

"Pah!" the frost pinnois spat. "Snails are for eating, not racing."

"I'll give you a storm to push you, one like you've never seen," Raindrop said. "And a well-placed storm might slow the Dark Circle's forces as well."

Marcus looked from the Fontasians to the frost pinnois and sighed. It was going to be an icy ride, and no matter how warmly they dressed, they would probably freeze to death on the way.

Then he looked at Kyja, who was grinning widely. The rain made her hair and clothes cling to her like a waterlogged scarecrow.

He wiped a hand across his face and grinned. "Let's do it!"

CHAPTER 44

THE FLYING WEASEL

ZHETHAR WASN'T JOKING about being fast. It was hours before sunset when the frost pinnois landed in the street outside The Seven-Fingered Lady, the inn where they'd stayed the last time they were there. Raindrop hadn't been kidding about the storm either. Kyja's arms were so cold she could barely bend them, and Marcus hobbled like an old man as he got down.

"I had no idea anything could fly so quickly," Kyja said.

The frost pinnois chuckled. "I was coasting on the last part. So you wouldn't think I was showing off."

People from the nearby buildings and streets were coming out to gawk at the huge ice creature. Several of them held swords and looked distinctly unfriendly.

"Maybe you'd better go," Marcus said.

"But thanks for your help." For once, Kyja didn't give the creature a hug. She was already cold enough. With a tinkle of frozen feathers, Zhethar flapped his wings and lifted into the air.

"Come on," Marcus said after the frost pinnois flew out of sight.

"Let's get to the wall to see if we can find that man we met—before people start asking questions."

"Did we actually meet him?" Kyja asked. "Or does that not count since we went back in time?" Were the two of them already inside the inn eating with Mr. Z? If so, they could give themselves advice that would help out a lot. But if they did, would they still be here now?

"No clue," Marcus said. "This whole time travel thing is way too confusing." Using the staff he'd found by the tower, he followed Kyja to the city wall.

Kyja thought the city felt warmer than the last time they were here. The streets were still icy, and the buildings were still covered with snow, but now the ice was slushy and the snow was melting from the roofs in a steady stream of water.

"Feels like the Fontasians are getting the weather straightened out," Marcus said.

It took them a while to find the man, but eventually they discovered him talking to three soldiers wearing heavy armor.

"Admiring our wall, be ye?" the man asked Marcus.

"Mined straight from the Altarian Mountains," Marcus said.

The man looked surprised. "Took ye for outlanders. Per'aps I was mistaken?"

"No," Kyja said. "You're not wrong. We're from Terra ne Staric."

"With the weather clearing up a mite, the view should be a good one."

"We aren't here for the view," Marcus said. "We've come with a warning. Your city will be attacked tonight."

"Attacked, is it?" One of the soldiers laughed. "Well, the odds be good on that. We be attacked at least thrice a week."

"Not like this," Marcus said. "A Summoner is on its way right now. With a bunch of Thrathkin S'Bae."

The soldiers' faces hardened. "Summoner? Never heard o' such a beast."

"You *have,*" Kyja said. "You just didn't know that's what it's called. Remember when one of the soldiers told you about a big, red creature with a body like a snake, huge wings, and teeth as tall as a man? With an army of undead?"

All four men burst into laughter. "Ye be spending too much time in ale houses, ye do. Listening to tall tales. There be no such creature."

"There *is,*" Marcus said. "And it's coming tonight with a bunch of dark wizards and Fallen Ones. You have to prepare."

"Listen here, lad." The man they'd met before laughed. "Even if there do be such a creature—and I not be saying there be or there don't—the city guard would stop it like that." He snapped his thick fingers.

"You don't understand," Kyja said. How could she make him believe her?

"If you don't prepare now," Marcus said, "your whole town will be destroyed."

The man from the wall stopped laughing. "Enough!" he snapped. "If it's a look ye be wanting, I'll have a man take ye up the wall. But I'll hear no more talk of make-believe creatures and destroyed cities. So either be up the wall, or be on your way."

Marcus turned to Kyja. "He won't listen. The Dark Circle is going to come, and Icehold will be destroyed just like Windshold."

That was it. *Windshold.* That's how they could convince him.

"Listen to me carefully," Kyja said. "I know this sounds crazy, but we've been here before on this night. You took us up to the wall and showed us how to—what did you call it?—*scry*, I think. You just don't remember."

The man opened his mouth. But Kyja couldn't let him interrupt. "Later that night—which is tonight—your town was destroyed by a Summoner, a dozen or more Thrathkin S'Bae, and the same kind of army that destroyed Windshold. I can prove it."

The man rubbed his chin. But at least he was listening. "And how would ye do that?"

"Your name is Freeman Arstel."

"Ye could'a heard that anywhere."

Kyja pointed to the leather string around his neck. "The medallion hanging from your neck—it's a flying weasel."

Freeman's eyes widened.

"It belonged to your brother," Kyja continued. "He called it his good luck charm. But he died in Windshold anyway. You wear the medallion in his memory."

The man stared at Kyja. "How could ye be knowing that?" he asked softly.

"We couldn't," Kyja said, praying he would believe her. "Not unless we're telling you the truth."

He nodded slowly. "Ye speak true. But be ye sure o' this *Summoner?*"

"Does a friddersnap sheer ferns?" Marcus asked.

———◄◆►———

"Do you see anything?" Kyja asked for the tenth time in as many minutes.

"Nay," Freeman said, staring into the scrying window, which Kyja couldn't see. "Ye still be sure o' this attack?"

Kyja nodded. But what if she was wrong? What if something had changed this time, and the Summoner chose another target? Or if the golems' defeat changed the Dark Circle's plans? The entire city of Icehold was armed and waiting for an attack, with guards stationed every twenty paces along the outer wall and hundreds more manning catapults, ballistas, and barrels of oil, ready to be lit at a moment's notice.

Every man, woman, and child not manning the walls had spent the last few hours clearing snow around the outside and inside of the walls in case the Thrathkin S'Bae came from underground in their snake form.

How would Kyja explain if she ended up being mistaken? Even worse, what if, while the Aerisians were on their way here, the Summoner turned back to Terra ne Staric, which was now unprotected?

"They're almost here," a voice said from only a few feet away.

"Rock and bone!" cried a soldier, dropping the ladle he was about to dip in a water barrel.

A blue head with white hair rose from the barrel, and Freeman raised his crossbow, his mouth an O of disbelief and terror.

"It's only Cascade!" Marcus shouted. "The water elemental we told you about."

Freeman carefully lowered his weapon, his finger still close to the trigger. "Aye, I see that now. But ye didn't be telling me he'd be climbing out o' me water barrel. Next thing there'll be ghosties comin' out o' me wife's butter churn."

Kyja hurried over to Cascade, who was watching the soldier with a look of concern.

"Where are they?" she asked.

Cascade looked out into the darkness and pointed to the

southeast. "Sixteen Thrathkin S'Bae are half a league that way. Twenty more, the same distance to the northeast. As soon as they get near the wall, they'll turn into giant snakes and tunnel underground. Watch closely, and you can see the ground rising above them."

Freeman rubbed the back of his hand across his lips. "Never have I seen men tha' could turn to snakes. Then again, never did I see little blue men peeping out o' me water barrel."

He turned to the soldiers beside him. "Ye there, move the ballistas to the corners o' the wall. And set a dozen'a me best archers to watch. At the first sign o' movement, fire into the ground."

"Aye." The soldier nodded and ran off down the wall, glancing back over his shoulder at Cascade, still sticking halfway out of the water barrel.

"What about the Summoner?" Marcus asked. "That's what we have to focus on. We have to keep it busy, or it'll start summoning an army of undead inside the city."

"It's headed straight for the Eastern gate," Cascade said. "Don't bother trying to use magic on it. It's practically immune."

"Ye be sure o' this?" Freeman shook his head in wonder. "I can't believe I be taking battle advice from a blue head."

"He's right," Marcus said. "Arrows won't hurt a Summoner much unless you get a lucky shot."

"How close are the Aerisians?" Kyja asked Cascade.

"They're on the way," he said, "But I don't think—"

A horn sounded, interrupting him. "Attack, attack!" a man screamed. Before anyone could react, the Summoner was on them.

"Look out!" Marcus shouted as a ball of flame crashed into the city gate.

"Aim, fire!" Came the commands farther down the wall, and

a cloud of arrows launched from both the top of the wall and inside the city. The Summoner screamed in surprise and fury, then wheeled away.

Below, a horn sounded twice, and huge blocks of stone covered in burning pitch catapulted into the air. One of them hit the Summoner's right wing, and this time its scream was of real pain.

"Beware the snakes!" yelled Freeman, pointing at the ground.

Kyja looked down to see ridges of dirt coming straight toward the walls. Prepared, the archers opened fire, at least some of the arrows finding their marks.

After that, it was hard to keep track of the action. At least some of the Thrathkin S'Bae got under the walls. Blue fire blasted buildings and people alike. And, despite the attacks against it, the Summoner managed to raise at least part of its undead army.

Kyja turned to watch the battles in the city streets, echoing with fires and screams of pain. But it was nothing like the last time. Fully armed and ready, the citizens met the attacks head on, cutting down the undead anywhere they appeared from the ground.

"I think they're going to do it." Kyja grinned, wishing she was down below, fighting with them. "I think they're—"

"Look out!" Marcus screamed. Kyja spun around to see burning red eyes right in front of her. Sharp talons ripped her from the wall and lifted her into the sky.

"No!" Marcus shouted, casting spells at the retreating Summoner. A handful of arrows flew through the air. But it was too late. The Summoner carried Kyja into the night, squeezing her so tightly she could barely breathe.

"Clever to prepare the city for ussss," the creature hissed. "My army will be dessstroyed. But the massster will be mossst pleassssed with you."

Kyja knew she should be terrified, but she wasn't. Was it because she knew this wasn't how she was supposed to die? She didn't think so. Cold wind buffeted her face as she stared up into the Summoner's red eyes. "You're the one Marcus calls Bonesplinter."

"No!" screeched the Summoner. "He is gone. I am a Summoner. Almighty. All powerful."

But he wasn't gone. Kyja had been so frightened the first time she saw a Summoner that she'd never realized before that something—or someone—was trapped deep inside the creature. "You want to escape, don't you? You didn't want to be like this."

"Be sssilent!" the Summoner hissed.

Kyja sensed she might be able to pull out whatever or whomever was trapped inside the monster, the same way she always pulled Marcus from Earth to Farworld. Was that part of the magic Master Therapass said was inside her?

"I think I can help you." She closed her eyes and reached.

"No!" the Summoner howled. "Stop, or I'll—" Distracted by what Kyja was doing, the Summoner didn't recognize the Aerisians until they were right on top of it. Suddenly, the wind currents it had been flying on disappeared. At the same time, powerful drafts of air forced it toward the ground.

Panicked, it opened its claws, blew fire at the horrible creatures on their silver steeds, and clawed for the sky.

Kyja plummeted toward the ground. "Help!" she screamed. Just before she hit the ground, a pair of arms closed around her.

"That was fun," Divum said. "Would you like to try it again?"

Kyja turned to look for the Summoner, but she couldn't see it anywhere. Was it dead, or had it escaped? She needed to find out more about what she'd sensed, understand what it meant.

A moment later, Divum had landed with her on the walls of

Icehold. Marcus came running up to Kyja, his eyes wet with tears. "Are you—? You're not—?"

"I'm fine." Kyja laughed. "I'm better than fine. We did it. We saved Terra ne Staric *and* Icehold."

"You are alive." Marcus searched her as though looking for some mortal wound he'd missed. When he was finally convinced she was really all right he pulled her tight against him. "I *think* we did it. I think we changed the future. I'm not going to kill you."

"Oh, good." Kyja laughed. "That's a relief."

CHAPTER 45

GOOD-BYE

WHEN MARCUS ENTERED the royal dining hall, it was already crowded from wall to wall with everyone from the high lord to stable boys. It had been only two days since the golems were destroyed—barely enough time for families to bury their dead—and rebuilding would take years. But for now, everyone was here to celebrate the fact that there was still a city *to* rebuild, and that so many of them had survived the terrible battle.

He stopped just inside the doorway and leaned on his staff, enjoying the sights of men, women, and children laughing and joking. There was a delicious aroma of cooked food, and precious water flowed everywhere.

His body still ached, and he couldn't walk far without tiring, but now all of that was for normal reasons, not because Farworld was on the brink of destruction.

"What are *you* supposed to be? Some kind of prince?" a sarcastic voice asked.

"Very funny." Marcus looked up at Riph Raph, who was

clinging to a chandelier and eating small cooked fish. Marcus tugged self-consciously at the white cape with gold trim, which hung from his shoulders. With his blue silk pants and ruffled shirt, he felt like he should be in a movie or trick-or-treating.

"Where's Kyja?" he asked.

Riph Raph popped another fish noisily into his beak and flapped a wing toward the far side of the room. "She's been over there talking to that crazy air woman forever. Personally, I don't know how she can stand it. Those Aerisians go on and on, talking about this and that. Blah, blah, blah. Until you just want to tell them to stop talking for a minute so your ears can rest."

Marcus rolled his eyes. "I certainly can't imagine how that would feel."

"I know," Riph Raph said, completely missing the sarcasm. "Then there's her missing friend—what was his name? Cracker? Curtain? Crouton?"

"Caelum," Marcus said. "He still hasn't shown up?"

"I'm afraid not," Master Therapass said, coming through the doorway behind Marcus. "It would appear that he has joined Tide and Nizgar-Gharat in siding with the Dark Circle."

Marcus couldn't believe it. After he and Kyja had freed the Aerisians from Air Keep, how could he turn his back on them? "They promised that if we freed them, they'd fight against the Dark Circle and help us open a drift."

Master Therapass nodded, and Marcus again noticed how old the wizard looked lately. The battles and late nights poring over scrolls and books had taken their toll. "Apparently Caelum feels the Aerisians kept the first part of their bargain by fighting against the golems here and against the Summoner in Icehold. We wouldn't have survived without their help. Divum has committed to join you in your attempt to open the drift. And I think she feels disappointed by Caelum's actions as well, but she would never say so out loud."

Two little girls ran by, chasing a boy with a wooden sword. One of the girls waved a hand, turning the boy's ears into tiny brown owls, and the girls exploded into giggles.

"I still don't understand why any of the elementals would side with the Dark Circle," Marcus said. "What's in it for them?"

Master Therapass shifted his weight, seeming as uncomfortable in his fancy robe as Marcus was in his clothes. "Wicked men have always been good at discovering what others desire and then using it to their advantage. What one desires isn't always the same thing for another. For one, it could be power, for another, freedom from the rules of normal society. For the Aerisian, it may be as simple as the opportunity to player a bigger game with higher stakes."

The wizard reached into his robe and pulled out a stoppered vial filled with gray liquid that Marcus thought looked sort of like rat guts. "This is for you."

Marcus opened the vial, sniffed, and wrinkled his nose. "It's not more goblin slime, is it?"

Master Therapass chuckled. "No. In my research on the realm of shadows, I have yet to find a way for you to jump between worlds without some level of danger. Mr. Z's suggestion of jumping when there is little or no shadow in either world appears to work. I have no idea why. I did, however, discover a way to extend your stay on Farworld, and Kyja's visits to Earth. Two drops of this potion will double the number of days you can go without getting sick. Four will triple it. Never take more than that."

"Awesome." Marcus tucked the vial in his pocket. "Speaking of Mr. Z, have you seen him?"

"No. As a creature of pure magic, he can probably spend only so much time around humans without getting bored."

Servants came into the hall, carrying platters and bowls of steaming food that made Marcus's stomach gurgle. He and the wizard headed toward the table reserved for them near the front of the room.

"I guess we're just lucky he lost that bet," Marcus said, squeezing past two men with hanging bellies and triple chins.

"Bet?" Master Therapass made an almost unnoticeable motion with one hand, and the men's chairs scooted tightly against their table, forcing them to suck in their considerable guts with a surprised *whoof*—so he could pass behind them.

"Yeah," Marcus said. "The only reason Mr. Z helped us at all was because he made a wager that his racing snail could beat one of the Aerisians' creatures, and he lost."

The wizard burst into laughter, but Marcus didn't understand what the joke was. "Highly unlikely," Master Therapass said, still smiling. "No creature on air or land is faster than a good racing snail."

"But the Aerisians said Mr. Z lost a bet with them. That's how they convinced him to bring us to Air Keep so we could open the Exsalusentia."

Suddenly, Marcus remembered Mr. Z's answer in the *Was* when asked about the bet. *Not all wagers are created equal.* "They didn't convince Mr. Z to help them. He tricked *them* into bringing Kyja and me there. He knew about the box and everything. He must have lost the bet on purpose so they'd think it was their idea the whole time."

"Imagine that," the wizard said, with a twinkle in his eye.

By the time they reached the table, every seat but theirs had been taken. Kyja sat by Divum. Cascade sat across the table from them, next to Breslek Broomhead. Tankum, who had several major chunks of stone missing from his body—and many cracks—sat on a stone chair constructed especially to hold his weight.

"Looks like you could use a good stonemason," said a skinny woman seated next to him.

"Ha!" roared the warrior. "I always wanted a quick way to take off weight. Looks like I found it."

The woman smiled uncomfortably and fiddled with her silverware.

The only ones missing from the celebration were Graehl and Lanctrus-Darnoc. "Have you heard back from the search party yet?" Marcus asked Master Therapass. "I still can't believe we forgot to warn Scr—I mean Graehl, about the flying octopus things the Aerisians showed us over the Windlash Mountains."

"I have heard nothing yet." Master Therapass slid out his chair and lowered himself carefully onto it. "I wouldn't worry, though. Graehl explored every inch of those mountains as a cave trulloch, and Lanctrus-Darnoc is as powerful as he is wise. I'm sure they'll be fine."

Marcus hoped so. He'd never had a chance to give Graehl a real thanks for the wand, or to apologize for the way he'd doubted him. "You look great," he told Kyja as he sat beside her.

"What?" Kyja blinked.

"I said you look awesome."

She wore a dark-blue gown with tiny gems sewn into the fabric, and her dark locks were braided and curled around her head with blue flowers that matched her dress.

"Who did your hair?" he asked. "It looks sort of familiar."

"My hair?" She touched her head and smiled distractedly. "Oh, Divum helped me with it."

"It looks nice."

Their table and all the others were filled with so much food Marcus couldn't imagine how anyone could eat it all. He piled his plate with roasted chicken, fish in a buttery crust so light it dissolved on his tongue, potatoes that made their own creamy gravy whenever you cut into them with a fork, a fruit that looked a little like a star-fish but changed flavor with every bite, and so many other things he couldn't count them, let alone taste them all.

"Have you thought about how we're going to find the fire elementals?" he asked Kyja between bites.

She didn't seem to be eating much, and he wondered if she'd been down in the kitchen sneaking food before the dinner. "Actually," she said, jabbing at a piece of melon with her fork. "That's what I've been talking to Divum about. Caelum didn't want her to tell us until we freed them, but now that she's on our side, she says that the fire elementals are blocked from coming to Farworld—like the Aerisians were. Reaching Air Keep was tricky, but getting to Fire Keep will be much harder."

Marcus took a bite of a roll that grew piping hot and swelled in his mouth. He fanned his lips. "Does Divum have any idea how we can get to Fire Keep?"

"Yes." Kyja stared at her plate before looking up and smiling. "She knows a way for you to send me there. Once I'm inside, I can pull you over. And then, when we free the fire elementals, we can come back together."

"Great," Marcus said. What was so hard about that?

More kitchen workers arrived, carrying away the dinner plates and bringing in pies, cakes, crystalized sugar balls filled with jams and jellies, and many other desserts. Marcus clasped his stomach and groaned. "I'm going to weigh five hundred pounds when I get out of here."

High Lord Broomhead stood and tapped his glass with the edge of his spoon. "Quiet, everyone! Quiet!"

Around the hall, conversations slowed, and then they died out completely as parents hushed their children.

"These desserts look delicious, and I'm sure you'd rather eat them than listen to me."

Laughter filled the room, and someone shouted, "Keep it short!"

"I intend to," Breslek called back, to a rousing cheer. "But first I want to thank a few people who made it possible for us to be here now. First, for the sumptuous meal, our cook, Bella, and her staff."

"Huzzah!" the crowd shouted. Bella, who stood near the kitchen in a food-stained apron, curtsied.

"Second, for protecting our city, the guards and our good friends the stone warriors and wizards."

"Huzzah!" Marcus joined in.

Tankum raised his stone hands to his mouth. "We just wish we could enjoy the food as much as you!"

Breslek rubbed his belly. "Third, our good friends the Aerisians, the Fontasians, and the land elementals, whose names I'm afraid I can't pronounce."

Another *huzzah,* mingled with laughter.

"And you, the people of Terra ne Staric. Because every man, woman, and child did their part to hold out against the golems. You should all be proud of yourselves."

Marcus hooted along with the rest of the room, clapping until his palms ached.

"Lastly," Breslek said, looking directly across the table at Marcus and Kyja, "the two people who freed the Aerisians, removed the land curse from Water Keep so the Fontasians could free Land Keep, saved Terra ne Staric, rescued Icehold, and generally saved Farworld. Am I missing anything?"

Marcus's face turned bright red as the room went wild, cheering and stomping. Many people wiped tears from their eyes, as they clapped furiously.

Master Therapass lifted his hands, signaling Marcus and Kyja to stand. Holding the table for support, Marcus pushed himself to his feet. "Kyja," he whispered when he realized she was still sitting.

"What?" she looked around, noticed everyone was watching her, and quickly stood next to Marcus.

"Toast!" someone shouted. "Give a toast." And soon the whole room was repeating it. "Toast, toast, toast."

Marcus lifted his glass. "To Master Therapass, who sent me away when I was a baby, but did bring me back." The crowd howled with laughter as the wizard took a pretend bow. "To Mr. Z, wherever you are." Polite clapping and some confused whispers, as most of the people in the room had no idea who Mr. Z was. "And most of all, to Kyja, who taught me the real meaning of trust." He lifted his glass and drank the sweet berry juice in it, while the crowd roared with approval.

Kyja lifted her goblet before realizing it was empty. Marcus reached for a pitcher to fill it, but Kyja pointed to a small silver decanter in front of Divum. Marcus grabbed it and filled her glass with a gold liquid that smelled like flowers. He would have liked to try some of it himself, but there was barely enough to fill Kyja's glass halfway.

Kyja held up her goblet and waited for the crowd to grow quiet. "To all of the people here tonight. For so long, I thought I didn't fit in here. That because I couldn't do magic, I was alone." The crowd was silent, and more than a few of them looked down at their plates.

"But I was wrong. I'm not alone. I may not know who my birth family is. But you, you, you, all of you, are my family. I know that now." She turned to Marcus. "Thank you for helping me remember that even the things we think of as our weaknesses—our flaws—can become our strengths if we trust others enough to help us through them."

The crowd started to clap, but Kyja held up a hand to stop them so she could continue. Marcus noticed her hand was trembling slightly. "I also want to say that even if I have to leave for a while, know that I love you all. And . . ." She swallowed and brushed her eyes with the back of her hand. "And I will always be here. Even if you can't see me."

There was a smattering of confused applause as Kyja quickly drank the liquid from her goblet and sat down.

"What was that about?" Marcus whispered to her, taking his seat. "Where are we going?"

Kyja rested her hands flat on the table. "Mortals can't enter the doorway to Fire Keep. It's . . ." She took a deep breath and relaxed back into her seat. "It's designed to keep humans out and fire elementals in."

"Then we'll figure a way around that," Marcus said. "Maybe Mr. Z can help us."

"He can't," Kyja said, looking up with her deep green eyes. "No one with magic can enter into the doorway. That's why *I* need to go first and then pull you over."

"Are you all right?" Marcus asked. Her face seemed too pale, and her breathing was slowing down.

"I'm fine." Kyja smiled softly. "The last rule about Fire Keep is that I can't go through the door by myself. I have to be sent by somcone I love." She reached out and squeezed his hand. Her fingers were ice cold.

Suddenly, Marcus remembered where he'd seen her hairstyle before. The flowers, the braid resting on a silk pillow in the glass coffin. He looked from her empty goblet to the silver decanter. The decanter he had poured her drink from.

I couldn't go through the door myself. I had to be sent by someone I love.

"No!" he screamed. "You can't do this. There has to be another way."

Kyja smiled at him one last time. She whispered, "I . . . love . . . you," then closed her eyes and stopped breathing.

CHAPTER 46

THE CELL

MARCUS HEARD THE FOOTSTEPS on the wet stone floor, but he didn't look up.

Breslek Broomhead stopped outside his cell door. "You shouldn't be here. You should be out there, at her funeral." He waved his hands at the dripping dungeon walls. "You don't belong here. Master Therapass told us everything and no one blames you for what happened."

Marcus gazed at his hands—filthy from the grime and dirt of the unwashed floors and walls. They were the hands that had killed Kyja by pouring the poison into her goblet. He would never wash them again. "This is where I belong. The law against murder is clear. If you let me go, you'd have to let every killer go too."

Breslek knelt before the cell and gripped the iron bars. "Did you do it?" he asked "Did you kill her?"

"Yes," Marcus repeated the words he'd heard twice before—the words he'd sworn he would never have to say. "I did it. I murdered her."

Something rustled in the upper corner of his cell. "You didn't know what was in the glass," Riph Raph said. "Even a turnip head like you should understand that it wasn't *murder*."

"I *should* have known!" Marcus snapped, the nails of his fingers cutting into his palms. "If I'd figured out what she was doing even a few minutes earlier, I could have stopped her. I could have thrown the poison away. We could have figured out something else, another way." He frowned up at the skyte. "You don't have to stay here with me. You didn't kill anyone."

Riph Raph's ears drooped. He flew down from the torch bracket he'd been perching on to land beside Marcus. "Since the day she rescued me, I've spent every waking moment of my life with her." Tears dripped from his gold eyes, spattering on the muddy floor. "When she pulls you over, I'm coming."

"I know," Marcus whispered. "I'm sorry." He pulled the skyte onto his lap and hugged him to his chest.

"Master Therapass is placing powerful protections on the coffin," Breslek said. "Nothing will be able to open it until she returns. Her body . . ." He wiped his eyes and sniffed. "Her body will remain just as it was the moment she stopped breathing."

Marcus nodded. "I know."

"He wants to talk to you."

Marcus shook his head. "It's against the law. No one but the High Lord can visit a murderer."

Breslek stood. "Is there anything I can bring you?"

"No." Marcus stared at his hands until the High Lord disappeared.

"She'll come for you," Riph Raph said.

Marcus swallowed. "I know."

But what if she didn't? What if she couldn't? It had been five days since she died. Five days without a word. Without any tug in his stomach or any kind of signal at all that she was still out there.

He pulled out the silver box he and Kyja had opened together, running his fingers across its cool, smooth surface. "I trust you, Kyja," he whispered, "I do. But please come soon."

EPILOGUE

CAELUM WRINKLED HIS NOSE at the stink of sulfur in the dank room. Used to the clear mountain skies of Air Keep, the smoky chamber made him anxious and fidgety.

"You don't approve of my home?" the master asked.

Caelum glanced uncomfortably at the figure seated before him, wishing he could see the face hidden under the dark cowl. Instead he stared briefly at the glowing eyes before dropping his gaze to the wrinkled gray hands clutching the arms of the throne.

"The girl is still dead," Tide said.

The master looked at the land elementals. "Can you get to her?"

"She is protected," the purple lizard head hissed.

"The wizard's magic is strong."

The master cackled, his white tongue poking out between his withered, gray lips. "That surprises you, doesn't it? That a human could cast magic too strong for a mighty . . ." He made a sound that was a series of hisses, clicks, and pops. Caelum assumed it must be what the land elementals called themselves.

"I taught Therapass everything he knows. And I am ten times as powerful as he is." The master's red eyes glowed like fire. "Let that be a reminder to you. In case you ever think about leaving my service."

Caelum chafed, wanting to be outside again in the fresh air, but he didn't dare show it. "And if she doesn't come back?"

The master cackled again, clapping his wrinkled gray hands. "If the girl remains dead, the boy will soon follow, and Farworld will be ours. You will win your game. You'd like that, wouldn't you?"

Caelum had hated being trapped in Air Keep. The idea of an entire world to play his tricks on was almost too good to imagine.

"And if she does?" Nizgar-Gharat asked. "What happens if she manages to return from Fire Keep?"

Gleaming white teeth appeared inside the cowl as the master leaned forward. For just a moment, Caelum thought he caught a glimpse of what was inside the hood; his knees quivered.

"If she returns, the gates of the underworld will open. The fourth member of our group will join us, and we will rip a hole between Earth and Farworld that will never be closed."

He squeezed the arms of his throne until blood dripped from between his fingers. "And then Earth and Farworld will be ours. Imagine the fun you can have with a a new world to play your tricks on, Caelum. Imagine a whole new world of knowledge at your fingertips, Nizgar-Gharat. Technology beyond your understanding. Weapons more powerful than anything Farworld has ever seen.

"And you," he said, turning to Tide. "You will be ruler over all of them. How will it feel to have millions—no, billions—kneeling at your feet?"

Tide squeezed a small fish between his fingers, then popped it in his mouth, crunching it between his teeth. "That sounds very good indeed."

GLOSSARY

Air Magic: The most fragile of all elemental magic and yet the most versatile. It can deflect projectiles as a powerful shield, knock down doors, reveal the location of hidden objects, and even shift time. Defensive air magic can heal even the most grievous of wounds.

Amulet: Kyja wears an amulet given to her by Master Therapass on her eighth birthday. It has the same image as the one on Marcus's shoulder.

Aptura Discerna: A magical window that looks into the user's heart. Kyja can use this device because it doesn't require any magic, and it casts no spell on the user.

Aster's Bay: A city located along the Noble River.

Augur Well: The oracle that acolytes desiring to become land elementals were required to seek.

Bella: The head cook in Terra ne Staric.

Bonesplinter: A Thrathkin S'Bae of the Dark Circle.

Broomhead, Breslek: The high lord of Terra ne Staric. He replaced High Lord Umquit after the battle with the Keepers of the Balance.

Cascade: A water elemental who controls all moving water. He agreed to join Marcus and Kyja on their quest to open a drift. He was sent on an unknown quest by Master Therapass.

Cave Trulloch: A tall, humanlike creature found in the Windlash Mountains and other high-altitude climates. *See* Screech.

Dark Circle, The: A group of dark wizards intent on stopping Marcus and Kyja from opening a drift between Farworld and Earth.

Dawn Chimes: Small, bell-shaped flowers which sing at sunrise in Farworld. Not everyone can understand their words.

Doors of Eternity: The doors which lead to the land elementals.

Drift: The magical doorway Marcus and Kyja must create in order to save their own worlds.

Elder Ephraim: The head of the Greek Orthodox monastery where Marcus was found as a baby. Elder Ephraim gave Marcus his name. He died when Marcus was still young.

Elementals: Beings which control water, land, air, and fire magic. They are difficult to find and do not work well together.

Everwood, Char: The wife of Rhaidnan Everwood. Kyja watched her children when Rhaidnan went missing.

Everwood, Rhaidnan: A hunter who was captured by the Unmakers and rescued by Marcus and Kyja. When the Keepers of the Balance held his wife and children hostage, he betrayed Marcus and Kyja, but later gave his life to save them from Zentan Dolan.

Fallen Ones: The army of undead creatures raised by Summoners and led by Thrathkin S'Bae.

Farworld: A world where everyone has magic. It is where Marcus was born, and where Kyja was brought as a baby.

Fein Ter'er: The inner sanctum of the master of the Dark Circle.

Fire Magic: The most powerful of all offensive magic, it can call down meteors from the sky and summon raging lava from the deepest crevices. Fire magic can also be used to change the look, feel, and shape of inanimate objects. Defensive fire magic also protects—defusing or reflecting other magic.

Fontasians: Another name for water elementals.

Forest of Before Time: A forest of mammoth trees located at the edge of the Borderlands.

Frost Pinnois: A flying water-magic creature made entirely of ice. *See* Zhethar.

Galespinner: A mist steed summoned by Master Therapass.

Golden Rope: When Kyja pulls Marcus from one place to another, she usually pulls a golden rope she sees in her mind.

Goodnuffs: The family who raised Kyja after Master Therapass summoned her to Farworld. They were killed by a pair of Thrathkin S'Bae.

Graehl: Originally a Keeper of the Balance, Graehl was changed into a cave trulloch named Screech for speaking out against their practices. After Zentan Dolan was destroyed, he turned back into a man and vowed to help Marcus and Kyja. *See* Screech.

Harbinger: Fairy creatures in Land Keep that were turned into monsters by the Dark Circle. They were later returned to their fairy forms by the land elementals.

Heartstrong, Tankum: One of Terra ne Staric's greatest warriors. He helped Master Therapass save Marcus from the Dark Circle, but gave his life in the effort. A stone statue erected in his honor was brought to life by Lanctrus-Darnoc to fight the Keepers of the Balance.

Icehold: A Borderlands city located near the ruins of Windshold.

Innoris a'Gentoran: A gauntlet of immense power brought to Terra ne Staric from the realm of shadows.

Ishkabiddles: Small fuzzy creatures who can sense danger by spraying sparkling dust from their feelers.

Jaklah: A boy from Aster's Bay. He met Marcus in the cavern near Land Keep and later refused to give up his magic to the Keepers.

Kanenas, Marcus: Originally born in Farworld, he was targeted by the Dark Circle because of an unusual scar on his shoulder. Marcus was sent to Earth by Master Therapass, who believes one of Marcus's parents is a creature of shadows.

Keepers of the Balance: A group of wizards who believed in taking magic from the poor and weak and redistributing it to the rich and powerful.

Knowledge Illuminator: A librarian in Land Keep.

Kyja: Born on Earth, she was brought to Farworld to even the scales of balance when Marcus was sent to Earth. Just as Marcus is key to saving Farworld, Kyja is key to saving Earth. Being from Earth, she cannot do any magic and is immune to its effects.

Lake Aeternus: A large body of water located along the edge of Water Keep that flows into the Noble River. It is located roughly at the same point in Farworld where Lake Michigan is located on Earth.

Lanctrus-Darnoc: A land elemental composed of a boar and a fox. He joined Marcus and Kyja in their quest to open a drift between Earth and Farworld and was sent on an unknown quest by Master Therapass.

Land Keep: The home of the land elementals.

Land Magic: The oldest of all magic, it can commune with all minerals from the smallest rock to the tallest mountain, as well as learn from and aid plants and animals. Land magic has the ability to tear down walls and create massive barriers. Land magic wielders are the world's greatest teachers and students. The most powerful users of land magic can transform themselves into the form of a plant or an animal—especially if the plant or animal has had an important impact on the caster's life. Land magic can also bring life to stone and other minerals.

Lusia: A game played by Farworld children.

Master of the Dark Circle: The only dark wizard powerful enough to command Summoners. He wears a gold ring that bears the same symbol that is on Marcus's shoulder and Kyja's amulet.

Melankollia: A tree with leaves that make people feel sad.

Mimicker: A creature that can look like anything else, including creatures others are thinking about.

Mist: The water elemental who controls fog and mist.

Mist Steed: A magical mount with a body taller and broader than a horse. It has a birdlike head covered with golden scales and a gauzy mane.

Morning Dew: The water elemental who controls dew.

Mr. Z: An odd little man who owns a racing snail.

Noble River: A river flowing from Lake Aeternus to the Sea of Eternal Sorrows.

Olden: The oldest tree in the Westland Woods.

Plains of Thayer: The flat open area between the Windlash Mountains and the Noble River.

Raindrop: The water elemental who controls rain and storms.

Realm of Shadows: A mysterious gray area between Earth and Farworld. Marcus and Kyja's bodies become trapped here when they are in the other world. Master Therapass believes one of Marcus's parents may be from the realm of shadows.

Riph Raph: A small blue skyte. Kyja rescued him when he was a baby, and he was one of Kyja's few friends when she was growing up. When Kyja and Marcus jump to Earth, Riph Raph is temporarily changed to another Earth animal.

Screech: A cave trulloch. *See* also Graehl.

Sea of Eternal Sorrows: The sea into which the Noble River flows.

Singale: A one-armed man Kyja found outside the gates of Terra ne Staric. He may be romantically involved with Bella.

Skytes: Small dragon-like creatures with floppy ears and big golden eyes. They can blow small fireballs and do limited magic. *See* Riph Raph.

Snifflers: Large insect-like creatures brought to Farworld from the realm of shadows to draw magic from humans.

Summoners: Terrifying creatures of mythic power created from the souls of twisted wizards. They have red serpentine bodies, wings, and spearlike teeth. They are rumored to be able to create intense storms, hypnotize others, and raise the dead.

Teagarden, Principal: The principal of the Philo T. Justice School for Boys, which Marcus was attending before he was brought back to Farworld.

Terra ne Staric: Capital of Westland. Home to Kyja and Master Therapass.

Therapass, Master: A powerful wizard who saved Marcus's life by sending him to Earth and accidentally trapped Kyja on Farworld.

Thrathkin S'Bae: Literally translated as "Masters of the dead who walk," these wizards of the Dark Circle use corrupt magic to force the elements to obey their will instead of asking for their help.

Throg: A long-necked water creature that echoes what it hears.

Tide: The king of the water elementals, he controls large bodies of water.

Trill Stones: A game using colored stones and a circular board. Also the stones themselves. The red stones change into valuable gems when transported to Earth.

Ty: A boy from Chicago who helped Marcus and Kyja when they were trying to enter Water Keep.

Unmakers: Creatures from the realm of shadows. They are nearly invisible to humans. Unmakers feed on humans—first sucking away all emotion, then magic, and ultimately their will to live.

Valdemeer: A country located in the eastern borderlands.

Water Keep: Home to the water elementals, its geography on Farworld is roughly the same as Chicago on Earth.

Water Magic: The most graceful of all magic, it can transform water, mist, or ice into any object or creature, and animate it as long as it remains nearby. Water spells tend to focus on the power of vision and discernment, seeing long distances or through objects, and occasionally even delving into visions and dreams. Defensive water magic cleanses by removing curses and poisons.

Westland: The area of Farworld between the Windlash Mountains and the Borderlands.

Westland Woods: Home to the Weather Guardians, which are huge talking trees.

Windlash Mountains: A very tall and dangerous mountain range dividing Westland and the Plains of Thayer.

Windshold: The city where Marcus was born. It was destroyed completely by the Dark Circle.

Y'sdine's Feint: A strategy used in Trill Stones where one player learns the other player's attack strategy and sets a trap for him.

Zentan Dolan: The leader of the Keepers of the Balance, he was actually a demon from the realm of shadows.

Zhethar: A frost pinnois who carried Marcus and Kyja to the walls of Water Keep. *See* Frost Pinnois.

DISCUSSION QUESTIONS

1. Marcus and Kyja enter the *Is*, the *Was*, and the *Will Be*. If you could spend a day seeing the future, visiting the past, or hanging out in the present, which would you choose and why?

2. Before Marcus goes into the *Will Be*, he is told that seeing his future will lock it in place. If you could see one version of your future, knowing that would mean that version of the future was unchangeable, would you take the risk? Why or why not?

3. Master Therapass tells Kyja to wait before pulling Marcus to Farworld, but she disobeys and does it anyway. Have you ever done something you weren't supposed to do? What were the results?

4. Marcus and Kyja are surprised to learn they will be traveling by snail. They expect the snail to be very slow, but it ends up being fast. Have you ever expected one thing to happen and been surprised when something much different occurred? What did you learn from the experience?

5. On their way to Air Keep, Marcus, Kyja, and Riph Raph encounter a number of creatures with names that are actually puns (words that can have more than one meaning depending on how you think of them). Some of the pun creatures they face include a "frost bite," a "fruit fly," and a "rope burn." Can you think up any of your own?

6. The air elementals see almost everything as funny. They say they would rather laugh at something than cry over it. How is seeing the funny side of things good? Are there times when laughing at something, or someone, is not right?

7. In Air Keep, Caelum and Divum try to trick Marcus and Kyja into opening the box. Would it have been better if they had been honest about what they wanted in the first place? Has anyone ever tried to get you to do something without telling you the whole truth? How did it make you feel?

8. Marcus tells Kyja that he thinks her magic is getting people to help her. She tells him that people are nice to her because she is nice to them. Who do you think is right and why?

9. Marcus is afraid to tell Kyja what he sees in the future because he thinks she will hate him when she sees what he is going to do. Have you ever been afraid to tell someone the truth because you thought they wouldn't like you? What happened?

10. The air elementals are unable to open the box because they do not trust others. How would our world be different if no one trusted anyone else?

ACKNOWLEDGMENTS

This book has been a longer time coming than I, or my publisher, would have liked. Sometimes—especially when we're waiting on pins, needles, and other sharp sewing implements—things don't move as fast as we'd like them to. To those of you who have been hanging in there, thanks so much for your patience. Hopefully this book, and the two that will follow, will have been worth the wait. If it is, here's who you can thank.

Chris Schoebinger, Lisa Mangum, Heidi Taylor, and all the other amazing people at Shadow Mountain. Thanks for believing in this project and for all the incredible art, formatting, editing, advice, and encouragement.

Annette Lyon for turning rocks into diamonds.

Brandon Dorman for another cover that totally rocks. Thanks for peeking into my head and capturing the dreams there.

The women (and man) of Wednesday night: LuAnn, Sarah, Michele, Annette, Heather, and Rob. After more than a decade together, you guys are still the best critique group, bar none.

My family: Jennifer, Erica, Scott, Jake, and Nick. Thanks for being patient with all the hours I spent up in my office and for all your love and encouragement. Best. Family. Ever.

And lastly, to all you readers who waited with patience (and impatience) for this book to come out. You are the real reason I write. You are my inspiration. Thank you!